31143011449353
FIC Carrere, E
CarrÃ¨re, Emmanuel,
The kingdom /

Main

ALSO BY EMMANUEL CARRÈRE

THE KINGDOM

THE

KINGDOM

EMMANUEL CARRÈRE

TRANSLATED FROM THE FRENCH
BY JOHN LAMBERT

FARRAR, STRAUS AND GIROUX
NEW YORK

Farrar, Straus and Giroux
18 West 18th Street, New York 10011

Library of Congress Cataloging-in-Publication Data
Names: Carrère, Emmanuel, 1957– author.
Title: The kingdom / Emmanuel Carrère ; translated by John Lambert.
Other titles: Royaume. English
Description: First American edition. I New York : Farrar, Straus and Giroux, 2017. I
    "Originally published in French in 2014 by P.O.L., France, as Le Royaume" — Verso
    title page/
Identifiers: LCCN 2016041337 I ISBN 9780374184308 (hardback) I ISBN 9780374714031
    (e-book)
Subjects: LCSH: Carrère, Emmanuel, 1957– I Authors, French—20th century—
    Biography I Authors, French—21st century—Biography I Jewish Christians—
    Fiction. I Christian civilization—Fiction. I BISAC: FICTION / Literary. I
    FICTION / Christian / Historical.
Classification: LCC PQ2663.A7678 Z4613 2014 I DDC 843/.914—dc23
LC record available at https://lccn.loc.gov/2016041337

Designed by Jonathan D. Lippincott

Our books may be purchased in bulk for promotional, educational, or business use.
Please contact your local bookseller or the Macmillan Corporate and Premium Sales
Department at 1-800-221-7945, extension 5442, or by e-mail
at MacmillanSpecialMarkets@macmillan.com.

www.fsgbooks.com
www.twitter.com/fsgbooks • www.facebook.com/fsgbooks

1   3   5   7   9   10   8   6   4   2

CONTENTS

TRANSLATOR'S NOTE
ON SOURCES

One of the challenges of translating works by Emmanuel Carrère is finding the right balance between his personal use of his many sources and the text of the sources themselves. Where no translation exists, I translate directly. Where several translations exist, I seek the one that in my view best corresponds to Carrère's version. So, for example, I use the Bible of the United States Conference of Catholic Bishops, Robert Fagles's translation of *The Odyssey*, Charles E. Wilbour's translation of Ernest Renan, Grace Frick's translation of Marguerite Yourcenar, and David L. Schindler Jr.'s translation of Charles Péguy. Where Carrère distances himself somewhat from the works he cites, I go to the English sources and tweak them accordingly. And when he uses his own words, as notably with Edgar Allan Poe's "The System of Doctor Tarr and Professor Fether," I leave the text behind and follow him as he strikes out on his own.

PROLOGUE

(PARIS, 2011)

I

That spring, I collaborated on the script of a TV series. The logline ran like this: One night, in a small mountain town, some of the dead come back to life. No one knows why, nor why these dead and not others. They themselves don't even know they're dead. They discover it in the horror-stricken faces of their loved ones, next to whom they'd like to resume their natural place. They're not zombies, they're not ghosts, they're not vampires. It's not a fantasy film, but reality. It asks the question, seriously: What would happen if this impossible event *really did* take place? How would you react if, coming into the kitchen, you found your adolescent girl who died three years ago pouring herself a bowl of cereal and worrying she's going to get bawled out because she came in late, without remembering anything about what happened the night before? Concretely: What would you do with your hands? What would you say?

I stopped writing fiction long ago, but I can recognize a powerful fictional device when I see it. And this was by far the most powerful one I'd been offered in my career as screenwriter. For four months, I worked with the director Fabrice Gobert every day, morning to night, in a blend of enthusiasm and, often, a state of shock at the situations we created, the feelings we manipulated. Then, as far as my participation went, things took a turn for the worse with our backers. I'm almost twenty years older than Fabrice, and I took less willingly than he did to having to jump through hoops for twerps with three-day beards who could have been my sons, and who pulled blasé faces at everything we wrote. The temptation to say "Look, you guys, if you know so well how it should be done, then do it yourselves" was great. I ceded. Lacking humility and against the wise advice of Hélène, my wife, and François, my agent, I slammed the door halfway through the first season.

I started to regret what I'd done only a couple of months later, at a dinner to which I'd invited both Fabrice and Patrick Blossier, the director of photography who'd created the images for my film *La Moustache*. I was sure he'd be just right for *Les Revenants* and that he and Fabrice would hit it off from the start, which they did. But listening to them that night around the kitchen table talking about the series that was taking shape and the stories we'd imagined in my study—stories that were already becoming choices of sets, actors, and technicians—I could almost physically feel that enormous and exciting machine—a film shoot—being set in motion. I said to myself that I should have been part of the adventure and that I was to blame if I wasn't. All of a sudden I grew sad, as sad as that guy Pete Best, who'd been the drummer for a little Liverpool band called the Beatles and who'd left the group just before it got its first recording contract, and who I figure must have spent the rest of his life regretting it. (*Les Revenants* has been a huge global success. It won the International Emmy Award for best drama series and has now been remade in the United States as *The Returned*.)

•

I drank too much during that dinner. Experience has taught me that it's better not to go on and on about what you're writing if you haven't finished writing it, above all when you're drunk: such shared enthusiasm is sure to cost you a week of discouragement. But that night, no doubt to vent my sour grapes and show that I too was doing something interesting, I told Fabrice and Patrick about the book on the first Christians I'd been working on for several years. I'd put it aside to work on *Les Revenants*, and had just picked it up again. I gave them the story the way you pitch a series.

It takes place in Corinth, in Greece, around A.D. 50—but no one, of course, suspects that they're living "in the year of our Lord." It starts with an itinerant preacher who opens a modest weaver's workshop. Without leaving his loom, the man who would later be known as Saint Paul weaves his tale and, step by step, spreads it over the city. Bald, bearded, weakened by a mysterious sickness, he tells with a deep, evocative voice the story of a prophet crucified twenty years earlier in Judea.

He says that this prophet came back from the dead and that his coming back from the dead is the portent of something enormous, a mutation of humanity, both radical and invisible. The contagion comes about. The strange belief radiates out from Paul in the seedy parts of Corinth, and its followers soon come to see themselves as mutants disguised as friends and neighbors: undetectable.

Fabrice's eyes light up: "Told like that, it sounds like vintage Dick!" The science fiction author Philip K. Dick was a major reference during our screenwriting work. I can feel my audience is captivated and go a step further: yes, it sounds like Dick, and this story of the early days of Christianity is also the story of *Les Revenants*. What we tell in *Les Revenants* is the last days that Paul's followers were sure they would experience, when the dead come back to life and the judgment of the world is consummated. It's the community of outcasts and chosen ones that forms around this shocking event: a resurrection. It's the story of something impossible that nevertheless takes place. I get excited, pour myself glass after glass, insist on filling my guests' glasses as well, and it's then that Patrick says something that's basically pretty banal but which strikes me because it seems to come to him out of the blue, something that he's never thought about before and that takes him completely by surprise.

•

He says it's strange, when you think about it, that normal, intelligent people can believe something as unreasonable as the Christian religion, something exactly like Greek mythology or fairy tales. In ancient times, okay: people were gullible, science didn't exist. But today! Nowadays if a guy believed stories about gods turning into swans to seduce mortals, or princesses kissing frogs that become Prince Charmings, everyone would say he's nuts. But tons of people believe in something just as outrageous and no one thinks they're nuts. Even if you don't share their faith, you take them seriously. They play a social role, less important than in the past, but one that's respected and rather positive on the whole. Their pie-in-the-sky ideas coexist alongside perfectly level-headed activities. Presidents pay deferential visits to their leader. Really, it's kind of strange, isn't it?

2

Yes, it's strange, and Nietzsche, whom I read a couple of pages of every morning in a café after taking Jeanne to school, expresses exactly the same astonishment as Patrick Blossier when he says:

> When we hear the ancient bells growling on a Sunday morning we ask ourselves: Is it really possible? This, for a Jew, crucified two thousand years ago, who said he was God's son? The proof of such a claim is lacking. A god who begets children with a mortal woman; a sage who bids men work no more, have no more courts, but look for the signs of the impending end of the world; a justice that accepts the innocent as a vicarious sacrifice; someone who orders his disciples to drink his blood; prayers for miraculous interventions; sins perpetrated against a god, atoned for by a god; fear of a beyond to which death is the portal; the form of the cross as a symbol in a time that no longer knows the function and the ignominy of the cross—how ghoulishly all this touches us, as if from the tomb of a primeval past! Can one believe that such things are still believed?

And yet they are believed. Many people believe them. At church they recite the Creed, every word of which is an insult to common sense, and they recite it in their own language, which they're supposed to understand. My father, who took me to church on Sundays when I was little, regretted that it was no longer in Latin, both out of a sense of attachment to the past and because, I remember his words, "in Latin you can't hear how silly it is." You can always reassure yourself with the thought that they don't believe what they're saying. Just like they don't believe in Santa Claus. It's part of the heritage of beautiful, secular customs to which they're attached. In perpetuating them, they're proudly affirming a link with the spirit that inspired the cathedrals and the music of Bach. They mumble all this because it's the done thing, the way we middle-class liberals who've replaced Sunday Mass with yoga classes mumble a mantra recited by the teacher before starting to practice. In our mantra, however, we wish for the rain to fall when it should and for all men to live in peace. Pious sentiments, okay, but ones that don't offend reason, which you can hardly say for Christianity.

Of course, aside from those who don't worry too much about the words at Mass and let themselves be lulled by the music, there must also be those who pronounce them with conviction, fully aware of what they're saying. If asked, they would say they *really do* believe that a Jew who lived two thousand years ago was born of a virgin and resurrected three days after he was crucified, and that he will return to judge the living and the dead. And they say that they themselves place these events at the center of their lives.

Yes, it's strange all right.

3

When I deal with a subject, I like to approach it from several angles. Once I'd started writing about the first Christian communities, I got the idea that I should also write a piece for a magazine about what had become of their belief two thousand years later and take one of those cruises "in the footsteps of Saint Paul" organized by agencies specialized in religious tourism.

Before they died, my first wife's parents dreamed of doing just that, as well as of taking a pilgrimage to Lourdes. But whereas they went to Lourdes several times, the Saint Paul cruise remained a dream. I think at one point the children talked about chipping in to offer my widowed mother-in-law the cruise she'd have so loved to go on with her husband. But without him, her heart wasn't in it: the family insisted for a bit, then let it drop.

Of course, I don't have the same tastes as my ex-parents-in-law, and I imagined with a mixture of amusement and horror the half-day stop-overs at Corinth or Ephesus, the group of pilgrims following their guide, a young priest waving a little flag and delighting his listeners with his wry humor. That's a recurring theme in Catholic families, I've noticed: the priest's sense of humor, the priest's jokes. Just the thought of it makes me shudder. The chances of meeting a pretty girl in such a group were slim—and supposing I did, I wondered how I'd react to one who'd signed up for a Catholic cruise: Was I perverse enough to find that sexy? That being said, my project wasn't about flirting but about approaching the cruise participants as a sample group of committed Christians and methodically interviewing them for ten days. Was it better to do such fieldwork incognito and pretend you share their faith, like the journalists who infiltrate neo-Nazi milieus, or to put your cards on the table? I didn't hesitate for long. I don't like the first method, and in my view the second always gives better results. I'd tell the plain truth: I'm an agnostic writer who wants to know *what exactly* Christians believe today. If you want to share that with me, I'd be delighted; if not, I won't bother you any longer.

Knowing me, I'm sure it would have worked. Day after day, meal after meal, conversation after conversation, I'd have come to find these people—with whom on the face of it I had almost nothing in common—endearing, moving even. I saw myself kindly grilling a table of Catholics over dinner, for example taking apart the Apostles' Creed phrase by phrase. "I believe in God, the Father Almighty, creator of heaven and earth." You believe in God, but how do you see him? As a bearded old man up on his cloud? As a superior force? As a being so large that we're like ants beside him? As a lake or a flame at the bottom of your heart? And Jesus Christ, his only son, who "will come again in glory to judge the living and the dead, and his kingdom will have no end"? Tell me about this glory, this judgment, this kingdom. And, to get to the heart of the matter: Do you believe he *really was* resurrected?

•

It was the jubilee year of Saint Paul: the clergy on board the liner would no doubt outdazzle each other. The archbishop of Paris was among the invited speakers. Demand was high, many of the pilgrims were going as couples, and most singles agreed to share a cabin with a passenger of the same sex—something I had no interest in whatsoever. And if you did insist on a single cabin, the cruise wasn't exactly cheap: practically twenty-four hundred dollars. I paid half almost six months in advance. Already it was nearly sold out.

The date approached, I started to feel uneasy. It bugged me to find envelopes with the logo of Saint Paul Cruises on the pile of letters in the hall. Hélène, who already suspected me of being "Catholic around the edges," as she said, viewed my project with perplexity. I didn't talk about it with anyone and eventually realized that in fact it embarrassed me. What embarrassed me was the suspicion that I was going more or less to make fun of the whole thing, or at least was motivated by the sort of condescending curiosity you see in TV programs on dwarf tossing, psychiatrists for guinea pigs, or look-alike contests for the Singing Nun, that unfortunate Belgian nun with a guitar and pigtails who sang "Dominique, nique, nique" and, after her fifteen minutes of fame, died of an overdose of alcohol and barbiturates. When I was twenty, I wrote a few articles for a weekly that was trying to be trendy and provocative, and whose first issue included a feature entitled "Confessionals Put to the Test." Disguised as a devout Christian, that is to say, dressed as badly as possible, the journalist set out to trap the priests of various Parisian parishes, confessing to increasingly far-fetched sins. He told the story in an amused tone, implying as if it went without saying that he was a thousand times freer and more intelligent than the poor priests and their flock. Even at the time, I found that stupid, shocking—all the more so because anyone who did something like that in a synagogue or mosque would be immediately hit by a storm of protest from all sides. It seems Christians are the only people you can make fun of with impunity by getting all the laughers on your side. I started to think that although I claimed I was acting in good faith, my safari among the Catholics was a bit like that as well.

It wasn't too late to cancel my reservation and even to get my deposit back, but I couldn't make up my mind. When the letter arrived asking me to pay the second installment, I chucked it out. Other reminders followed, which I ignored. Finally the agency called me up, and I said that no, something had come up, I couldn't go. The woman politely pointed out that I could have told her sooner, because a month before the departure no one else would take my cabin: even if I didn't go I'd have to pay the full sum. I got annoyed, and said that half was already a lot to pay for a cruise I wouldn't go on. She quoted the contract, which left no doubt in the matter. I hung up. For a couple of days I thought I'd just lie low. There had to be a waiting list, surely some pious bachelor would be delighted to take my cabin, and in any case they'd never sue me. Or would they? The agency was sure to have a collection service, they'd send me registered letter after registered letter, and if I didn't pay, this would end up in court. I suddenly felt a flush of paranoia at the thought that the story could prompt a derisive little article and that after that my name would be associated with a ridiculous affair about my being too cheap to pay my way on a cruise for zealots. To be honest—though I know it's not necessarily any less ridiculous—added to my fear of being caught out was the knowledge that I'd planned something that increasingly struck me like a bad deed, and that it was only right that I should pay for it. So I didn't wait for the first registered letter to send the second check.

4

The more I've worked on this book, the clearer it has become to me that it's very difficult to get people to talk about their faith, and that the question *"What exactly* do you believe?" is a bad one. Moreover, although it took me a surprisingly long time, I finally realized that it was ludicrous to want to interview Christians the way I'd interview people who'd survived a plane crash, been struck by lightning, or been held hostage. Because in fact I've had very close access to one Christian for several years, someone, indeed, you could hardly be closer to, because it was me.

•

In a word, in autumn 1990 I'd been "touched by grace." It would be an understatement to say that it embarrasses me to put it that way today, but that's how I put it at the time. The fervor that was born of this "conversion"—I want to put quotes just about everywhere—lasted almost three years, during which time I got married in a church, had my two sons baptized, and went to Mass regularly—and by regularly I don't mean every week but every day. I went to confession and took Communion. I prayed, and urged my sons to pray with me—something they like to tease me about now that they're grown up.

Every day during these years I jotted down ideas on a few verses of the Gospel of John. These commentaries take up around twenty notebooks, which I've never opened since. I don't have very good memories of this period and have done my best to forget them. Miracles of the unconscious: I did such a good job that I was able to start writing on the origins of Christianity without making the connection, and without remembering that there was a time when I *believed* in this story that so interests me today.

Now I remember. And even if it scares me, I know it's time to reread these notebooks.

But where are they?

5

The last time I saw them was in 2005, and I was doing very, very badly. That was the last of my major crises, and one of the worst. For convenience's sake you could call it a depression, but I don't think that's what it was. The psychiatrist I was seeing at the time didn't think so either, or that antidepressants would help. He was right. The several I tried had nothing but unpleasant side effects. The only treatment that brought me any relief was an antipsychotic drug that, according to the leaflet, remedied "erroneous beliefs." Few things made me laugh at the time, but these "erroneous beliefs" did, though my laughter wasn't what you'd call cheery.

In my book *Lives Other Than My Own*, I described my visit to the old psychoanalyst François Roustang, but I only told the end. Here I'll tell the beginning—that was one dense session. I let it all out: the persistent pain in the pit of my stomach, which I compared to the fox devouring the young Spartan's entrails in the legends of ancient Greece; the feeling—or rather, the certainty—that I'd been checkmated, wasn't able to love or work, and harmed everything I touched. I said I was thinking of suicide. Despite everything, I'd come hoping Roustang might propose another solution, and since, to my great surprise, he didn't seem to want to propose anything at all, I asked if he'd accept me as a patient as a last-ditch effort. I'd already spent ten years on the couches of two of his colleagues, without any notable results—or so I thought at the time. Roustang replied that no, he wouldn't. First, because he was too old, and second, because in his view the only thing that interested me in analysis was confounding the analyst, something I clearly excelled at, and that if I wanted to demonstrate my skill a third time he wasn't going to stop me, but, he added, "not with me. And if I were you, I'd try something else."

"Like what?" I asked, with all the superiority of the incurable.

"Well," Roustang went on, "you talked about suicide. It doesn't get very good press these days, but sometimes it's a solution."

After that he was silent. So was I.

Then he went on: "Or you can live."

With these two sentences he shattered the system that had let me hold my two previous analysts in check. It was bold of him, the kind of boldness Jacques Lacan must have allowed himself on the basis of a similar clinical acumen. Roustang understood that no matter what I thought, I wasn't about to kill myself, and, bit by bit, without my ever seeing him again, things started to improve. Nevertheless, I went home feeling no better than when I'd gone to see him—that is, not really determined to kill myself but sure I'd do it anyway. There was a hook in the ceiling over the bed where I lay all day long, and I got up on a stepladder to test its strength. I wrote a letter to Hélène, another to my sons, a third to my parents. I cleaned out my computer, not hesitating to delete a few files I didn't want anyone to find after my death. However, I did wonder what to do with a box that had followed me from move to move without my ever opening it. That was the box with the notebooks from my Christian period, in which I'd written my commentaries on the Gospel of John every morning.

I'd always thought I'd reread them one day, and that I may well even gain something from them. After all, it's not so common to have firsthand access to documents on a period of your life when you were totally different from what you've become, when you were firmly convinced of something you now find absurd. On the one hand, I had no wish whatsoever to leave these documents behind me if I died. On the other, if I didn't kill myself I'd certainly regret having destroyed them.

Miracles of the unconscious, continued: I don't remember what I did. Or rather, I remember dragging my depression around with me for another couple of months, then starting to write what became *My Life as a Russian Novel*, which pulled me from the abyss. As for the cardboard box, the last I recall is seeing it unopened in front of me on my study carpet and wondering what I should do with it.

Seven years later I'm in the same study, in the same apartment, and I wonder what I did with it. If I'd destroyed it, it seems to me I'd remember, especially if I'd destroyed it dramatically, by tossing it into the flames. But maybe I did it more prosaically, and just took it down and chucked it out. And if I kept it, where did I put it? In a safety deposit box? That's like the flames: I'd remember. No, it must have stayed in the apartment, and if it stayed in the apartment . . .

I can feel I'm burning hot.

6

In my study there's a closet where we keep suitcases, stuff for working around the house, foam mattresses for when friends of our daughter, Jeanne, come and stay: things we need from time to time. But it's like in that children's book *A Dark, Dark Tale*, where in the dark, dark castle there's a dark, dark hall leading to a dark, dark room with a dark, dark cupboard, and so on. At the back of this closet there's another, smaller, lower one that's unlit and harder to get at, of course, where we keep things we never use, things that will stay there, practically beyond reach, until a next move forces us to decide on their fate. This is mostly the usual mix you find in any storage room: rolled-up old carpets, obsolete stereo equipment, a suitcase full of audiocassettes, garbage bags containing judo outfits, punch mitts, and boxing gloves, attesting to the successive passions of my sons and me for combat sports. Almost half the closet, however, is taken up by something not so usual: the investigation file on Jean-Claude Romand, who killed his wife, his kids, and his parents in January 1993 after pretending he was a doctor for over fifteen years, although in fact he was nothing at all—he spent his days in his car, at highway rest areas, or walking in the dark forests of the Jura Mountains.

•

The word "file" is misleading. It's not *one* file but fifteen or so, bound and cinched together, each one very thick and containing documents ranging from endless witness testimonies to expert reports to miles and miles of bank statements. I think everyone who has written about this kind of case has had—like me—the feeling that these tens of thousands of bits of paper tell a story, and that this story must be extracted the way a sculptor extracts a statue from a block of marble. During the difficult years I spent documenting and then writing about this case, these files were a source of fascination for me. In principle they were inaccessible to the public as long as the trial was still pending, so I was only able to consult them as a special favor on the part of Romand's lawyer, in his office in Lyon. Left alone with them for an hour or so in a little windowless room, I was allowed to take notes but not to make photocopies. It sometimes happened that—after I'd come all the way from Paris just to view them—the lawyer said: "No, it's not possible today, or tomorrow either. Come back in two weeks." I think he got a kick out of stringing me along like that.

After the trial, at the end of which Jean-Claude Romand was sentenced to life imprisonment, things were simpler: in accordance with the law, Romand became the owner of his file, and he allowed me to make use of it. Unable to keep it with him in prison, he'd entrusted it to a woman he'd befriended, a volunteer for a Catholic prison ministry. It was at her place in Lyon that I went to pick it up. I stowed these boxes in the trunk of my car and, back in Paris, in the studio apartment where I worked at the time, on Rue du Temple. Five years later *The Adversary: A True Story of Monstrous Deception*, my book on the Romand affair, appeared. The woman from the prison ministry called me up to say she'd appreciated the book's honesty but was saddened by one detail: that I say she seemed relieved to dump the macabre keepsake on me and happy the files were now under my roof and not hers. "It didn't bother me at all to have them. If it bothers you, just bring them back. We've got plenty of room for them here."

I thought I would as soon as I got the chance, but this chance never came up. I no longer had a car, had no particular reason to go to Lyon, it was never the right moment. As a result, in 2000 I hauled the three huge boxes in which I'd stored the files from Rue du Temple to Rue Blanche, then, in 2005, from Rue Blanche to Rue des Petits-Hôtels. There could be no question of tossing them: Romand entrusted them to me, and if he wants them I have to be able to give them back when he gets out. As he received twenty-two years and is a model prisoner, he's been eligible for parole since 2015. Pending his release, I decided that the best place to keep these boxes that I had no reason or inclination to open again was this inner closet in my study, which Hélène and I finally nicknamed Jean-Claude Romand's room. And, it struck me all of a sudden, the best place to stash the notebooks from my Christian period—if I hadn't destroyed them when I was thinking of killing myself—was right next to these files, in Jean-Claude Romand's room.

I

A CRISIS

(PARIS, 1990–1993)

I

There's a passage I love in Casanova's memoirs. Locked away in Venice's dark and humid Piombi prison, Casanova hatches an escape plan. He's got all he needs to bring it off except for one thing: hemp to make a rope, or a fuse for explosives, I forget which, but the key thing is that if he can get his hands on some he's saved, and if he can't he's lost. It's not as if hemp was easy to come by in prison, but all of a sudden Casanova remembers that to absorb the perspiration under his arms, when he had his suit made he asked the tailor to line the jacket with—guess what? *Hemp!* Casanova, who cursed his thin summer jacket that does so little to protect him from the cold prison air, understands that it was divine providence that made him wear it the day he was arrested. It's there, in front of him, hanging on a nail hammered into the crumbling wall. He looks at it, his heart beating. In a second he'll tear open the seams, search the lining, and freedom will be his. But just as he goes to grab it, he's seized by doubt: What if, in a moment of oversight, the tailor didn't do as he asked? Normally, that would hardly matter. Now it would be tragic. So much is at stake that Casanova falls to his knees and starts to pray. With an ardor he's forgotten since his childhood, he prays to God that the tailor has indeed sewn hemp into his jacket. At the same time his faculty of reasoning doesn't remain idle. It tells him that what is done is done. Either the tailor has sewn hemp into the lining or he hasn't. Either it's there or it isn't, and if it isn't there, his prayers won't change a thing. God is not going to put it there, or retroactively give the tailor the conscientiousness he lacked. These logical objections don't stop Casanova from praying like a lost soul, and he'll never know if his prayer had any effect, because the hemp really is in the jacket. He escapes.

•

In my case the stakes weren't as high. I didn't get down on my knees and pray for them to be there, but the archives from my Christian period really were in Jean-Claude Romand's room. Once they were out of their box, it took me a while to overcome the wariness I felt at the sight of these eighteen green and red bound notebooks. When I finally resolved to open the first one, two folded typewritten sheets of paper fell out, on which I read the following:

> Statement of intent by Emmanuel Carrère for his marriage with Anne D., 23 December 1990.
>
> Anne and I have been living together for four years. We have two children. We love each other and are as sure of this love as one can be.
>
> We were no less in love just a few months ago, when we didn't see the need for a religious marriage. I don't think that in opting out we were putting off or refusing a binding commitment. On the contrary, we saw ourselves as committed to each other, and intent, for better or for worse, on living, growing, and getting old together, and, consequently, on one of us being there when the other dies.
>
> Quite apart from any questions of faith, I believed that the goal of communal life was to discover yourself in discovering your partner, and to encourage your partner to do the same. I thought that the growth of one was the condition for the growth of the other, and that in seeking Anne's good I was in fact seeking my own—which I certainly didn't lose sight of. I even started to sense that this mutual growth happens according to the laws of love as John the Baptist described them: "He (in this case she) must increase; I must decrease."
>
> I'd stopped seeing this formula as reflecting the kind of masochism felt by someone who's incapable of elevating his partner without lowering himself, and had understood that I had to think of Anne, her happiness and her fulfillment, more than I thought of myself, and that the more I thought of her, the more I'd do for myself. I discovered, in short, one of the

paradoxes of Christianity that turn worldly wisdom on its head—namely, that you have every interest in scorning your own interest, and in losing sight of yourself to love yourself.

I found that hard. All our misery is rooted in self-esteem, and my self-esteem, exacerbated by my line of work (I write novels, one of the "delirious professions," as Paul Valéry said, based entirely on the opinion one has—and gives—of oneself), is particularly tyrannical. Of course I did my best to escape this quagmire of fear, vanity, hatred, and self-absorption, but my efforts resembled those of Baron Munchausen, who pulls himself out of a swamp by his hair.

I had always believed I could rely on no one but myself. Faith, which I was graced with just a few days ago, has delivered me from this tiring illusion. Suddenly I grasped that it is up to us to choose between life and death, that life is Christ and that his yoke is light. Since then I've felt this lightness constantly. I'm expecting it to spill over onto Anne, and that she'll respect Saint Paul's commandment as I would like to and be joyful always.

I used to think our union depended only on us: our free choice, our goodwill. That its endurance was contingent on us and us alone. I wanted nothing more than a life of love with Anne. But to accomplish that I relied only on our strength, and of course I was appalled at our weakness. Now I know that it is not we who accomplish what we accomplish, but Christ in us.

That's why today I feel we should put our love in his hands, and ask him to grace it and let it grow.

That's also why I consider our marriage my true entry in the life of sacrament, from which I have distanced myself since a first Communion which I received—let's say—absentmindedly.

And, finally, that's why it's important for me that our marriage be celebrated by a priest I met at the moment of my conversion. It was at his Mass—my first in twenty years—that I felt the pressing need to marry, and even at the time I thought it would be good to receive the marriage blessing from him in Cairo. I'm very thankful to the parish and diocese to which I now belong for understanding this project, which, although sentimental, is far from a whim.

2

Of course it shook me up to reread this letter. The first thing that strikes me is that it rings hollow from the first line to the last, and yet I can't doubt its sincerity. The second is that, leaving aside its religious fervor, the person who wrote it twenty years ago isn't so different from the person I am today. His style is a bit more pompous, sure, but it's still mine. Give me the beginning of one of these sentences and I'll finish it in the same way. Above all, the desire for a committed relationship and a love that lasts is the same. All that's changed is its focus. Its current focus suits me better: it's less hard to believe that Hélène and I will live together in peace and harmony. Nevertheless, the things I believe or want to believe today, and which are the pillar of my life, I believed or wanted to believe twenty years ago in almost identical terms.

•

Still, the key thing about the letter is what I don't say, namely, that we were very unhappy. We loved each other, true, but we did it all wrong. Both of us were afraid of life, and we were both terribly neurotic. We drank too much, made love as if we were gasping for air, and each tended to blame the other for our unhappiness. For three years I hadn't been able to write—which I considered my sole reason to exist at the time. I felt powerless, relegated to the suburb of life that is an unhappy marriage, bogged down in a long and dreary rut. I told myself that the best thing would be to leave, but I was afraid that would bring catastrophe and destroy Anne and our two little boys, as well as myself. To justify my paralysis I also told myself that what was happening to me was a test, that making a success of my life—our life—depended on my being able to plod on in this seemingly impossible situation, instead of throwing in the towel as common sense suggested. Common sense was my enemy. I preferred my mysterious intuition, and tried to convince myself that one day it would reveal another, far higher, meaning.

3

Now I have to talk about Jacqueline, my godmother. Few people have had such an influence on me. A very young—and very beautiful—widow, she never remarried. In the sixties several volumes of her half-amorous, half-mystical poetry were put out by prestigious publishers. Later, my godmother abandoned secular poetry and dedicated herself to hymns. A good number of the hymns sung in French churches since Vatican II were penned by her. She lived in a beautiful apartment on Rue Vaneau in the building formerly occupied by André Gide, and something about her evoked the kind of studious, almost austere, aura that you associate with the *Nouvelle Revue Française*—for which Gide wrote—between the wars. At a time when it was less common than it is today, she was well versed in Oriental wisdom and practiced yoga— thanks to which, until an advanced age, she was lithe as a cat.

One day, I must have been fourteen or fifteen, she told me to lie down on the rug in her living room, close my eyes, and concentrate on the base of my tongue. I found that very disconcerting, almost shocking. As an adolescent I was too cultivated, and obsessively worried that people were trying to take me for a ride. Very early on I'd made a habit of finding "amusing"—that was my favorite adjective—everything that in fact attracted or frightened me: other people, girls, a zest for life. My ideal was to observe the absurd turmoil of the world without taking part in it, with the superior smile of someone who's above all that. Actually I was terrified. My godmother's poetry and mysticism offered a perfect target for my perpetual irony, but I also felt that she liked me and, to the extent that I was able to trust anyone back then, I trusted her. At the time, of course, I made a point of finding it highly ridiculous to lie on the floor and think of my tongue. But I did what she asked, tried to let my thoughts flow without judging or holding on to them, and took the first step on the path that later led me to the martial arts, yoga, and meditation.

That's one of the many reasons for the gratitude I now feel for her. She gave me something that stopped me from doing really stupid things. She taught me that time was my ally. Sometimes I think that when I was born my mother sensed she could give me the arms I needed to face the worlds of culture and intelligence, but that for another, es- sential realm of existence she would have to defer to someone else. And that someone else was this woman who was older than she was, both eccentric and completely focused, and who had taken her under her wing when she was twenty. My mother lost her parents at a young age, she grew up in poverty, and what she fears above all else is counting for nothing in this world. For her, Jacqueline was a sort of mentor, the very picture of an accomplished woman, and above all a witness to this dimension that's . . . how to put it? "Spiritual"? I don't like the word; nevertheless, everyone knows more or less what it refers to. My mother knew it existed—or rather, she *knows* it exists, that this inner kingdom is the only one that's really worth aspiring to: the treasure for which the Gospel tells us to renounce all riches. But her difficult personal history made these riches—success, social status, popular acclaim—infinitely desirable for her, and she spent her life going after them. She succeeded, she got it all, she never said "That's enough." I'd be quite out of line to cast the first stone: I'm like that myself. I need all the glory I can get, I need to occupy as much room as I can in other people's minds. But I think that in my mother's mind there has always been a voice reminding her that another combat, the true combat, takes place elsewhere. It's to hear this voice that she's read Saint Augustine her whole life, almost in secret, and that she went to visit Jacqueline. And it's to let me hear it too that she entrusted me in a way to Jacqueline. Sometimes she'd joke about it prudishly. She'd say, "You were at Jacqueline's? Did she talk to you about your soul?" And I'd respond in the same mockingly affectionate tone: "Of course, what else is there to talk about with her?"

That was her role: she talked to you about your soul. We went to see her—and when I say "we," it wasn't just my mother and me: my father went too, and so did dozens of others, people of all ages and backgrounds, and not necessarily believers. We all went to see her on Rue Vaneau, always one-to-one, the way you go see a psychoanalyst or a confessor. With her there could be no posing, you could only talk heart-to-heart. And you knew not a word would leave her living room. She'd look, and listen. You felt yourself looked at and listened to like no one had ever looked at or listened to you before, and then she'd speak to you about yourself as no one had ever done.

•

In her last years my godmother slipped into apocalyptic flights of fancy that left me more than saddened. The whole logic of her life made you think her last days would be marked by an apotheosis of light, yet she sank into the darkness; it's something I don't like thinking about. But until she was eighty she was one of the most remarkable people I knew, and her way of being remarkable shook up all my points of reference.

At the time I admired and envied a single category of humanity: creators. I thought the only thing worth accomplishing in life was to be a great artist—and I hated myself, because in the best of cases I'd be a minor one. Jacqueline's poems hardly impressed me, but if there was anyone around I could consider an accomplished human being, it was her. The few writers and filmmakers I knew were no match for her. Their talent, their charisma, their enviable place in existence were special, narrow advantages, and, even if I didn't know in what way, it jumped out at you that Jacqueline was more *advanced*. I don't just mean she was morally superior: above all, she knew more, she put more things together in her mind. I can't put it any better than that. She was more advanced, the way you can say in biology that one organism is more evolved and consequently more complex than another.

The fact that she was a fervent Catholic only made her more mysterious in my eyes. Not only was I not a believer, but most of my existence had taken place in a milieu where it went without saying that you weren't one. As a child I went to Sunday school and took my first Communion, but this Christian education was so formal, so routine, that it wouldn't make sense to say that I lost my faith at any given moment. For my mother, matters of the soul were just as little a subject of conversation as matters of sex. And as for my father, as I've already said, while respecting the formalities he made no bones about poking fun at the ideas behind them. He was a man of the old school, adhering vaguely to the ideas of Voltaire and the conservative thinker Charles Maurras. So he was the very opposite of a Marxist, but on one point Voltaire, Maurras, and Marx all agree: religion is the opium of the people. When I was growing up, I never broached the subject with any friends, lovers, or acquaintances, no matter how distant. It was situated beyond the pale, totally outside the realm of our thoughts and experience. I could get interested in theology, but, as Borges says, as a branch of fantastic literature. I would have found someone who believed in the resurrection of Christ as strange, as Patrick Blossier said, as someone who's not only interested in but also *believes in* Greek mythology.

So what did I do with Jacqueline's faith? Nothing at all. What for her was her very essence, her very life, I chose to neglect as a strange peculiarity, while picking and choosing what suited me from our conversations. I went to see her to hear her talk about me, and she did that well enough for me to put up with her also talking about our Lord—as she called God. One day I told her just that, and she answered that it was the same thing. In talking to me about me, she was talking about Him. In talking to me about Him, she was talking about me. One day I'd understand. I shrugged: I didn't want to understand. When one of my friends was a child, he'd heard about a boy his age who'd been touched by grace and later became a priest. This edifying tale so frightened him that he prayed each night that he be spared from receiving God's grace and becoming a priest. I was like him. That didn't throw Jacqueline off. "You'll see," she said.

•

I think that as an adolescent and young man I was terrifically unhappy, but I didn't want to know it, and consequently I didn't. My defense system, based on the irony and the pride of being a writer, worked rather well. It was only once I'd turned thirty that this system jammed up on me. I could no longer write, I didn't know how to love, I knew I wasn't particularly likable. Just being me became literally unbearable. When I went to see Jacqueline in this state of acute distress, she wasn't particularly surprised. She saw it as progress. "Finally!" I think she even said. Stripped of the ideas that had allowed me to keep up a pretense, naked, skinned, I became accessible to my Lord. Just a while beforehand I would have fought that tooth and nail. I would have said that I didn't give a shit about my Lord, that I had no interest in consolations for the weak and defeated. Now I was suffering so much, every additional second I spent being me was such torture that I was ready to hear the words the Gospel addresses to all those whose burden is so great that they can't go on.

"Try reading it now," Jacqueline said, handing me the New Testament from the Jerusalem Bible—the one I still have on my desk, and which I've opened twenty times a day since I started this book. "And try not to be too intelligent."

4

Jacqueline gave me another present, at the start of the summer of 1990. She'd long been telling me about her other godson, saying that it would be good for us to get to know each other one day. But as soon as she said it she'd shake her head and change her mind. Would it be such a good idea? Would you have anything to say to each other? Probably not. It's too early.

That summer of agony she felt it was no longer too early, and suggested I call him. Two days later a guy a little older than me rang the doorbell at our apartment on Rue de l'École-de-Médecine. He had blue eyes and his red hair was going gray—it's completely white now, Hervé's just turned sixty. He's the kind of guy who looks like a little boy for a long time, and then like an old man, and never really like an adult. The kind of guy who doesn't really strike you the first time you see him: nondescript, without any apparent sparkle. We started to talk—that is, I started to talk, about myself and the crisis I was going through. I rambled on and on, feverish, confused, mocking. I smoked cigarette after cigarette. Even before starting a sentence I corrected it, qualified it, warned that it would be inexact, that what I wanted to say was in fact far more immense and complicated. As for Hervé, he spoke little and without hesitation. Later on, I got to appreciate his sense of humor, but what threw me off the first time we met was his total lack of irony. Everything I said and thought at the time, even the most sincere expression of distress, was steeped in irony and sarcasm. I think this trait was quite common in the little world I lived in, that of journalism and publishing in late-eighties Paris. No one said anything without a little smile at the corners of their mouths. It was tiring and stupid, but we didn't see that. I only realized it once I was friends with Hervé. He wasn't ironic, he didn't bad-mouth anyone or play the wise guy. He didn't care what people thought of him or play social games. He tried to state precisely and calmly what was on his mind. In saying this, I don't want readers to imagine some kind of sage, unaffected by life's ups and downs. He's had his share of miseries, obstacles, and secrets—and still does. As a child he wanted to die. As a young man he took a lot of LSD and his perception of reality was permanently altered. He was lucky enough to meet a woman who loves him as he is, to have a family with her, and to find a career—he's worked at Agence France-Presse his whole life. Without those two strokes of luck, he could have become a complete misfit. He adapted to the minimum. The only things he really cares about in life are of a—again I trip over this terrible word, with everything it entails in the form of pious inanity and otherworldly claptrap, but there you go—"spiritual" nature. Let's say that Hervé belongs to that group of people for whom being isn't something you take for granted. Since his childhood he's wondered: What am I doing here? And what's "I"? And what's "here"?

A lot of people can live their whole lives without ever being bothered by such questions—or if they are, it's only very fleetingly, and they have no problem getting over them. They manufacture cars and drive around, they make love, talk at the coffee machine, get pissed off because there are too many foreigners in their country, or too many people who think there are too many foreigners in their country, plan their vacations, worry about their children, want to change the world or be successful—and when they are they're afraid of becoming less successful—make war, know that they're going to die but think about it as little as possible, and all of that is quite enough to fill a life. But there's also another type of person for whom it's not enough. Or too much. In any case, who aren't content with things as they are. You can argue all you want about whether they're more or less wise than others, but the fact is that they've never gotten over their astonishment, and can't live without asking why they're living, what it all means, and whether it means anything at all. For them, existence is a question mark, and even if they don't exclude the possibility that there's no answer, they go on searching, they can't help it. As others have searched before them—and some even claim they've found it—they listen to their testimonies. They read Plato and the mystics, they become what are known as religious minds—outside of any church, in Hervé's case, even if, at the time I got to know him, like me he was under the influence of our godmother and for that reason oriented toward Christianity.

•

At the end of this lunch, Hervé and I decided to become friends, and that's just what we did. As I write these lines, our friendship has lasted twenty-three years, and its form, strangely, hasn't changed in all that time. It's a close friendship: I just wrote that, like everyone, Hervé has his secrets, but I think he doesn't have any from me. What makes me think that is that I have none from him. Nothing is so embarrassing to me that I can't tell him about it without feeling the slightest shame. That may seem appalling, but I know it's true. It's a calm friendship that has gone through neither crisis nor eclipse, and developed quite apart from any social interference. Our lives are as different as our characters, and we only see each other alone. We have no common friends. We don't live in the same city. Since we met, Hervé's worked as correspondent and then as bureau chief with Agence France-Presse in Madrid, Islamabad, Lyon, The Hague, and Nice. I went to visit him at each of these posts, and he comes to see me sometimes in Paris, but the real locus of our friendship is a village in the Valais region in Switzerland, where his mother has an apartment in a chalet and where, ever since we first met, he's invited me to come and stay at the end of the summer.

5

So it's now been twenty-three years that Hervé and I have got together each spring and fall in a village called Le Levron. We know all the paths that crisscross the neighboring valleys. In the past we used to leave the chalet before dawn on daylong hikes rising over three thousand feet. Today we're less ambitious, a few hours is enough. Fans of bullfighting use the word "*querencia*" to identify that part of the arena where the bull feels safe amid the terrifying tumult. With time, Le Levron and Hervé's friendship have become the safest of my *querencias*. I go there feeling troubled, I come back calm.

That first summer I was completely stressed out when I arrived. The vacation had been a catastrophe. Following Jacqueline's advice, I'd resolved to abandon all my literary plans and dedicate myself to my wife and son. To use all the energy I'd have otherwise put into my literary work to be available, attentive, and caring—in a nutshell to live well instead of writing poorly. That would change me, I was sure. To help me along, I planned to read a bit of the Gospel every day. I tried, it didn't work. Anne was pregnant, as tender as she could be but sad and worried, with good reason too, because I couldn't hide my panic at the thought of the arrival of our second child. It had been the same with the first, it would be the same fifteen years later before Jeanne was born. All things considered I don't think I've been a bad father, but expecting a child terrifies me. We took long naps from which Gabriel—who was three—tried to wake us by making as much of a racket as he could. I emerged from this depressive torpor only to brood over my misery, once again torn between the clear fact that Anne and I were unhappy together and the conviction that I had made my choice and that for me success depended on how well I could stick to it. Before the summer I'd seen a psychoanalyst several times, and decided to start therapy at the end of the vacations. This idea should have given me cause for hope. But in fact it only distressed me all the more, because I was afraid I'd have to admit that what I'd resolved to do and what I really wanted to do were two separate things. As for the Gospel, I forced myself to read it, as I'd promised Jacqueline. I found it quite beautiful, but I thought that I was far too unhappy for philosophical or moral teaching—to say nothing of religious belief—to be of any help at all. I almost canceled the trip to Le Levron at the end of August. The idea of going to visit a guy I'd only had lunch with once at his mother's place in Switzerland seemed absurd. The other option was to get put away in a psychiatric hospital and have my brain numbed on medication. I'd sleep, I'd be out of circulation, what more could you ask for?

I went to Le Levron, and in the end—and against all odds—I felt almost all right there. Hervé didn't judge me or try to give me advice. He's so aware that we're all out of balance, that we live poorly and do what we can but can't do much, that in his presence I stopped endlessly justifying and explaining myself. What's more, we didn't talk a lot.

6

A path above the village led to a tiny chalet made of black wood, which belonged to an old Belgian priest. He came there every summer to relax and get away from his parish in the blazing furnace of Cairo, where for the rest of the year he used what strength he still had to help the poor and needy. He finally died not so long ago, but when I met him he already seemed very old and very ill. All of his deeply wrinkled face had taken on the sooty color of the shadows around his shiny, black, inquiring, almost sardonic eyes. There were only two rooms in the chalet, and the bottom one, where the hay used to be kept, had been turned into a chapel, with icons covering the walls. Father Xavier belonged to the Melkite order, an increasingly marginal Middle Eastern denomination combining Catholic dogma and Byzantine rites. I was told how this heir to a grand Walloon family ended up becoming a Melkite priest, but I've forgotten. Each morning he said Mass, attended by four or five people in the village, including Pascal, a boy with Down syndrome who acted as altar boy. From his mother, who accompanied him, I learned how proud Pascal was of the responsibilities he'd been given. He eagerly awaited the priest's return each summer, and it warmed the heart to see him hanging on his every gesture, waiting for the blink of an eye indicating that it was time to ring the bell or swing the incense.

The only memories I had of Masses from my childhood were of stress and boredom. This one, celebrated by a tired old man for a handful of Valais mountain dwellers and a boy with Down syndrome whose every gesture indicated that he was right where he belonged and wouldn't exchange his place for anything in the world, moved me so much that I came back the following days. In this converted hay shed I felt protected. I dreamed, I listened. I thought back on my last conversation with Jacqueline before the summer. I no longer felt like saying no to her faith. I was willing to try anything that could improve my situation, I'd said, only I thought it wasn't within my grasp. "Ask," she'd answered. "Ask and you'll see. It's a mystery, but it's the truth: everything you ask for will be granted. Knock on the door. Dare to knock." What did it cost me to try?

•

Father Xavier read a passage from the Gospel of John. Right at the end. It takes place after Jesus' death. Peter and his companions have gone back to their trades as fishermen on the Sea of Tiberias. They're discouraged. The big adventure of their lives went wrong, and even its memory has gone sour. They threw their nets all night but didn't catch a thing. In the early morning hours, a stranger calls out to them from the shore. "Children, have you caught anything to eat?" "No." "Cast the net over the right side of the boat and you will find something." They throw the net. It's so full of fish that all three have to pull to get it back in the boat. "It is the Lord," murmurs the disciple whom Jesus loved, and who wrote the Gospel. "It's the Lord," repeats Peter in stupefaction, and he does something charming, something Buster Keaton could have done: he is naked, he puts on his coat and jumps fully dressed into the sea to go join Jesus on the shore. Jesus says: "Come, have breakfast." They grill up some fish, which they eat with bread. "None of them," says the evangelist, "dares to ask him, 'Who are you?,' knowing that it is the Lord." Three times, Jesus asks Peter if he loves him. Peter swears he does, and Jesus asks him to feed his sheep—an injunction that leaves me somewhat cold because I'm not a shepherd by vocation. But to finish up he says something mysterious:

Amen, I say to you,
when you were younger, you used to dress yourself and go
    where you wanted;
but when you grow old, you will stretch out your hands,
and someone else will dress you
and lead you where you do not want to go.

I think that everyone who converts to Christianity must have a sentence of their own, one that's made for them and is waiting to be discovered. This was mine. It says first of all: Let yourself go, it's no longer you who leads. And once you've taken the step, what could be considered an act of abdication can also come as an immense relief. That's what's called abandonment, and I had no other desire than to abandon myself. But this passage also says that the thing—or the person—to whom you abandon yourself will lead you where you do not want to go. It's this part of the sentence that was addressed most personally to me. I didn't understand it very well—who could?—but I grasped with an obscure certainty that it was for me. What I wanted the most in the world was that: to be led where I didn't want to go.

7

From Le Levron I sent this letter to my godmother:

Dear Jacqueline,
    I know you prayed for what has happened to me, and this letter will bring you much joy. This summer I tried to convince myself that if I knocked often enough the door would open—without being entirely certain I wanted to go in. Then all of a sudden, in the mountains with Hervé, the words of the Gospel took on life for me. Now I know where Truth and Life reside. Relying only on myself for almost thirty-three years, I've never stopped being afraid. Today I discover that it's possible to live without fear—not without suffering, but without fear—and I

can hardly believe this good news. I remind myself of a wrinkled tablecloth covered with crumbs and more or less appealing leftovers, which all of a sudden is shaken out and flaps joyously in the wind. I'd love this joy to last, even though I'm well aware that things aren't that simple, that darkness will return. Nevertheless I'm confident: it's Christ who leads me at present. I'm not very good at bearing his cross, but just the thought of it makes me feel light! There. I wanted you to know quickly, and also how grateful to you I am for having so patiently shown me the way. xo.

I'd completely forgotten this letter, a rough draft of which is in my first notebook. It has a false ring to it, which embarrasses me today. That doesn't mean I was insincere when I wrote it—of course I was sincere—but I can't help believing that someone deep inside me thought what I think now: that all of this is only autosuggestion according to the Coué method, Catholic double-talk, and that all these capital letters and exclamation marks, this tablecloth flapping joyously in the breeze, are simply not like me. But that's exactly what enchanted me: that the whole thing wasn't like me. That the mocking, worried little guy I could no longer stand being had been reduced to silence and that another voice was welling up inside me. The more different it was from my own, the more, I thought, it would *really* be mine.

•

When I get back from Switzerland I'm happy, and convinced I'm entering a new life. The next day I tell Anne that we have to talk, without saying about what, and take her out to dinner at our favorite Thai place, near Place Maubert. I must seem different, a little strange, but not uneasy like someone getting ready to tell their partner that they've "met someone," as they say. Nevertheless, I have met someone, just someone I would never leave her for. On the contrary: he's her ally, our ally. Anne is surprised, to say the least, but takes it well, all in all. Far better, of course, than I'd take it today if the woman I loved came to me and said, with shining eyes and a strangely sweet smile, that she's understood where Truth and Life reside and that we'll now love each other in Our Lord Jesus Christ. I think that if something like that did happen, it would throw me into a complete panic, and Anne has better reasons to panic than most people. Unlike me, she grew up in a family that was Catholic to the point of bigotry. Her parents' most cherished hope was that she would become a nun and, ideally, die very young like Saint Thérèse of Lisieux, her patron saint—Anne's first given name is Thérèse. She inherited the whole package of religious neuroses: an abhorrence of sex, agonizing scruples, overarching sadness. As soon as she was old enough to rebel, she fled this nightmare on the double: she was a crunchy granola type in her adolescence and a night clubber as a young adult. When I got to know her, most of her friends were regulars at discos like Le Palace or Les Bains Douches, people whose relationship with Christianity was limited to laughing their heads off at Monty Python's great parody *Life of Brian*. Since we've been living together, she's had lots of things to hold against me, but certainly not that I've tried to bring her around to the gloomy rituals of her childhood. From that perspective she has nothing to worry about as far as I go. Or so she thought. Anything can happen: the egocentric and mocking Emmanuel Carrère can even start talking about Jesus, with that forced smile you have to make to pronounce the first syllable (you have to try hard to say "gee" without doing it), and which, even at the time of my greatest devotion, always made the name vaguely ridiculous to me. In retrospect, I think she had to be pretty devoted to me—and willing to do everything she could to save our relationship—to greet the news of my conversion with anything other than sarcasm. She must have hoped that something good would come of it. And that's how it was at first.

8

To bolster my nascent faith, Father Xavier advised me to read a passage of the Gospel every day, to meditate on it, and, as I'm a writer, to jot down in a few lines the fruit of my meditation. At Gibert Jeune bookstore on Boulevard Saint-Michel, I buy a big notebook, several big notebooks, because I want to have enough to keep me going for a while—in two years I'll fill eighteen of them. As for the Gospel, I choose to attack the Book of John because that's the one with the bit on going where you don't want to go. I had a vague idea, as well, that it's the most mystical, the deepest, of the gang of four. Starting with the first verse, I'm proved right: "In the beginning was the Word, and the Word was with God, and the Word was God." That's a bit much, especially for someone looking less for metaphysical flashes than rules of conduct, and I wonder if it wouldn't be better to switch horses before leaving the stable. Compared to the thoroughbred whose first reaction was to try to buck me off, Mark, Matthew, and Luke strike me as robust draft horses, better suited for a beginner. But I don't cede to what appears to me as a temptation. I no longer want to obey my own preferences, I no longer want to do the things I'd normally do. I take my initial reaction to the Gospel of John as proof that I must stick to it.

•

One verse a day, no more. Some shine with extraordinary brilliance, themselves deserving the words of the Roman soldiers who arrested Jesus: "No one ever spoke like this man." Others, at first glance, seem to have little meaning, like simple narrative stopgaps, small bones without much to chew on. You'd like to pass over them and move on to the next, but it's precisely here that you have to take your time. An exercise in attention, patience, and humility. Above all humility. Because if you accept—as I decide to do that fall—that the Gospel is not just a fascinating text from a historical, literary, and philosophical point of view, but also the word of God, then you also have to accept that nothing in it is random or incidental. That what looks like the most banal fragment contains more treasures than Homer, Shakespeare, and Proust together. If John tells us, say, that Jesus went from Nazareth to Capernaum, it's anything but anecdotal. Rather, it's a precious asset in the combat of the soul. If nothing more remained of the Gospel than that one modest verse, one Christian's life would not be enough to plumb its depths.

Aside from these verses that are content to remain unobtrusive, I quickly run across others that completely repel me, against which my conscience and critical spirit rebel. These too, above all, I vow not to neglect. To ponder them until their truth appears to me. I think: many of the things I now believe are true and vital—no, not that "I believe": that I *know* are true and vital—would have seemed grotesque to me a few weeks ago. It's a good reason to suspend my judgment and tell myself that I'll understand all that remains closed to me—or even shocks me—if I'm given the grace to persevere. Between the word of God and my understanding, it's the word of God that counts, and it would be silly of me to retain only what jibes with my limited understanding.

Never forget: it's the Gospel that judges me, not the opposite. Between what I think and what the Gospel says, I'll always come out ahead by siding with the Gospel.

9

When I go to see her, Jacqueline doesn't waste time delighting in my conversion. Right away she puts me on my guard: "What you're going through now is the springtime of the soul. The ice breaks, the water flows, the trees bud, you're happy. You see life as you've never seen it before. You know that you're loved, you know that you're saved, you're right to know it. It's the truth. That truth now appears to you in the full light of day, enjoy it. But beware: it won't last. Sooner or later, and certainly sooner than you think, this light will grow dim. Today you're like a child who feels totally safe because his father is holding him by the hand. But a time will come when he'll let go. You'll feel lost, alone in the darkness. You'll call for help, no one will answer. You might as well prepare yourself—but no matter what you do, you'll be caught unawares, and you'll buckle. That's what the cross is like. No joy is entirely free of its shadow. Behind joy is the cross, you'll see that soon enough, in fact you know it already. What you'll take longer to discover—perhaps all your life, but it's well worth it—is that behind the cross is joy: breathtaking, unobstructed joy. The path is long. Don't be afraid, but expect to be afraid. Expect to doubt, to despair, to accuse the Lord of being unfair and asking too much of you. And when you think that, remember this story: A man rebels, and complains as you've complained in the past, and as you'll complain in the future, that the cross he bears is heavier than others'. An angel hears him and bears him on his wings to the place in heaven where all the crosses are stored. Millions, billions, of all sizes. The angel says to him: Choose the one you want. The man lifts a few of them, compares them, and takes the one that strikes him as lightest. The angel smiles and says: That was yours.

"No one," my godmother concluded, "is ever tempted beyond his strength. But you must arm yourself. You must know the sacraments."

•

Leaving the living room where we were sitting, she goes into her study to get a book on the Eucharist. I follow her into the comfortable, somewhat dark room, where she often works late into the night and which I feel I've known forever. I feel good there, and sit on the sofa while she searches through the shelves that cover the walls from floor to ceiling. Things don't often move around at her place. For thirty years I've seen the same goblet in her front hall, which must be for holding sacred wafers, the same box with Monteverdi's *Vespers of the Blessed Virgin* beside the record player, and the same reproductions of Italian and Flemish Madonnas on the shelves. Such permanence is reassuring, like her presence in my life. But that day I can't take my eyes off an image I've never seen before. Black spots dotted irregularly over a white background, which seem to me to depict a face. Or not, depending on the angle from which you look at it, like those drawings where you have to find the hunter hidden in the landscape.

I blink two or three times and ask, "What's that?" Jacqueline glances over at what I'm looking at and says after a while, "I'm glad."

Then she tells me the story behind the image.

•

Two women, one of them very devout, the other not, go walking in the countryside. The nonbeliever tells her friend that she'd like to believe as well but unfortunately that's just the way it is: she doesn't. For her to believe she'd need a sign. Suddenly, just as the words are leaving her lips, she stops and points up at the leaves of a tree. Her face is motionless, her expression wavers between awe and ecstasy. The other woman looks at her, dumbfounded. As she has her camera with her, she hits on the idea, God knows why, of pressing the shutter release in the direction her friend is looking. A few months later, her friend joins the Carmelite Order.

When it's developed the photo captures the play of light in the foliage. It shows an almost abstract set of spots in high contrast, in which certain people see what the woman saw when she was so suddenly touched by grace. Jacqueline sees it, some of her visitors see it, others don't. The reproduction of the photo has been there on the bookshelf for twenty years. I've come in there twenty times without noticing it, but now the time has come, the scales have fallen from my eyes. I've seen the face of the man hidden in the leaves. He's lean and bearded. And he looks the way he does in his other, almost photographic portrait, the one that appears on the Shroud of Turin.

•

"That's good," is all Jacqueline says.

Almost terrified, I murmur, "Once you've seen it, you can't not see it."

"Don't fool yourself," she answers. "It's easy not to see it. But you can also pray that you continue seeing it, it and only it."

"Pray how?" I ask.

"As you like, as it comes. The greatest prayer, and one you'll always come back to, is the one the Lord himself gave us: the Lord's Prayer. And then there's the Book of Psalms in the Bible, which contains all possible prayers for any situation or state of mind. For example . . ." She opens the book and reads:

Do not hide your face from me,
lest I become like those descending to the pit.

I nod my head, I recognize myself. I am one of those who would descend into the pit. In fact the pit is my natural habitat.

But, in another psalm, God says to man:

It's when you no longer saw me that I was the closest to you.

10

I leave Jacqueline's place with the mysterious photo, of which she always keeps a couple of copies in reserve, just in case. I put it, as if on an altar, on a shelf in the studio apartment that serves as my office on Rue du Temple.

That's where I spend the better part of my day. I've always lived by writing, first as a journalist and then as an author of books and television screenplays. I am proud to earn my living—and my family's—without having to depend on anyone, the sole master of my time. While I have pretensions of being an artist, I also like to see myself as an artisan, tied to his workbench, punctually filling orders to the full satisfaction of his customers. But over the past two years, this rather pleasant self-perception soured. I hadn't been able to write novels for some time, and I felt like I'd never be able to again. Even if I was still able to put food on the table thanks to my screenplays, my life had become tinged with helplessness and failure. I'd come to see myself as a failed writer and blamed it on my unhappy marriage, and I constantly repeated to myself Céline's terrible phrase: "Not much music left inside us for life to dance to . . ." I'd never allowed life to dance very graciously, nevertheless there had been a bit of music inside me—frail, not at all exhilarating music—but now it was over. The music box was broken. The days in my studio stretched on interminably. I worked just to put the food on the table, slogging away without conviction. Long, groggy spans punctuated by masturbation. I devoured novels like drugs, to numb the pain and disappear.

•

All of that was before my trip to Le Levron. Before my conversion. Now I get up full of joy, take Gabriel to school, go swimming at the pool for an hour and there I am, after climbing the seven flights, in my quiet studio where, like Louis XIV's industrious finance minister Jean-Baptiste Colbert as related in schoolbook imagery that my generation must have been the last to appreciate, I rub my hands in pleasure at the thought of the work that lies ahead.

The first hour is dedicated to the book of John. One verse at a time, I'm careful to avoid letting my commentary become a sort of diary, full of psychological introspection and above all a record of what's happening to me. No, I want to march boldly forward, guided by the word of God, without obsessively thinking as I've always done in the past that whatever happens to me, sooner or later it will come out in book form. Banning from my mind any idea of a book to come, I force myself to concentrate on the Gospel. Even if Christ talks to me about myself in it, from now on I'm determined to think about him, and not about me.

(When I reread these notebooks today I skip over all the theological reflections I thought were so important, the way you skip over the bits on geography when you read Jules Verne. Of course what interests—and often appalls—me is what I say about myself.)

Then comes prayer. I've often wondered whether it's better to pray before or after I read the Gospel, the way I'll wonder a few years later if it's better to meditate before or after my yoga exercises. And in fact prayer is a lot like meditation. The same posture: cross-legged with a straight back. The same need above all to focus your attention. The same effort—usually vain, but it's the effort that counts—to tame the incessant roving of your thoughts and attain calm, if only for a moment.

The difference, if there is one, is that in prayer you address someone—
the person whose mysterious photo I've placed on the shelf in front of
me. Depending on my mood, I recite the mantras we call psalms, which
my godmother helped me discover, or I speak freely to Him. About
Him, about me. In my notebook I write "Him" with a capital "H." I
ask Him to teach me to know Him better. I tell Him that I want His
will to be done, and that if it runs counter to my own, that's good. I
know that that's how He teaches His chosen ones.

•

Before that, I often went out for lunch, with one friend or another.
Mostly we spent the time talking about literature: extolling the great
works, swapping the latest book dirt, and in any case drinking too
much wine. We'd order by the glass to be reasonable, and as the glasses
progressed, we'd say we should have just ordered a bottle. By the time I
got back to my studio, the drunken elation I'd felt when we left the restaurant had already turned into anguished depression. I'd spend the afternoon promising I'd never do it again, and just a day or so later I'd start
over. Then, from one day to the next, I quit this deplorable habit. I turn
down all lunch invitations and content myself with a bowl of brown rice
that I eat slowly, taking care to chew each mouthful seven times, while
reading with no less concentration—me the voracious reader—some
edifying tract: Augustine's *Confessions, The Way of a Pilgrim, Introduction to the Devout Life* by Saint Francis of Sales. Some of Augustine's
phrases send a shiver down my spine. I murmur them to myself as if I
were whispering in my ear: "Where was I when I looked for you? I
could not find myself, much less find you." This book, which foreshad-
owed Montaigne and Rousseau—and the first in which someone strug-
gles to come to terms with who he has been, what has made him himself
and no one else—is entirely written in the vocative. As I have been sens-
ing vaguely for years that one day I'll have to switch from the third to
the first person singular, this striking use of the second person comes
as a revelation. Emboldened by this example, when I write in my notebooks now I address myself directly to the Lord, with the result that my
daily reflections on the Gospel increasingly resemble prayer, but
also—when I reread them from the perspective of a nonbeliever—have
an emphatic, artificial tone that embarrasses me to no end.

In the afternoon I turn my attention to the screenplay I happen to
be working on. I no longer see this as a secondary occupation, some-

thing you resign yourself to for lack of anything better, but as a sort of higher duty that I carry out cheerfully and with care. If one day God gives me the grace to write books again, so be it. It doesn't depend on me. And if he wants me to write TV screenplays, what I can do is write good ones. What a relief!

I I

In fact things aren't quite that simple. A few really quite colorful pages of my second notebook stand out in sharp contrast to my interminable prayers, and describe a visit to the bookstore La Procure. Bookstores are dangerous terrain for a writer who can no longer write. Aware of this, I've avoided them ever since my conversion—the same way I've avoided publishers' cocktails, literary supplements, and conversations on this fall's books: everything that could hurt me. But La Procure, situated right across from the Church of Saint-Sulpice, is a religious bookstore, and I want to buy a book on John the Apostle, so I risk it. I spend a moment at the "Bible, Exegesis, Church Fathers" section, flipping through thick works on the Johannine milieu. I exchange glances over the table with a priest who's leafing through the same kind of stuff and I feel safe: I like being this grave, fervent guy who takes a discreet interest in Johannine literature without letting the whole world know. Along with a commentary on Saint John, I choose the letters and diary of Thérèse of Lisieux, which Jacqueline has recommended to me. Left to myself I would have been more inclined to read Teresa of Ávila, whom I see as the height of mystical chic, while Thérèse of Lisieux reminds me of my parents-in-law's stodgy piousness, and everything covered by the adjective "Sulpician." But when I told her that, Jacqueline gave me the look of pity she put on from time to time: "My poor boy, even saying such a thing! Saint Thérèse of Lisieux's writings are the height of beauty." I wouldn't want people to think Jacqueline didn't like Teresa of Ávila. On the contrary, she loved her—to the point of having heart-to-heart talks with her in Spanish during her prayers. But for her, Thérèse of Lisieux's "little way," her pure humility and submissiveness, are just the answer to my all-encompassing intellectual disdain. That and a pilgrimage to Lourdes. Instead of going into raptures over Rembrandt and Piero della Francesca, who are accessible to the first aesthete who comes along, to her mind it would do me good to discover all the splendor and devotion contained in the crassest plaster statue of the Virgin Mary. In any event, Saint Thérèse of Lisieux and John the Apostle under my arm, I head for the cash register. The problem is that to get there I have to pass the section with nonreligious books, including a table covered with all the novels that have come out this season. I wasn't expecting that. I'd like to flit by the way a seminarist caught up with carnal thoughts averts his eyes when he passes a poster for a skin flick, but it's too much for me: I slow down, take a look, stretch out my hand, and there I am flipping through book after book, reading the back covers, immediately plunged into a hell that's all the more hellish in that it's ridiculous. My own personal hell: this mixture of powerlessness, resentment, and all-consuming, humiliating envy of everyone who's doing what I passionately wanted to do, was once able to do, and can't do anymore. I stay there for an hour, two hours, hypnotized. The idea of Christ, of life in Christ, becomes illusory. What if this were reality? This vain restlessness, these dashed hopes? What if the real illusion were the You of the *Confessions* and the fervor of prayer? Not just mine, which is so feeble, but that of Thérèse of Lisieux, of Teresa of Ávila, of Augustine, of the Russian pilgrim? What if the real illusion were Christ?

•

I leave the store in a wretched state. Walking down the street, I try to gather myself, to cut my losses. The charade consists of telling myself firstly that most of the books that just caused me so much grief are bad, and secondly that if I can't write any longer it's because I've been called upon to do something else. Something higher. A big book, perhaps, the fruit of these cruel, fallow years, something that will blow everyone away and expose the insignificance of the paltry crop of books that I'm reduced to envying today. But maybe that is not God's plan for me. Maybe what he really wants is for me to stop being a writer and to serve him by becoming, let's say, a stretcher bearer at Lourdes.

Here all the mystics agree: what is asked of us is what we least want to give. You have to look into yourself and find what you're the least willing to sacrifice, and that's it. For Abraham, it's his son Isaac. For me, it's my work, glory, having my name ring in people's ears. That for which I would have gladly sold my soul to the devil. But the devil didn't want it, and all that's left for me to do is offer it to the Lord for free.

Still, I'm reluctant.

•

I find refuge in the Church of Saint-Séverin, the last station of my day before returning home, where I attend the seven-o'clock Mass every evening.
Since not many people attend, it doesn't take place in the large nave but
in a chapel in one of the wings. Everyone there is a regular, and they're
all very fervent, very different from the public at Sunday Mass. Almost
everyone takes Communion, but not me. Even though Jacqueline has
assured me that you become intimate with God far quicker and far
more profoundly by participating in the Eucharistic mystery. You'll be
amazed, she promised. I believe her, but I don't feel ready. Such scruples
tick her off: if you had to be ready before opening yourself to Him, no
one would ever get that far in the first place. That's also what people
acknowledge when they celebrate the mystery: "Lord, I am not worthy
to receive you, but only say the word and I shall be healed." Still, I prefer
to wait until I really feel the need. I know it will come when the time is
right. I stay in the background, near a pillar, and wonder how I could
have found all this boring in the past. Now I find it—or persuade myself
that I find it—a thousand times more absorbing than any book or film.
Each time it seems exactly the same, each time it is entirely different.

1 2

Before meeting Dr. C., on whose couch I've agreed to lie that fall, I met
several of her colleagues, and each time there was at least one thing
about their offices that I found very off-putting. One had a plaque with
his last name followed by his first at the front door of his building—Dr. L.,
Jean-Paul—another had hung frighteningly ugly paintings on the
walls, a third left books in his waiting room that I would have blushed
to have people see at my place. One could think that such a lack of taste
or cultivation has no bearing on an analyst's competence; I didn't, and I
had a hard time seeing myself developing a positive transference toward
someone I considered a total clod. I had no problems with the way
Dr. C. decorated her office, her way of speaking, or how she looked.
She's a woman of around sixty, mild-mannered, reassuring, pleasantly
neutral. But as the day of our first session approaches, I'm taken by a
desire to cancel it. If I don't, it's a bit out of politeness and a lot thanks to
Hervé. Why deprive yourself of something that could be useful without
even trying it?

•

Instead of lying on the couch as I was supposed to, I sit in the chair, facing Dr. C. She doesn't react to this gesture of defiance, waits for me to make the first move. I take the plunge and say, Okay: something has happened since the last time we spoke. I've met Christ.

Having let that one go, I figure the ball is in her court. I wait, watching her expression. She remains neutral. After a moment's silence, she lets out a little "Mmm?," a typical little analyst's "Mmm?," to which I respond quite aggressively: "That's exactly the problem with psychoanalysis. Saint Paul himself could walk in here and tell you what happened to him on the road to Damascus, and you wouldn't ask yourself whether it's true, just what it's the symptom of. Because of course that's what you're wondering, right?"

No answer. Everything's as it should be. I go on, and explain that all summer I've been afraid that instead of improving my love relationship, analysis would force me to admit that it's a failure. Now things have changed. I no longer see the need for her services because I consider myself cured. Well, maybe not exactly cured: I wouldn't be that presumptuous. Let's say on the way to being cured. Like every morning, this morning I read a passage from the Book of John before coming to this meeting, and I came across a sentence I liked. Jesus says to a certain Nathanael, who's come to listen to him out of curiosity: "I saw you under the fig tree." We don't know what Nathanael was doing under the fig tree. Maybe he was whacking off, maybe what he was doing there sums up all his secrets, all his shame, everything he finds hard to bear. Jesus saw all that, and Nathanael is delighted. That's what makes him decide to follow Jesus.

"I'm like Nathanael," I say to Dr. C. "Christ saw me under the fig tree. He knows far more about me than I do, far more than I could learn from analysis. So what's the point?"

Dr. C. doesn't say a thing, not even "Mmm?" She looks a bit sad, but then again she always does, and to my surprise my voice is also quite sad when I start speaking again. All the aggressiveness I felt at the start is gone.

"Of course you don't say anything. You're not supposed to let me see what you think, but I've got a pretty good idea. I think that Christ is truth and life. You think that that's a comforting illusion. And if I stay here what you'll try to do—with the best intentions in the world and no doubt with a lot of professional acumen—is cure me of this illusion. But I don't want your cure, you see? Even if you proved to me that it's a sickness, I'd prefer to remain with Christ."

"What's forcing you to choose?"

I was no longer expecting her to talk. What she says surprises me, in a positive way. I smile, the way you smile at chess when your opponent makes a good move. I'm struck by an anecdote, which I tell her. As a young girl, Thérèse of Lisieux was asked to choose among several Christmas presents. What she says could be taken for the words of a child, but Catholic commentators interpret it as the sign of her insatiable spiritual appetite: "I don't want to choose. I want it all."

"I want it all?" Dr. C. repeats thoughtfully while motioning to the couch with her hand.

I lie down.

•

Five years later, at the end of what I'll later call my first bout of analysis, Dr. C. will evoke the rule of thumb according to which every therapy is summed up in its first session. Mine, she'll say, was a striking case in point. I've had to piece it together from memory, because the eighteen notebooks I filled in the first two years make almost no mention of it whatsoever. During these years, I went to her practice in the 19th arrondissement twice a week to talk about anything and everything that went through my head for exactly three-quarters of an hour—Dr. C. was an old-school Freudian. In the same period I wrote for at least an hour a day about the Gospel and what happened in my soul. These two activities were vital for me. Nevertheless, I made sure to erect a watertight partition between them, and in retrospect I can easily see why. I tell myself I should have seen it at the time, that it stared you in the face, but the fact is that I didn't. I was scared stiff that my faith would be destroyed by analysis, and I did all I could to protect it. I remember I once said very explicitly to Dr. C. that there could be no question of me discussing my conversion in our sessions. Anything else, fine, but not that. I could just as well have said: We can talk about anything you like, but I'd like to keep my private life to myself.

Looking at things from her point of view, I imagine I didn't exactly make things easy—all the more so because I'm horribly intelligent. Make no mistake: I'm not committing the sin of pride in saying this. On the contrary, I mean it mischievously, the way my godmother meant it, and the way Dr. C. meant it when, sitting behind me in her chair one day, she exclaimed in despair: "Why must you always be so intelligent?" What she meant was, incapable of simplicity, convoluted, hairsplitting, anticipating objections that no one was thinking of making, not being able to think something without at the same time thinking its opposite, then the opposite of its opposite, and exhausting myself with these mental gymnastics for no purpose whatsoever.

13

Our second son, Jean Baptiste, was born that fall. Anne wasn't particularly wild at the thought of naming him after an unkempt zealot basically known for his farouche manners, his ascetic life in the desert, his imprisonment under the cruel King Herod, and, in the end, his beheading. Plus it sounded extremely Catholic. As for Jean Baptiste, when he grew up he sided with his mother: apart from when he's with his family, everyone calls him Jean. But I stuck to my guns. In my readings of John the Apostle, I'd gotten as far as the account of John the Baptist, who is both the last of the prophets of Israel and the precursor of Jesus. The greatest of the Old Covenant, the smallest of the Covenant to come. The one who summed up love according to Christ in this dazzling, almost unacceptable formula: "He must increase; I must decrease." The day Jean Baptiste was baptized, I wanted his godfather Hervé to read the song of thanksgiving intoned by John the Baptist's father, the old Zechariah, the day his son was circumcised. It's given in the Gospel of Luke and is called the Benedictus:

And you, child,
will be called prophet of the Most High,
for you will go before the Lord
to prepare his ways,
to shine on those who sit
in darkness and death's shadow,
to guide our feet
into the path of peace.

14

A couple of days after this baptism, our au pair girl leaves us without notice. That's a real problem. Anne works a lot, so do I in my way. Both of us spend all day out of the house. We've simply got to have someone to pick up Gabriel at daycare, and now to take care of Jean Baptiste. Feverishly we place ads and start interviewing candidates. As the school year has already started, we can't be too picky. All the charming, dynamic students have found something, the only candidates left are the ones no one was willing to take: foot draggers whose only motivation is that they can't find anything better, on the lookout for the first occasion to leave without notice. It's a discouraging, almost comical pageant, and we feel like we're scraping the bottom of the barrel, when one bleak December afternoon we open the door to Jamie Ottomanelli.

The other applicants for the position of au pair girl at least have one thing going for them—namely, that they are girls, I mean young. Jamie is over fifty, she's big and fat, with greasy hair and dressed in an old sweat suit that doesn't smell very good. Not to put too fine a point on it, she looks like a bum. Anne and I have worked out a kind of code for discreetly trading impressions and preventing interviews from going on for too long. This time the verdict's clear—not on your life—but we can't send her back out into the rain without at least having the semblance of a conversation. We offer her a cup of tea. She sits down in an armchair near the fireplace, spreading her fat legs as if she were getting ready to spend the rest of the day there. After a moment's silence, she notices a book on the coffee table and says in French but with a strong American accent: "Oh, Philip K. Dick . . ."

I raise my eyebrows: "You know him?"

"I knew him, way back when, in San Francisco. I babysat his little daughter. He's dead now. Often I pray for his poor soul."

•

I read Dick passionately as an adolescent, and, unlike most adolescent passions, this one never waned. I regularly read and reread *Ubik, The Three Stigmata of Palmer Eldritch, A Scanner Darkly, Martian Time-Slip, The Man in the High Castle.* I felt—and still do—that their author is something like the Dostoyevsky of our time. Like most of his fans, however, I was rather embarrassed by the books of his last period—the way

Dostoyevsky's fans are embarrassed by *A Writer's Diary*, Tolstoy's by *Resurrection*, and Gogol's by *Selected Passages from Correspondence with Friends*. In a nutshell: at the end of his chaotic life, Dick had a sort of mystical experience, only he couldn't be sure if it was a *real* mystical experience or the final expression of his legendary paranoia. He tried to deal with it in strange books full of quotes from the Bible and the Church fathers. For a long time I really had no idea what to make of them, but in the past few months I've been giving them a fresh look. That said, the last thing I expected was for an interview with an au pair girl to morph into a discussion about Dick.

As we talk, it comes out that like Dick, Jamie was raised in the San Francisco Bay Area, that she grew up in a community of hippies and experimented with all the trips of the sixties and seventies: sex, drugs, rock and roll, and above all Oriental religion. After ordeals she prefers not to go into, she converted to Christianity. She wanted to become a nun and did long stretches at convents, where she discovered that it was not her vocation. For the past twenty years she's been moving from place to place, guided by the sentence in the Gospel about the birds in the sky who do not sow or reap, who gather nothing into barns, and yet the heavenly Father feeds them. In her case, however, the heavenly Father hasn't really come through. Jamie is very poor—at the end of her tether, in fact. Which is why she's come to see us: according to our ad, the job comes with a room on the top floor, that caught her interest. This naïve admission prompts Anne to bring the discussion away from Dick, the *I Ching*, and Saint Francis of Assisi, where it's been for the past hour, and around to the matter at hand. Apart from her pressing need for a roof over her head, has Jamie ever looked after kids?

Oh, yes, of course, often. Most recently those of an American diplomat. "Oh, perfect!" I say cheerfully. I'm ready to hire her on the spot, but Anne is firm and says she'd like to think it over. She asks Jamie for the diplomat's number, and we spend the evening hashing things out after Jamie leaves—me won over, Anne countering that while Jamie is certainly an endearing character, she does look *very* lost. I'm wise enough not to come right out and admit what's really on my mind, namely, that this woman who prays for the poor soul of Philip K. Dick has been sent to us by God. Instead, I tell Anne about the *niania* who took care of me and my sisters when we were kids. A Russian *niania* is anything but a maid: she's a wet nurse, a housekeeper, part of the family, and in general she stays until the end of her days. I adored ours—my sisters less so, because she favored me shamelessly. I'm sure that this Jamie, who's been so subject to life's ups and downs but who's remained candid and starry-eyed, will become for our boys what my *niania* was for me. That she'll give all of us precious lessons in joy and a disregard for material things. Moved by my conviction, Anne calls the American diplomat, who has nothing but praise. Jamie's a marvelous woman: far more than an employee, she's a longtime friend. The kids are going crazy, they've been crying every night since she left. Well, then why did she leave? In fact they're the ones who are leaving, the American diplomat explains. After four years in Paris, he's leaving his post and returning stateside.

15

Jamie no longer lives at the American diplomat's place but she's left her stuff there, and I go with her to pick it up. The concierge of a grand building in the 7th arrondissement greets us in an extremely surly way, and follows us down to the basement as if she suspected us of being thieves. Jamie's things are stored in a huge metal trunk, which we load into the car and then haul up to the maid's room on the top floor at our place, not without difficulty, because it's extremely heavy. Before I leave to let her get settled in, Jamie opens the trunk, which contains very few clothes but reams of paper, tattered yellow photos, and painting equipment—because she paints icons, she tells me. She takes out a thick manuscript: since I'm a writer this might interest me.

While she's getting installed I spend the afternoon playing with Jean Baptiste, and, when he goes to sleep, thumbing through *Tribulations of a Child of God (by Jamie O.)*. It's not exactly an autobiography, more of a diary interspersed with poems and illustrated with all kinds of drawings, photo collages, and parodied advertisements, typically reminiscent of the seventies. The drawings look like psychedelic album covers, and are both insipid and hideous. But Jacqueline has lectured to me about the importance of purity of heart in artistic matters and the narrow-mindedness of professed experts, telling me with a smile that their punishment in hell will be to drool for all eternity over the ghastly paintings they so scorned here on earth. A series of photos taken in a booth shows Jamie, younger but already fat, making faces alongside a skinny guy with a beard and round glasses. I gather that he was her husband and that he's dead. The whole thing is chaotic and extremely hard to bear, and full of a gnawing anger at the whole world that I find somewhat alarming.

•

The previous night we had some friends over for dinner and told them about our colorful new nanny. I said that she bears a striking resemblance to Kathy Bates—the actress who stars in *Misery*—and everyone got a kick out of imagining the Stephen King version of our story: the adorable fat lady who heaps kindness upon kindness on the young couple and gradually crushes them with her monstrous tyranny. While not explicitly rejecting this horror scenario, I maintained with a straight face that Jamie was a sort of saint, someone whose life's twists and turns and no doubt a secret vocation have forced her, from deprivation to deprivation, to let go of her ego and put herself for better or worse in the hands of providence. In fact, one look at her pathetic manuscript is enough to see that the poor girl hasn't at all let go of her ego—which on the contrary is alive and kicking—and that far from having achieved the Franciscan joy I ascribed to her, she suffers cruelly from the humiliations that life hasn't stopped heaping on her: the rejection of her attempts at literature and photography; the shock of seeing her fat, unattractive body in the mirror. But determined as I am to consider her life, and her entry into ours, from a spiritual point of view, I prefer to see in her bitter and revengeful blathering the echo of the many psalms where Israel, all the while complaining about present injustice, expresses his confidence in the coming of the Messiah, who will put the powerful in their place and uplift the poor, the humiliated, the eternally rejected. And at the same time I'm in a bit of a jam: she's given me her manuscript, author to author, she expects an answer, and I wonder what I can say to encourage her without being too much of a hypocrite.

16

The first day when Jamie takes care of the children on her own, we come back to find the entire apartment hung with multicolored daisy chains, cut out with the help of Gabriel, who seems to have thoroughly enjoyed himself. That's good. What's less good is that all the rooms— not just the kids'—are in an indescribable mess, and Jean Baptiste is wailing because he hasn't been changed for hours. We've planned a sort of welcome dinner and asked Jamie not to do a thing. She takes our instructions literally and lets herself be served without lifting a finger to help. Our discreet suggestions—"reproaches" or even "observations" would be too strong—about how we'd like to find the house when we return home are met with a benevolent, Buddhist smile, a bit too detached, to Anne's mind and even to mine, from the contingencies of this world. When she goes back upstairs, leaving us alone with the dishes, Anne and I get into an argument. Annoyed and feeling responsible, I admit that we have to find a more fitting tone. Treat her like a friend, yes, but not overdo it. Of course we'd never ask her to serve us at dinner, but we also want to avoid the absurd situation where we serve her—no matter what Jesus has to say on the subject. I promise to talk to her, and spend the whole next day going over what I'll say. At five o'clock I get a call at my studio from Gabriel's daycare: his nanny hasn't come to pick him up.

I frown, I don't understand. That very morning I showed Jamie around, introduced her to the people who work there, there's no reason for anything to go wrong. Nevertheless, that's how it is: she hasn't come. I call home, no one answers. I call Anne at her office and there's no answer there either—of course this all takes place in the remote days before mobile phones. I run to the daycare to pick up Gabriel and take him home. Jean Baptiste and Jamie aren't there. The weather isn't good enough for them to be out at a playground: I'm starting to get worried.

I go up to the top floor, where I find her door wide open. Jean Baptiste is sound asleep in his bassinet—I breathe a sigh of relief: that's the key thing. As for Jamie, she's busy covering the wall with a sort of fresco that must represent the Last Judgment: paradise in her room, hell and its procession of the damned spilling out into the hallway. I'm not quick-tempered, perhaps not quick-tempered enough, but this time I blow up. The firm but good-natured words of reproof I've prepared turn into a torrent of rebukes. Forgetting one of the children she's been entrusted with! On the very first day! I don't have time to cut into my second accusation—namely, that neither we nor the landlord have asked her to decorate her room or the hallway, because much to my surprise, instead of hanging her head and admitting her mistake or stammering an apology, Jamie starts shouting louder than me, calling me an evil man, and worse, someone who derives pleasure from driving people mad. Rising to her full stature in her old sweat suit, her eyes flashing, sputtering her words, she brandishes a copy of my novel *The Mustache*, crying: "I know what you do! I've read this book! I know what perverse games you play! But that won't work with me. I've known worse devils than you, you won't be able to drive me mad!"

•

As Michel Simon says in *Bizarre, Bizarre*: "If you write enough horrible things, horrible things start to happen."

17

Of course the wisest thing would be to leave it at that and, after this disastrous trial, to go our own separate ways. The problem is that having found a couple of square feet for her trunk and herself, Jamie has no intention of leaving. She no longer comes down to our place, Anne and I have to go up to talk to her. Behind her locked door in the hallway covered with gremlins, we try in vain to get her to come around to our point of view. We appeal to her good sense, stress our need to find and lodge a replacement. We offer her a month's salary, two, three. All in vain. Most of the time she doesn't answer. We don't even know if she's in there. Other times she screams at us to go to hell. She explains that it's not Anne she's really mad at, but me. Anne's like a boss who looks out for her own interests: she pays, she demands a service, fine. Of the two of us, I'm the real shit. Playing at being Mr. Nice Guy, all sanctimonious, wanting to have it both ways: kicking people out in the middle of winter only to be plagued by my delicate conscience and suffer pangs of remorse.

She hit the bull's-eye there: my notebooks are full of afflicted soul-searching. I recopy phrases from the Gospel, such as "Why do you call me 'Lord, Lord,' but not do what I command?" I feel like those whom Jesus condemns with the words "I was hungry and you gave me no food, I was thirsty and you gave me no drink, a stranger and you gave me no welcome, naked and you gave me no clothing, ill and in prison and you did not care for me." When they respond, "Lord, when did we see you hungry or thirsty or a stranger or naked or ill or in prison, and not minister to your needs?" he answers, "What you did not do for one of these least brothers of mine, you did not do for me. And whatever you did for one of these least ones, you did for me."

Irrefutable Gospel logic. Nevertheless, I try to justify my position: we need someone we can count on, the situation has become unbearable, moreover she's more of a burden for Anne than for me, so to protect my wife I must be tough—brutal if need be. But that's worldly wisdom, the wisdom of the boss who wants his money's worth for services rendered. Christ asks for something else. That we put other people's interests above our own. That we recognize him in Jamie Ottomanelli, with her poverty, her confusion, the looming threat of her madness. I know she's praying up there, three floors above us, barricaded in her little room, and I tell myself that in her prayers she's closer to Christ than I am. "Seek first the kingdom of God," Jesus says, "and all these things will be given you besides." After all, isn't seeking the kingdom of God remaining true to the trust we felt when we hired Jamie, rather than betraying it in the name of reason? If you want to live according to the Gospel, can you be *too* trusting?

•

While I turn these scruples over in my head, Anne takes more concrete steps. As a desperate measure she'd be willing to go to the police, but we don't have a work contract with Jamie, we thought we'd pay her under the table, so it's a bit delicate. She tries to contact the American diplomat, who can't be reached. She leaves increasingly urgent messages, at his home, at his office, but he doesn't call back. Has he gone back to the States already? Small surprise at the embassy: he's not going back to the States at all. Finally his wife, Susan, calls back and arranges to meet Anne in a café. She arrives wearing dark glasses—it's December and raining—and comes out with the truth.

Jamie's a sort of friend, it's true. Roger, her husband, knew her at college. They ran into her by accident in Paris. She was completely adrift, but she's a touching character so Roger wanted to help her out for old times' sake. They let her stay in the studio apartment where they put up friends, and in exchange she was to help their daughter with her homework. "She's got a good education, you know, she could have gotten by fine in life, but she's had a hard time. After a couple of days, things became absolutely impossible. No need to go into detail, it's been the same with you and must be like that with everyone." Susan demanded that Roger get Jamie out of there at any price, and that price was to do this disgusting thing: to recommend Jamie when she answered an ad. *"C'était dégeulasse,"* Susan repeats in her American accent, without Anne being sure if she knew she was imitating Jean Seberg in Jean-Luc Godard's film *Breathless*. They were ready to do anything to get rid of Jamie, and now they feel terrible about putting such a nice young couple in such a fix. Well, she feels terrible. Roger's a bit of a coward, like all men—to which Anne, I suppose, nods in agreement. Susan says she'll ask Roger to do something and get things sorted out. If, despite everything that's happened, anyone still has any authority over Jamie, it's him.

•

Anne returns home skeptical, though touched by Susan's honesty. Three days later, we don't know what strings Roger pulled, but when I go upstairs for another round of talks the room is empty, swept clean, with the key in the door. The only trace of Jamie's passage is the Last Judgment on the wall, which we spend the weekend scrubbing off. We then hire a sluggish, apathetic Cape Verdean, who speaks no French and just a little English. After the nightmare we've just been through, she's a pearl. Anne calls Susan to thank her. Susan doesn't answer or call back—like those FBI agents who disappear without a trace once their mission's done, and I predict half-jokingly that if we call the embassy we'll be told Roger X doesn't exist and never has.

18

During the Christmas vacation Anne and I go to Cairo to get married, in Father Xavier's parish. I've chosen the most classic reading you can find for such an event: the hymn to love from the First Letter of Saint Paul to the Corinthians. For reasons I analyzed at length and for the most part vainly during analysis, I don't want our families to be present at the ceremony. The only witnesses are the church sexton and a street sweeper. As we didn't even bring a bottle of wine to offer them a glass, Father Xavier goes to his room to fetch some stale port that was given to him by one of his parishioners. It's sad, almost secretive: we get married as if it embarrassed us. Anne cries that night. We cross the Sinai Desert by car and watch the sunrise at Saint Catherine's Monastery. I read from the Book of Exodus. I imagine the people of Israel, out of Egypt but still far from the Promised Land, wandering on this gravelly sand for forty years, and I compare their ordeal to my own. The words "desert crossing" comfort me. Despite my submission to the divine will, I don't stop asking myself if and when I'll be able to write a new book. A vague, very vague, idea starts taking shape: a portrait of a sort of savage mystic who's a bit like Philip K. Dick and Jamie Ottomanelli, an old hippie— or rather an old hippie girl—scarred from drugs and misfortune, who has a mystical illumination one day and wonders until her dying days if she met God or if she's crazy, and if there's a difference between the two.

•

Right after we get back from Egypt, a guy on Boulevard Saint-Michel hands me a poorly printed tract on what he calls the Revelation of Arès. It's sectarian claptrap, and I read a few lines with the pitying disdain of someone who spends his time with Meister Eckhart and the Church fathers. One argument makes me smile: "If the recipient of the Revelation of Arès is not the prophet sent among twentieth-century man, the equal of Abraham, Moses, Jesus, and Muhammad, everything contained in the Revelation would be false. And that's impossible." I shrug, then realize that the argument echoes Saint Paul word for word: "If Christ is preached as raised from the dead, how can some among you say there is no resurrection of the dead? If there is no resurrection of the dead, then neither has Christ been raised. And if Christ has not been raised, then empty too is our preaching; empty, too, your faith." That throws me off. I reason with myself: if you believe as I do that God exists, it is beyond question that the message of Saint Paul is light-years from what the guy who received the Revelation of Arès says, or even from what Dick says from deep in the mystical delirium of his last years. Paul was inspired, the other two clearly misguided. The one was grappling with the real thing, the other two with pitiful illusions. *But what if there is no real thing?* If God doesn't exist? If Christ was not raised from the dead? At best you can say that Paul's undertaking was more successful, that it's worthier from a philosophical and cultural point of view—but deep down it's exactly the same B.S.

19

One night Anne returns home extremely agitated. She met Jamie in the stairway of our building. Yes, Jamie. In her baggy sweat suit, carrying a shopping bag from the supermarket. What's she doing here? Troubled as if she'd met a ghost, Anne lacked the presence of mind to ask her, and Jamie avoided her eyes and hurried on her way. Gabriel, who's listening, pipes up. He's seen Jamie as well. "Here in the building?" "Yes, here. Is she going to come back and live with us?" he asks hopefully, still remembering the great time he had cutting out the daisy chains.

I go up to inspect the top floor with the maids' rooms. Right at the end of the hall, past the small washroom that we repainted to give our employee the most basic amenities, I discover a kind of nook under the sloping roof. Not a room, more like an alcove. I had no idea it even existed, simply because I'd never gone that far down the hall: no one in this old, rather impractical building has any reason to. There's not even a door, just a bit of cloth pinned up with thumbtacks. In the film adaptation of a book by Stephen King, this is where the music would grow more and more oppressive. You'd want to cry out to the reckless protagonist to get out of there as fast as he can, rather than pulling on the curtain as, of course, he's going to do, as I do. And in this tiny garret is, you guessed it, Jamie's trunk. On it is a cardboard tray with what's left of a takeout meal. A candle—unlit, luckily—in front of one of Jamie's icons. Her painting supplies and, already, one of her vile psychedelic frescos half finished on the peeling wall.

Zoom in on a laughing demon. The camera plunges into its shadowy mouth while the kettledrums of *Dies Irae* roll. End of shot: with any luck the spectators are riveted to their seats.

•

We never found out exactly what happened. Did Jamie leave on Roger's orders only to come back on the sly, having spotted this fallback solution long ago? Or, having promised his wife that he'd clear Jamie out of our room, did Roger interpret this commitment in the narrowest sense and advise her to sit tight a couple of yards farther down the hall in this rat hole that's of no use to anyone, thinking: Well, I've done what I can, don't expect me to do anything else? Whatever the case, she's squatting three floors above us and it's horribly nerve-racking. What should we do? Call the police? Tell the landlord? As we were the ones who brought her in there in the first place, that could turn against us. Worse, Jamie could also turn against us. Seek revenge. Take it out on the children. Snatch Jean Baptiste from his cradle. Lure Gabriel, who adores her, into her lair. Flee with him, and we'll never see him again. Our poor little boy will grow up goodness knows where, raised by this nutcase, rummaging through garbage cans, fighting stray dogs for food, returning to the state of nature. We give the Cape Verdean girl a warning worthy of out-and-out paranoiacs. We make Gabriel promise he won't talk to Jamie, accept anything from her, or follow her anywhere.

"But why?" he asks. "Is she a bad person?"

"No, she's not a bad person, not really. But you see, she's very unhappy, and sometimes very unhappy people do . . . how to put it? . . . things they shouldn't do."

"What kind of things?"

"I don't know . . . things that could hurt you."

"So you shouldn't talk to very unhappy people? Or accept anything from them?"

I wanted to bring up our son in a spirit of confidence and openness: each word of this conversation is sheer torture.

•

After this climax, the film comes to a quick end. I suppose that will come as a disappointment for readers. But as we expected one horror after the next, for us it's a relief. Far from harassing us, Jamie avoids us. No doubt she chooses the hours when she stands the least chance of running into anyone to come and go, leaving the building at dawn, coming back after dark. Despite her size she's as elusive as a ghost, so discreet that we wonder if we didn't dream the whole thing up. But no, her trunk is still there. I feel as if misfortune is lurking in the building, as if a menace is hovering overhead, but little by little this impression fades. Whereas before we thought about her obsessively, now we can go for several hours—and soon several days—without thinking about her at all. One night I see her at Mass, at the Church of Saint-Séverin. I'm afraid she'll get aggressive, but when she looks over I nod to her and she nods back. I see that she's going to take Communion, which I don't yet do. I think of Christ's words: "If you bring your gift to the altar, and there recall that your brother has anything against you, leave your gift there at the altar, go first and be reconciled with your brother, and then come and offer your gift." As we leave I head over to her. We exchange a few words, without bitterness. I ask how she's doing, she says things are tough. I sigh: I understand. Is there anything we can do? I'm no longer really sure how things ended. I remember vaguely that we asked the parish to help her out, that we gave her a bit of money, and that before she left she even came down to kiss us goodbye. I never saw her again, and I have no idea if she's still alive.

20

Once the moment of open crisis has passed, there's no further mention of her in my notebooks. Or rather: there is, but it's no longer really her, Jamie Ottomanelli. It's the character in the book I thought about all that winter. In fact, I did more than think about it, I got to work on it. The problem is that no trace of it exists. Now that we write—and even read—more and more on screens and less and less on paper, I have a telling argument in favor of the second medium: in the more than twenty years that I've been using computers, everything I've written by hand is still in my possession, for example the notebooks I base this book on, while without exception everything I typed directly onto the screen has disappeared. Of course, I made all kinds of backups, and backups of my backups, just like everyone said I should, but only the ones I printed out on paper have survived. The others were saved on floppy disks, sticks, external drives—all supposedly much safer but ultimately obsolete one after the next—and are now as inaccessible as the tapes we listened to in our youth. Anyway: deep in a computer that gave up the ghost long ago there was once the first draft of a novel that, if I could get my hands on it, would nicely round out my notebooks. I'd borrowed a title from the filmmaker Billy Wilder, who left us with so many great one-liners. Coming out of the movie *The Diary of Anne Frank*, Wilder was asked how he liked it. "Very beautiful," he said with a serious look. "Really very beautiful . . . Very moving." (A pause.) "Still, you'd like to know the adversary's point of view."

•

As far as I can remember, *The Adversary's Point of View* featured Jamie in a long monologue up in her garret like Job on his dunghill. Like him, she scratches her boils and obsessively rehashes the same themes: the injustice of fate that inflicts hardships on those of goodwill while the evil triumph and indulge themselves; the revolt against God, whose justice we praise and yet who tolerates such cruel injustices; the effort to submit to his will despite everything, to believe that there's a meaning to this chaos that will one day be revealed, and that finally the righteous will rejoice and the evil will gnash their teeth.

To compose this monologue I'd put together what I could remember of Jamie's autobiography *Tribulations of a Child of God*, alongside quotes from the psalms and the prophets. This montage worked quite well, because the psalmist's supplications are universal, and the prophets, who after the fact were venerated by the Hebrews, must in their day have been pigheaded oddballs much like Jamie, bellyaching to no end, indecently displaying their sores, and getting on everyone's nerves with their demands and their misery—it's no coincidence that the name Jeremiah gave the word "jeremiad." That said, my great idea, and the one that justified the title, was not just to represent Jamie as one of these poor, humiliated wailers to whom Jesus promises the kingdom of heaven but also to depict myself as I would appear in her eyes. And even if I've lost this text, even if I've forgotten almost all of it, I have no problem imagining that here my taste for self-flagellation must have really come into its own. Although interwoven with biblical references, the story itself was realistic, piecing together Jamie's slow nosedive between sixties California—where, of course, she crossed paths with Philip K. Dick—and nineties Paris, where she wound up working as an au pair for a couple of young intellectuals who were as odious as they were well intentioned. The wife was feverish, never at rest, prey to perpetual worries. Just being in the same room with her was exhausting, but she was nothing compared to the husband. Oh, the husband! The young writer with the romantic lock of hair who spent his time gazing at his own navel, nursing his neuroses, full of a sense of his own importance and—worst of all—of his humility. He's found a new way of finding himself interesting: being Christian, commenting devotedly on the Gospel, and assuming a gentle, benign, sympathetic air, which doesn't stop him from plotting with his wife to call the police in the middle of winter to kick a poor, fat, washed-up old vagrant out of their tiny garret room with toilets on the landing. And when he finally drops the idea it's not out of kindness but because it could attract the landlord's attention. Since they're just subletting their lovely, book-filled apartment, they don't want to create a scandal or make waves. You've got to wonder what the two of them would have done if she'd been Jewish during the occupation . . .

How long, Lord, will you forget me?
How long will you hide your face from me?
How long must I carry sorrow in my soul,
grief in my heart day after day?
How long will my enemy triumph over me?

My soul is filled with troubles;
my life draws near to Sheol.
My couch is among the dead,
why do you reject my soul, Lord,
and hide your face from me?
I have been mortally afflicted since youth,
I have borne your terrors and I am made numb,
my only friend is darkness.

Lord, my heart is not proud;
nor are my eyes haughty.
I do not busy myself with great matters,
with things too sublime for me.
Rather, I have stilled my soul,
like a weaned child to its mother,
weaned is my soul.

21

My notebooks from 1991 deal for the most part with Communion, which I'm fervently preparing for. In the Gospel of John, I've got as far as the feeding of the multitude and Jesus' grand discourse on "the bread of life." It contains such stunning, and in fact even shocking, lines as "Whoever eats my flesh and drinks my blood remains in me" and "Unless you eat the flesh of the Son of Man and drink his blood, you do not have life within you." What does it mean to have life within you? I don't know, but I know it's what I aspire to. Without knowing it, I pine for another way of being present to the world, to others, and to myself than this blend of fear, ignorance, narrow self-interest, and inclination to do evil when we in fact want to do good, which is our common sickness and which the Church names with a single, generic word: "sin." A short while ago I learned that there's a remedy for sin, as efficient as aspirin is for head-aches. Christ assures us that there is, at least in the Gospel of John. Jacque-line never stops telling me about it. What's surprising, if it's true, is that everyone's not rushing to get their hands on it. As for me, I'm all for it.

•

How it's done is no secret. It started two thousand years ago and hasn't stopped since. In bygone times—and even today according to certain rites—real bread is used: the most basic kind, straight from the baker. Nowadays the Catholics use little white rounds that feel and taste like cardboard, called the host, or holy wafers. At one point in the Mass, the priest declares that they have become the body of Christ. The faithful line up to receive one each, on their tongue or in the palm of their hand. They go sit back down with their eyes lowered, thoughtful, and, if they believe it, transformed. This incredibly strange rite, which harks back to a precise event that took place around the year A.D. 30 and that is at the heart of Christian worship, is celebrated today all over the world by hun-dreds of millions of people who, as Patrick Blossier would say, are *in other respects* not stark raving mad. Some, like my mother-in-law and my god-mother, do it every day without exception, and if they happen to be so sick that they can't go to church, they have the sacrament brought home to them. The strangest thing is that, chemically speaking, the host is noth-ing but bread. It would be almost reassuring if it were a magic mushroom or a tab of LSD, but it's not: it's just bread. At the same time, it's Christ.

•

Of course, you can see the ritual in a symbolic, commemorative sense. Jesus himself said: "Do this in memory of me." That's the light version, the one that doesn't shock our sense of reason. But hardline Christians believe in the *reality* of transubstantiation—which is what the Church calls this supernatural phenomenon. They believe in the *real* presence of Christ in the host. This is the razor's edge that divides the two camps. Believing that Communion is just a symbol is like believing that Jesus is just a wise master, grace a kind of autosuggestion, and God the name we give to an inner moral sense. At this moment in my life, I can't go along with that: I want to belong to the other camp.

At one rather similar moment in his own life—he could no longer write, was the same age as me, married to a woman with the same name, and afraid he was going mad—Philip K. Dick also turned to the

Christian faith, he too with no reservations. He convinced his Anne to marry him in church, had their children baptized, and devoted himself to pious readings—with a predilection for the Apocryphal Gospels, although he hardly knew the canonical ones. I've since written his biography, and today I'm unable to say how much of the chapter on these years is really him, and how much of it is a projection of my own experience. In any case, one scene I like a lot is when he explains what Communion is.

•

His wife's daughters don't really get it. In fact the idea shocks them. When Jesus calls on his followers to eat his flesh and drink his blood they're horrified, as if it were a kind of cannibalism. To calm them down, their mother says it's an image, a bit like the expression "to lap up someone's words." When he hears that, Phil protests: What's the point of becoming Catholic if it's just to reduce all the mysteries to platitudes?

"What's the point of becoming Catholic," Anne responds bitterly, "if it's just to treat the religion like one of your science fiction stories?"

"That's exactly what I'm getting at," Phil says. "If you take the New Testament seriously, you have to believe that in the nineteen-odd centuries since the death of Christ, humanity has been undergoing a sort of mutation. Maybe you can't see it, but that's how it is, and if you don't believe it, you're not Christian, that's all. It's not me who says it, it's Saint Paul, and there's nothing I can do about it if it really does sound like science fiction. The sacrament of Communion is the agent of this mutation, so don't go telling your poor girls that it's like some kind of stupid commemoration. Listen to me, girls: Do you know the story of the prime rib roast? A woman invites some people over for dinner. She puts a superb five-pound roast on the kitchen counter. The guests arrive, she talks with them for a while in the living room, they drink a few martinis. Then she slips out to the kitchen to prepare the roast . . . and sees it's disappeared. Who does she see licking its chops in a corner? The cat."

"I know what happened," says the elder daughter.

"All right, what?"

"The cat ate the roast."

"You believe that? You're not dumb, but wait. The guests come rushing in and discuss what's happened. The five-pound roast has disappeared into thin air, the cat looks happy and well fed. Everyone concludes the same thing as you.

"Then one of the guests suggests, 'What if we weighed it, just to be sure?'

"They're all a bit drunk, and think it's a great idea. They take the cat into the bathroom and put it on the scale. It weighs exactly five pounds. The guest who suggested weighing the cat says, 'There you go, the numbers add up. Now we can be sure of what happened.'

"But then another guest scratches his head and says, 'Okay, now we know where the five-pound roast is. But then *where's the cat?*'"

•

Blaise Pascal, peeved: "How tiresome are the souls who throw up obstacles to believing in the Eucharist! If Jesus is the son of God, where is the difficulty?"

(You could call this the "now that we've come this far . . ." argument.)

And Simone Weil: "Certitudes of this kind are experimental. But if you don't believe them before experiencing them, or at least if you don't act as if you believe them, you'll never have the experience that leads to such certitudes. That's how it is with all knowledge that's useful for spiritual progress. If you don't adopt it as a rule of conduct before having verified it, if you don't spend a long time attached to it through a faith that's mysterious at first, you'll never transform it into certitude. Faith is the essential condition."

•

Simone Weil, whom I read a lot of at this time and from whose works I recopy entire pages into my notebooks, felt a compelling urge to take Communion. But while even the humblest of Christians consider themselves invited to the Lord's table, this brilliant, saintly woman believed until her death that she was destined to remain away from it. To remain on the side of those whose way is barred. With—in her own words— "the immense, unhappy crowd of unbelievers."

22

Still . . . At first you're struck by certain of Jesus' dazzling turns of phrase. Like the guards charged with arresting him, you acknowledge that "no one ever spoke like this man." From there you go on to believe that he was resurrected on the third day, and was—why not—born of a virgin. You decide to commit your life to this mad belief: that Truth with a capital "T" took on the flesh of man in Galilee two thousand years ago. You're proud of this madness, because it's not natural, because in adopting it you surprise and surrender yourself, because no one around you shares it. You rule out as ungodly the idea that the Gospel contains makeshift contingencies, that there's both good and bad in Christ's teaching and the account given of it by the four inspired narratives. And why not, while you're at it—*now that we've come this far*— also believe in the Trinity, original sin, the Immaculate Conception, and papal infallibility? Under Jacqueline's influence that's what I apply myself to this season, and I'm appalled to find such zany reflections in my notebook as:

"The sole argument that can allow us to admit that Jesus is the truth and life is that He says it, and since He is truth and life, He must be believed. He who has believed will believe. He who has a lot will be given more."

And: "An atheist *believes* that God does not exist. A believer *knows* that God exists. One has an opinion, the other knowledge."

And: "Faith consists in believing what one doesn't believe, and not believing what one does." (This sentence isn't mine, it's by Lanza del Vasto, a Christian disciple of Gandhi whom I read a lot of at the time. I respectfully recopied it. Today I notice that it's similar to—and almost as funny as— Mark Twain's quip: "Faith is believing something you know isn't true.")

And, why not, one for the road: "I have to learn to be truly Catholic, that is, to exclude nothing: not even Catholicism's most repelling dogmas; not even the rebellion against these dogmas." (The last bit of this sentence is defiant. It's more like me than the rest, and reassures me somewhat.)

•

When I start defending Church dogma to Hervé, he doesn't laugh or shrug his shoulders: that's not his style. No, he listens to what I have to say, weighs my words, tries to extricate what is sound in what I say from its straightjacket of intolerance. He's no fan of criticism for criticism's sake, even less of polemics, but, faced with my almost fundamentalist flights of religious ecstasy, this true friend of God nevertheless plays the role of skeptic. He could espouse the words Edmund Husserl addressed to his student Edith Stein, a Carmelite and mystic who died at Auschwitz: "Promise me, my dear child, that you'll never think anything just because others have thought it before you." When, in the elation of my conversion, I wanted to cancel the appointment with the analyst that I'd made long ago, Hervé was the one who dissuaded me: Why say no to something that could be useful? If God's grace is really working inside you, analysis certainly won't stop it. And if analysis frees you from an illusion, so much the better. And it's with the same, very Swiss equanimity that he tempers my dogmatic slide. Unlike me, he doesn't love himself to the point of hatred, and he doesn't hate himself to the point of wanting to believe something he doesn't believe. He's the least fanatic of human beings, and the least pretentious. It doesn't bug him at all to take what suits him from the Gospel, and to put together his own credo where the words of Christ jostle with those of Lao-tze and the *Bhagavad Gita*— which for twenty years I've seen him slip into his bag before heading up into the mountains and take out to read a few lines each time we stop. It's always the same little blue, almost square book. When one copy falls apart, he goes to get another from the shelf where he's got a good twenty stored away, the same way he stores Kleenex for his sinusitis.

•

Jacqueline, our godmother, has been pestering us for some time about Medjugorje. Medjugorje is a village in Yugoslavia—which still exists as a country at this time. Terrible things are starting to happen there, but personally I couldn't care less: the Serbs, Croats, and Bosniaks can slit each other's throats for all I care, I'm reading the Book of John. The Virgin Mary is believed to have appeared in Medjugorje in the seventies, and, speaking through the peasant children who witnessed her apparition, she warns the world that it is heading for disaster. These peasant children have now become very sought-after—and prosperous—preachers, invited to give talks all around the world. One of these talks will take place in Paris, and Jacqueline wants us all to go. My first reaction is one of prejudice—or reason? I'm happy to read the Gospel, but not to go in for this sort of religious quackery. You've got to draw the line somewhere, or else with one thing leading to another you end up scouring the esoteric bookstores for works on Nostradamus and the mystery of the Templars. But wait a second! Second reaction: What if it were true? In that case, wouldn't it be tremendously important? Wouldn't you have to drop everything else and dedicate your life to spreading the word of Medjugorje?

A good ten pages of my notebook record this back-and-forthing, to which Hervé isn't subject in the least. He's reserved, but curious: What skin is it off our back to go spend an hour at this talk? In this respect he's like Nicodemus, that inquisitive figure who appears only in the Gospel of John. Nicodemus is a Pharisee, and as such he's got strong reservations against Jesus. What he's been told reeks of superstition, sects, maybe even a hoax. No matter, not satisfied with what he's been told, he prefers to find out for himself. He goes to see Jesus, at night. A note in the Jerusalem Bible insinuates that it's cowardice on his part that makes him go at night, so as not to compromise his reputation. But I'm not at all shocked by such discretion. On the contrary, what strikes me is the nobleman's open mind. He questions Jesus, interrupts him, makes him repeat what he hasn't understood—and you've got to admit, what John has Jesus say is difficult to understand. Nicodemus returns home thoughtful, if not converted. "Come, and you will see," Jesus often says. Nicodemus, at least, went and saw.

Hervé and I, finally, went and saw the Yugoslavian spokesman for the Virgin Mary. What he said in her name struck us as both ominous and dull.

23

To enter what Jacqueline calls the sacramental life, I have to make a general confession, and before that I must undertake an in-depth examination of conscience. Through one of those coincidences that start multiplying like rabbits as soon as you decide to see divine grace at work in your life, Gabriel asks me: "What's the worst thing you've ever done?" In fact, I don't think I've done a lot of bad things, if by that you mean deliberate evil. Most of the bad things I've done I did to myself, despite myself, making me feel more sick than guilty. The priest Jacqueline sends me to is hardly thrilled by this way of seeing things: for him it's just my strictly psychological point of view, whereas the whole idea behind the general confession is to escape this point of view and put yourself under the eye of God. To do that, you have to go right back to the Decalogue. Yes, the Decalogue: the Ten Commandments, in the light of which I examine my entire life for a week.

•

I also examine it in the light of the three theological virtues: faith, hope, and charity. The first was recently granted to me through an unexpected grace. For the moment it's just a tiny, fragile seed, threatening at any moment to become lost among the brambles. However, I believe this seed will become a large tree, and that the birds in heaven will come and nest in its branches. Does it not require hope to believe that it can grow? If so, I have plenty of it. In fact, I have so much that it's suspicious. Maybe I'm mistaken in giving the noble word "hope" to something that's more like wishful thinking: the vague conviction that whatever inconveniences I encounter, everything will go my way in the end. That after the ordeal of drought I'll wind up bearing fruit—that is, concretely, writing a book that was worth all the trouble. Maybe the best thing would be to get rid of this vile form of wishful thinking to allow true hope to flourish. That leaves charity, which Saint Paul calls the most important of the three. Here, however, there's nothing, zilch, nada. No charity. Not the slightest inclination to do even the smallest act of kindness, although they say this can move mountains. The encounter with God has changed my soul—and my opinions—but not my heart. I continue to love no one but myself, and badly at that. But even that is planned for. The prayer I need comes from Ezekiel. I repeat it nonstop:

"Lord, remove my heart of stone and give me a heart of flesh."

•

I write:

Lord, I am not worthy to receive you, nevertheless I ask you to establish in me your dwelling place. To make room for you I must decrease, I know, something I resist with every breath I take. I'll never be able to do it alone, you can't decrease alone. Left to ourselves, we take up all the room there is. Help me decrease so that you can increase in me.

Lord, maybe you don't want me to become a great writer, maybe you don't want me to have an easy, happy life, but I'm sure you want to let me feel charity. I ask you with a thousand ulterior motives, a thousand hesitations that I waste too much time analyzing, nevertheless I ask you. Give me the ordeals and the opportunities that will open me little by little to a sense of charity. Give me the courage to bear the first and seize the second, and to recognize that the same event may be both at the same time. I can't say I want nothing else, that wouldn't be true. Far more than that, I want to realize my desires. I want to be big, not small. But I'm not asking you for what I want. I'm asking you for what I want to want, for what I want you to let me want.

I accept everything in advance. Saying that, I know I'm speaking like your disciple Peter, who was so certain he wouldn't deny you and yet did so nonetheless. I know that in saying this all I'm doing is preparing the place where I will deny you, but I say it anyway. Give me what you want to give me, take from me what you want to take from me, do with me what you will.

Simone Weil: "In spiritual matters, all prayers are granted. He who receives less has asked for less."

And John of Ruysbroeck, the Flemish mystic: "You are as holy as you want to be."

•

I draw up a list of those I've hurt. The first I remember is a guy I went to school with: knobby-kneed, not really slow-witted but strange, whom everyone made fun of, I in a more sophisticated way than the rest. I wrote little texts about him that I embellished with caricatures and passed around. He found out. He left the school at the end of the first semester; people said he'd been sent to a home for problem kids. My talent for writing is at the origin of the first real harm I can remember doing to someone, and when I think about it, of much more harm besides. In the last novel I published, *Hors d'atteinte* (Out of Reach), I traced a cruel and mean-spirited portrait of a woman—Caroline—who had loved me and whom I had loved, and I can't help thinking that my inability to write for the past three years is punishment for abusing my talent like that. Before approaching the holy table I would like to make peace with my victims. No doubt it would be possible to find the boy I made fun of in eighth grade. He had a double-barreled name that was as strange as he was and there can't be tons of them in the phone book, but all of that's too far away now—and moreover, confusedly, I'm too afraid I'll find out that he's dead, that he died in the asylum not long after leaving our school, and that it's my fault. But I do have Caroline's address. I write her a long letter saying how sorry I am. She doesn't answer, but a few years later she'll tell me how shocked and full of pity she was to get "this spate of Catholic guilt"—her exact words—that I regret not being able to present here as a testimony.

•

One night, on the Feast of the Conversion of Saint Paul, I go as usual to the seven o'clock Mass at Saint-Séverin, and this time I advance between the pews with those wishing to take Communion. I'm somewhat preoccupied, but not surprised that I am. I feel nothing. That's normal: the kingdom is a grain of mustard seed that grows in the darkness of the earth, in silence, unbeknownst to us. What counts is that now it's part of my life. For over one year I'll take Communion every day, just as I go to the analyst twice a week.

24

Despite Communion and the joy it's supposed to procure, I suffer on Dr. C.'s couch. I whine, blame, gripe. I don't say anything about all that in my notebooks, as if the person who wrote them was somehow above all that. With one exception: one morning I arrive for my appointment after reading a short article in the paper that didn't just floor me—it literally devastated me. It's about a little boy just four years old—Gabriel's age. He went into the hospital for a minor operation but an anesthesia accident left him paralyzed, blind, deaf, and dumb for life. He's now six. For the past two years he's been living in utter blackness. Walled up alive. In desperation, his parents stay by his bedside. They talk to him, touch him. They've been told that he can't hear anything but that maybe he feels things, that maybe the contact of their hands on his skin does him good. No other communication is possible. All that's known is that he's not in a coma. He's conscious. No one can imagine what's going on in his head, how he interprets what's happening to him. There are no words to express that. Words fail me. I who am so articulate, so prone to saying what I feel, don't know how to express what this story has set in motion within me. My voice trembles, I start sentences that I can't finish, an enormous sob wells up in my chest, rolls, bursts, and I start crying like I've never cried in all my life. I cry and cry without being able to stop. There's no comfort in these tears, no consolation, no relaxation, they're tears of terror and despair. This lasts ten or fifteen minutes. Then I can talk again. I don't calm down, what I babble is interspersed with tears and sobbing. I ask what kind of prayer someone like me who wants to believe in God can pray after reading something like that. What he could ask of this Father, whose son Jesus says: "Ask and it will be given to you." A miracle? For it never to have happened? Or that he fill this trapped child with his tender, loving, reassuring presence? That he illuminate his darkness, and make this unimaginable hell his kingdom? And if not, what then? If not, you've got to admit that the reality of reality, the bottom line, the last word, is not his infinite love but the absolute horror, the unspeakable terror of a little four-year-old boy who wakes up in eternal darkness.

"That's enough for today," says Dr. C.

•

Three days go by. I remember, my sessions were on Tuesdays and Fridays, and the next Friday is Good Friday. I'm sure Dr. C. thought about me a lot during those three days. We come back to my fit of tears, what the terrible story about the walled-in child awakens in me, but what interests her most is what I said about the Father. I'm reluctant, I'd like to close this door that I imprudently opened during the last session. She insists. Okay, I talk about the Father, but talking about him in this setting seems to me almost obscene. By a tacit agreement we've never brought up the subject of my faith ever since our first strange session. Until now Dr. C. hasn't mentioned it or let on anything about what she thinks. Now, with much precaution, she invites me to consider the following hypothesis: Is it not possible that this all-powerful, all-loving, all-healing Father who came into my life at the precise moment when I started treatment—and whom I brought into the first session like a sort of unwieldy joker that I refused to play—is merely a passing figure that's necessary for a while in the process of analysis? A crutch that I'm using on the journey toward an understanding of the place occupied in my life by my own father?

This idea makes me uneasy, but I can't reject it with as much conviction as I would have done six months earlier. It must have matured inside me without my knowing. I shrug it off as if I've already been through all that a hundred times, as if the matter was settled long ago and there's really no point going over it again. I say: So? Of course faith has psychological foundations. Of course to reach us, God's grace uses our deficiencies, our weaknesses, our childish desire to be consoled and protected. What does that change?

Dr. C. doesn't say a thing.

•

I suppose that to many readers the doubts I'm describing here seem totally abstract, speculative, disconnected from the true problems of existence. But they completely ripped me apart, and I'm writing this book to remember just that. I'm tempted to be ironic about the person I was, but I want to remember the confusion and terror I felt at the thought that the faith that had changed my life and to which I held above all else was endangered. It's no coincidence that it's Good Friday, the day Jesus cried out: "Father, Father, why have you forsaken me?"

Intellectually, nothing new. I've been around the block. I've read Dostoyevsky, I know what Ivan Karamazov says and what Job said before him about the suffering of the innocent, the scandal that bars the possibility of believing in God. I've read Freud, I know what he thinks and what Dr. C. no doubt also thinks: that of course it would certainly be very nice if there were an all-powerful Father and a Providence that cares for each and every one of us, but that conveniently this construction corresponds so precisely to what we want when we're children. That the root of religious desire is nostalgia for the father, and the childish fantasy of being at the center of the world. I've read Nietzsche, and I can't deny that I feel targeted when he says that the big advantage of religion is that it lets us escape reality and makes us interesting to ourselves. Nevertheless, I thought: Of course you can say that God is the answer we give to our anxieties, but you can also say that our anxieties are his way of making himself known to us. Of course you can say that I converted because I was in despair, but you can also say that God granted me despair to make me convert. That's what I want to think with all my strength: that the real illusion isn't faith, as Freud *believes*, but what makes faith subject to doubt, as the mystics *know*.

I want to think that, I want to believe it, but I'm afraid I'll stop believing it. I wonder if wanting so much to believe it isn't the proof that I no longer do.

25

We go to spend the Easter weekend with my mother-in-law in Normandy. Late at night the television shows a documentary on Béatrix Beck, a writer I like a lot and whose novel *The Passionate Heart* I adapted as a screenplay. It's an autobiographical book on her conversion, and Jean-Pierre Melville has already made it into a movie starring Jean-Paul Belmondo and Emmanuelle Riva. It was excellent but that didn't stop us from doing it again, and so much the better because I really enjoyed working on that adaptation. In retrospect, I like to see this work, which I did a year before my conversion, as one stage in a subterranean process, and the producer who asked me to do it as an agent of divine grace in my life. The book was written in the 1950s, and everything about it rings true. The profound change experienced by the heroine is all the more convincing in that she describes it prosaically, without the wooden language of Christianity, and often in a very funny way. Béatrix Beck, who lived well into her nineties, was a free—and disconcerting—spirit. Asked at one point if she still believes, she answers that she doesn't: it was a moment in her life, it's over. She speaks about it the way a former communist might talk about his commitment, or the way you talk about a great love of your youth. A stormy passion that you're happy to have experienced, all things considered, but that now belongs to the past. She talks about it because she was asked to, in fact she no longer thinks about it at all.

For me that's terrible. Not for her, clearly, but I'm appalled at the idea that faith can pass and that you're no worse off for it. I thought: The grace that you let slip by will destroy your life. If it doesn't change it completely, it will wreak havoc on it. Refusing it and distancing yourself from it once you've caught a glimpse of it means condemning yourself to a life in hell.

But maybe not.

•

The next day is Easter Sunday. We'll look for Easter eggs in the garden with the kids. We'll go to Mass, in the large, beautiful abbey attended by all the region has to offer in terms of grand Catholic families, dressed in navy-blue blazers and pastel dresses. I'll go, there can be no question of me not going, but this bourgeois, provincial Christianity that has no room for doubt, this Christianity of pharmacists and notaries that I've taken to observing with indulgent irony, suddenly revolts me. At dawn I slip out of bed, where I tossed and turned all night without getting a wink of sleep while Anne lay peacefully beside me. I leave the house without waking a soul, and head over to the community of nuns where my mother-in-law often goes to Mass because it's just next door. From time to time I've gone along with her. At seven o'clock they say the morning prayers. The chapel is gray and ugly, lit by a dull light. The thick stone walls drip with humidity. The community now has no more than ten or so nuns, all old and wobbly on their feet. One of them is a dwarf. Their voices falter and crack as they sing, and the bleating of the young priest who looks like the village idiot and who's come to bring them Communion isn't any better. It's terrible to say, but in his mouth even the sublime passage in the Gospel of John telling how Mary Magdalene takes the resurrected Christ for the gardener on Easter morning sounds stupid. No one really seems to be listening. The bleak, lost look in their eyes and the trickle of spit on the corner of their mouths must be in anticipation of breakfast. As my pious mother-in-law admits almost gaily, Mass with the nuns isn't exactly cheerful. In fact, it's enough to fill you with sadness, and it would have sent me packing in the past—supposing I'd ever gone in there in the first place. Anne, who grew up in the shadows of this twilight home, thinks I'm perverse to go there and wallow in the scent of diapers and disinfectant. But I say to myself: This is it, this is the kingdom. Everything that is weak, despised, and wanting: that is the dwelling place of Christ.

While the service drags on, I repeat like a mantra these lines from a psalm:

That I may dwell in the house of the Lord
all the days of my life.

But what if I were chased out? Or, worse still, if I were happy to leave? If one day I considered this time when I wanted to dwell in the house of the Lord all my life, and when I found nothing more beautiful than attending Mass with a group of old nuns, three-quarters of whom had reverted to a second childhood, as an embarrassing episode, morose in some ways and in others rather comical? A whim I was lucky enough to have put behind me? Or rather, not a whim but an interesting experience, provided you came out the other side? I'd talk about my Christian period the way a painter talks about his pink or blue period. I'd pat myself on the back for having been able to evolve and move on.

It would be horrible, and I wouldn't even know it.

•

It's funny: while writing this chapter I visited a country house where I ran across a book I could have read at the time called *An Initiation to Spiritual Life*. It was published in 1962 by the Catholic publishing house Desclée de Brouwer, and bears the *Nihil obstat* with which the Church declares that it's not opposed to publication. And in this case it's hard to see why it should be, because it's a long, boring text on the infinite wisdom of the Church, through which the Holy Spirit expresses itself infallibly and which consequently is always correct. The author, a Jesuit, is named François Roustang. At first I thought it was a coincidence, then I checked: it's the same François Roustang whom I consulted so successfully forty-three years after this book was published, and who had in the meantime become one of France's most heterodox psychoanalysts. This *Initiation to Spiritual Life* does not appear on the "By the same author" page in his recent books. I imagine that the elderly Roustang must be a little embarrassed by it, and doesn't like it when people remind him of this time in his life. I also imagine the young Roustang, who wrote this exceedingly dogmatic work, so sure he was in possession of the truth. He would have been quite surprised to see what a skeptic he'd become. Not just surprised: horrified. I'm sure he would have prayed as hard as he could for that not to happen. And today he must be glad it did. Like those people who go on dreaming they're writing their final exams well into their old age, this old Taoist master must sometimes dream he's still a Jesuit, talking gravely about sin and the Trinity. And when he wakes up he must say: "Man, what a nightmare!"

26

Not long after my conversion, I jotted down the following in a notebook I'd just bought: "The fact that Christ is truth and life simply stares you in the face—sometimes something has to stare you in the face for you to see it at all. But a lot of people still don't see it. They've got eyes and don't see. I know, I was one of them. And I'd like to talk with the little me I was just a few weeks ago who's now receding into the past. In examining his ignorance, I hope to have a better grasp of the truth."

I felt I was in a strong position. To my mind the little me, the unbeliever who was receding into the past, wasn't a particularly formidable adversary. But a formidable adversary is on the horizon: not the me I've put behind me but the me to come, a me who is perhaps just around the corner, who will no longer believe and will be more than happy not to. What could I say to him to put him on his guard? To prevent him from leaving the path of life for the path of death? How to make him listen to me, although I already know how sure he'll be of his superiority?

•

Starting this Easter weekend, I believe my faith is in great peril. To protect it, I declare a state of siege. Curfew and brainwashing. I take a weeklong retreat to the Benedictine abbey Saint-Marie de la Pierre-qui-Vire in Burgundy. Vigils at two a.m., lauds at six, breakfast at seven, Mass at nine, reading and commentary on the Book of John at eleven, lunch at one, walk in the forest at two, vespers at six, dinner at seven, compline at eight, bed at nine. Always the good obsessive, I'm thrilled. I don't miss a thing. Very soon, I no longer need the alarm to wake up for the vigils. Back in Paris, I do my best to adapt the Rule of Saint Benedict to city life. No more newspaper with my coffee after taking Gabriel to school: I now consider that a waste of time. As soon as I get to my office, an hour of yoga, thirty minutes of prayer, an hour dedicated to the Gospel of John, an hour of (pious) reading with my brown rice and yogurt. Five hours of hard work in the afternoon—soon I'll say about what. Evening Mass at seven at Saint-Séverin, back home at eight. That's where I have the most work cut out for me, and I do my best to put my good resolutions into practice: Never do two things at once. Leave my worries at the office, so as to be there—and in a good mood—for my family. See daily life as a series of opportunities for choosing between two paths: vigilance or distraction, charity or egotism, presence or absence, life or death. And, as I'm prone to insomnia, follow the example of Charles de Foucauld, who got straight down to work when he jumped out of bed, no matter what the time.

I'm not sure if this draconian program made me any better a husband or father. In fact, I'm even sure it didn't. Disturbing notes of mine comparing my family life with a cross I have to courageously bear make me think that in my own way I must have behaved like those somber puritans in Hawthorne's novels, who subject their loved ones to a veritable domestic hell with implacable kindness, all for the good of their souls.

•

I read a lot, with a preference for French authors of the seventeenth century like Fénelon, Saint Francis of Sales, and the Jesuit le Jean-Pierre de Caussade. Accomplished stylists, suave and subtle, they all say that what is happening to me is planned, set down, part of a program. It's reassuring, and not all that far removed from psychoanalysis. If I believe I'm losing my faith, it's because my faith is maturing. If I no longer sense the presence of God, which just last fall made me feel like I was advancing in spiritual life like the Tibetan mages described by Alexandra David-Néel, leaping over mountains in five-hundred-yard strides, it's because God is educating me. The drought of the soul is a sign of progress. Absence is presence squared. I recopied dozens of variations on this theme, here just a small compendium:

> God never leaves the soul until He has rendered it supple and pliable by twisting it all manner of ways. The more we fear to do these things, the more we have need to do them. The repugnance which our wisdom and self-love manifest to them is a sufficient evidence that they are of grace.
> (Fénelon, *Christian Perfection*)

> We have a happy condition in this warfare that we shall always be victorious as long as we want to fight.
> (Saint Francis of Sales, *Introduction to the Devout Life*)

> By the very means that seem like privations, God bestows graces and favors on faithful souls. God teaches the soul by pains and obstacles, not by ideas. To whatever the soul attaches itself, God upsets its plans, and allows it to find, instead of success in these projects, nothing but confusion, trouble, emptiness, and folly. Therefore darkness itself is a light for our guidance; and doubts are our best assurance.
> (Jean-Pierre de Caussade, *Abandonment to Divine Providence*)

I'm divided when I reread these texts, but I was also divided when I first read them. Even at the time I found them outrageous, and I still find them magnificent. It seems clear to me that they are inspired by experience, I mean that the men who wrote them aren't talking rubbish: they know what they're saying. At the same time, they're teaching a disdain for experience, for the testimony of the senses and of common sense that is as radical as the immortal sentence by the Bolshevik Pyatakov: "For the party's sake you can and must at 24 hours' notice change all your convictions and force yourself to believe that white is black."

27

Since it pleases God to put my faith to the test, I decide to not shy away from this ordeal. I want to experience it to the full. I want to relive anew the meeting between Jesus and the tempter.

Nietzsche is very good in the role of the tempter. The best, even. He makes you want to go over to his side. It both horrifies and enchants me when he murmurs in my ear that wanting—as I reproach myself for doing—to be glorious or powerful, to be admired by your peers, to be very rich, or to seduce all women, are perhaps crude ambitions, but at least they aim at real things. They occupy a terrain where you can win or lose, conquer or be conquered, whereas the inner life along Christian lines is above all a tried and tested way of telling yourself stories that run no risk of being contradicted, and in any case of making yourself interesting in your own eyes. Thinking that everything that happens to us has a meaning, and interpreting everything in terms of ordeals set by a God who organizes people's salvation like a kind of obstacle course is nothing but naïveté, cowardice, and vanity. People, Nietzsche says, are judged—and, as opposed to what Jesus says, you *must* judge—by their ability to not tell themselves stories: to love reality and not the comforting fairy tales they create in its place. They are judged *by the dose of truth they're able to bear.*

•

But for Simone Weil: "Christ wants us to prefer the truth to him, because before being Christ he is the truth. If you turn from him to seek the truth, you won't go far before you fall back into his arms."

Fine. I'll accept the wager. I'll run the risk. I open a new file—which like the first one I've subsequently lost—and once again give it the title that I clearly like a lot: *The Adversary's Point of View.* That's the project I work on for five hours each afternoon.

•

A year earlier, talking with my friend the philosopher Luc Ferry, I said that it's impossible to foresee not only what the future holds in store, but even what will become of us, what we'll think. Luc responded that, for example, he could be sure he'd never become a member of the far-right National Front. I answered that that didn't seem at all likely for me either, but that I couldn't be sure and that, as distasteful as the example was, I considered this uncertainty the price of my liberty. At that time although the Christian faith didn't inspire the same hostility in me as the National Front, I would nevertheless have been almost as surprised if I'd been told I'd convert to Christianity one day. But it happened. Everything takes place as if I'd caught a disease—although I really didn't belong to a risk group—the first symptom of which is that I take it for a cure. So what I propose to do is observe this disease. To keep a journal of it, as objectively as possible.

•

Pascal: "See the open war between men, where each has to choose his side and of necessity declare himself either for dogmatism or Pyrrhonism, for he who thinks to remain neutral will be a Pyrrhonian par excellence."

Pyrrhonian: disciple of the philosopher Pyrrho, meaning a skeptic. Or, as we say today: relativist. Which means shrugging your shoulders like Pontius Pilate when Jesus assures his listeners that he's the truth, and saying: "What is truth?" There are as many truths as there are opinions. Fine, I won't pretend to be neutral. I'll take a Pyrrhonian look at my dogmatism. I'll tell the story of my conversion the way Flaubert describes the aspirations of Madame Bovary. I'll put myself in the skin of the person I most dread becoming: the one who, returned from faith, examines it with detachment. I'll piece together the maze of defeats, self-hatred, and panicked fear at life that led me to believe. And perhaps then, and only then, I'll stop telling myself stories. Maybe I'll have the right to say, like Dostoyevsky: "If anyone could prove to me that Christ is outside the truth, and if the truth really did exclude Christ, I should prefer to stay with Christ."

2 8

François Samuelson, my agent, says to me one day: "You haven't written for three years, you look miserable, you've got to do something. Why not write a biography? That's what all writers do when they get a block. Some of them it helps. Of course it depends on the subject, but I can certainly get you a good contract."

Why not? A biography is a more modest project than the big novel that's still haunting me, and more exciting than grinding out one teleplay after the next. Maybe a good way of using the talent that the good Lord gave me, and that he would rather see us squander than hoard. In my notebook, I jot down this sentence from the Bible: "Anything you can turn your hand to, do with what power you have" (which, I realize today, could also be read as an invitation to masturbate), and I ask François to find an editor interested in the life of Philip K. Dick.

•

I write a note of intention ending with the words "It's tempting to consider Philip K. Dick as a type of misguided mystic. But even talking about misguided mystics suggests that there is such a thing as a true mystic, and thus a true object of mystical knowledge. That's a religious point of view. If, worried about coming to that conclusion, we prefer to adopt an agnostic point of view, we must admit that while there is perhaps a difference of human and cultural elevation, of audience and respectability, between Saint Paul, Meister Eckhart, and Simone Weil on the one hand and a poor visionary hippie like Dick on the other, there is no difference in nature. He himself, incidentally, was perfectly aware of the problem. A writer of fiction, and of the most extravagant fiction at that, he was convinced that he was writing nothing but *reports*. The last ten years of his life he slaved away at an interminable, unclassifiable *report* that he called his *Exegesis*. This *Exegesis* aimed to give an account of an experience that, depending on his mood, he interpreted as his meeting with God ('It's a fearful thing,' Saint Paul says, 'to fall into the hands of the living God'), the delayed effect of all the drugs he'd taken over the course of his life, the invasion of his mind by extraterrestrials, or a pure paranoid construction. Despite all his efforts, he never managed to draw the line between delusion and divine revelation—assuming there is one. Is there one? Strictly speaking, the question can't be decided one way or the other, and it goes without saying that I won't try to do so here. But telling the life of Dick means forcing yourself to come to grips with this line. To approach it from all sides, as attentively as you can. And that is what I would like to do."

•

It took me a bit more than a year to write this book, which, bearing in mind its length and the huge amount of information it deals with, strikes me in retrospect as quite the exploit. I worked like a dog, and I remember loving every minute of it. There's nothing better in the world than working, than being able to work, especially when you haven't been able to for a long time. Everything I'd tried in vain to do during the dry period that preceded it now took on meaning. I lost the two files called *The Adversary's Point of View*, the one on Jamie's life and the other on my conversion told by a future me who's since lost the faith, but in any case I'd abandoned them, and all the questions that these failed works attempted to deal with very naturally found their place in the biography of Dick. Instead of distressing me, they captivated and some-times even amused me. Dick's life, despite—or maybe because of—his awkward genius, was a catastrophic, never-ending series of excesses, separations, internments, and psychological breakdowns, but I never stopped being fond of him. I never stopped saying to myself that from wherever he was ten years after his death, he was looking over my shoulder and watching what I was doing, and that he was happy some-one was talking about him the way I was doing.

•

Another trusted counselor accompanied me from the beginning to the end of this project: the *I Ching*, the ancient Chinese book of wisdom and divination so loved by Confucius and the hippies of my generation—or rather, of the previous generation, but I've always sided with people older than myself. Dick himself used it to put together one of his novels, *The Man in the High Castle*. When he was blocked he consulted the *I Ching*, and it got him out of his jam. I did the same, quite successfully. One day, when I was completely snowed under by everything I had to bring together and thought I'd never be able to cope, the *I Ching* gave me this sentence that still serves me as a guideline for the poetic arts: "Perfect grace consists not in exterior ornamentation of the substance, but in the simple fitness of its form."

29

Of course, my notebooks of Gospel commentary bear the brunt of this breakthrough. I didn't really drop them, but the rhythm slackened. I filled fifteen the year after my conversion and only three in the year I spent writing the book on Dick, and when you flip through those three, it's clear that my heart isn't in it anymore. I take from the Gospel what can help me for my book. I still go to Mass, but not every day. I still take Communion, though I have to force myself a bit. On good days I think that's not such a bad thing. The Father isn't some kind of slave master. When I take Gabriel and Jean Baptiste to the park, I'm happy to watch them run around on the playground, climb the ladders, and slide down the slides. I'd be worried if instead of that, they spent the whole time with me, watching me, wondering what I'm thinking and if I'm happy with them. I like them to forget about me, to live their little boys' lives. If I, who am not the best father in the world, can show my sons such tenderness, how much tenderness must the Father have for me? But there are days of doubt and hesitation, when I tell myself that the pleasure—enthusiasm, even—I feel working on Dick's biography is nothing but a smug illusion that only gets me further from the truth. A boon, and so a curse: it's what Jesus seems to say in the Beatitudes, which are at the very heart of his teaching. I'm no longer sure the Beatitudes are true. I no longer see what this systematic inversion of anything and everything is supposed to mean. Convincing yourself that when you're at the bottom of a hole it's the best thing that can happen to you might help you out in a pinch, even though it could be wrong. But believing as soon as you're slightly happy that *in fact* you're doing terribly, that things *are* very bad: I don't see the point. I prefer the *I Ching*, which says something that's both very similar and very different. The bottom line is that there's no point getting too excited when you throw a positive hexagram: if you're at the top, you're bound to come back down; if you're down, you'll no doubt rise again. If you go up on the sunny side, you come down on the shady side. Night follows day, day night, the good cycles follow the bad, and the bad the good. It's simply *true*, not morally loaded, Nietzsche would say. It says that when you're doing well, it's wise to expect unhappiness, and vice versa: not that it's *bad* to be happy and *good* to be unhappy.

•

At Le Levron there's a golden book in which Hervé's mother likes each visitor to leave a trace of his or her visit. I like that too. Twenty years ago I imagined myself flipping through it twenty years later, remembering past stays. These twenty years have now passed, more than that even, and I look back on our bygone visits. I like the fact that our friendship has lasted all that time. I like to look at our lives the way you look back on the path you've climbed when you reach the highest point on a hike: the bottom of the valley where you started out, the forest of firs, the scree slope where you twisted an ankle, the snowfield you thought you'd never get across, the alpine pasture where the shadows are already growing longer. I came to Le Levron alone in the fall of 1992 and worked there nonstop for ten days, then Hervé came to join me. The golden book bears witness, as does my notebook with Gospel commentary—too often neglected—in which I relate one of our conversations.

I'm complaining, as usual. Before I complained about not being able to write, now about enjoying it too much and distancing myself from Christ. Qualms, scruples, anxieties that feed on whatever they can find. The desire for calm gets me all worked up. The Gospel strikes me as a dead letter. What I considered the only reality has become a vague abstraction. After climbing a very long, very steep slope in the glaring sun, we reach a mountain lake where we stop for lunch. We pull out our sandwiches on a clump of grass in the middle of the snow, and Hervé pulls out his *Bhagavad Gita*. We're silent for a long time, and then, out of the blue, he says that it always surprised him a lot in his childhood that his grandmother's parrot never tried to escape when the cage was opened. Instead of flying away, it stayed there stupidly. His grandmother explained the trick: all you have to do is put a little mirror in the bottom of the cage. The parrot is so happy looking at its reflection, so absorbed by what it sees, that it doesn't even notice the open door of the cage and the possibility of freedom outside, attainable with a flap of its wings.

Deep down, Hervé's a Platonist. He believes that we live in a cave, a cavern, in a labyrinth, and that the object of the game is to get out. As far as I'm concerned, I'm not sure there's an outside to fly to. True, there can be no telling for sure, Hervé says, but supposing there is: it would be a shame not to go have a look. How to get there? By praying. Just a year ago Hervé countered my Catholic dogmatism with Taoist flexibility and said we should obey the spontaneous movements of the heart; and here he is insisting on the need to pray. Even without really wanting to, even without benefiting from it. Even if he is immediately swept away by the current of centrifugal, parasitic thoughts—little monkeys that never stop jumping from branch to branch, as the Buddhists say—every instant of prayer, every effort at praying goes to justify the day, he now argues. A light in the tunnel, a tiny refuge of eternity snatched from the hands of nothingness.

•

Twenty years later, Hervé and I still go walking on the same paths, and our conversations still turn around the same subjects. What we used to call prayer we now call meditation, but it's still the same mountain we're headed for, and it still seems to me just as far away.

30

I'm reaching the end of these notebooks. My book on Dick has come out. It wasn't as successful as I hoped it would be. I must have been disappointed but I don't talk about it. Once again I'm at loose ends and morose. I try to come back to the Bible and prayer. At least for a few moments each day I try to relate with what I'm now reluctant to call God, or even Christ. I no longer like these words, but I still want to feel an affinity for what they evoke within me. As always, this desire is inspired by anxiety. The impression that my life is ebbing away, that time is passing, thirty-five years, thirty-six, thirty-seven, without my living up to the talent I'd shown. If I do try to pray it's to convince myself that despite all appearances, everything will mysteriously turn out for the best. It's becoming harder and harder.

I've finished the Gospel of John and move straight on to that of Luke. I comment on the Beatitudes without conviction. What can they tell me, in my bitter, absent state?

Rather than denying, I shrug my shoulders.

I've taken the mysterious image of Christ in the foliage off my shelf. Not because I no longer see his face, but because I'm afraid of the embarrassment I'd feel if a visitor noticed it and asked what it is. I blame my "natural faults," as Montaigne says: the ones that can't be mended. I lack dynamism and staying power. I'm mean-spirited, deprived of everything, even deprivation. How to pull yourself together when that's the stuff you're made of? When you have no hold, when everything is sliding all around you?

•

Easter 1993, last page of my last notebook:

Is this what losing your faith is? No longer even feeling like praying to keep it? Not seeing this loss of interest that settles in day after day as an ordeal to be overcome, but as a normal process? The end of an illusion?

It's now that you should pray, the mystics say. It's in the night that you should remember the light you've caught a glimpse of. But at the same time it's now that the mystics' advice seems like brainwashing, and true courage appears to be turning away from them to confront reality.

Is the real world one in which Christ was not resurrected?

I write this on Good Friday, the moment of greatest doubt.

Tomorrow night I'll go to the Orthodox Easter Mass, with Anne and my parents. I'll kiss them and say *Christos voskres*, "Christ is resurrected," but I'll no longer believe it.

I forsake you, Lord. Please do not forsake me.

II

PAUL
(GREECE, 50–58)

1

I've become the person I was so afraid of becoming.

A skeptic. An agnostic—not even enough of a believer to be an atheist. A man who thinks that the opposite of truth isn't falsehood but certainty. And the worst thing, from the point of view of the person I was, is that I'm doing fine.

So, case closed? It can't be completely, because fifteen years after storing all my notebooks with biblical commentary in a cardboard box, I've once again been taken by the urge to explore this central and mysterious point in our common and my personal history. To come back to the texts, that is, to the New Testament.

Will I now retrace as a novelist the path I followed as a believer? Or as a historian? I still don't know, I don't want to make a decision, I don't think the title is all that important.

Let's say as an investigator.

2

If it doesn't enlighten, the figure of Jesus blinds. I don't want to tackle it head-on. Even if it means putting off following the spring back to its source, I prefer to open the investigation a little downstream and start by reading, as attentively as I can, the letters of Saint Paul and the Acts of the Apostles.

•

The Acts of the Apostles is the second part of an account attributed to Saint Luke, the first being the Gospel that bears his name. Logically speaking, these two books that biblical canon has separated should be read one after the other. The Gospel tells the life of Jesus, the Acts of the Apostles what happened during the thirty years that followed his death, that is to say, the birth of Christianity.

Luke wasn't a companion of Jesus. He never met him. He never says "I" in his Gospel, which is a secondhand account written half a century after the fact. But he was a companion of Paul, the Acts of the Apostles is to a large extent a biography of Paul, and at one moment in this biography something surprising happens, without warning or explanation: a sudden switch from the third to the first person.

It's a brief moment, you could miss it altogether, but when I noticed it I was spellbound.

Here it is, in chapter 16 of the Acts:

During the night Paul had a vision. A Macedonian stood before him and implored him with these words, "Come over to Macedonia and help us." When he had seen the vision, *we* sought passage to Macedonia at once, concluding that God had called *us* to proclaim the good news to them. *We* set sail from Troas, making a straight run for Samothrace, and on the next day to Neapolis.

Just who is covered by this "we" is unclear: maybe an entire group comprising the narrator and companions he feels aren't important enough to name. Be that as it may, for the last sixteen chapters we've been reading an impersonal account of Paul's adventures, and here all of a sudden *someone* appears who's telling the story. Then after a couple of pages this someone disappears, returning to the sidelines of the narrative. There he will stay for the next couple of chapters, only to reemerge and take part in the events through the end of the book. In this way, which is both abrupt and discreet, Luke tells us what the evangelist never says: *I was there.* What I'm telling you I saw firsthand.

•

When I'm being told a story, I like to know who's telling it. That's why I like narratives in the first person, that's why I write in the first person and would even be incapable of writing anything differently. As soon as someone says "I" (although, if need be, "we" does the job as well), I want to follow him and discover what's hiding behind this pronoun. I realized that I was going to follow Luke, that what I was going to write would be largely a biography of Luke, and that these few lines in the Acts of the Apostles were the door I'd been looking for to enter the New Testament. Not the main door, not the one that opens onto the nave, facing the altar, but a small, hidden side door: exactly what I needed.

I tried to zoom in—the way you do with Google Maps—on the exact point in space and time when this person who says "we" in the Acts appears. Regarding the time, and according to a method of counting that no one yet has any inkling of, it is around the year 50, give or take a year or two. As for the place, it's a port situated on the eastern coast of Turkey, which was called Asia in those days (today we say Asia Minor): Troas. At this precise moment in space and time, two men meet. They will later be called Saint Paul and Saint Luke but for now are simply named Paul and Luke.

3

A lot of things are known about Paul, who, for better and for worse, and perhaps even more than Jesus, has shaped twenty centuries of Western history. Unlike with Jesus, we know for certain what he thought, how he expressed himself, and what he was like, because the authenticity of most of his letters is uncontested. We also know what he looked like, something we have no idea about as far as Jesus is concerned. No one painted Paul's portrait during his lifetime, but all of the painters who have represented him know from his own account that he was just plain ugly, with a burly, ungainly body, that he was stocky but at the same time tormented by sickness. As one, they paint him bald and bearded, with a bulging forehead and eyebrows meeting above the nose, his face so far from any aesthetic convention that you simply say he must have looked like that.

•

About Luke we know far less. Almost nothing, in fact. Even though a legend I'll come back to later makes him the patron saint of painters, there is no clear pictorial tradition regarding what he looks like. Paul mentions him three times in his letters. He calls him "Luke, our dear doctor." Of course, back then they didn't say Luke, but Loukas in Greek, and in Latin, Lucanus. Similarly, Paul, whose Hebrew name was Shaul, as a Roman citizen bore the name Paulus, meaning "little one." One tradition has it that Luke was a Syrian born in Antioch. But the place where he met Paul between Europe and Asia and the fact that he served, as we'll soon see, as a guide in Macedonia, in cities he was familiar with, suggest that he was Macedonian. Last clue: according to scholars—I'm not in a position to judge—the Greek in which his two books are written is the most elegant in the New Testament.

To sum up: we're dealing with a lettered doctor whose language and culture are Greek, and not a Jewish fisherman. However, this Greek must have been attracted to the Jewish religion. If not, he'd never have come in contact with Paul. He wouldn't have understood what Paul was saying.

4

A Greek attracted to the Jewish religion: what is that?

First of all, it was common. As the Roman philosopher Seneca notes with contempt and the Jewish historian Josephus with satisfaction: Everywhere in the Empire—that is, in the world—there are people who observe the Sabbath, and these people are not only Jews.

Now I know you have to be careful about making facile comparisons, but for me this infatuation with Judaism, so widespread on the Mediterranean coast in the first century, is a little like the interest in Buddhism today: a religion that was both more humane and more refined, with that extra bit of soulfulness that was lacking in the waning paganism of the day. I have no idea just how fervently the Greeks in Pericles' day believed in their myths, but it's certain that five centuries later they no longer did, and neither did the Romans who conquered them. Or, in any case, most people no longer believed in them, just like most of us no longer believe in Christianity. That didn't stop them from observing the rites and sacrificing to the gods, but they did it the way we celebrate Christmas, Easter, or Pentecost. People believed in Zeus hurling bolts of lightning the way children today believe in Santa Claus: not for long, and not really. When Cicero famously wrote that two Roman augurs could not look each other in the face without laughing, he was not expressing the audacity of the freethinker but the average opinion—which must have been even more skeptical than it is today, because as dechristianized as our era is, no one nowadays would write the same thing about two bishops. Without necessarily believing what they say, at least we believe that they believe it. All of this explains, back then as much as today, the interest in Eastern religions. And the best thing on the market in terms of Eastern religions was the Jewish one. Their single God was less picturesque than the gods of Olympus, but the aspirations he fulfilled were higher. Those who worshipped him spread the faith by example. They were serious, industrious, totally lacking in frivolity. Even when they were poor, and they often were, the exacting, warm love that bonded their families made people want to be like them. Their prayers were true prayers. Those who were dissatisfied with their own lives felt that theirs were denser, weightier.

The Jews called all non-Jews *goyim*, which translates as "Gentiles," and "proselytes," the Gentiles attracted by Judaism. These they welcomed. If they really wanted to become Jews, they had to be circumcised and observe the Law in its entirety. Back then, as today, that was quite the undertaking, and few people went down that route. Many were content to observe the Laws of Noah: a light version of the Law, reduced to the major commandments and without the ritual prescriptions that serve above all to separate the children of Israel from other peoples. This minimum allowed the proselytes to enter the synagogues.

And there were synagogues everywhere, in all the ports, in all cities of any size. They were nondescript buildings—often merely private homes—and not churches or temples. The Jews had a single Temple, like they had a single god. That Temple was in Jerusalem. It had been destroyed, then rebuilt: it was magnificent. The Jews who were dispersed around the world, those who were known as the Diaspora, sent yearly offerings for its maintenance. They didn't feel obliged to go there on pilgrimages. Some did, but for the others the synagogue was enough. Since the days of their Babylonian exile, they were accustomed to having their relations with their god take place not in a remote, majestic building, but in the words of a book. And the synagogue was the modest, nearby location where, each Sabbath, they took out the scrolls of the book that wasn't called the Bible, and even less the Old Testament, but the Torah.

•

This book was in Hebrew, which is the ancient language of the Jews, the language in which their god spoke to them, but even in Jerusalem many no longer understood it: it had to be translated for them into their modern tongue, Aramaic. Everywhere else the Jews spoke Greek, like everyone else. Even the Romans, who had conquered the Greeks, spoke Greek—which, when you think about it, is as strange as if the British, having conquered the East Indies, had learned Sanskrit and adopted it as the dominant language throughout the world. In all of the Empire, from Scotland to the Caucasus, cultivated people spoke Greek well and the common people spoke it poorly. They spoke what was known as Koine Greek, which means "common" in the dual sense of "shared" and "vulgar," and which was the exact equivalent of our broken English. As early as the third century B.C., the Jews of Alexandria started to translate their sacred texts into this language that had become universal, and tradition has it that the Greek king of Egypt, Ptolemy Philadelphus, was so enchanted by these first texts that he ordered a complete translation for his library. It's said that on his request the grand priest of the Temple of Jerusalem sent six representatives of each of the twelve tribes of Israel, in all seventy-two learned men, to Pharos, an island off the Egyptian coast, and that although they each got down to work on their own, they came up with absolutely identical translations. Proof, it was said, that they were inspired by God, all of which explains why this Greek Bible bears the name of the Septuagint.

•

It's this Bible that Luke must have read, or rather heard read aloud when he went to the synagogue. Above all he knew the first five books, the most sacred, known as the Torah. He was familiar with Adam and Eve, Cain and Abel, Moses and the Pharaoh, the plagues of Egypt, the wandering in the desert, the parting of the Red Sea, the arrival in the Promised Land, and the battles for the Promised Land. He then got a bit lost in the histories of the kings who came after Moses. David and his sling, Solomon and his justice, Saul and his melancholy, he knew them the way a French schoolboy knows the kings of France—if he knows that Louis XIV comes after Henry IV, he's already ahead of the game. Even if he listened to them with respect and did his best to learn something in the process, he must have hoped when he went into the synagogue that he wouldn't have to hear one of those endless genealogies that the old Jews follow with closed eyes, nodding their heads as if lost in a trance. These litanies of Jewish names were like songs that they'd heard since their earliest days. But it wasn't the same for Luke, who didn't see why he should get interested in the distant folklore of another people when he wasn't interested in that of his own. Patiently he awaited the commentary that followed the reading, and focused on the philosophical meaning of these exotic, childish, often barbaric tales.

5

The thread running through these stories is the Jews' passionate relationship with their god. In their language this God is called Yahweh, or Adonai, or yet again Elohim, but the Jews of the Diaspora see no problem with the proselytes calling him *Kyrios* in Greek, meaning Lord, or *Theos*, which simply means God. He's their version of Zeus, but unlike Zeus he's not a skirt-chaser. He's not interested in women, just in his people, Israel, whom he loves exclusively, paying much more heed to their affairs than the Greek and Roman gods pay to those of their people. The Greek and Roman gods live among themselves, with their own intrigues and affairs. They're about as concerned about humans as humans are about ants. All dealings with them are limited to a few simple rites and sacrifices. Once that's out of the way, everything's in order. The god of the Jews, by contrast, asks the Jews to love him, to think of him nonstop, to do his will, and he is very demanding. He wants the best for them, which as it turns out is always the most difficult thing. He gave them a Law full of interdictions that prevent them from mixing with other people. He wants them to walk on craggy paths—in the mountains, in the desert, far from the welcoming plains where the other people lead quiet lives. The people of Israel regularly grumble and complain, want to take a break and mix with other people, and lead a quiet life like them. Their god then becomes angry, and either heaps hardships upon them or sends them inspired, difficult men to remind them of their vocation. These critics and finger-pointers are the prophets. They are named Hosea, Amos, Ezekiel, Isaiah, Jeremiah. They wield the carrot and the stick, above all the stick. They stand up to their kings and shame them for their conduct. To the unfaithful they promise terrible catastrophes in the immediate future and, later, provided they get back on the right track, a happy ending that basically comes down to the reign of Israel over all other nations.

•

This reign will be only a restoration, think the Jews, who live in the memory of a legendary time when their kingdom was powerful. A Greek like Luke can understand them. As different as they are, the Jews and Greeks are in the same boat under the Roman yoke. Their glorious cities of yore have become Roman colonies. Neither the Greek agora nor the Jewish Temple have any power anymore. But some of their past glory does subsist, because it is situated on another level. The Romans are the best conquerors whom the world has known since Alexander, and they're far better than he was at administering what they've conquered. That doesn't stop the Greeks and Jews from being unrivaled in their own fields, which today we'd call culture and religion. The Romans have no doubts about that as far as the Greeks go: they adopted their language, copied their statues, and imitated their refined ways with a zeal bordering on obsequiousness. By contrast they're less good at singling out the Jews among the mass of querulous and bizarre Oriental peoples whom they subjugate. But the Jews couldn't care less: they know they're superior, chosen by the true God. They delight in the contrast between the darkness of their present condition and the incommensurable grandeur of their calling. Certain Greeks, like Luke, are impressed.

•

Careful: When I say "Greeks," and when Saint Paul says "Greeks," it doesn't just refer to the small aristocratic people who invented democracy in the fifth century b.c., but to all of the people who lived in the countries conquered by Alexander the Great two hundred years later, and who spoke Greek. Starting in the third century, you became Greek by cultural assimilation, which had to do neither with blood nor with the soil. This civilization, which became known as "Hellenistic," developed in Macedonia, Turkey, Egypt, Syria, and right across to India. In many ways it resembled our own, and like ours it could be called globalized. It was a subjugated, frivolous, troubled civilization that had outlived its own ideals. The ideal of the city, which had made Greece great in the time of Pericles, had long been out of vogue. No one believed in the gods anymore, but many believed in astrology, magic, and evil spells. The name of Zeus was still invoked, but while the commoners demonstrated a very new-age syncretism in grafting it onto any Oriental divinity that happened to suit the purpose, for the lettered it was a pure abstraction. Three centuries earlier, Greek philosophy had asked what was the best way to govern a city. Now it knew that it had no say in the matter. It was now no more than a recipe for individual happiness. As the city could no longer be autonomous, it was up to man to take up the slack, or at least to try. The school of Stoicism, which was the dominant ideology of the time, invited adherents to protect themselves from the world, to become islands and to cultivate negative virtues: apathy, which is the absence of suffering, and ataraxy, which is the absence of agitation and gives its name to Atarax, an anxiolytic that I consumed in large doses at one period in my life. Nothing is more desirable, says Stoicism, than the absence of desires: that alone procures the tranquility of the soul. We're not far from Buddhism.

•

Luke would have no reason to be interested in the long domestic quarrel between Israel and the God of Israel if he didn't see it as an allegory for the relationship between man—lazy, fickle, scattered—and something grander, either within him or outside of him. The ancient writers called this *something* indifferently gods or god, or nature, or destiny, or Logos, and the hidden figure of each person's life is the relationship he maintains with it.

In Alexandria there was a very famous rabbi named Philo, whose specialty was reading his people's scriptures in the light of Plato, and retelling them as a philosophical epic. Instead of seeing the first chapter of Genesis as being about a bearded God busying himself in a garden and creating the universe in six days, Philo said that the number six symbolized perfection, and that it's not for nothing if, against all apparent logic, this book tells two contradictory stories of creation: the first about the birth of Logos, the second about the fashioning of the material universe by the demiurge also described in Plato's *Timaeus*. The cruel story of Cain and Abel set the stage for the eternal conflict between love of self and love of God. As for the tumultuous relationship between Israel and its god, it was transposed on the personal level to that between each person's soul and the divine principle. Exiled in Egypt, the soul languished. Led by Moses into the desert, it learned thirst, patience, discouragement, rapture. And when it arrived in view of the Promised Land, it had to battle against—and brutally massacre—the tribes that had settled there. According to Philo these weren't real tribes, but evil passions that the soul had to subdue. Again, when Abraham is traveling with his wife Sarah and the two are put up by sinister Bedouins, to avoid any problems Abraham offers that they sleep with Sarah. Rather than putting this act of pimping down to the harshness of desert life or the rough customs of yore, Philo maintained that Sarah was the symbol of virtue, and that it was a fine thing on Abraham's part not to want to keep her to himself. The rhetoricians named this way of reading allegory. Philo preferred to call it *trepain*, meaning passage, migration, exodus, because if the reader's spirit were persevering and pure, it would emerge changed. It was up to each individual to go on his own spiritual exodus, from flesh to spirit, from the darkness of the physical world to the luminous realm of the Logos, from slavery in Egypt to freedom in Canaan.

Philo died an old man, fifteen years after Jesus, whose name he certainly never heard, and five years before Luke met Paul in the port of Troas. I have no idea if Luke read him, but I think the version of Judaism that Luke was familiar with was strongly Hellenized, and tended to transpose the story of this small exotic people that you could hardly find on a map into terms that were accessible to the Greek ideal of wisdom. For Luke, going to the synagogue was less like embracing a religion than attending a philosophy class—just as when we practice yoga or meditation we become interested in Buddhist texts without feeling obliged to believe in Tibetan divinities or turn a prayer wheel.

6

The scene takes place in the synagogue in Troas. Luke is traveling on business that is no doubt linked to his work as a doctor. When visiting another city he made a habit of going to the synagogue on the day of the Sabbath. He doesn't know anyone, but he's not fazed, because synagogues are the same everywhere. A simple room, almost empty. No statues, no frescoes, no ornaments. That too pleases and calms him.

After the usual reading of the Laws and the Prophets, the head of the synagogue asks if anyone wants to address the gathering. According to custom, he first asks the new arrivals. Although he's new there, Luke's not the type to volunteer. I even imagine him afraid to be noticed, and worried that the head of the synagogue might pick him out of the crowd. But he doesn't have time to fret, because a man gets up and goes to the center of the room. He introduces himself as Paul, a rabbi from the city of Tarsus.

He looks at those around him like a gladiator at the spectators before a fight. His voice is deep, he speaks slowly at first, but as he warms up his words come out faster, becoming vehement, disjointed.

"Men of Israel," Paul starts, "and you others who are God-fearing, listen. The God of this people Israel chose our ancestors and exalted the people during their sojourn in the land of Egypt. With uplifted arm he led them out of it and for about forty years he put up with them in the desert..."

Those present nod their heads, so does Luke. They know the story. And they know what comes next, which the orator reels off without showing any great talent for concision but with a praiseworthy attention to chronology. After the forty years in the desert, the establishment of the twelve tribes in the land of Canaan, then the government of the judges, then that of the kings, the greatest of whom was David, son of Jesse, a man after the Lord's heart...

"Among the descendants of David," Paul continues, God promised that a child would be born who, when he became a man, would be a light for his people..."

More nodding. That too they know back to front.

"And now," the orator goes on, "now, men of Israel, listen! Learn that God has kept his word. Learn that he has given his people the savior they were waiting for. He has brought to Israel a savior, Jesus."

At this point Paul pauses and inspects his audience, who need a bit of time to grasp the full significance of what they've just heard.

There's nothing unusual about bringing up the savior who will come one day, reward the good, punish the evil, and restore the kingdom of Israel. A proselyte like Luke has often heard the name, or rather the title, of this Khristos: the savior, the Messiah, the one who has received the divine unction. As a Greek, he's not particularly interested. When it's brought up in the synagogue he doesn't really pay attention. He tends to class it together with the more folkloric than philosophical odds and ends of Judaism that interest only the Jews. In any case, what everyone says is that he *must* come. But it's another thing altogether to say that he *has* come. That he has another name than Khristos, a perfectly banal Jewish name, in the original version Yeshua. And after the majestic list of all the Samuels, Sauls, Benjamins, and Davids, this name is about as incongruous as if, after listing the kings of France, you said the last one was Gerald or Patrick.

Jesus? Who's that, Jesus?

Everyone raises their eyebrows, frowns, exchanges perplexed looks. But that's not all. This is just the beginning.

"Jesus was the Christ," Paul resumes. "The inhabitants of Jerusalem and their leaders failed to recognize him, and by condemning him they fulfilled the oracles of the prophets that are read Sabbath after Sabbath. They refused to listen to him. They mocked him. They weren't content just to mock him. Without a motive, they sentenced him and had him die on the cross."

A stir goes through the crowd: "On the cross!"

The cross is a horrible punishment, and above all a humiliation, used only for the dregs of humanity: bandits, escaped slaves. Again transposed into today's context, it's as if you announced that in addition to being named Gerald or Patrick, the savior of humanity was jailed for being a pedophile. It's shocking, but captivating. Instead of speaking louder, as a less-skilled orator would do, Paul lowers his voice. The people are forced to remain still, and even to move closer.

"They put him in a tomb.

"And after three days, as it's written in the Scriptures, the Lord raised him from the dead.

"He appeared first of all to his twelve closest companions, and then to many others. Most of them are still alive and can testify to what they saw. I too can bear witness, because I am the last to whom he appeared, although I'm just a runt and didn't even know him when he was alive. They saw him, I saw him, breathing and speaking although he was dead. Anyone who has witnessed such a thing can do nothing but testify to what he has seen. That is why I travel the world telling people what I have just told you. The Lord has fulfilled the promise made to our fathers. He resurrected Jesus, and he will resurrect us as well. All of this will happen soon, far sooner than you think. I know it's difficult to believe. Nevertheless, you are the ones who are asked to believe. You, children of the stock of Abraham, you to whom the promise was made, but not only you. What I say also holds for the Greeks, the proselytes. It holds for everyone."

7

I've tried to reconstruct what Paul said: the typical discourse heard in the synagogues of Greece and Asia around A.D. 50 by people who converted to a belief that was not yet known as Christianity. I've compiled and paraphrased the most ancient sources. For those interested in knowing how I composed this cocktail, there's a bit of the grand profession of faith from Paul's First Letter to the Corinthians, and much of a long tirade that Luke, forty years later, has Paul say in chapter 13 of the Acts of the Apostles. Without being able to claim that this is what Paul said word for word, I think it's very close to the truth. Paul started on familiar territory, recapitulated Jewish history, reminded his listeners of the promise it held, then all of a sudden he proclaimed that this promise had been fulfilled. The Messiah, the Christ, had come and was called Jesus. He died ignominiously, then was resurrected, and those who believed that would be resurrected too. From a familiar, even somewhat conventional discourse, he shifted without warning to something whose scandalous nature we—accustomed as we are to its extravagance—have difficulty grasping.

•

Luke's accounts of reactions to Paul's preaching always follow the same scenario. After a moment of stupefaction, one part of the crowd is filled with enthusiasm while the other cries blasphemy. Such hard and fast reactions didn't surprise Paul. What he announced cleaved the world as neatly as the blow of an axe. Those who believed, those who didn't believe: two separate humanities.

Luke wasn't scandalized. Did that mean he immediately believed what Paul was saying? I have a hard time accepting that. But almost as an aside, he evokes a third reaction in the Acts: that of those who walked a few paces with the apostle and asked him questions outside the synagogue. Perhaps because that would also be my reaction, I can well imagine Luke belonging to this third group: those who neither tear their clothes in indignation nor prostrate themselves in front of Paul, but are intrigued, engrossed by the speaker's conviction, and, without committing themselves, want to know more.

•

Today the discussion would continue in a café, and maybe Luke did sit down with Paul and his two companions in a tavern in the port of Troas.

Boats in the background, fishnets drying, grilled octopus in a dish, a pitcher of resinated wine: you get the picture. Soon the two others will go off to bed. Luke remains alone with Paul. They talk until sunrise, or rather Paul talks and talks, and Luke listens. The next morning everything seems different to him. The sky is no longer the same, the people are no longer the same. He knows that a man came back from the dead and that from now on his own life will no longer be the same.

Maybe that's how it happened. Or . . .

I think I have a better idea.

8

Luke was a doctor. Paul was sick. He mentions that several times in his letters. In the one he wrote to the Galatians, he recalls how he stayed with them for a long time because of this sickness and thanks them for showing neither disdain nor disgust at his ravaged body—although it wasn't easy for them. He puts a lot of stress on that: just going near him deserved credit. In another letter he complains of a "thorn in the flesh." Several times he begged God to rid him of it, but God didn't want to, contenting himself to say: "My grace is sufficient for you."

Thousands of pages have been written on this "thorn in the flesh." During Paul's fits the mysterious sickness made his body so repulsive and caused him such suffering that he prayed to God to cure him. What could it be? Paul's description makes you think of a skin disease, one of those conditions that make you scratch until you bleed—eczema, psoriasis—but also of what Dostoyevsky says about his attacks of epilepsy, or Virginia Woolf about her dives into depression. I think of that simple, poignant entry in her diary: "Today, the horror returned." We'll never know what illness Paul had, but reading him it's clear that it was horribly painful, even shameful. Something that always came back, even after long periods of remission when he could believe he was cured. Something that tied him in knots, body and soul.

Second version, then: Luke is witness to the scandal in the synagogue. Deep in thought, he returns to his inn and goes about his business. The next day, some people come to get him because another traveler is sick. This other traveler is Paul. Devastated by fever, crippled with pain, his body and perhaps his face covered with a blood-and-pus-stained cloth. Luke thinks he's going to die. He looks after him and does what he can to soothe him, but nothing seems to work. For two days he doesn't leave the dying man's side. In a semi-delirium and with a hoarse, wheezing voice, this man says things even stranger than what he said in the synagogue. And in the end he doesn't die. Then we come back to the earlier version of the scene, the conversation between the two men, which is more intimate and more full of trust because of what has just happened. And now it's time to ask just what Paul said when the two were alone.

9

Those familiar with the endless political debates that followed May '68 in France and the anti–Vietnam War protests in the States will remember the ritual question: "Where are you coming from?" I still find it pertinent. To be touched by a thought, I need it to come from somewhere, to come from someone, and to know what they mean by it. Paul belongs to the group of people who don't have to be asked twice to say where they're coming from—that is, to talk about themselves—and it didn't take long before Luke heard his story, which was as disturbing as his speeches.

•

Paul tells Luke that he used to be named Saul, after the first king of Israel. He was an extremely pious young Jew. His parents, wealthy merchants from the large eastern city of Tarsus, wanted him to become a rabbi and sent him to study with Gamaliel, the grand Pharisee teacher of Jerusalem. The Pharisees were the doctors of the Law, erudite men of faith whose opinions, like those of the *ulama* in Islam, were deemed authoritative. Saul dreamed of becoming a second Gamaliel. He read and reread the Torah, examining each word with fervor.

One day, he heard talk of a sect of Galileans who called themselves "those who follow the Way" and held a strange belief that set them apart from other Jews. For reasons that remain somewhat obscure, a few years earlier their master was put to death on the cross. That was shocking enough, but rather than playing it down, they boldly asserted it. And even more shocking: they refused to believe that he was dead. They said they'd seen him laid in the tomb, and that afterward they'd seen him alive, talking and eating. They said he'd been raised from the dead. They wanted everyone to worship him as the Messiah.

Saul could have shrugged that off, but he reacted exactly the way the most pious of his listeners now react: by crying blasphemy. And he didn't joke around when it came to blasphemy—he took piety to the point of fanaticism. Not content to see a follower of this crucified one stoned before his eyes, he wanted to get in on the action himself. He kept watch on the houses where his sources told him that the followers of the Way congregated. Those he suspected of belonging to the group he denounced to the high priests and had arrested and thrown in prison. By his own account, he breathed threats and murder. One day he decided to leave for Damascus, where he'd been told that some were staying, planning to bring them back to Jerusalem bound in chains. But as he was traveling at noon along the rocky road, a bright light suddenly blinded him, and an invisible force knocked him down. A voice whispered in his ear: "Saul! Saul! I'm the one you're persecuting. Why are you persecuting me?"

When he got up he couldn't see a thing. He staggered around as if drunk. Those who were accompanying him led him blind and reeling to the house of strangers where he remained for three days, shut up in a room, alone, without eating or drinking. He was afraid. What scared him wasn't any external danger but what was stirring, like a beast, in his soul. Often, in the uneasy dreams of his youth, he'd felt something enormous and menacing prowling around him. Now it was no longer around him. It was crouched deep within him, ready to devour him from the inside. After three days, he heard the door of the room open and someone approach. Someone stood by him, in silence. For a long time. He heard the beating of his heart, the throbbing of blood in his veins. Finally the man spoke: "Paul, my brother, it's the Lord who sends me. He wants your heart to awaken."

While the stranger spoke these words, the man who still went by the name of Saul tried to resist. He struggled with all his might, horrified by this enormous, menacing thing that was growing in him and trying to expel him from himself. He would have liked to remain himself, to go on being Saul, not to let himself be invaded, not to surrender. He cried, he shook. Then, all of a sudden, everything gave way. He accepted the invasion. And instead of destroying him, the enormous and menacing thing that had grown within him started to lull him like a child. What he had so dreaded now struck him as the greatest happiness, one that had been unimaginable just a few moments ago and that was now patent, unassailable, eternal. He was no longer Saul the persecutor, but Paul, who would one day be persecuted, and who was glad that he would be persecuted. And, one by one, the brothers who would share in his persecution entered the room and surrounded him.

They embraced him, and added their tears of joy to his own. There was no need for words. Their hearts responded to each other, silent, ecstatic. Gone were the rifts, the misunderstandings, the obscurity. Everything that separates men from one another had disappeared, as had everything that separates them from the deepest realm within them. Everything was now transparency and light. Paul was no longer himself, he was finally himself. Thick scales had fallen from his eyes. He could see again, but what he saw bore no resemblance to what he had seen before. Horror and pity seized him when he saw in a flash who he had been until his deliverance, and what a world of shadows he had lived in believing it was real. Horror and pity also seized him at the thought of the many souls still wandering in this world of shadows without knowing or suspecting a thing. It was then that he swore to help them, not to abandon a soul, to triumph over their fear of this metamorphosis as Jesus himself had triumphed over his own.

•

Blessed by the brothers of Damascus, Saul returned to Jerusalem. Going by his new name Paul, he went to the synagogues to announce that the man who had been crucified a few years ago really was the Christ: the Messiah that Israel was waiting for. His teachers and friends among the Pharisees renounced him, and those he had hounded with his hatred were wary, fearing a ruse. Finally he convinced them of his sincerity, and they sent him beyond the borders of Israel to announce not only to the Jews but also to the Gentiles that the Christ had died and been resurrected, as a prelude to the death and the resurrection of all humanity.

•

What Paul did was a world apart from seeking to demonstrate the validity and credentials of a new doctrine on the basis of the Scriptures. He said: You are sleeping, wake up. Let your heart hear me and you will awaken. Your life will be completely transformed. You will no longer even understand how you lived that oppressive life of darkness, and how others continue to live it as if there were nothing more to life, without suspecting a thing. He said: You are a caterpillar destined to become a butterfly. If you could explain to a caterpillar what awaits it, it would have a hard time understanding. It would be afraid. It's not easy for anyone to cease being who he is, to become something other than himself. But that is what the Way is. Once you're on the other side, you no longer even remember the person you once were, the person filled with mockery or fear—it's the same thing. Some of them do remember: they're the best guides. That's why I, Paul, am telling you this.

10

Paul also said that the end of the world was near. He was absolutely convinced of that, and it's one of the first things he made clear to those with whom he spoke. The end of the world was near because this man he called the Christ had been resurrected. And if this man he called the Christ was resurrected, it's because the end of the world was near. It wasn't near in an abstract way, the way you can say that death is near for all of us, at every moment. No, Paul said, it will happen in our lifetime. To us, who are talking now. None of us here will die without having seen the Lord fill heaven with his power and separate the good from the evil. If those he was talking to shrugged their shoulders, there was no point going on. It would be just as vain to explain the path of Buddha to someone who showed no interest in the first of his noble truths—all of human life is change and suffering—and even less in the next: Is there a way to escape this sequence of change and suffering? Someone who refuses to go along with this diagnosis and doesn't ask what remedies there might be, someone who finds life fine as it is, has no reason to get interested in Buddhism. In the same way, in the first century A.D. someone who didn't want to believe that the world would soon end wasn't a good customer for Paul.

•

I don't know how widespread this idea was at the time. But it seems to me that today it's very widespread indeed. Sticking to what I know—my country, my small sociocultural milieu—it seems to me that a lot of people think in vague but certain terms that for whatever reason, we're heading straight for the wall. Because there are too many of us for the space we've been allotted. Because the more we devastate it, the more this space is becoming uninhabitable. Because we have the ability to destroy ourselves and it would be surprising if we didn't. This statement gives way to two families of ideas, represented in our home by Hélène and myself. The first, to whose moderate wing I belong, thinks that we are heading if not for the end of the world, then at least for a major historic catastrophe that will entail the disappearance of a significant part of humanity. Those who hold this belief have no idea how it will happen or what it will lead to, but they think that if not they themselves, then at least their children will be in the front row. The fact that that doesn't stop them from having children shows how easily—through their moderate wings, which have the most adherents by far—the two families coexist. At the dinner table when I repeat what I read in a book by a German sociologist on the nightmarish wars that won't fail to come about as a result of the climate change, Hélène, a member of the second party, responds that yes, of course there are historic catastrophes, the Great Plague, the Spanish flu epidemic, the two world wars—yes, major changes take place, changes of civilization and, as we say today, of paradigms. But, she continues, ever since humanity's earliest days, one of its favorite pastimes has been to dread and announce the end of the world, and there's no more reason for it to happen now or tomorrow than in the thousand times in the past when people like me had been sure it would.

•

One lunatic, Caligula, had just ruled over Rome. Soon another, Nero, would appear. Earthquakes were frequent, volcanoes covered entire cities with dust, and sows giving birth to clawed monsters gave rise to dark premonitions. Is that enough to conclude that the first century was more prey to apocalyptic beliefs than any other? Israel, yes, no doubt, but the Greco-Roman world at the height of its power and stability? The world to which someone like Luke belonged?

I don't know.

11

Paul was traveling with two companions at the time, named, as the Acts of the Apostles tells us, Silas and Timothy. For the moment I'm not quite sure what to do with these second roles, what I care about is that until Troas this trio is called "they," and when they leave Troas it becomes "we": Luke appears on the scene.

The Acts also tells us that when they meet, Paul hesitates about what direction he should take. Having started out from Syria, he's just spent five years traveling through Cilicia, Galatia, Pamphylia, Lycaonia, Phrygia, Lydia. These exotic names belong to ancient Hellenistic kingdoms that had become far-flung districts of the Roman Empire. From east to west, they basically cover the area now occupied by Turkey. Straying from the populous coastal regions and ports, Paul made his way inland. He went on foot and, when lucky, on the back of a mule, on bad roads infested with bandits. All he owned fit into one bag, his coat served as his tent. Maps didn't exist, the horizon of one village extended as far as the next, beyond that lay the unknown. Paul was headed for the unknown. He climbed steep and craggy mountains, trekked over high passes, saw the strange rocky concretions that still today enthrall tourists visiting Cappadocia, and reached sleepy villages on the vast Anatolian plateau where Jewish colonies nevertheless existed. But these were such rustic, naïve Jews, so far removed from everything that unlike those living in the big cities, they welcomed Paul's words and adopted Christ without a murmur. After five years, judging these communities faithful enough to be able to get along without him, he decided to return to more civilized areas. His goal was to continue his mission in Asia, meaning the coastal area in western Turkey.

Then the Spirit of God blocked his way.

•

That's how Luke describes it, with a straight face and without giving any details as to just how the Spirit went about it. Consequently, the scene is quite hard to imagine. Hoping to learn more, I referred to the notes of the Jerusalem Bible and the Ecumenical Translation of the Bible, which from now on I'll just call JB and ETB. These two translations are the ones I always have on my desk. Near at hand on a shelf I also have Louis Segond's—Protestant—translation, the one by Lemaistre de Sacy, known as the "Port-Royal Bible," as well as the most recent one put out by Bayard Publishing House, referred to as the "Writers' Bible," which I will no doubt refer to again because I participated in writing it. The notes in the JB and the ETB are abundant and generally very good, but if you want to know how the Spirit of God blocked Paul's way, you have to admit that they're a bit of a letdown. While the two advance slightly different hypotheses about the apostle's route, neither goes any further than saying that the Spirit stopped Paul from going to Asia because it was his destiny to go to Europe.

Luckily, there's a more rationalist version of the story: the one by Ernest Renan. The apostles lived in a world of signs and wonders, he says, and in all circumstances believed they were obeying divine inspiration. They interpreted their dreams, chance experiences, and all the incidents that occur while traveling as so many divine injunctions. According to this version, Paul said to Luke that he felt he was at a crossroads and didn't know what direction he should take. Luke, who was going back home to Macedonia, offered to serve as a guide and introduce him to people who might be interested in his message. Paul concluded that Luke was sent to him by the Holy Spirit. Maybe he dreamed of him the following night. The passage of the Acts that got me into the story in the first place mentions a Macedonian who appears in a dream to Paul and invites him in the name of his compatriots to go over to the other shore. What if this mysterious Macedonian is Luke himself? For me the story loses nothing in being told in this way.

12

I just appealed to the authority of Renan, and I'll do it again. He's one of my companions on this voyage to the land of the New Testament. I have his two large tomes right next to my Bibles, and I think it's time I introduced him to readers who may be unfamiliar with him.

Ernest Renan was brought up in a fervently Catholic family from Brittany, and was destined to become a priest. During his studies in the seminary, his faith started to waver. At the end of a long and painful struggle, he renounced serving a God he was no longer certain he believed in. He became a historian, a philologist, an Orientalist. He thought that to write the history of a religion, the best thing was to have believed it and no longer believe. It's in this frame of mind that he undertook his grand oeuvre whose first volume, *The Life of Jesus*, sparked a huge scandal in 1863. A peaceful scholar spurred on by a love of knowledge, Renan was one of the most hated men of his time. He was excommunicated and stripped of his chair at the Collège de France. All the major pamphleteers of the Catholic right dragged him through the mud. Here as an example are a couple of lines by the novelist Léon Bloy: "Renan, the god of cowards, the potbellied wise man, the fine scientific latrine from which radiates the greasy odor of a soul cast out from the toilets where he was born."

People whose taste I respect without sharing it consider Bloy a great writer. Those are the same people who above all quote the Bible passage from Revelation saying that God "spits out the lukewarm." It's true, Renan left himself open to this caricature. Fat and meek-mannered, wedged into his armchair by soft little cushions, he had the face of a vicar and the same, perhaps deceptive, look of a hypocrite that did such a disservice to Pope Benedict XVI. That said, it strikes me, and should, I think, strike a large number of my readers, that what made several generations of people think of him as the antichrist—to the point where they went straight to confession after merely *seeing* one of his books in a store window—is an essential minimum of rigor and reason. (That's what I think today, of course: if I'd read Renan twenty years ago when I was a dogmatic Catholic, I would have hated him and been proud of it.)

•

Renan's whole project seeks to give a natural explanation to events that are deemed supernatural, to bring the divine down to a human scale, and to situate religion on the plane of history. Renan is anything but sectarian and very much in favor of everyone thinking and believing what they want, he just thinks every man to his trade. He chose to be a historian and not a priest, and the historian's role is not and cannot be to say that Jesus was resurrected, nor that he's the son of God, just that a group of people at a certain time and in circumstances that deserve to be recounted in detail got it into their heads that he had been resurrected, that he was the son of God, and even managed to persuade others of the same. Refusing to believe in the resurrection, and more generally in miracles, Renan tells the life of Jesus while trying to come to terms with *what could really, historically, have happened*, which the first narratives deform according to their belief. With each episode of the Gospel, he sorts and selects: this yes, this no, this maybe. In his writings, Jesus becomes one of the most remarkable and influential men who ever lived, a moral revolutionary, a master of wisdom like the Buddha—but not the son of God, for the simple reason that God doesn't exist.

•

The Life of Jesus remains a more instructive and more enjoyable read than 99 percent of what comes out on the subject every year; nevertheless, it has aged poorly. What was new about it is no longer new, its elegant but dated style often turns syrupy, and it's hard for contemporary readers not to be annoyed when Renan praises Jesus for having been the prototype of the "gallant man," for having "possessed to the highest degree what we regard as the essential quality of a distinguished person, and by that I mean the ability to smile at what he has done," or when he prefers Jesus' subtle skeptical jibes to the obtuse and fanatical belief of Paul—his pet peeve. But *The Life of Jesus* is just the tip of the iceberg. The most enthralling of Renan's works are the next six volumes of *The History of the Origins of Christianity*, in which he tells in detail this story that is far less well known: how a small Jewish sect, established by illiterate fishermen and bound by an absurd belief on which no one in their right mind would have bet a sesterce, devoured the Roman Empire from the inside in less than three centuries, and against all likelihood has endured to the present day. And the fascinating thing is not just the extraordinary story that Renan tells, but also the extraordinary honesty with which he tells it: his way of explaining to the reader how he goes about his work as a historian, what sources he uses, what he does with them and on the basis of what presuppositions. I like his way of writing history, not *ad probandum*, as he says, but *ad narrandum*: not to prove something, but simply to tell what happened. I like his stubborn good faith, the scrupulous care he puts into distinguishing between the certain and the probable, the probable and the possible, the possible and the dubious, and the calm with which he responds to his fiercest critics: "As for those persons who would have, in the interests of their belief, that I am an ignoramus, an evil genius, or a man of bad faith, I do not pretend to be able to modify their opinions. If such opinions are necessary for the peace of mind of certain pious people, I would make it a veritable scruple to disabuse them of them."

13

The boat connecting Asia with the shores of Europe drops Paul and his companions in the port of Neapolis, from where they head to Philippi

in Macedonia. It's a new city, built by the Romans who have occupied
the former kingdom of Alexander the Great for the past two centuries.
From one end of the Empire to the other, from Spain to Turkey, Roman
roads, paved so solidly that many still exist today, connect Roman cities,
which are all built according to the same model: large avenues crossing
at right angles; gymnasium, baths, forum; an abundance of white marble; Latin inscriptions although the people speak Greek; temples dedicated to the emperor Augustus and his wife Livia, whose purely formal
worship—which doesn't require any more commitment than our cere-
monies marking Remembrance Day or Thanksgiving—coexists peacefully with that of the local deities. You can't say that the Romans
invented globalization, because it already existed under Alexander's empire, but they brought it to a point of perfection that lasted for five centuries. It's like McDonald's, Coca-Cola, shopping malls, and Apple
Stores today: wherever you go, you find the same thing. Of course, there
are grouches who deplore this cultural and political imperialism, but all
in all most people are happy to live in a pacified world where you can
move around freely, where you're never out of your element, where wars
are fought by professional soldiers on the distant borders of the Empire
and have no more repercussions on people's lives than the festivities and
celebrations that mark their victories.

•

A city like Philippi is populated half by native Macedonians and half by
Roman settlers. No doubt there aren't many Jews, because there's no
synagogue. But there is a little group that gathers outside the walls on
the banks of a river, to celebrate the Sabbath in an informal way. Its
members aren't Jews, they only have a very vague knowledge of the
Torah. For me they're like people who do yoga or tai chi in a small town
and find a way to practice although there are no teachers: with a book,
a couple of videos, or under the guidance of the only one who's taken a
few courses or attended a workshop. In general such groups are composed
mostly of women, and, as unorthodox as it sounds when transposed onto
a religion in which the service can be celebrated only in the presence of
at least ten men, that's the case in Philippi: in his account Luke mentions only women. It could be that he knows them already, that he's already attended their meetings, and that he knows just what he's doing
when he brings his three new friends to see them.

•

"When the student is ready, the teacher will appear": an adage well known in the milieu of the martial arts. Clearly in this case the students were good and ready, because they immediately recognized in Paul the master they'd been waiting for. Luke speaks in particular of a certain Lydia, who was apparently the leader of the group. "She listened," he writes. "The Lord opened her heart to pay attention to what Paul was saying."

Despite her passion for Judaism, Lydia has never thought of having her husband and sons circumcised—and no one has asked her to either. But as soon as Paul evokes the rather peculiar rite by which you affirm your faith in the belief he tells her about, she insists on going through with it. You have to admit that unlike circumcision, it's painless and doesn't leave any traces. You wade out into the river, you kneel down, the person carrying out the service keeps your head underwater for a few moments and says in a loud voice that he's wetting you in the name of Christ, and then it's over, you'll never be the same. It's called baptism. After receiving it, Lydia wants her family to receive it too. She wants the new guru and his companions to stay at her place. Paul starts by refusing, because he makes a point of depending on no one, but Lydia is so enthusiastic, so warm, that he lets her twist his arm.

Lydia, Luke tells us, is a merchant of purple cloth, that is, of the dyed fabric that's a specialty of the region and a good export product. Not the wife of a merchant: a merchant. You get the idea: a prosperous business, an energetic woman, a matriarchal environment. Four religious visionaries who come and stay in the comfortable home of such an energetic woman and convert her whole family would certainly get people talking in a French provincial town today, and I see no reason to think that it didn't get people talking in a Macedonian provincial town in the first century.

•

A small circle gathers around Paul and his companions at Lydia's place. A few years later, Paul will write a letter to the inhabitants of Philippi in which he makes sure to greet Euodia, Epaphroditus, and Syntyche. I'm pleased to write the names of these minor characters who have come down to us over twenty centuries. There must have been others, I'd say ten or twenty. Paul's charisma and Lydia's authority are so effective that they all start to believe in the resurrection of this Jesus whose name they didn't even know just a few days ago. They all have themselves baptized. In doing so it never occurs to them that they're betraying Judaism, which they adopted with a zeal that was as vibrant as it was ill-informed. On the contrary: they thank God for having sent them such a learned rabbi to guide them and show them how to worship in spirit and truth. Of course, they continue to observe the Sabbath, they put down their work, light candles, and pray, and Paul does all of that with them, but he also teaches them a new ritual. It's a meal that Paul calls the agape and that takes place not on the day of the Sabbath but the day after.

The agape is a real meal, a festive meal, even if Paul insists that no one should eat or above all drink too much. Everyone is supposed to bring a dish they've prepared at home. These instructions probably didn't work too well in Philippi because meals were served at Lydia's place, and as I imagine her, Lydia was the kind of hostess who's both generous and tyrannical, who always wants to do everything herself, to prepare three times too much to eat, and if someone wants to help she says no, no, that's kind, but that's not the way we do things here. "Leave that, I'll do it, you go sit down with the others." At one point in the meal, Paul gets up, breaks a piece of bread, and says it's the body of Christ. He raises a goblet filled with wine and says it's Christ's blood. In silence, the bread and the wine are passed around the table, and everyone eats a piece of bread, drinks a mouthful of wine. In memory, Paul says, of the last meal that the savior ate on this earth before being crucified. Afterward, they sing a sort of hymn about his death and Christ's resurrection.

14

"One day," Luke continues, "as we were going to the place of prayer, we were met by a slave girl who had a pythonical spirit." My Bibles and Renan agree: "had a pythonical spirit" means possessed with a gift for prophesy and divination like the Python of Delphi. The slave girl goes up to Paul, Timothy, Silas, Luke, and perhaps some of their Philippian followers. She calls out to them, she follows them, she shouts that they are slaves of the Most High God who proclaim the way to salvation. She starts again the next day, and the days after that. Paul, who would prefer more discreet publicity, passes her by and averts his eyes. Then, as her calls become louder and louder, he loses his patience and commands the spirit to come out of her in Christ's name. Spasms, jerks, then prostration. End of the hysterical fit.

To believe Luke, Paul does such things on a regular basis, but he thinks twice before displaying his powers. On the one hand, it's impressive and calms suffering. On the other, the people it tends to convert aren't the most desirable. More often than not, it only brings trouble.

There's another story like that in the Acts. Luke doesn't witness it: Timothy must have told it to him because it took place two years earlier in Lystra, Timothy's hometown in the mountains of Lycaonia. There Paul cured a paralytic, and, seeing this miracle, the inhabitants of Lystria threw themselves down with their faces to the ground. They took Paul and his disciple for Zeus and Hermes who had descended to earth.

When I ran across this passage it made me think of the wonderful story by Rudyard Kipling, *The Man Who Would Be King*, and of the film made by John Huston. Two ex-officers of the Indian Army—played by Sean Connery and Michael Caine—seek their fortune in the Hindu Kush, which first-century Lycaonia must have largely equaled in terms of savagery. As the local inhabitants have never seen white men, it doesn't fail; they're worshipped like gods. Michael Caine, who plays the role of Sancho Panza in the story, would like to take advantage of the misunderstanding, swipe the loot in the temple, and make a run for it. Sean Connery, who plays the role of Don Quixote, thinks that these mountain dwellers don't lack brains. He lets it go to his head and starts to think he really is a god, and the whole thing ends very badly. The last images show the village children playing soccer in the dust with his head wrapped in bloody rags.

Unlike Michael Caine, Paul didn't want to take advantage of the Lycaonians' gullibility—or at least not in the same way. He was interested in their souls, not their gold. But he did experience the giddiness felt by Sean Connery, at whose feet the crowds prostrate themselves, and the anger of this crowd when they discover that the one they are worshipping is just a man. In Lystra, Paul was stoned and left for dead in a ditch, and that almost happens to him again in Philippi, where the masters of the possessed slave don't take kindly to his intervention. They exploited the poor girl's gift, taking money each time she told the future. Once exorcised by Paul, she's like an Indian beggar cured of his repulsive

but lucrative infirmity: she's no use at all anymore. Furious at this interference in their affairs, the masters seize Paul and Silas, drag them before
the magistrates, and accuse them of disturbing the public order. "These
people," they say, "are Jews and are disturbing our city, and are advocat-
ing customs that are not lawful for us Romans to adopt or practice."

•

The accusers don't differentiate between Jews and Christians, and neither do the magistrates. Above all they couldn't care less. The Empire
practiced an exemplary secularism in the countries it conquered. There
was complete freedom of thought and religion. What the Romans called
religio had little to do with what we call religion, and implied neither a
professed belief nor spiritual effusion, but an attitude of respect toward
the institutions of the city, demonstrated by rites. Religion in the sense that
we know it, with its bizarre practices and misplaced fervor, they disdainfully called *superstitio*. That was something for Orientals and barbarians,
who were free to practice as they saw fit so long as they didn't disturb
the public order. Disturbing the public order, however, is just what Paul
and Silas are accused of, which is why the tolerant magistrates in Philippi
had the two stripped, beaten with rods, and thrown into prison with their
feet in leg irons.

•

What are Luke and Timothy doing in the meantime? The Acts is silent
on that question. You have to assume they were keeping a low profile.
What the Acts does say, on the other hand, is that during the night, in
their cell, Paul and Silas pray loudly and sing hymns to God, which
their fellow prisoners listen to in wonder. Suddenly an earthquake
shakes the foundations of the building, breaks open the doors, and even
pulls their chains loose. The prisoners could seize the chance and escape,
and maybe the others do, but not Paul and Silas. That impresses the
jailer so much that he too starts to believe in the Lord Jesus Christ and
invites the two men to his home. He bathes their wounds, sets a meal
before them, and has himself and his whole family baptized.

    The next day, having thought things over, the magistrates order
that the troublesome prisoners be discreetly released. Paul answers disdainfully: "What do I care if I am pardoned? I am a Roman citizen, I've
been flogged and imprisoned without judgment, that's against the law.
You are in the wrong and there can be no question of me leaving like a

thief. No, as long as you have not come to apologize I will stay in prison. I'm fine here."

•

The moving force behind this comic scene is Paul's Roman citizenship. At first the magistrates in Philippi had no idea that Paul was a Roman citizen, and when they find out, they see they've gotten themselves into a pickle. An obscure Jew could be flogged without prior judgment, but not a Roman citizen: he could complain and cause them trouble. Jérôme Prieur and Gérard Mordillat, who directed the famous documentary series on the origins of Christianity, *Corpus Christi*, rightly found it suspicious that, mistreated by the authorities, Paul waited for so long before invoking this status that would have spared him a beating and a night in jail. They wonder if he really was a Roman citizen. And, now that we're asking difficult questions, the two directors also observe that what both Luke and Paul say about Paul's first exploits as a persecutor of Christians—obtaining letters signed by the high priest of Jerusalem, "binding men and women and delivering them to prison"—is totally implausible in the context of first-century Judaism. As the sole police authority, the Roman administration was careful to remain neutral in religious quarrels and would never have let a fanatic young rabbi have people thrown into prison in the name of his faith. And if he had tried to pull off something like that, Paul's the one who would have been arrested. If you want to take what Paul says seriously, you have to imagine a whole different scenario: that he was a sort of collaborator working in the service of the occupying army. A historian whom I'll come back to put forward this audacious thesis. For now, however, there's no need to take things that far to draw instructive conclusions about Paul's psychology and sense of drama. Maybe he never was this Jewish Terminator that he so likes to describe, "breathing threats and murder" and spreading terror in the church whose pastor he will one day be, but he knows that told like that the story is more gripping, the contrast more striking. Paul the Apostle is all the grander for having been Saul the inquisitor, and it seems to me that this trait fits in well with the picture given by the episode in Philippi: the pleasure he feels at letting himself be flogged when a word would suffice to be freed—but before saying it, he waits until he's bruised and bloody, and those who had him beaten are up to their necks in guilt.

•

The test of wills ends in favor of Paul, who comes out of prison with his head held high though the magistrates nevertheless ask him to get out of town. He takes his leave of Lydia and her group and urges them to prove themselves worthy of their baptism, then continues his journey with Silas and Timothy. Their further adventures are told in the Acts, but Luke drops out of his own account at this point. Either because he didn't want to follow Paul or because Paul didn't want him to go with him, Luke goes back into the wings of the story and only reemerges a full three chapters and seven years later. Only then will he return to the "we" of the eyewitness, and in the same whereabouts. Which makes me think, together with Renan, that he was Macedonian and that he remained in Philippi for seven years. And what I'd like to do now is to imagine these years far from the theater of operations, in this northern, Balkan Greece where Theo Angelopoulos's slow, hazy films take place. How one of these little churches that Paul scattered behind him like stones developed in his absence. What those who remained behind knew of Paul's travels, what they heard of his letters. And how, over the course of this long winter, what he had sown took root and grew.

15

What was a "Christian church"? Were these words already in use? Yes, no doubt. In his letters Paul talks about his "churches," which, to be less clerical, one could simply call "groups."

And "Christian"? Also yes. The word was coined in Antioch, in Syria, where Paul started to preach ten or so years after the death of Jesus. Under his authority, the number of conversions multiplied and people started calling *khristianos* the followers of this Khristos, who many, starting with the Roman authorities, considered a rebel leader who was still alive. This urban legend eventually made its way to Rome, where as early as the year 41, Emperor Claudius saw fit to issue a decree against the Jews, accusing them of provoking strife in the name of their leader, Chrestos.

•

Rome, Antioch, and Alexandria were the capitals of the world. But even in as far-flung a corner of the Empire as Macedonia, where Luke lived, a couple of dozen people in a few villages thought of themselves as the Church of Christ.

These few dozen weren't poor, illiterate fishermen as in Galilee, where the Church originated—and of whom they knew nothing. Nor were they among the powerful. Rather they were traders, like Lydia the cloth merchant, or artisans, or slaves. Luke makes a big thing of a few recruits of a higher rank, Romans in particular, but Luke is a bit of a snob and inclined to name-dropping, fully capable of pointing out that Jesus wasn't only the son of God but also from an excellent family on his mother's side.

Some were Hellenized Jews, most were Greeks with an interest in Judaism. But after meeting Paul they all, Jews and Greeks alike, thought they belonged to a particularly pure and authentic branch of the religion of Israel, and not to a dissident movement. They continued to go to the synagogue, provided they didn't meet with too much opposition there. That said, opposition arose as soon as there was a *real* synagogue, a *real* Jewish settlement, *real* circumcised Jews. That wasn't the case in Philippi, but it was the case in Thessalonica, where Paul went right afterward. The Jews there took it very badly that the newcomer attracted some of their followers. They denounced him to the Roman authorities as a troublemaker and forced him to flee, and this scenario was repeated in the neighboring village of Berea. What could Paul's converts do? Either keep going to the synagogue, as they had in the past, and meet discreetly among themselves to follow their new guru's instructions. Or they could go all out and open another synagogue.

•

Really? Was it that simple? For us it's a bit hard to believe. Right away we think schism, heresy. That's because we're accustomed to thinking of all religions as more or less totalitarian, although in antiquity that wasn't the case at all. On this point as on many others having to do with Greco-Roman civilization, I defer to Paul Veyne, who is not just a great historian but also a marvelous writer. Like Renan, he has accompanied me through all the years I've spent writing this book, and I've always enjoyed his company: his vitality, his humor, his great love for detail. And, Veyne writes, places of worship in the Greco-Roman world were small private enterprises: the temple of Isis in one city had as much to do with the temple of Isis in another as, let's say, two bakeries. A foreigner could set up a temple to a divinity from his country the way he would open a restaurant with exotic specialties today. The public had the final say by going or staying away. If a competitor showed up, the worst that could happen is that he attracted some customers—as Paul was accused of doing. The Jews were already less relaxed about such issues, but it was the Christians who invented religious centralization, with its hierarchy, its all-binding credo, its sanctions for those who deviate. In the period we're dealing with, this invention wasn't even in its infancy. Rather than a religious war—something the ancients were simply incapable of conceiving—what I'm trying to describe more resembled a phenomenon you see quite often in yoga or martial arts schools, and certainly in other circles as well, but I'm talking about the ones I know. An advanced student decides to teach, and takes a number of his fellow students with him. The master sulks more or less openly. In a spirit of harmony, some students take one course here and another there, saying that's how to get the best of both approaches. In the end, most choose one or the other.

16

These little congregations that developed in Macedonia in the years after Paul came through didn't live in a community—the way Jesus' disciples and family did in Jerusalem. The apostle's instructions were that everyone should remain where they are and not change anything outward in their lives. First, because the end of the world was near, and while waiting there was no point getting all agitated or making plans. Second, because the real change was taking place elsewhere: in the soul. If you're a slave, said Paul, don't try to seek your freedom. Because in summoning you the Lord will free you, while the free men will become slaves. If you're married, stay married. If you're not, don't look for a wife. If you're Greek, don't have yourself circumcised. If you're Jewish, stay circumcised—I was surprised to learn it, but to avoid embarrassment at the baths, some Hellenized Jews had their foreskins surgically restored: an operation known as epispasm.

•

It comes as no surprise to us to read that they called each other "brothers" and "sisters." But it should. Centuries of sermons starting with "My dear brothers" have familiarized us with this custom, but in antiquity it was perfectly incongruous. It was possible to call someone "brother" by extension or metaphor, to underscore the intimate nature of a relationship, but the idea that all men are brothers is a brainchild of this little sect, and must have been very shocking in its early stages. Imagine a priest today addressing his congregation as "wives and husbands," as if all men were the husbands of all women, and vice versa. That would not sound any stranger than the "brothers and sisters" used in Paul's churches, and it's not surprising that people often considered their meetings incestuous, and in any case debauched.

On this point, they were wrong. The first Christian churches were anything but lewd places. At the start of the second century, Pliny the Younger, appointed governor of the far-flung region of Bithynia on the Black Sea, would write to Emperor Trajan a perplexed letter that is one of the first documents on the Christians stemming from pagan sources. On taking up his post, Pliny discovers that the civic religion is in decline, the temples are empty, no one at the marketplace wants to buy meat that's been sacrificed to the gods, and from what he's gathered, the principal reason for this sad state of affairs is the success of a sect he's never heard of before: the disciples of Christus. They get together in secret. Pliny's chief of staff thinks it's to have group sex. But Pliny is not content to listen to rumors. He makes inquiries, sends someone, and the results of his investigation are disconcerting. When they get together, these people limit themselves to sharing a frugal meal, smiling, and singing hymns. So much mildness is worrying. Pliny would have preferred debauchery, but he has to face the facts: no one's sleeping with anyone.

This almost alarming purity of morals disturbs us—or rather, it disturbs me—as much as it disturbed Pliny. Well-meaning authors have tried to amend the dreadful reputation of killjoy that Paul suffers from in modern times. To defend him against the accusations of prudishness, machismo, and homophobia that rain down on him on the basis of his letters, they make a point of casting him as a moral revolutionary who expounds a true love of the human body in a world that's bent on degrading it. I have no problems with that, except that the same line of defense is also used by people who believe the full veil is the height of respect for women who are demeaned by Western pornography. Paul was not just a bachelor—something that is already contrary to Jewish morals, which hold that an unmarried man is incomplete. He was chaste; he prided himself on being a virgin and proclaimed that it was by far the best choice. In one letter he halfheartedly admits that "it is better to marry than to burn"—and by burn he means what he calls *porneia*, which means exactly what you think it does—and that, regarding such questions, he is the one who is speaking, "not the Lord." Sometimes you can't help wondering on the basis of what criteria he does it; nevertheless, the fact is that Paul clearly distinguishes between questions on which he is talking as a spokesman for the Lord and those on which he is expressing his own personal view. Accordingly, it's only Paul who, "in view of the present distress," esteems that it's best to remain a virgin. The Lord is less demanding: he simply says that you should remain in the state you were in when you received the calling. Married if you were married, et cetera. As for Paul, he specifies: "From now on, let those having wives act as not having them, those weeping as not weeping, those rejoicing as not rejoicing, those using the world as not using it fully. For the world in its present form is passing away—and I should like you to be free of anxieties."

17

Already everyone got together for the Sabbath, then they gathered for the Lord's Supper, the day after the Sabbath, and then little by little they started meeting every day. There was so much to talk about! So many new experiences to share and compare! Outwardly, they did the same thing as at the synagogue: they read and interpreted the Scripture. But now they had a new—and prodigiously exciting—approach. In the often obscure words of the prophets, they looked for announcements: of the death and resurrection of the Christ, of the impending end of time. And when they looked for them, of course, they found them. They read, interpreted, egged each other on. Above all, they prayed. They prayed like they'd never prayed before.

•

Here I would like readers to ask themselves what the word "prayer" means to them. For a first-century Greek or Roman, it was something very formal: an invocation said out loud in the context of a rite, addressed to a god they believed in, yes, but the way you believe in an insurance company. There were specialized contracts, like the one with the god of wheat rust. You sought his protection and thanked him for granting it. Then if the wheat was damaged by rust you blamed his negligence; and once you'd turned your back on the altar you were quits, no need to give the matter any more thought. For many people such minimal dealings with the divine were all they needed.

Just as eras can be more or less religious (I think that the era I'm dealing with wasn't any more religious than our own, and that it was religious in pretty much the same way), temperaments can be more or less religious as well. Some people have a taste and talent for such things—the way you can have a taste and talent for music—while others congratulate themselves for being able to live perfectly well without them. In the Greco-Roman world of the first century, the pious souls didn't have much to sink their teeth into, which is why they liked Judaism so much. No longer just a simple recitation, with the Jews, prayer became an exchange in which the heart could unburden itself. Their god was a conversation partner, or better, all possible conversation partners: a confidante, a friend, a sometimes tender, sometimes tough father, a jealous husband from whom you could hide nothing—although it was tempting at times. Raising your eyes to him, you plunged them deep within yourself. That was already a lot, but Paul demanded more. He demanded incessant prayer.

•

There's a little book written near the end of the nineteenth century called *The Way of a Pilgrim*. I read it again and again during my Christian period, and I still come back to it. The narrator is a poor muzhik who hardly knows how to read, who has one arm shorter than the other and who one fine day, in church, hears the priest read this sentence spoken by Paul: "Pray without ceasing." He's thunderstruck. He understands that more than being important, it is essential. More than essential, it is vital. It's the only thing that counts. But, he asks: How can you pray without ceasing? And off the little muzhik goes, traveling the Russian roads in search of men more educated and more pious than he is, to find out how to do it.

The Way of a Pilgrim is a marvelous vulgarization of a mystical current that has existed for fifteen centuries in the Orthodox Church, which the theologians call hesychasm, or "inner prayer." And it has had unexpected modern progeny: the two stories in J. D. Salinger's book *Franny and Zooey*, which was one of the biggest literary passions of my youth. The heroine, a sexy, neurotic young girl, comes across this anonymous Russian book in the bohemian New York of the 1950s. She too is thunderstruck, and much to her family's dismay, she starts mumbling morning to night, "Lord Jesus, have mercy on me." To find out how her brother, a young, pretentious, and brilliant actor, frees her from this whim while at the same time approving of it to its final consequences, you'll have to read Salinger's book. It too was inspired by this saying of Paul's in the First Letter to the Thessalonians, which was taken at face value for the first time in these lost churches of Macedonia and Anatolia around A.D. 50: "Pray without ceasing."

•

Like the little muzhik, the brothers and sisters of Thessalonica, Philippi, and Berea worried at the start: "But we don't know what to say. We don't know what to ask for."

Paul answered: "Don't worry, the Lord knows what you need better than you do yourselves. Don't ask for material things, don't ask for prosperity, don't even ask for virtue. Just ask Christ to grant you the gift of prayer. It's as if you wanted to have children: first you have to find the mother, and prayer is the mother of all virtues. It's by praying that you learn to pray. Don't get lost in long sentences. Simply put your whole heart into repeating *Marana-tha*, which means: 'Come, Lord.' He will come, I promise you. He will descend upon you, he will make his abode in you. It will no longer be you who lives, but he, the Christ, who will live in you."

If they said, "Fine, I'll try," he shook his head: "Don't try. Do."

•

Paul hadn't stayed long in Thessalonica, Berea, or Philippi, but he had left instructions and the mantra. Thus equipped, the brothers and sisters practiced with zeal and passion, and compared their experiences among themselves. One got up earlier and went to bed later, and as soon as he had a moment, he retired to his back room, where he sat cross-legged and alone, repeating *Marana-tha* until the blood beat in his temples, his belly grew warm, and he no longer remembered the meaning of what he was saying. Another repeated it in silence, and so he didn't need to be alone at all. He could do it all the time, anywhere, in a crowd of people. He prayed while walking, while sorting seeds, while talking with customers. He said to the first, the one who needed to sit cross-legged: "Do you retire to your room to breathe? No. Do you stop breathing when you work? When you talk? When you sleep? No. So why not pray like you breathe? Your breathing can become prayer. You breathe out and you call Christ. You breathe in and you welcome Christ. Even your sleep can become prayer. 'I sleep but my heart is awake,' says the bride in the Song of Songs. The bride is your soul. Even asleep, let it remain awake."

•

Paul had said this as well: "We must stay awake," and some did their best not to sleep. Voluntary insomnia gave them visions. They got so fired up that they went into a trance. In these trances, some praised God in Greek: that was called prophesying. Others cried out, sighed, or moaned. Sometimes they uttered sounds that were like words and even sentences, but which no one understood. They gave the name "speaking in tongues" and attached much value to this phenomenon, which psychiatrists call glossolalia. Was this an unknown language that they simply couldn't identify, or even a language that didn't exist, spoken by no one on earth? Impossible to know, but there could be no doubt that those who spoke it were inspired by God, and not possessed by a demon like the Philippi slave girl with the pythonical spirit. They tried to transcribe these mysterious sounds, to save them and decipher their meaning.

•

(After his mystical experience, Philip K. Dick started thinking and dreaming in an unknown tongue. He jotted down what he could. Going from his notes, he did research and finally identified it. Guess what it was.

Koine Greek, the language spoken by Paul.)

18

Ecstasy, trances, tears, prophesies, speaking in tongues . . . These phenomena that flourish in most sects past and present were cultivated with a disorderly enthusiasm in the first Christian churches. Some followers had dabbled in other Oriental religions where you took drugs, mushrooms, ergot fungi, and other ecstasy-inducing beverages. They were a little disappointed that the body and blood of Christ consumed during the agape were only bread and wine. They would have preferred something more mysterious—without realizing that the most mysterious thing was just that. They wished for magic powers. Paul, meanwhile, preached prudence and a sense of discernment. In his letters he said what good yoga teachers say when their students believe they can feel their stomach moving all by itself, and that their kundalini is awakening. Yes, that exists and is a sign of progress, and yes, at a certain level of practice you acquire powers. But you shouldn't attach too much importance to them, otherwise they become a trap and you regress instead of advancing. He said that all gifts have a function, like the parts of the body, that none are inferior, and that the person who is speaking in tongues should not look down on those who are still speaking Greek like everyone else. "I too can speak in tongues for hours on end, but rather than ten thousand words in a tongue that will leave you speechless, I prefer to speak five words in Greek that will be useful to you." Finally, and above all, he said that gifts are all very well and good, but that one alone really counts and surpasses all others: the one he calls *agápē*.

•

Agápē, from which Paul derived the word "agape," is the nightmare of translators of the New Testament. In Latin it's translated as *caritas* and in French as *charité*, or "charity," but after centuries of loyal service, charity is clearly no longer cut out for the task. So "love," quite simply? But *agápē* is neither carnal, passionate love, which the Greeks called *eros*, nor the tender, peaceful love of married couples or parents for their very young children, which they named *philia*. *Agápē* goes beyond that. It's the love that gives rather than takes, the love that makes itself small rather than taking up room, the love that wants the good of others rather than one's own, the love that is freed from the ego. One of the most astonishing passages in Paul's astonishing correspondence is a sort of hymn to *agápē* that is traditionally read out loud during wedding Masses. Father Xavier read it when Anne and I got married in his poor parish in Cairo. Renan believes—and I agree—that it's the only passage in the New Testament that's on a par with the words of Jesus, and Brahms put it to music in the last of his sublime *Four Serious Songs*:

If I speak in the tongues of men or of angels, but do not have love, I am only a resounding gong or a clanging cymbal.

If I have the gift of prophecy and can fathom all mysteries and all knowledge, and if I have a faith that can move mountains, but do not have love, I am nothing.

If I give all I possess to the poor and give over my body to hardship that I may boast, but do not have love, I gain nothing.

Love is patient, love is kind. It does not envy, it does not boast, it is not proud. It does not dishonor others, it is not self-seeking, it is not easily angered, it keeps no record of wrongs. Love does not delight in evil but rejoices with the truth. It always protects, always trusts, always hopes, always perseveres. Love never fails.

Where there are prophecies, they will cease; where there are tongues, they will be stilled; where there is knowledge, it will pass away. For we know in part and we prophesy in part, but when completeness comes, what is in part disappears.

When I was a child, I talked like a child, I thought like a child, I reasoned like a child. When I became a man, I put the ways of childhood behind me. For now we see only a reflection as in a mirror; then we shall see face-to-face. Now I know in part; then I shall know fully, even as I am fully known.

And now these three remain: faith, hope, and love. But the greatest of these is love.

19

Of course it was neither new nor foreign to the ancients' morals to say that it's better to be good than bad. Greeks and Jews knew the Golden Rule, about which Hillel, a rabbi contemporary of Jesus', said that it summed up in itself all of the Law: "Do not do unto others what you would not have them do unto you." There's nothing scandalous in the idea that it's better to be modest than a braggart, either. More humble than haughty: same thing, it's a commonplace of worldly wisdom. But with one thing leading to another, taking Paul seriously you'd soon say it's better to be small than big, poor than rich, sick than healthy. And at this point the Greek spirit was completely at a loss, while the new converts were delighted by their own audacity.

•

Chronologically speaking, it's premature to bring it up, but one of the scenes that to my knowledge best evokes the sort of shock that this code of conduct must have caused is found in Henryk Sienkiewicz's *Quo Vadis*, once an immensely popular historical novel on the first Christians in the days of Nero. The hero, a Roman officer, behaves very badly during the entire first part of the book. I can't remember the details, but his file includes persecution, rape, blackmail, and perhaps murder. When the plotline has him fall into the hands of the Christians who have such good reason to be angry with him, he's not exactly bursting with confidence. He expects them to do what he would do without batting an eyelid if he were in their place: torture then kill him. He wouldn't do it because he's bad, but because that's what any normal man does when he's severely harmed and then gets a chance for revenge. It's the rule of the game. But what happens? Instead of stirring the coals with a red-hot iron and applying it to his eyes or his balls, the head of the Christians, whose adoptive daughter the officer had personally handed over to Nero, unties his hands, embraces him, calls him his brother, and frees him with a smile. At first the Roman believes his foe is taking cruelty to the limit, then he understands that it's not a joke. The man who should be his worst enemy really has pardoned him. In running the huge risk of letting him go, the Christian has placed his trust in him. He has abdicated his position of strength and put himself at his mercy. At that moment a shift takes place in the Roman officer's heart. He realizes that these miserable, persecuted people are stronger than he is, stronger than Nero, stronger than everything, and all he wants is to be one of them. In the name of their faith, which in that instant also becomes his own, he is ready to let himself be thrown to the lions—which promptly happens.

The Acts of the Apostles is full of adventures and miracles, but there are no episodes like this. Nevertheless, I'm convinced that the Christian sect's force of persuasion had a lot to do with its ability to inspire astonishing acts—and not just words—that ran counter to normal human behavior. People are constituted in such a way that the best of them want good for their friends, while all of them want evil for their enemies. They prefer to be strong rather than weak, rich rather than poor, big rather than small, dominant rather than dominated. That's the way it is, that's normal, no one ever said it was bad. Greek wisdom doesn't say it, nor does Jewish piety. Now, however, men are not only saying the exact opposite, they're also doing it. At first they're not understood, no one sees the interest of this extravagant inversion of values. And then people start to understand. They start to see the interest, that is to say, the joy, the power, the intensity of life, that the Christians draw from this apparently aberrant behavior. And then they have only one desire, to do as they do.

•

In the days when they used to go to the synagogue, the proselytes in Philippi and Thessalonica were filled with a solemn and gentle sense of piety, more focused on peace and tranquillity than elation. The more or less strict observance of the Law gave form to their lives and dignity to everything they did, but they expected a progressive development rather than a sudden change. Once they became disciples of Paul, things were different. The impending end of the world completely altered their perspective. They were the only ones aware of something enormous. They alone were awake among the sleeping. They lived in a supernatural world, one that was all the more remarkable in that you had to make sure you didn't let it show, and to act—again, Paul put great stress on this—in a completely normal way. The contrast between this extraordinary thing that was growing within their group and the zealous, scrupulous attempt to lead the most ordinary of lives had an intoxicating effect, and I suppose that when Paul's disciples met with those who had remained faithful to the synagogue, the most sensitive of the second group must have observed in the first a change that left them bemused and vaguely envious.

20

The Acts gives only a sketchy chronicle of Paul's adventures between his departure from Philippi and his return seven years later. And for good reason: Luke wasn't there. But to complement his narrative, there are other documents of an absolutely exceptional value, because Paul wrote them himself: his letters to his churches.

In all the editions of the New Testament they come right after the Gospels and the Acts, under the somewhat high-sounding name "epistles"—which simply means "letters." This order is misleading: they predate the other two by at least twenty to thirty years. They're the oldest Christian texts, the first written traces of what was not yet known as Christianity. They're also the most modern texts in the Bible, by which I mean the only ones whose author is clearly identified and speaks in his own name. Jesus did not write the Gospels. Moses did not write the Pentateuch, nor King David the Psalms that pious Jews attribute to him. By contrast, even according to the strictest criteria, at least two-thirds of Paul's letters are definitely authored by him. They express his thought as directly as this book expresses my own. We'll never know who Jesus really was or what he really said, but we do know who Paul was and what he said. To get a feel for his turns of phrase, we don't have to put our trust in intermediaries who covered them with thick layers of legend and theology.

Paul didn't write to create a body of work, but to keep in contact with the churches he founded. He sent his news, and answered questions that were put to him. Maybe it's not what he expected when he wrote the first, but his letters very quickly became circulars, bulletins rather similar to those that Lenin wrote to various factions of the Second International from Paris, Geneva, and Zurich before 1917. The Gospels didn't yet exist: the first Christians had no sacred book, but Paul's letters served the purpose. They read them aloud during the agape before sharing the bread and the wine. The church that had received an original letter preserved it piously, but the followers made copies that circulated in the other churches. Paul insisted on them being read by everyone, because, unlike many gurus, he celebrated neither low nor secret masses. He had no taste for esotericism, and had no problems adapting to his audience: here too he resembles Lenin, who believed that you have to "work with the existing material." Everyone was free to receive his teaching and take from it what they could. What he wrote to the Thessalonians concerned *the entire* church of Thessalonica, and the other churches of Macedonia. Even if he never referred to them in the Acts, Luke must have attended meetings where these letters were read out loud, and probably even recopied them.

•

For a theologian, Paul's letters are theological treatises—you could even say that all of Christian theology is based on them. For a historian, they are sources of incredible richness and freshness. Thanks to them you get an immediate feeling for what the daily life, problems, and organization of these first communities were like. And thanks to them you also get an idea of Paul's comings and goings from one Mediterranean port to the next between A.D. 50 and 60. And whatever their obedience, when specialists of the New Testament try to reconstitute this period, they all have Paul's letters and the Acts of the Apostles on their desks. They know that in case of contradictions it's Paul who must be trusted, because original archive material has more historical value than later compilations. As to what they do with them, everyone—myself included—can decide that for themselves.

2 1

After leaving Philippi, Paul went to Thessalonica, then from Thessalonica to Berea, and everywhere it was the same scenario. The day of the Sabbath he addressed the synagogue, converted a few Greeks who'd been leaning toward Judaism, and aroused the hostility of the real Jews who did all they could to rid themselves of this disloyal competition. If the story were told in a comic strip, you'd see him leaving each town covered with tar and feathers. These repeated setbacks finally convinced him to try his luck in a big city. So it came to pass that, smuggled out of Berea in a hurry by his disciples, he took the boat for Athens, where an even worse fiasco awaited him.

•

One thing's for sure, Athens was not the place for him. The names of Pericles, Phidias, Thucydides, or of the great tragic playwrights, probably didn't mean much to him. And even going on the unlikely hypothesis that he had entertained sweet dreams about the splendor of ancient Athens, in any case he would have been deceived. For the last two centuries the city had been no more than a provincial hub of the Roman Empire, politically subjugated and already transformed into a museum. The sons of good families were sent there to study for a year. They admired the Acropolis and the statues that had escaped the pillage of the city by Sulla's legions. They listened to educators, rhetoricians, and grammarians arguing about grand philosophical problems while pacing the agora the way Plato and Aristotle had done in bygone days. Paul was shocked by the statues: as a good Jew, for him any representation of the human figure was idolatry. Nor did he like the blabbermouths or the snobs. But he could have thought naïvely that people who spent their entire days debating elevated topics would be good customers for him. He too started to talk in the agora, taking on Stoic and Epicurean philosophers who were professionals above all in the art of argumentation, if not of persuasion. In his poor foreigner's Greek, he talked to them about Christ and the resurrection. And as "resurrection" is *anastasis* in Greek, they thought Paul was talking about a person, Anastasia, who was Christ's companion. In the same way a plaque on a building in Nice informs visitors: "Here lived Friedrich Nietzsche and his tormented genius." Another charming couple.

He was considered a "preacher of foreign deities," meaning a sort of Hare Krishna. "What is that parrot cackling about?" some said. And in fact you can just see him, chattering away with his hackles raised, pestering his listeners, preaching "in season and out of season," as he himself writes in a letter.

•

Nevertheless, some listeners who are more curious than the rest invite Paul to expound his doctrine to the Areopagus. That was the city's high court of appeal, the one that had condemned Socrates four and a half centuries earlier. You have to believe it had no more important business that day. Paul must have prepared his speech like an oral exam, and he found a truly clever point of attack. "Athenians," he said, "I see that you are rather too religious than not enough. I have walked through the streets and visited your temples, and there I discovered an altar inscribed "To an unknown god." (Such dedications existed: it was a precaution to avoid offending a god no one had thought of.) Well, it is of this god that you worship unknowingly that I have come to speak."

An excellent start, followed by a little sketch of the god in question. His traits are well suited to please philosophers. He doesn't live in a temple, doesn't need sacrifices. He is the primordial breath, he drew the whole human race from the One, he gives order to the cosmos. Men grope around for him, but he is close to everyone's heart. All in all, then, he's a congenially abstract god about whom it would be difficult to quarrel.

Not a word about the less consensual features of the god of the Jews: jealous, vindictive, only concerned about his own people. So they listen to Paul with unenthusiastic approbation. Perhaps they were expecting something more eccentric. But then, all of a sudden, things go off the rails. Like in the synagogue in Troas. Like in Metz in 1973, when Philip K. Dick gave a speech to a group of French science fiction aficionados on his mystical experience entitled "If You Find This World Bad, You Should See Some of the Others," and said in essence that everything in his novels was *true*.

"Because," Paul continues, "God has set the day, and this day is near, when the man he has appointed will judge the world. For that he has raised him from the dead."

Paul doesn't have the time to say who this man is, because the judgment of the world and the raising of the dead are enough for those present to close the case. The Athenian skeptics aren't even shocked, like the Jews in the synagogue or the science fiction buffs in Metz. They smile, shrug their shoulders, say fine, we'll talk about it another time. Then they depart, leaving the orator alone, even more offended by this amused tolerance than he would have been by a scandal followed by stoning.

2 2

Humiliated, Paul didn't stick around Athens for long. He left for Corinth, which is in every way the exact opposite of Athens: an enormous, densely populated, dissolute port city, with neither a glorious past nor prestigious monuments, but with narrow streets teeming with people, and stalls where anything can be bought or sold in any language. Half a million inhabitants, of whom two-thirds are slaves. Temples to Jupiter for the form, but at every street corner shrines to Isis, Cybele, Serapis, and above all Aphrodite, whose cult of worship is overseen by priestess-cum-prostitutes with the pretty name of *hierodules*, known for transmitting a pox that the entire Mediterranean Basin calls with a snicker the "Corinthian disease." It's a city of debauchery, profit making, and impiety, but Paul breathes easier here than in Athens, because at least the people work hard and don't think themselves better than the common run of mortals. And here, the Acts tells us, he meets a couple of pious Jews named Priscilla and Aquila, who were chased out of Italy by

Emperor Claudius' famous edict ordering all Jews to leave Rome. As Priscilla and Aquila ply the same trade as Paul, he moves in with them and shares their workshop.

•

I haven't yet had the chance to say it, because in Philippi he made an exception and allowed himself to be lodged and fed, but Paul didn't just preach: he worked, and he took pride in it. "If anyone is unwilling to work," he liked to say, "neither should he eat." Like Eduard Limonov, who traveled the world with a sewing machine and made a living by altering pants wherever he went, Paul earned his keep by weaving a cloth that was rough and resistant, and that served to make tents, sails, and bags for transporting merchandise. For someone who liked to travel and to depend on no one but himself, it was a good choice, and ensured that he'd never be short of work. But it was all the more surprising on the part of someone from a well-to-do Jewish family who had wanted to become a rabbi. In his letters Paul puts a fair amount of stress on the fact that he not only works to make a living, but that he also works *with his hands*, to make it clear that he wasn't obliged to do so, that it was a choice he had made. If you think about it, such cases are rare. Some great intellectual figures of the last century, Simone Weil, Robert Linhart, the worker-priests, took on factory work to share a condition to which fate did not compel them. It seems to me that nowadays far fewer of us understand why they did it. And what's certain is that aside from Paul, the ancients wouldn't have understood it at all. Whether Epicureans or Stoics, all the wise men taught that fortune is changing, unpredictable, and that we must be ready to lose all we have without a murmur. None of them, however, would have recommended or even entertained the idea of getting rid of it on purpose. They all considered what they called *otium*—that is, leisure and the free use of one's time—to be an absolute condition of human accomplishment. Seneca, one of Paul's most famous contemporaries, says something quite nice on that topic: if by some mischance he were reduced to working for a living, no big deal; he'd just kill himself.

23

As usual, Paul started by speaking in the synagogues of Corinth each Sabbath, using the Scriptures to demonstrate that Jesus was the announced savior. As usual, the Jews were shocked, and things didn't get any better when Paul sent them all to the devil, declaring that if that's how things were he'd bring the news to the pagans, and opened a rival school in the home of a Greek whose house was next to the synagogue. In their fury, the Jews once again complained to the Roman authority, who once again dismissed them, saying, "If this were an offense or a crime, I would welcome your grievances. But this dispute is about words, names, and your own Law. Sort this out among yourselves. I'm not getting involved."

•

These wise words delight not only partisans of secularism but also historians of the New Testament, because Luke gives the name of the Roman proconsul who spoke them. His name was Gallio, and an inscription attests that he exercised the function of proconsul in Corinth from July A.D. 51 to June A.D. 52. Of course, those aren't the dates that are marked on the inscription, because no one back then suspected that they were living "Anno Domini." But they can be reconstituted and are the only ones in this whole story that are absolutely certain. It's on the basis of them—and only them—that historians slide their chronologies of Paul's travels back and forth in time. And, of course, Luke had no idea about the standards of modern historiography. But history existed in his day too, and that's what he considered himself to be writing. Nothing demonstrates that better than the eagerness with which, anytime he could, he connected his clandestine, subterranean chronicle of the little Jewish sect that would become Christianity with the official and public events of his day, the ones that might attract the attention of real historians. Luke is well aware that outside their little sect, no one has any idea who the heroes of his narrative—Paul, Timothy, Lydia, and even Jesus—are. And unlike the other evangelists, he's bothered by that, because he's writing for readers outside the sect. That's why he's so happy when, to back up the story of these obscure people and events, he can cite other people and events that everyone knows, or at least important people, people who leave a trace of their existence, as was the case with the proconsul Gallio. I think that with his taste for name-dropping, Luke would have been even happier if he'd known and been able to tell us that the proconsul Gallio was the brother of Seneca, whom I mentioned a few lines ago, and the person to whom the famous philosopher's treatise *On the Happy Life* was dedicated.

●

This *On the Happy Life* is a strange book. At first sight, it's a short summary of Stoic philosophy, which was what we'd call today a method of personal development. I think this explains why it was almost as successful as Buddhism is among the moderns, who, like the Romans of the first century, have bid farewell to collective ideals and have no other point of anchor than the ego. As Seneca describes its charms to his brother Gallio, the happy life depends entirely on the practice of virtue and the peace of mind it procures. Its guiding principles are abstention, withdrawal, and quietude. Happiness resides in putting yourself beyond reach. The idea is that by practicing it every day, at all times—the Latin name for this exercise is *meditatio*—you can free yourself from the hold of the affects: to not regret, not hope, not anticipate, to distinguish what we can change from what we cannot. If it should happen that your child dies, to persuade yourself that there's nothing you can do about it and that there's no reason to wallow in sadness. To see each of life's circumstances (above all those that seem unfavorable) as a chance to practice, and by progressing constantly from common folly to soundness of mind to attain the ideal of the sage—of which the Stoics admitted without embarrassment that examples were few and far between, perhaps one every five hundred years.

The book goes on like that in noble, well-balanced prose for thirty or so pages, and then at one moment, out of the blue, this calm, doctrinal tract transforms into a vehement *pro domo* appeal. Seneca gets angry, his voice goes up a notch, and there's no need whatsoever to read the preface or footnotes to understand what's going on: he's defending himself tooth and nail against a campaign accusing him of living contrary to his philosophical principles.

His accusers did have a point. Seneca was a Spanish-born member of the equestrian order who had had a brilliant career in Rome. Which says a lot about integration in the Empire: he was regarded as the very embodiment of the Roman spirit, and no one would ever have thought of him as Spanish—any more than you'd think of Saint Augustine as being Algerian. A man of letters, the author of successful tragedies, a grand popularizer of Stoicism, he was also a courtier driven by ambition.

Favored under Caligula, he fell into disgrace under Claudius, then was once again favored under the reign of Nero. And, finally, he was a shrewd businessman who used his sizable income and networks to become a sort of private bank, amassing a fortune assessed at 360 million sestertii—by today's standards easily the equivalent of the same number of dollars. When you knew that—and everyone did—it was hard not to laugh at his sententious works in praise of detachment and frugality, and at his recommended method of practicing a life of poverty: eating brown bread and sleeping rough.

What does Seneca say to defend himself from this ridicule that finally snowballs into a conspiracy? That he never claimed he was an accomplished sage, and that he's just trying to become one at his own speed. That even without having gone the whole distance, it's a good thing in itself to point the way forward for others. That when he talks about virtue he doesn't propose himself as an example, and when he talks about vice he's primarily thinking of his own. And what the hell! No one ever said a sage has to refuse the gifts that fortune provides. He must put up with sickness when it hits, but take delight when he is in good health. Not be embarrassed if he is frail or misshapen, but prefer to be sound of body. As to riches, they procure him the same satisfaction as favorable winds to the navigator: he can do without them, but he prefers it when they're there. So what if he eats from a plate of gold, if through *meditatio* he can be sure he'd enjoy the food just as much from a crude bowl?

I laugh a little too, but deep down I pretty much agree: that sort of wisdom suits me fine. Paul, however, didn't agree. For him that was worldly wisdom, and he was proposing another, radically different kind of wisdom, one neither Seneca nor his brother Gallio would have understood—if they'd listened.

•

According to his contemporaries, Gallio was a kindly, cultivated man, the best possible version of a high Roman functionary. Much better than Pontius Pilate, who exercised the same functions in Jerusalem twenty years earlier and found himself in a similar situation. That said, in answer to those who demanded that he crack down on Jesus of Nazareth, Pontius Pilate tried to give the same answer as Gallio gave to those who brought Paul before him, bound hand and foot: that he refused to get involved in their religious quarrels. If in the end he was obliged to pass judgment on Jesus, it's because Jerusalem was a chaotic, colonial hotbed of nationalist rebellion, whereas Roman order ruled in Corinth, and you could afford to be tolerant. But what Pilate and Gallio did have in common is that neither for a moment suspected the significance of the events that were unfolding before their eyes. Jesus and Paul were obscure, flea-ridden Jews who were brought before their tribunal by other obscure, flea-ridden Jews. Gallio had Paul released, and forgot the whole thing a minute later. Pilate had to have Jesus crucified, and maybe the knowledge that he'd allowed an injustice to be committed in the name of preserving the peace caused him a sleepless night or two. That's all. And that's always how it is. It could well be that even as I write, some obscure character who will change the world for better or for worse is stirring things up in a suburb or township. It's also possible that for one reason or another he'll cross paths with a prominent figure, someone considered by all accepted standards as one of the most enlightened figures of his day. You can bet your bottom dollar that the second will pass by the first without so much as noticing him.

24

Over the course of the winter a year after Paul's visit, word got around in Macedonia that Timothy was back in Thessalonica. The brothers and sisters anxiously awaited the glorious return of the Lord, but for now they'd make do with the return of Paul, and failing that, they must have been happy that he was sending his assistant. If, as I believe, Luke was living in Philippi—a day on horseback from Thessalonica along the wide Roman road that crossed northern Greece and three or four on foot—it would be surprising if he didn't make the journey.

•

Timothy was then a very young man. Born of a Greek father and a Jewish mother, he was fully Jewish according to the Law of Israel. But he wasn't circumcised when Paul visited his family at Lycaonia and converted his mother, grandmother, and him—whether his father was also converted isn't known. The boy was so fervent that he begged Paul to take him along when he resumed his travels. Paul said yes, and the night before they left he circumcised Timothy with his own hands. He decided to do that, Luke writes, somewhat embarrassed, "because of the Jews who were in those places." And it's true, Paul had enough hassles with them without the walking scandal posed by an uncircumcised Jewish gofer. No doubt he didn't regret it: as things turned out, Timothy was the ideal disciple, the most faithful of the faithful. We know he acted as Paul's secretary, my guess is that he was also his valet. And, finally, he became his emissary.

Having known two great masters quite well—one in tai chi and one in yoga—I'm also acquainted with this inevitable figure of disciple-cum-dogsbody. And, even if I'm willing to listen to everything I'm told about this relationship of absolute subjection between master and disciple being a tradition in the East, the necessary condition for a true transmission, I can't help finding pathetic these people whose only desire is to *depend* on someone. That said, there are two sorts of right-hand men. The first are rigid devotees, filled to the point of cruelty with the small amount of power they get from being the master's favorite, while the others are nice, harmless types. I prefer to imagine Timothy as belonging to the second group. Of all the brothers and sisters gathered to honor him in Thessalonica, it was Luke who had known him the longest. He must have been proud of this close relationship, and even made a bit of a deal of it in front of the others. And as for Timothy, I can see him understanding this and treating Luke like an old comrade-in-arms, not missing a chance to remind everyone that without him, without their chance meeting in Troas and his invitation to Philippi, the Macedonian churches wouldn't exist at all.

•

What does Timothy say? That Paul blesses everyone. That he would have liked to come in person, but that Satan, alas, prevented him (just how Satan did this is no clearer than how the Spirit of God blocked Paul's way to Asia, and in my less generous moments I'm tempted to think Paul used it as a handy excuse: "Sorry guys, tried to come, but you know how Satan is . . ."). That it's a great comfort to Paul to think of his dear Macedonian disciples, the purity of their ways, and the freshness of their climate, plunged as he is in the cauldron of Corinth where he has his hands full, what with the debauched pagans and the acrimonious Jews. Regarding the pagans, there's not much to say: they're pagans. But it's the Jews who give him the hardest time. The Jews don't want to hear the message that's first and foremost destined for their ears. The Jews don't stop making trouble for him, hauling him before the Roman courts and threatening to have him stoned. The Jews had the Lord Jesus killed, and the prophets before him. They're the enemies of all men. They do not please God, who will bring his anger down upon them.

Perhaps Timothy didn't say that, but Paul did, in a passage in his First Letter to the Thessalonians that embarrasses a lot of Christian exegetes. As for the anticlericalists, they love it. They use it to trace the long and damning tradition of anti-Semitism in the Church right back to Paul. And it's hard to prove them wrong, even if, luckily for the Christian exegetes, Paul said kinder things about the Jews in other letters. Maybe I'm wrong, but I think that this kind of diatribe must also have embarrassed the Thessalonians—or at least Luke as I imagine him. It's strange, after all: Paul was Jewish, Timothy was Jewish, the people they addressed weren't, and yet it's Paul and Timothy who didn't stop griping about the Jews. Someone like Luke liked Judaism and what he knew about Jewish life. It must have bothered him to hear them being denigrated all of a sudden, and to hear these two Jews say "the Jews," as if they weren't Jews themselves, and "their prophets," as if they weren't theirs as well. The more he heard it repeated that God would give to pagans like him the gift that he'd prepared for his unworthy people, the more Luke must have felt the way you'd feel if a capricious billionaire decided to leave you his entire fortune just to spite a son he's taken a disliking to. Even if it's difficult to refuse the windfall, it's a little embarrassing all the same.

25

Another thing embarrasses the Thessalonians—and "embarrasses" is putting it very mildly: it devastates them, shakes the very foundation of their faith. A few weeks earlier, a member of their community died. But before he left, Paul had said something that Jesus also said, in any case that the Gospels have him say, something extremely imprudent that can be summed up as follows: What I am announcing to you, you will see very soon, and you *all* will see it. None of you will die without having seen it. According to the version attributed to Jesus: "This generation will not pass away until all these things have happened." This solemn, exceedingly short-term promise does much to explain the new converts' feverish sense of urgency. There's no point starting projects, all there is to do is pray, keep vigil, and be as charitable as possible while waiting for Judgment Day.

•

Toward the end of her life, my godmother was unfortunately inclined to making this kind of pronouncement. I remember talking to her one day about a trip I was planning to take in six months. She gave me that look she sometimes put on, the look of someone who knows and who is saddened to discover so much ignorance, and said: "My poor boy, in six months no one will travel, no one will take the plane." She didn't say anything more, and I didn't want to know any more either, all the more so because I'd already heard her make such predictions and I considered them the price to be paid for the great blessings I received from my conversations with her. I was never tasteless enough to remind her of them later, once the dates she fixed with such precision had passed. She must have forgotten them herself, and, in any case, it didn't seem to bother her to see them lapse without the expected cataclysms ever taking place. Of course, as always there were earthquakes, floods, atrocious wars, and terrorist attacks. But she didn't point to them as arguments in her favor, because what she was announcing was something completely different from this daily grind of worldly chaos. She was announcing the end of the world, really, and all that went with it: the return of Christ in heaven among the angels, the judgment of the living and the dead. This wonderfully intelligent and cultivated woman, one of the people who influenced me the most in this world—to the point that in certain circumstances I still wonder what she'd advise me to do—literally believed what the little group of Thessalonians converted by Paul had believed twenty centuries before her. She would have reacted just as they did to the death of one of their members: by saying that in just three more days—the length of time separating the death of Christ and his resurrection—it would be *the* Day, the day of the greatest darkness and the greatest glory.

•

During these three days, the Thessalonians must have kept vigil over the deceased, resolutely waiting for him to rise on the evening of the third, to cast off the sheet that covered him and to order the dead in the graveyard to rise as well. And not just the dead in the graveyard: *all* the dead. Those who died yesterday, those who died the day before, all those who had been born, who had lived and who had died since the dawn of time. For three days they stayed with the bony, bloated, perfumed corpse of the man they alone knew was the last in line, the last man to die before they were all reborn. They wondered what form he would take, what form they would all soon take when they were reborn. They wondered if those who had been no more than dust for so long would come back as they had been when they were alive, and if so—a not unimportant question—whether they would come back as they were when they died or at the most glorious moment of their lives. They wondered if they would come back in the wizened bodies of old people or in the vibrancy of youth, with hard muscles, firm breasts, and even, although Paul was against the idea, if they would want to make love. They wondered all of this while watching over the corpse, and when after three days he did not arise, when after four days he started giving off a strong odor and there was no getting around the fact that he had to be buried, they didn't understand. They didn't dare return home. They dragged their feet, murmured insults, resented each other for having let themselves be taken in. The first of their dead, who was to have been the last of the dead among men, was in fact just another dead person. He had not seen the Day of the Lord. And neither would they, no doubt.

•

What tone did they strike when telling Timothy of their deception? Were they timid, or like people who've been duped by a sweet-talker and want an answer now? Timothy promised to defer the matter to Paul.

26

One thing that surprises me as I advance in this story is that it has done so little to inspire religious imagery. Before getting started I would have sworn that everything in the New Testament had been depicted, again and again, in art. But while that's true of the life of Jesus and those of the saints who followed him—preferably if they suffered some gruesome martyrdom—leaving aside the conversion of Paul on the road to Damascus, almost the entire book that I scour page after page, the Acts of the Apostles, strangely escapes representation. Limiting myself to the scenes I've already evoked, why is it that as fervent a reader of the Bible as Rembrandt never painted a *Circumcision of Timothy*, a *Paul Chasing the Demon from the Pythonical Slave Girl*, or a *Conversion of the Philippian Jailer*? Why did no early Italian or Flemish painter portray the small silhouettes of *Lydia and Her Companions Listening to Paul Along the Riverfront*, in a green Arcadian landscape? Why are there no bombastic paintings in the Musée d'Orsay showing *The Lycaonians Mistaking Paul and Barnabus for Gods*, and why does the Louvre not have a masterpiece by Théodore Géricault showing *The Thessalonians Grieving Their First Dead*? Pale, swollen bodies of drowned fishermen, painted using corpses stolen from the morgue, their arms twisted toward the blackened sky rent by a thunderstorm—can't you just see it?

In this gallery of phantom paintings, there's one I miss more than the rest. The scene it depicts is decisive in the history of the Christian Church, and at the same time so picturesque that I find it astonishing that it hasn't been painted, filmed, and narrated a thousand times, and that it isn't as much a part of the collective imagination as *The Adoration of the Magi* or *The Annunciation Made to Mary*. The title could be: *Paul Dictates His First Letter to Timothy*.

•

The scene takes place in Corinth, in the workshop of Priscilla and Aquila. It's the sort of shop you still see in poor neighborhoods of Mediterranean cities, with one room opening out onto the street, where the artisans work and receive their customers, and another in the back where the whole family sleeps. Bald and bearded, his forehead creased with wrinkles, Paul bends over his loom. *Chiaroscuro*. A ray of light comes from under the doorstep. The young Timothy, still covered in dust from his trip, winds up the story of his mission in Thessalonica. Paul decides to write to the Thessalonians.

Back then, writing was no trifling matter. You had to buy a small board to which ink pots are attached, a stylus, a scraper, and a roll of papyrus—no doubt the least expensive of the nine varieties listed by Pliny the Younger in one of his own letters. Timothy, the board on his knees, is sitting cross-legged at Paul's feet—if it's Caravaggio who painted it, his feet are dirty. The apostle has let go of his shuttle. He raises his eyes skyward, and starts to dictate.

This is the start of the New Testament.

27

I read in a scholarly article that scribes in antiquity wrote about seventy-five words an hour. If that's true, it means that Paul spent no less than three hours, without taking a break, perhaps walking to and fro in the workshop, dictating the long opening paragraph in which he congratulates the Thessalonians for spurning their idols to serve the true God and await the return of his resurrected Son. But Paul doesn't just congratulate the Thessalonians. He encourages them, he galvanizes them, he appeals to their competitive spirit: they're doing everything right, all they have to do is do it even better. They're a model for the other teams in Greece. That's also because they've got a great coach. On this topic—his own merits, that is—Paul is inexhaustible. There are no errors in what he says. He says it to please God, not men. He is a stranger to cunning and flattery. For the believers of Thessalonica, he's like a father to his children, tender or severe according to their needs. And he's never cost them a cent.

This we'll hear again and again. As an apostle, Paul could live off his followers. All the priests of all the temples, whether Jews or pagans, live handsomely from the offerings of their faithful. The shepherd who takes his flock to pasture is fed by their milk and clothes himself with their wool. Not Paul. As we know, he works with his hands, which allows him to ask nothing of anyone, to announce the Gospel for free, and in the goodness of his heart he doesn't even mention it. Or at least that's what he says: in reality he never stops mentioning it. He comes back to it in practically every one of his letters; he must have repeated it day in, day out, and I imagine his close acquaintances—even the most pious, even Timothy, Priscilla, and Aquila—exchanging a look of amused resignation each time he mentions it. Paul was a genius, and also the kind of guy who time and again says things like "I have to admit, I have one big fault: I'm too honest" or "I'm the most modest guy around." He was a boor, in fact, and on this point like on many others, the opposite of Jesus—that gentleman, as Renan would say.

•

All of this doesn't answer the question that so troubles the Thessalonians: If one of them has died and did not rise from the dead, what to make of Paul's promise? How to believe that the dead will be resurrected?

Paul isn't someone to shirk an issue. He'll respond. He'll respond with much authority, but before hearing his answer I'd like to dwell for a few moments on this strange notion of resurrection.

It is strange, and was even stranger twenty centuries ago. Accustomed as we are to the relatively recent religions of Christianity and Islam, we think that it's the nature of a religion, its raison d'être even, to promise its followers a life after death, and if they've behaved well a better one. But that's wrong, just as wrong as thinking that by nature, religions seek to convert.

The Greeks and the Romans believed that gods were immortal and men were not. A Roman tomb reads: "I did not exist, I existed, I do not exist, so much for that." Their version of the hereafter, which they called Hades, they thought of as an underworld where men's shadows lead a sort of half-life: slow, comatose, larva-like, hardly aware. It wasn't a punishment to end up there, it was the common lot of all the dead, whatever their crimes or virtues. No one was interested in them any longer. In the *Odyssey*, Homer tells the story of Odysseus' descent into this dismal dungeon. There he meets Achilles, who preferred to live a brief, intense life rather than a run-of-the-mill one. From where he is now, Achilles is kicking himself: it's better to be a living dog than a dead hero.

As different as they were from the Greeks and Romans, the Jews agreed with them on that point. They called their Hades *Sheol*, a place they didn't spend much time describing because they didn't much want to think about it. They prayed that God should establish his kingdom "in our life and in our days," not after. They expected the Messiah to restore the glory of Israel in this world, not in heaven. But unlike the Greeks and the Romans, who adapted better to injustices that they ascribed to chance or fate, the Jews believed that God treats men according to their merit. That he rewards them when they are just and punishes them when they are cruel, and all of that, again, in this world and this life: they imagined no other. It took them a long time to realize that things don't necessarily happen like that; in fact, they rarely happen like that. The course of this perplexity is traced in the Bible, and expressed with overwhelming eloquence in the Book of Job.

For a people as a whole, it's always possible that they will obtain future compensation for their present misfortunes, and the Jews weren't above entertaining such hopes. But it's more difficult with a single person, when you're forced to admit that someone was heaped with woes despite his merits: his harvests burned, his wife raped, his children slaughtered, and that he himself died amid dreadful physical and moral suffering. He has good reason to complain, as does Job scratching his sores among the ashes. In their search for an explanation to this scandalous state of affairs, the Jews didn't hit on the idea of karma and reincarnation—which strikes me, at least intellectually, as the only satisfactory one. But at the time I'm talking of, they started to forge the idea of a hereafter in which each person is rewarded according to his merit: of a heavenly Jerusalem, and thus of a resurrection of the dead. This still refers to the resurrection of *all* the dead on a far-off Judgment Day, and not of a single dead person who defies the laws of nature. To judge how frankly scandalous that idea is, just imagine how it would madden even those of us who claim to be Christians if they were told that someone they know, all alone and just yesterday, came back from the dead. I repeat: when Jesus' disciples started talking about it three days after his death, and when Paul took it up for the benefit of the Greeks interested in Judaism, this whole thing about resurrection was far from the sort of pious idea that comes naturally to mind as consolation for a painful loss—it was an aberration and a blasphemy.

•

But—Paul answers—it's at the very heart of his message. All the rest is incidental, and to drum it into the heads of the Thessalonians, he develops the circular argument that already gave me food for thought twenty years ago. You remember: the Revelation of Arès. And if you don't remember, go back to page 53:

> If Christ is preached as raised from the dead, how can some among you say there is no resurrection of the dead? If there is no resurrection of the dead, then neither has Christ been raised. And if Christ has not been raised, then empty too is our preaching; empty, too, your faith. If for this life only we have hoped in Christ, we are the most pitiable people of all. If the dead are not raised, then those people are right who say: Let us eat and drink, for tomorrow we die.

(In fact that is just what a lot of us do think: that resurrection is a chimera like the Judgment Day, that you should enjoy life while you're alive, and that the Christians really are a pitiable lot if Christianity comes down to what Paul taught.)

28

It's a well-known phenomenon, one often observed by historians of religion: rather than destroying a faith, denying reality tends to reinforce it. When a guru announces that the world will end at a precise day and time in the not-too-distant future, we can't help chuckling. We're amazed at his recklessness. We think that unless he's proven right against all odds, he'll be forced to admit he was wrong. But that's not what happens. For weeks or months, the guru's followers pray and do penance. They prepare for the event. In the bunker where they've taken refuge, each one holds his breath. Finally the fateful day arrives. The hour sounds. The followers resurface. They expect to be the sole survivors in a devastated, vitrified world, but that's not how it is: the sun is shining, the people go about their business just like they did before, nothing has changed. In the normal run of things, the followers should be cured of their crazy ideas and leave the sect. Some of them do, in fact: the reasonable ones, the lukewarm, and good riddance. But the others persuade themselves that it's only in appearance that nothing has changed. In fact, a radical transformation has taken place. If it remains invisible, it's to put their faith to the test and separate the wheat from the chaff. Those who believe what they see have lost, those who see what they believe have won. They have nothing but contempt for what their senses tell them: if they free themselves from the demands of reason, if they're ready to look like fools, they've passed the test. They are the true believers, the chosen: the kingdom of heaven is theirs.

•

The Thessalonians passed the test. Steeled by this ordeal, they close ranks. Paul breathes easier—but not for long. He can never breathe easily for long. His letters show him running ceaselessly from one crisis to the next, stopping a leak here, fighting a fire there. No sooner has he staved off an attack on the terrain of common sense than another even more dangerous one appears on the domain of legitimacy. Now it's time to discuss the Galatian affair.

29

The Galatians are the pagans on the Anatolian highlands whom Paul converted on his first trip to Asia. While he was there he suffered from an attack of his mysterious illness, and he always thanks them for taking care of him without showing repugnance. Others would have chased him away like a leper, but they welcomed him "as an angel of God, as Christ Jesus." Paul hasn't seen these good Galatians for a long time, but he often thinks of them with tenderness and nostalgia. Now, however, one day in Corinth in the year 54 or 55, he receives extremely alarming news. Some troublemakers came and led them away from the true belief.

•

I imagine these troublemakers going around in pairs, like Jehovah's Witnesses or killers in detective films. They come from far away, their dark clothes are dusty from the road. Their faces are stern. They stick their feet in the door if you try to slam it shut. They say that to be saved you have to be circumcised, according to the Law of Moses. It's nonnegotiable. If Paul tells his followers that they don't have to be circumcised, he's misleading them. He promises them salvation, but in fact he's taking them down the road to perdition. He's a dangerous man, they say, a wolf disguised as a shepherd.

At first the Galatians aren't alarmed. These accusations aren't new. They've heard them from the heads of the synagogue, and Paul taught them to answer: "We are not Jews, why should we be circumcised?" But the visitors aren't satisfied with that as an answer. "If you're not Jews, what are you?" they ask. "We're Christians," the Galatians proudly reply. "We belong to the Church of Jesus Christ."

The visitors exchange the kind of knowing, sorrowful look that two doctors give each other at the bedside of someone who's seriously ill but doesn't know it. Then they turn the knife in the wound. They know the Church of Jesus Christ well, they say: they even come in its name. The *true* Church of Jesus Christ, that is, the one in Jerusalem, the church of the friends and family of Jesus Christ. And the sad truth is that Paul is fraudulently usurping its name. He is misrepresenting its message. He's an imposter.

•

The Galatians are devastated. In fact, they only have a very vague idea about the origins of their religion. Paul told them a lot about Christ but very little about Jesus, a lot about his resurrection but nothing at all about his life, and even less about his friends or family. Paul has always presented himself as an independent master, preaching what he calls "my

Gospel," and only evoking in a very vague way the existence of a parent
enterprise whose representative he is. For the Galatians as for the Thessalonians, there was Timothy, who was Paul's emissary and who was
accountable to Paul, and the chain stopped there. Above Paul there was
no one. Or rather, there was Khristos, the Christ, and Kyrios, the Lord,
but no one human.

And now there are these people from Jerusalem, who first of all
introduce themselves as Paul's superiors, and secondly say that he's no
longer part of the business. They had to let him go, they say, because
this isn't his first transgression. He's already opened up shop here and
there under their prestigious logo, even though they've forbidden him
from using it. He's been uncovered several times, but he always goes
farther and finds new dupes. Luckily, the headquarters has zealous
inspectors who follow in his footsteps, open the eyes of those he's taken
in, and offer them the real thing in place of the counterfeit. When they
arrive, the swindler has generally flown the coop.

•

I'm reminded of the play by Nikolai Gogol, *The Government Inspector.*
The pinnacle of nineteenth-century Russian theater, it tells how a fake
government inspector arrives in a small provincial town and hoodwinks
everyone. He promises, charms, menaces, he knows everyone's soft spot.
Of course, anyone with anything to hide fears his inspection, and breathes
a huge sigh of relief when they discover that it's possible to come to am-
icable terms with him, between civilized people. Things go on like this
and everyone's happy until the last scene, when the fake inspector disappears. They look for him everywhere, and start to worry. It's then that a
valet enters the mayor's drawing room and announces in a booming
voice the arrival of the real government inspector. At this moment all of
the actors are supposed to freeze onstage in a pantomime of horror that
Gogol—who was both a comic genius and an over-the-top zealot—
explicitly saw as representing the Last Judgment. Generations of Russian
audiences have busted their guts laughing at this play, which they insist
on seeing as an irresistible satire of life in the provinces. They were dead
wrong, if you believe its author, who to the end of his days wrote no end
of preachy prefaces explaining its true meaning. The small town is our
soul. The corrupt officials, our passions. The audacious little scoundrel
who passed himself off as the government inspector and accepted bribes

from the corrupt officials while promising to turn a blind eye is Satan, the prince of this world. And the true inspector is, of course, Christ, who will come at a moment when no one is expecting him. And then, woe to those whose affairs aren't in order! Woe to those who thought they could hedge their bets by cutting a deal with the false inspector!

•

The Galatians must have felt the same shiver of astonishment as the characters in *The Government Inspector* when the *real* representatives of Christ arrived all the way from Jerusalem to tell them that for several years they had been the victims of an imposter. The big difference between their story and the play, however, is that while the false inspector scrams without further ado, Paul did not play dead or use trickery, or even do anything that someone with a guilty conscience might have done. On the contrary, he took a stand in the most striking way possible by writing to the Galatians the most jealous and the most passionate of his letters, which starts with the words:

> I, Paul, apostle, sent not by men or by a man but by Jesus Christ himself, am amazed to see you turn away from him who called you for a different Gospel. But there is no other Gospel! There are only some who trouble you. There are only those who want to destroy in you the Gospel of Christ.
>
> Listen to me. Even if an angel from the heavens came to preach something other than what I have preached, you should not believe him. Even if I came to preach something other than what I have preached, you shouldn't believe me. You should curse that angel, you should curse me. Because what I told you I did not receive from a man but from Jesus Christ directly.

30

After which, to put things straight, Paul launches into a long flashback.

He starts with his education in Judaism, his zeal for the Law, his feverish persecution of the followers of Christ, and suddenly, the grand turnaround on the road to Damascus. All of that we know already, the Galatians knew it too—that's not what Paul's writing about. What he is writing about is his relationship with this church of Jerusalem about which the Galatians, by contrast, knew nothing whatsoever until its messengers came to stir up trouble.

On that issue Paul is categorical: he owes nothing to the church of Jerusalem. Christ himself converted him on the road to Damascus, not someone from the church of Jerusalem. And once converted by Christ, he did not go to pledge his allegiance to the church of Jerusalem. No, he retreated alone to the deserts of Arabia. It was only after three years that he went to Jerusalem, where, he admits somewhat reluctantly, he spent fifteen days with Cephas, and briefly saw James.

•

The person whom Paul calls Cephas, and whose existence the Galatians certainly discovered in this letter, was in fact called Simon. Jesus had given him this nickname, which means "rock" in Aramaic and translates as Petrus in Latin and Peter in English, to signify that he was as solid as a rock and could be counted on. In the same way, he had given the nickname Boanerges—son of thunder—to Yohanan (whom we call John) because of his impetuous character. Peter and John, who like Jesus came from Galilee, were his first and most faithful disciples. Yaacov, whom we call James, was another story: the brother of Jesus. His brother, really? Exegetes and historians are at each other's throats over this. Some say the word "brother" had a wider connotation and could be used for cousins. Others reply that no, there was a word for cousins and brother means brother, period. Of course this linguistic quarrel hides another dispute, about Mary's virtue and, in technical parlance, her perpetual virginity. Did she have other children after Jesus, and in a more natural way? Or, as a compromise, did Joseph have other children, which would make James a half brother? Whatever your view on these important questions, one thing is certain—namely, that in the 50s of the first century, no one was asking them. The cult of Mary didn't exist, and neither did concerns about her virginity. Nothing that was known about Jesus opposed the idea that he could have brothers and sisters, and it's as the "brother of the Lord" that James was honored on equal terms with the companions of the first hour, Peter and John.

All three—James, Peter, and John—were very pious Jews, strictly observing the Law, praying in the Temple, no different from the other very pious Jews in Jerusalem, apart from the fact that they believed that their brother and master was the Messiah, and that he had been raised from the dead. Of course all three had good reasons to look askance at this Paul, who after having persecuted them was now affirming that he'd switched sides and joined their ranks. This Paul, who said he'd had the privilege of an apparition by Jesus, although Jesus had only appeared to his closest companions, and that only in the weeks after his death. This Paul, who said he'd been converted by Jesus, was only accountable to Jesus, and had received from Jesus the glorious title of apostle, which was reserved for the historic disciples.

•

To transpose: imagine that around 1925 an officer of the White Army, who had distinguished himself in the fight against the Bolsheviks, asks to be received by Stalin in the Kremlin. He explains that a personal revelation has given him access to the pure Marxist-Leninist doctrine, and that he plans to see it triumph all over the world. To that end he demands that Stalin and the politburo give him full powers, but refuses to submit to their authority.

Get the picture?

3 1

Paul doesn't give details about how James and Peter welcomed him. All he says is that he only saw them in Jerusalem, and that after fifteen days he left for Antioch in Syria. End of the first flashback.

The second, Paul specifies, starts fourteen years later. Following a revelation, he thinks the time is right to return to Jerusalem to report on his fourteen years of activity in the field—"for fear that I might be running in vain."

This note is important. It shows that, as independent as Paul is, he absolutely needs the approval of the troika composed of James, Peter, and John, whom he calls the "pillars" of the Church. They owe their authority to historical reasons to which Paul, deep down, attaches little importance. Nonetheless, without the pillars' approval, he feels he will have "run in vain." You don't break with the Party.

This time Paul comes accompanied by two Christians from Antioch: Barnabas, who's Jewish, and Titus, who's Greek, and their discussions immediately focus on circumcision. Of course it goes without saying that Christians of Jewish origin, like Barnabas and Paul himself, are circumcised. But in order to follow Christ, should those like Titus who aren't Jewish be forced to have themselves circumcised—and not only to have themselves circumcised but also to observe all of the prescriptions of Jewish Law? The pillars say yes. They insist. Paul could submit to their authority: after all, he circumcised Timothy with his own hands. But in Timothy's case it was out of a situation-based pragmatism—to avoid needless hassles with the local Jews—while circumcising Titus would set a precedent. Giving in here would have incalculable consequences, Paul thinks, and he says no.

•

As Paul tells it in the Letter to the Galatians, what historians call the Conference of Jerusalem, and more often the Council of Jerusalem, was an exceedingly violent clash. Almost half a century later, Luke will give a distinctly more peaceful version, bringing to mind those Soviet history manuals where everyone is retrospectively shown to agree with what later became the Party line, and where leaders who were in fact at each other's throats embrace each other and propose heartfelt toasts to the friendship among peoples and the dictatorship of the proletariat. Luke's version tells of nothing but mutual assurances of tolerance and under-standing between Paul on the one hand and Peter and James on the other. There's no mention at all of circumcision, although it was the major bone of contention, and all of this fine harmony leads to a letter of recommendation in due form addressed to the Gentiles by the pillars, giving Paul carte blanche.

I have a hard time believing that the pillars ceded on all points. Nevertheless, both Luke and Paul confirm that they ratified the fol-lowing division of labor: Peter would preach the Gospel to the Jews, and Paul to the pagans. Peter would get his circumcision, Paul his fore-skin, and it's a deal. So the second episode ends with what seems to be a victory for Paul. Further developments show that he was deluding himself.

32

Third episode of the flashback: Having secured something he is deter-mined to consider an agreement, Paul hurries back to Antioch, his base camp. Neither the Acts nor the Letter to the Galatians explains why

Peter comes to join him there, although in principle they've reached an accord on the repartition of the territories between the apostle of the foreskin and the apostle of circumcision. Is it a friendly visit or an inspection? An inspection masquerading as a friendly visit? In any event, everyone is waiting to see if Peter will sit at the Greeks' table and share the agape with them when he arrives.

•

The question of meals was as charged as that of circumcision. In accepting an invitation from a Greek, a Jew could not be sure that the meat served was slaughtered according to the rules. Worse, he couldn't be sure that it didn't come from animals sacrificed to pagan gods. Because the pagan temples recovered and sold the meat after sacrifices, which made them prosperous butchers as well as places of worship. A Jew who respected the Law would have rather died than eat meat sacrificed to idols. When in doubt he abstained, and the ban on eating together was one of the reasons why Jews and pagans lived separately.

In Antioch as elsewhere, most of Paul's converts were Greeks: the question didn't concern them. And to those of Jewish origin, Paul simply said that they should do what they felt was best, and that such food-related issues have no importance regardless what the Law says. Idols are just idols: what counts isn't what enters the mouth, be it kosher or unkosher, but only what comes out—that is, the quality of the words spoken. The truth, Paul said to Jews and Greeks alike, is that *everything is permitted*. Everything is permitted, but, he added, everything is not opportune. Eat what you want, but if you find yourself at a table with someone who believes such matters are important, take care not to shock him. Even if the interdictions he observes seem childish to you, observe them too out of respect for him. Freedom doesn't dispense with tact. (It's not the case with all of Paul's positions, but this one strikes me as remarkably sensible.)

•

When Peter arrives in Antioch, he goes along with the customs of the community and eats what he's given without asking questions. Everyone is happy, Peter not the least, until James's emissaries arrive from Jerusalem. Seeing Peter at a table with pagans, they pale. Do they wait until the meal is over, or do they make him get up before he's emptied his bowl? In any case, they take him aside to tell him how impiously he's behaving. Peter, the most faithful of the faithful, the rock on which Jesus wanted to build his church, eating impure meat! Neglecting the Law of Moses! Offending God! How pernicious Paul's influence must be for Peter to fall so low! How naïve Peter must be to let himself be hoodwinked by someone who couldn't care less about circumcision, and who may not even be Jewish, for all anyone knows! On top of which he says he's had a vision of Jesus that puts him on a par with the apostles. A vision of Jesus! How pretentious! In his place an honest man would learn from Jesus' real disciples: those who knew him and spoke with him, some of whom were even family. Not Paul. If he found himself face-to-face with Moses he'd start laying down the law. Nothing stops him. It was imprudent to give him a hand, now he wants an arm, soon it will be the entire body. He can't be allowed to go on like this, something must be done.

•

Jewish historians don't make much of James, the brother of the Lord, whom they consider a renegade. As for Christian historians, they tend to present him as the punctilious head of a strictly Jewish church closely affiliated with the Temple, whose members are certain they possess the truth and prefer to keep it to themselves. To this respectable but somewhat slow-on-the-uptake apostle, they oppose the grand figure of Paul: a visionary, inventor of universality, who threw open all doors, knocked down all walls, abolished all differences between Jews and Greeks, circumcised and uncircumcised, slaves and free men, men and women. Peter, meanwhile, is somewhere in between: less radical than Paul, more open than James, but a little like the "liberals" whom Kremlinologists like to contrast with the "conservatives" in the Soviet politburo. He must have had a hard time in Antioch. Siding easily, the way I see him, with the last person who's spoken, and not really knowing which side to take, he withdrew to his home and stopped going out to avoid all contact with the pagans. As soon as the emissaries from Jerusalem had their backs turned, it seems that he left his retreat and went back to eating with the others. But after being bawled out by James's minions, he then turned around and got a roasting from Paul. "In front of everyone," Paul stresses in the Letter to the Galatians, and amid a commotion that he perhaps exaggerates a little. As we will soon see, it's a reproach the Corinthians will also soon level at their apostle: accusing him of being full of authority when he writes everything down after the fact, and notably less so when dealing with people face-to-face.

•

Peter must have been impressed by Paul: he must have respected him and even recognized his right to tell him off. But he must also have thought that there was something to what James was saying. They had known and loved Jesus, Paul hadn't, and now Paul was telling them what they should think of him. Paul wasn't interested in their anecdotes or memories, or in any of the little things they had to say about the man who had lived and taught, and whose meals and life they had shared, shoulder to shoulder, for three years. He knew that Christ had died for our sins, that he redeemed us and justified our lives, that all of the power in heaven and on earth would soon pass on to him, and that was enough. His soul was in permanent communication with that Christ, that Christ lived in him and spoke through him, so he had no time for the worldly facts and gestures of Jesus of Nazareth, and even less for the memories of the clods who had surrounded him in his lifetime. He had no interest in knowing "Christ according to the flesh," as he said—a little like the critics who prefer not to read the books or see the films they review, to be sure that their judgment won't be swayed by the work in question.

•

Renan makes a brilliant remark about Paul: he was a Protestant for himself, and a Catholic for everyone else. His was revelation, immediate contact with Christ, total freedom of conscience, a refusal of all hierarchy. It was up to everyone else to obey without a murmur, and to obey Paul, because Christ had charged him with the task of guiding them. Paul could get on your nerves, there can be no doubt about that. Before the episode at Antioch, James saw Paul as a free electron with whom the church in Jerusalem had been far too lenient. Afterward, Paul became for him the equivalent of Trotsky for Stalin. A campaign was mounted against him, emissaries were sent halfway around the world to denounce his deviationism. No one mentioned the heretic's name in the entourage of the Lord's brother. Some started to call him Nicolas—the Greek equivalent of the Hebrew Balaam, which is the name of a prophet but also of the devil. His followers became the Nicolaitans, and his churches were called Satan's synagogues. To give an idea of the hostility he faced,

Renan quotes an impressive passage from the Letter of Jude. Jude was also one of Jesus' brothers, less well known than James. Although it is out of the question that the letter that bears his name was written by him, it is part of the New Testament. Listen:

> There have been some intruders who are blemishes on your love feasts, as they carouse fearlessly and look after themselves. They are waterless clouds blown about by winds, fruitless trees in late autumn, twice dead and uprooted. They are like wild waves of the sea, foaming up their shameless deeds, wandering stars for whom the gloom of darkness has been reserved forever. They are complainers, disgruntled ones who live by their desires; who utter bombast and cause divisions, devoid of the Spirit . . .

(No historians today agree with Renan that these second-century maledictions are aimed at Paul; nevertheless, they're so striking that I'll include them for good measure.)

33

There, end of the flashback. Now we know the story behind the troublesome preachers who were sicced on Paul. Following his trail into deepest Asia Minor, they threw the candid Galatians into disarray—and not only the Galatians: the apostle's furious letter applies to all of the communities where the parent enterprise's envoys were sent to undermine his activities:

> O stupid Galatians! Who has bewitched you? Are you so foolish? Having started out with the spirit, are you now ending up with the flesh?

Careful: the flesh is not the body, nor the spirit that immaterial thing that is said to inhabit, outlive, and extend beyond it. This isn't Plato. In Paul's terminology, the spirit is faith in Christ. As for the flesh, it comprises the dictates of the Law regarding foreskins, impure meat, and the like. From there, carried away by his passion for opposites, Paul goes on to equate the spirit with life, the flesh with death, and almost without anticipating it, I suspect, he's confronted with the correlation: the Law is death. But he's not one to be stopped by the boldness of what he writes, so he goes on:

> Before the coming of Christ, we were placed under guard by the Law like a child who will inherit a grand domain but may not enjoy it, and who is in the custody of a guardian. You are adults now, you no longer need a guardian. You are adults and you want to return to childhood? You are free and you want to be slaves once more? You know God and you want to go back to vain and childish observances? But now there is neither Jew nor Greek, neither slave nor free man, neither man nor woman. There is only Christ, and you in Christ, and Christ in you!
>
> You claim to live according to the Law, but you don't understand it. Remember Abraham. He had two sons. One with the slave Hagar, and another with a free woman, Sarah. The child of Hagar is the child of the flesh, the child of Sarah is the child of the spirit. It's only normal for the child of the flesh to hold a grudge against the child of the spirit. The Scripture said that the child of the slave would not inherit with the child of the free woman, and you are the children of the free woman. It's for your freedom that Christ came. So, my children, you whom I do not cease to give birth to in suffering so that Christ may take shape in you, do not place yourselves once more under the yoke of slavery! How I would like to be near you, to speak with you in person, for I no longer know how I should address you!

34

Even if an angel from the heavens came to preach something other than what I have preached, you should not believe him. *Even if I came to preach something other than what I have preached, you shouldn't believe me.* You should curse that angel, you should curse me.

In writing these words at the start of the letter, Paul imagines something even worse than what has just happened. Enemies came to the Galatians to discredit Paul in their eyes. That's bad. But something even more serious could happen, and no doubt will happen: these enemies could visit the Galatians not in the name of the church of Jerusalem, but in his name, in the name of Paul. Or they could seek out other innocent souls who have never seen him in person, and even pass themselves off as him. Or they could send his disciples letters signed with his name that say the very opposite of what he taught them, telling them that this version of his teaching replaces the previous one, and that anyone pretending to be Paul and wanting to contest them should be considered an imposter.

To ward off such threats, Paul took what precautions he could. "See with what large letters I am writing to you in my own hand!" he wrote in the same Letter to the Galatians. It's touching to read that, because no original manuscripts of Paul's letters exist. The oldest date from after 150, they're copies—or rather copies of copies—and I wonder what went through the mind of a second-century copyist who was piously writing out in his own hand a sentence whose only purpose is to say "I am written in Paul's hand." There are sentences like this in several of his letters, because Paul had entrusted his churches with samples of his writing so that they could tell that the letters he sent were actually his. Nevertheless, what was initially meant to confound forgers must have made things easier for them later on. It was a habit of Paul's, all they had to do was copy it.

•

Similarly, we read at the end of the Second Letter to the Thessalonians: "This greeting is in my own hand, Paul's. This is the sign in every letter; this is how I write."

What spices the whole thing up—and here I require a little attention—is that the Second Letter to the Thessalonians, which so loudly proclaims its own authenticity, is not authentic. And what's more, as many biblical commentators eventually admit after a lot of hemming and hawing, it is meant to discredit the first—whose authenticity is unquestioned.

This is what we read (in the Second Letter): "Don't be shaken or alarmed either by a spirit, or by an oral statement, or by a letter allegedly from us to the effect that the day of the Lord is at hand." Such an "oral statement, or letter allegedly from us to the effect that the day of the Lord is at hand" very much resembles what Paul *really* said and wrote in the early 50s, in particular in the First Letter to the Thessalonians. He believed with absolute certainty that the end of the world was imminent, and that the process had been set in motion. That all of creation was suffering the pangs of this birth. The Thessalonians believed it, all of the communities believed it. But as the years went by and the world didn't end, to avoid being considered completely mad, it became necessary to explain what was holding things up, and, where possible, to interpret or tone down the texts where this unrealistic prophesy was the most vividly expressed. Which is what the anonymous, later author of the Second Letter to the Thessalonians zealously goes about doing.

In the First Letter, Paul described the Last Judgment as being both sudden and imminent. Without transition, apparent peace would give way to a catastrophe. All those who read the letter would witness the event. The author of the Second Letter describes a long, complex, laborious process. If Jesus is late in coming, he explains, it's because the Antichrist must appear beforehand. And if the Antichrist is also late in coming, it's because something or someone else is "restraining him, that he may be revealed in his time." What is this something or someone that is restraining the Antichrist from appearing as long as his time has not come? For two thousand years exegetes have been baffled by the question. In fact, no one has the slightest idea, and clearly the real goal of the letter is to muddy the waters by maintaining that all of this is going to take a lot of time. So have patience, and above all don't let yourself be fooled by visionaries.

Clearly the author of this second letter wasn't a forger in the modern sense—no more than a painting done by the school of Raphael is a forged Raphael. He wasn't an enemy of Paul's who was trying to lead Paul's church astray, but a member of this church who was trying to resolve in Paul's name problems that arose after his death. He wrote to be true to Paul, not to betray him. Nevertheless, not satisfied with merely saying the opposite of what Paul said, he goes about discrediting what he wanted to say and, in passing Paul's authentic letter off as a forgery, justifies all of his worries.

These worries, I believe, went even further. Paul didn't just fear the work of enemies, imposters, and forgers. No, you have to give the screw an additional turn: he was afraid of himself.

•

There's a story by Edgar Allan Poe, "The System of Doctor Tarr and Professor Fether," whose narrator visits a private madhouse. Before commencing the visit of cells where the dangerous patients are kept, the superintendent puts him on his guard. The patients, he says, have developed a strangely coherent collective delirium: they believe they're the superintendent and the nurses, locked up by the lunatics who have taken over the asylum and are masquerading as them. "Really?" says the visitor, "how interesting." At the start he does find it interesting, but as the visit goes on he feels less and less comfortable. The patients say as one what the superintendent said they would. They beg the visitor to believe them, as unbelievable as it may seem, and to tell the police to save them. The discussions take place in the presence of the superintendent, who listens to the patients with a benign smile and occasional wink to the visitor, who is increasingly confused. He suspects that the patients could well be telling the truth, and starts looking at his guide with a growing sense of terror. As if picking up on this, his guide only adds to his confusion: "What did I tell you? They're convincing, no? And just wait: the most convincing of all is the superintendent. A remarkable, truly remarkable patient! I'll bet my bottom dollar, after five minutes with him you'll think I'm the dangerous lunatic! Ha ha ha!"

•

Fantastic literature has come up with thousands of variations on this harrowing theme. Some of the most memorable were penned by Philip K. Dick. In real life, especially after his religious experience, Dick subjected friends who called him on the phone to a whole barrage of questions aimed at proving that they were really who they said they were, and not FBI agents or aliens. He was fascinated by the Moscow trials, in which the accused denied what they had affirmed their whole lives, insisting that what they were saying now was the truth—Stalin is right, I'm a monster—and that everything they'd said before—I'm right, Stalin's a monster—should be considered null and void.

Paul of Tarsus was neither Philip K. Dick nor Stalin, even if he did share some of the traits of these two remarkable men. The centuries that separate him from them did a lot to bring paranoia to new heights. Be that as it may, when I read this sentence in the Letter to the Galatians: "Even if I came to preach something other than what I have preached, you shouldn't believe me," I recognize the germ of a terror unknown to the ancient world. That's because what had happened to Paul was unknown to the ancient world, and he must have dreaded, more or less consciously, that it could happen to him again.

Saul had undergone a mutation on the road to Damascus: he had been transformed into Paul, his opposite. The person he once was had become a monster to him, and he had become a monster to the person he once was. If the two could have met, the person he once was would have cursed him. He would have prayed to God to let him die, the way the heroes of vampire movies make their friends swear they'll drive a stake through their hearts if they're ever bitten. But that's what they say before it happens. Once contaminated, their only thought is to bite others in turn, in particular those who come at them with a stake to make good the promise they made to the person who no longer exists. I think that Paul's nights must have been haunted by a nightmare of this kind. What if he became Saul once again? What if, in a way that was as astonishing and unexpected as when he became Paul, he became someone else? What if this person who was different from Paul but who would have Paul's face, Paul's voice, Paul's art of persuasion, one day visited Paul's disciples with the intention of stealing them away from Christ?

•

("It's yourself you're talking about," Hervé says. "When you were a Christian, what you feared the most was becoming the skeptic that you're only too happy to be now. But who says you won't change again? Who says that in twenty years' time you won't reread this book that you find so sensible with as much embarrassment as when you reread your commentaries on the Gospel today?")

35

Slandered and persecuted by the church of Jerusalem, Paul could have broken with it completely. Until now his whole strategy had consisted in pursuing his missionary activities as far as possible from the Church headquarters, in places where it had no subsidiaries. He had set up bases in isolated, far-flung regions like Galatia, and then in large cities like Corinth. Since James's partisans were giving him so many hassles, and since for him the Law they so ardently defended was outdated, he could have set himself up on his own and founded an entirely new religion. He didn't. He must have sensed that his teaching would lose its vitality if it were detached from Judaism. So he sought a compromise, and as a gesture of goodwill he got the idea of organizing a fund-raising among the relatively prosperous churches in Asia and Greece in favor of the church of Jerusalem, which was chronically short of money. To his mind it was a positive gesture, and a sign of unity between Jewish and pagan Christians.

He had left Corinth for Ephesus, in Asia, from where he sent letter after letter to his churches, announcing the collection and recommending that they not be too stingy. These letters were read out on Sundays during the agape. At the end, everyone put money in the kitty. The idea was that each church should choose a delegate when the time came, and that the entire delegation should travel to Jerusalem under Paul's leadership to give the funds they'd collected to the "poor" and the "saints"—as James's disciples called themselves. I imagine that in Lydia's house in Philippi, the prospect of going on such a trip must have been the stuff of dreams.

36

While he was in Ephesus, Paul got other worrying news from Corinth. This time the problem wasn't emissaries sent by James, but another Christian preacher named Apollos. Although the two had never met, their paths were continually crossing. Apollos was in Ephesus while Paul was in Corinth, then Apollos went to Corinth as Paul was traveling to Ephesus, so that each one found himself in terrain prepared by the other. That wasn't much to Paul's liking. Like many demanding masters, he tended to prefer students who had received no training at all to ones who had been trained by someone else, with whom he had to undo bad habits. Paul and Apollos were both highly cultured Jews, a rare thing among early Christians. But whereas Paul came from the Pharisee tradition of Jerusalem, Apollos hailed from that of the Hellenists of Alexandria. He was a Platonic philosopher, a student of Philo's. Judging from the way Luke stresses his eloquence, one imagines him more charismatic than the intense and rough-hewn Paul. Of all the members of this first Christian generation, Apollos was probably the only one who could compare with Paul in terms of intellectual breadth of vision, and you have to wonder how Christianity would have developed if Luke, its first historian, had met Apollos instead of Paul on his travels, and if the Acts had been a biography of Apollos and not of Paul.

There was no overt rivalry between Apollos and Paul. Each was careful to praise the other's merits and to say that in any case it wasn't the individuals who counted, but Christ. That didn't stop factions from forming in Corinth. Some claimed they followed Paul, others Apollos, still others Peter or James. "Me? I'm for Christ," said those who had best understood the lesson.

•

Of all the communities Paul wrote to, it was the Corinthians who worried Paul the most. They drank, fornicated, transformed the agapes into orgies, and now on top of everything else they were divided as well. "Is Christ divided?" Paul rails in the first letter of rebuke he addressed to them. Apollos, Peter, Paul, James . . . : such petty quarrels are fine for the philosophical schools, the Stoics or Epicureans who bombard each other with names and quotes. Fine for those lovers of wisdom who believe you can achieve happiness by living your life according to the demands of reason. Paul doesn't name Apollos—that would be tricky in a text aimed at denouncing any kind of polemicizing—but you can guess that he puts him in the same boat. And the more you read on in the letter, the more you understand that it's not division that Paul is attacking, but wisdom, pure and simple.

Wisdom, however, is what everyone is after. Even the fast livers, the pleasure seekers, and the slaves of their desires yearn for wisdom. They say that there's nothing better, and that they'd be philosophers if they could. Paul doesn't agree. He says that wisdom is a wretched goal, and that God does not approve of it, or of reason, or of the will to be the master of one's life, and that if you want to know God's opinion you just have to read the book of Isaiah: "I will destroy the wisdom of the wise, and the intelligence of the intelligent I will reject."

Paul goes even further than that. He says that God has chosen to save the men who listen not to wise words, but to foolishness. He says that the Greeks go astray in seeking wisdom and the Jews go astray in asking for signs, and that the only truth is this crucified Messiah who is a scandal for the Jews and foolishness for the Gentiles. For the foolishness of God is wiser than human wisdom, and the weakness of God is stronger than human strength.

Not many of the brothers in Corinth were wise. Or powerful, or noble of birth. Paul himself didn't win them over with seductive words or fine philosophic discourses. The Paul he showed them was stripped of all prestige, as if naked. And it's in this way, weak, afraid, trembling, that he teaches them that the wisdom of the world is foolishness before God. That the foolish of the world were chosen by God to shame the wise. That the weak were chosen to shame the strong. That what is lowly and despised in the world—*the things that are not*—was chosen to bring to nothing the things that are.

·

What Paul writes here is stunning. No one wrote anything like it before him. You can look all you like. Nowhere in Greek philosophy, nowhere in the Bible will you find such words. Maybe Jesus said such audacious things, but at this time there's no written trace of them. The people Paul is writing to aren't familiar with any. What they hear—mixed with moral exhortations, reproaches, and threats that I don't want to go into—is something absolutely new.

37

Titus, whom Paul sent to take his letter to the Corinthians, comes back a couple of weeks later saying that he was well received, that the collection is advancing, but also—and it takes Titus longer to admit this—that people in Corinth are saying strange things about Paul. That he's vain: always boasting about the wonders the Lord works in him. Fickle: always saying he'll come to visit and continuously putting it off. Hypocritical: always changing his tune depending on whom he's addressing. A bit of a nutcase. And finally—I've already touched on this—that the force and severity of his letters contrast with the mediocrity of his appearance and spoken words. Commanding from afar, gutless close up. Well then, let him come! We'll see if he keeps putting on airs when we have him face-to-face!

In the second letter he wrote to the Corinthians, Paul doesn't reply to these accusations right away. He plays them down and comes back to recent events, assuring his readers that Titus has reassured him completely, and congratulating them on their good conduct. And when he's finally done with the diplomatic preliminaries, he focuses very specifically on the collection. In fact, we learn in passing, it was the Corinthians themselves who first launched the idea. And bearing that in mind, Paul feels, they could be more generous—as generous as the churches of Macedonia and Asia. "Imitate our Lord Jesus Christ," he says to the Corinthians, "for your sakes He became poor, so that you through His poverty might become rich." Give generously, give with joy, because "whoever sows sparingly will also reap sparingly," and you'd look pretty silly to the other churches if you turned out to be the most stingy . . .

Thereupon starts the most extraordinary part of the letter, which a charming heading in the JB sums up as follows: "Paul is forced to boast." In fact, he defends himself against the accusations of duplicity and folly that Titus told him about. The whole thing is stunning, reminiscent of Dostoyevsky's grand monologues. The style is conversational: full of repetition, stalling, petty details, and shrill notes. You get the feeling you're hearing Paul dictating to Timothy, correcting himself, getting mad, turning in circles . . .

Here's a bit that I translate freely:

You can't put up with a little foolishness on my part? Come on! Put up with it! Put up with me! I'm as jealous of you as God is. I'm afraid you'll be seduced, it's true. I'm afraid you'll be led astray. I'm afraid another Jesus will be preached to you than the one I have preached. I'm afraid your thoughts will be corrupted. I'm afraid you will listen to other preachers than me.

Nevertheless, I'm in no way inferior to the super-apostles you speak of. True, I'm no good at speaking. But as far as knowledge and understanding what I'm talking about go, it's a different matter. I showed you that, didn't I? But perhaps I was wrong to lower myself to elevate you, by announcing the Gospel free of charge . . . [A familiar theme, I'll skip fifteen lines]. And don't believe I'm foolish. Or rather, do believe it. Go on, believe it, and let me be foolish for a moment. Let me boast a little. It's not the Lord speaking now, it's me. Me the fool, me the bragger. Everyone boasts, why shouldn't I? You are wise, that should make you indulgent toward fools. You're full of tolerance for people who make you their slaves, who eat you, who cheat you, who look down on you, who strike you in the face. They are Hebrews? So am I. Jews? So am I. Descendants of Abraham? So am I. Ministers of Christ? I know I sound like a fool, but I'm a far better one. I've sweated far more blood. I've spent far more time in prison. I've suffered more blows, and faced more mortal danger. Five times I've received the thirty-nine lashes of the Jews. I've been beaten with rods three times, stoned once, ship-wrecked three times, and I've spent one night and one day adrift at sea. I've traveled on foot, and known all kinds of dangers. Dangers from rivers, dangers from robbers, dangers from my own people, dangers from others, dangers from the city, dangers from the desert, dangers from the sea, dangers from false brothers. I have been hungry, I have been thirsty, I have been cold, I have spent sleepless nights, I have agonized for you, for my churches, and if I boast of one thing, it is only of my weakness.

I could boast about my visions. I could boast about my revelations. I could tell you about a man who was taken up to the third heaven fourteen years ago. Was it in my body, was it out of my body? I don't know, the only one who knows is God. This man was lifted up to paradise and there he was told things that are so grand that he has no right to repeat them. I could boast about that: it wouldn't be folly, it would just be the truth. But I won't. The only thing I boast of is my weakness. What I heard up there was so grand that to overcome my desire to boast I was given a thorn in my flesh. Three times I asked the Lord to cure me, but he said: "No, my grace is enough. My power needs your weakness to reach its full potential." Fine, I'll take pleasure in weakness, in insults, in misery, in persecution, in fears, because by being weak I am strong!

I played at being the fool. You pushed me to it. I'm nothing, but that is more than your super-apostles. Everything an apostle is supposed to do I did when I was with you. Signs, wonders, miracles. The only thing I didn't do [here we go again], was to live at your expense. I should have, that's all you respect. But I won't. I'll come to visit you again, it will be the third time, and

I won't live at your expense. I don't want your money, I want you. Children shouldn't have to put money aside for their parents, just the opposite. I will give you all I have, all I am, and the more I love you, the less you will love me. I know you'll say that I'm crafty, that the less I ask for the more I'll obtain . . . Oh! I'm afraid that when I come I'll be disappointed in you, and that you'll be disappointed in me. I have no doubts as to what I'll find: discord, jealousy, anger, rivalry, backbiting, arrogance, and all manner of unrest. I will be humiliated. I will weep. But I will come nonetheless, for the third time, and you will see, I won't be easy on you. You want the proof that Christ speaks in me? He will speak, and he is not weak. Look at yourselves, mend your ways. I hope with all my heart that I'm wrong, and that you will prove me a liar. All I want is for me to be weak and for you to be strong. All I want is for you to progress. That's why for now I prefer to write you—to advise you and give you a chance—rather than having to take drastic action when I'm there. The Lord put me here to nurture you, not to destroy you. So rejoice and let peace be with you.

38

Luke's second appearance in the Acts is as unsensational as the first. We've seen him appear beside Paul in the port of Troas in the form of an enigmatic "we," then act as narrator for a chapter in Macedonia, and then vanish when Paul leaves Philippi. Seven years go by, and we're again in the port of Troas. Paul reappears, accompanied not by two but by ten or so disciples, who have been delegated by the churches of Greece and Asia to bring the money they've collected to the poor and the saints of Jerusalem. Sopater is there from Berea, Aristarchus and Secundus from Thessalonica, Gaius from Derbe, Trophimus from Ephesus, Tychicus from Galatia, and, of course, the most faithful of the faithful, Timothy. "*As for us*," Luke goes on calmly, "we left Philippi by sea after the feast of unleavened bread, and met up with them in Troas, where we stayed for seven days before setting sail."

It's difficult to be any less conspicuous. He wasn't there, now he's there. You don't notice him any more than the last time; nevertheless, starting with this sentence, Luke is in the saddle again, and he stays there until the end. Everything is more precise, more alive, more detailed: you can sense it's an eyewitness account.

•

He's part of the expedition as a delegate of the church of Philippi, the way Sopater represents the church of Barea, Aristarchus and Secundus that of Thessalonica, et cetera. I try to imagine these second-order delegates, these foot soldiers of the Church whose names have come down to us over twenty centuries thanks to Luke. None of them has ever set foot in Judea, none of them knows the Jewish Scriptures aside from the Septuagint, none of them knows anything more about Jesus than what they've gathered from Paul's teaching, which is personal to say the least. They are not professional disciples like Titus or Timothy, who left everything years ago to follow their guru, and who are accustomed to the discipline and ordeals of evangelism. In Berea, in Thessalonica, in Ephesus, they must have gone to church but otherwise lived normal lives, with trades, families, habits. Was there much competition in these churches to become a delegate? How were they chosen? How did the delegates imagine the adventure they were embarking on? Did they think they'd left for three months, six months, a year? I picture them like fervent yoga practitioners, leaving Toulouse or Dusseldorf for a long trip to the ashram of their master's master in India: For months they haven't thought of anything else, haven't talked about anything else. They've bought a quick and easy guide to Bengali and they know the Sanskrit names of all the postures. Their yoga mat rolled up tight to take up the least possible space, they've packed and repacked their bags ten times and spent entire nights going over the contents in their heads, afraid of taking too much, and then of not taking enough. Before closing the door, and then opening it again to make sure they really did turn off the gas, they burned incense sticks one last time in front of their little altar and chanted *Om shanti* on their meditation cushion—just as Luke makes a point of telling us that he left after celebrating the feast of unleavened bread, even though he's not Jewish. They meet their traveling companions in Troas, where everyone gathers for the departure. The four Macedonians already know each other: Philippi, Thessalonica, and Berea are all quite close. The others come from Asia and Galatia. No Corinthians—unless Luke forgot to put them on his list—and as the

Corinthians are above all known for the terrible browbeating that Paul gave them on account of their frivolity, debauchery, and stinginess, it's tempting to snicker that it's no big surprise. But Paul forbade bad-mouthing, so everyone is careful to be on their best behavior and greet each other with a *Marana-tha* loaded with the maximum of kindness and goodwill. Nevertheless, whether Macedonians or Galatians—and not forgetting that the Galatians also got a good roasting in their time—they feel like they're part of an elite: those whose love of Christ and generosity in the collection Paul regularly cites as examples in his letters. Each of them must have looked to see how much the other was bringing when the offerings were counted and sealed. Paul is very punctilious on this point: he's not the kind of person to misappropriate a drachma to cover his costs.

39

One night, Paul talks with the delegates in an upper room in the house where they're staying, near the port. Night falls. The oil lamps are lit and they're served a few small dishes: olives, grilled octopus, cheese, and wine. A group of followers surrounds the master, who speaks in a muffled, choppy voice. A little way off, an adolescent is sitting listening on the windowsill. His name is Eutychus, and he's not part of the group. He's probably the boy of the house, taking advantage of the travelers' visit to stay up late. He was told to behave himself, and he is behaving himself. No one pays him any more attention than if he were a pet. The hours go by, Paul talks at length. Eutychus nods off. He sways. The dreadful sound of his body hitting the ground interrupts Paul. It takes them a while to understand what's happened, then they run down the stairs. In the courtyard, three stories down, they bend over the boy's contorted body. He's dead. Paul, the last one down, takes him in his arms and says, "Don't be alarmed. His soul is still in him." Then he goes back upstairs and talks until daybreak. "As for the boy," Luke goes on calmly, "he was taken home alive, to everyone's great relief."

•

I find this passage terribly embarrassing. Not because there's no rational explanation for it. On the contrary, it's clear: everyone thought Eutychus was dead, Paul sees that he's only badly hurt, so much the better. Then all night in their quarters the naïve delegates from Asia and Macedonia whisper together and convince themselves that they've witnessed a resurrection. What's embarrassing is that Luke relates this resurrection as if it were no big deal, or rather as if it were remarkable, yes, but no more than a surprising recovery. You get the impression that Paul resurrected people from time to time. That he didn't overdo it, so as not to get people talking, but that for him it was all part of the job. In his letters, however, Paul never boasted that he could do such things, and I'm sure he would have put someone firmly in his place for suggesting that he could. That's because he took resurrection very seriously. He thought the same thing we do: that it's impossible. That all kinds of things are possible, including what he called signs and we call miracles, like a paralytic who starts to walk, but resurrection: no. There's a fundamental difference between a paralytic who starts to walk and a man who comes back from the dead. And this difference was very clear to Paul, but apparently less so to Luke. In the same way you can admit that a man whose arm was paralyzed might start to use it again, but not that an amputated arm can grow back. Paul's entire doctrine—if you can call something so intensely lived a doctrine—is based on just that: resurrection is impossible, and yet a man has been resurrected. At one precise moment in time this impossible event happened, which divides history in two: before and after. At the same time it divides humanity in two: those who don't believe and those who do. And for those who believe— those who have received the incredible grace of believing this incredible thing—nothing they believed before makes sense anymore. They have to start again from scratch. But what does our Luke make of this unique, unprecedented, inimitable act? For him it's just one in a series of events. God resurrected his son, Jesus. Paul resurrected the young Eutychus. Things like that happen, and Sopater and Tychicus must think that if they watch closely enough they can get the hang of it themselves. I imagine how Paul would have reacted if he could have read the biography written about him twenty or thirty years after his death by his former traveling companion. What an idiot! Maybe he wouldn't have been surprised, though. Maybe that's how he saw this worthy Macedonian doctor: as a nice, naïve oaf at whom it took a huge amount of effort—not always crowned with success because Saint Paul was anything but a saint—not to blow his top.

40

Paul talked and talked that night. Luke doesn't say what he talked about, but the Letter to the Romans gives a fair idea of what it could have been, since it was written at the same time and must have made up a lot of his conversation.

This letter, which opens the canonical collection of Paul's epistles, is not like the others. Despite its title, it's not specifically addressed to the Romans, and doesn't deal with any problems the Romans might have brought to his attention. Unlike the Galatians or the Corinthians, if the Romans did have problems, it would never have occurred to them to address them to Paul, who hadn't established their church and who knew full well that it was developing under the guidance of Peter and James. Taking the initiative of writing to their flock instead of to his own was first of all an incursion into their domain, and second it meant giving to his text the status of an encyclical, whose validity extends beyond Rome to all churches. To get it all down, Paul took advantage of the relatively calm winter that preceded his departure for Jerusalem. You can feel him get comfortable, like a thinker who has been too busy to write anything but articles and who now takes the time to work on a real book. And that's what it is: it's as long as the Gospel of Mark. It was dictated to a certain Tertius, who at the end takes the opportunity to greet the reader in his own name, but it must have been copied and recopied for the other churches—and why not by Luke?

•

Imagining the Luke whom I imagine faced with this text is a way of justifying my own lack of appetite, because I think that much of this austere, doctrinal position paper must have been over his head—as it is over mine. Luke was fond of anecdotes and human traits; theology bored him. He could get excited about Paul's quarrels with the Corinthians, because the Corinthians were Greeks like him, and because the problems that they ran up against trying to introduce Christianity in pagan surroundings concerned him directly. The Letter to the Romans, by contrast, deals with the emancipation of Christianity from Jewish Law. On the one hand that isn't really Luke's problem, and on the other he must have been a bit lost in all the biblical references and rabbinical subtleties that Paul brings up to substantiate the break with the synagogue.

In fact, the key idea of the Letter to the Romans is already found in the Letter to the Galatians—but, as one Swiss exegete nicely says, the Letter to the Galatians is like the Rhône River before Lake Geneva, and the Letter to the Romans like the Rhône after Geneva: above it a mountain torrent, below it a majestic river. The Letter to the Galatians was written in anger in one brilliant sitting, while the Letter to the Romans was written slowly, after dipping the pen repeatedly in the inkwell. And since it greatly embarrasses Paul to write his key idea in black and white, he gets caught up in lengthy juridico-theological quibbles, explaining that a married woman is bound by the Law to her husband for as long as he is alive, but that when he dies she is released from the law of marriage, so that if she sleeps with another man in the first case it's adultery, while in the second she cannot be reproached. After beating around the bush for a while, Paul nevertheless ends up saying what's really on his mind, which can be summed up very simply: the Law is finished. Since Jesus came, it has lost its purpose. The Jews who hold on to it like a privilege that comes with being the chosen ones show in the best of cases their deafness, in the worst their bad will. The Jews were called first, the Gentiles afterward, but as of now all of them can be saved only by the grace of Jesus. "That's how it is. He shows mercy on whomever he wants. He hardens those he wants to harden."

But then, if it pleased God to harden them, what will become of the Jews? Paul is full of mercy for them. The time for railing that they displease the Lord and that he will bring his wrath down upon them is past. No, Paul has taken a step back, and his new idea is that it's a godsend for the Gentiles if the Jews in their folly (he calls it a "stumbling") let them inherit that which rightfully belongs to them, but that things don't stop there. Israel's resistance will last until all the Gentiles have entered the Church, and then the Jews will enter in turn, and this will be the sign that the times have changed. To illustrate this, Paul tries his hand at a parable in the style of Jesus, evoking a gardener who grafts new shoots onto an olive tree. However, he doesn't burn the branches that were broken off, and once the new shoots have grown he will gather them up as well and graft them back onto the tree. Horticulturally speaking, the metaphor is particularly unconvincing, but you get the idea: the Jews are the branches that have been broken off the olive tree. However,

Paul warns, the newly grafted shoots must not boast against the branches! "You do not support the root, the root supports you."

•

What could have touched someone like Luke if he read, copied, or heard this theological treatise that consummates the rupture of the Church with the synagogue on the eve of his departure to Jerusalem? Perhaps—because he was of a conciliatory nature—the idea that despite everything, things would work out, that there would always be a place at God's side for the old, failed people, if that's how he saw Israel. Without any doubt—because he preferred practical instructions to abstractions and because he had a taste for the established order—the passage where Paul all of a sudden gets down off his high horse to settle the question that was certainly raised by all Jewish nationalists who were up in arms against the Empire: Do you have to pay taxes? Paul is very clear: Yes, you do. "For the authorities are ministers of God, attending to this very thing. And everyone must submit to the authorities, for there is no authority except from God, and those that exist have been established by God." (No need to insist on the havoc this sentence could cause.) Finally, what he read about Jesus preferring to forgive sinners must have warmed Luke's sentimental heart. What he likes most are stories about lost sheep, and later he'll tell dozens of his own.

Aside from that, I imagine him nodding his head in approval without really getting the drift.

4 I

If Paul himself didn't stress several times in this letter that he was writing it just before going to Jerusalem "to make a contribution for the poor and the saints," it would be very difficult to believe. To recapitulate: on the one hand, this marginal dissident, viewed with the greatest suspicion by the head office, sets out on a long and perilous journey to present his respects, bring money, and show that, despite appearances, he's loyal and reliable; on the other—and at the same time—he writes a long and peremptory circular to all of the subsidiaries explaining that all of the principles put forward by Peter, James, and John, the historic fathers of the Church, are now obsolete and that it's time to move on.

A little while back I imagined a former Czarist officer demanding that Stalin give him carte blanche to spread Marxism-Leninism abroad. Now he comes back to Moscow for the Party congress just after publishing a series of articles much noted in the West entitled "The End of the Class Struggle, the End of the Dictatorship of the Proletariat: Marxism Is Dead, Long Live Marxism!" It's what you'd call sticking your head into the lion's mouth, and I don't know what the good Sopater, Tychicus, Trophimus, et cetera, think about it, or if these trusty traveling companions are so excited at the prospect of leaving for the dreamed-of Holy Land with their master that they don't sense just how much the whole venture smells of trouble. I think Paul does suspect the sort of welcome that awaits him in Jerusalem. But, he seems to be thinking, it's just got to be done. Once it's over, he'll be able to pursue his mission and travel as far to the west in the inhabited world as he's been to the east. After having done the rounds of the Greek world and the Orient, his project is to go to Rome, where his letter will have preceded him, and from there, God willing, as far as Spain.

42

Luke's memories are remarkably precise as far as the circumstances of the grand departure go, and I like this passage of the Acts all the more because I know the area like the back of my hand. For several years I've gone to the Greek island of Patmos together with Hélène and the kids. After toying with the idea of buying a place in the South of France, that's where we now dream of having a home away from home. As I write this chapter, at the start of May 2012, we've just come back from a trip spent looking for one, unsuccessfully, unfortunately, or at least not entirely successfully, because everything's complicated with the Greeks. You never quite know where you stand, what's possible and what isn't, how much things cost, who owns what, so that sometimes we're so exasperated that we think the huge financial crisis they're now going through is just what they deserve. I do hope we'll have found the house we're looking for before the end of this book. In the meantime, when I read that "we"—that is, Luke and his companions—"left Troas for Assos, where Paul was going on foot," and that "the next day we set sail from there and arrived off Chios. The day after that we crossed over to Samos, and on the following day arrived at Miletus," I'm thrilled, and feel like I was there.

I love these marvelous rocky crags that are strung like beads off the coast of Turkey, a coast that for political reasons is not shown on many Greek maps, so that the islands of the Dodecanese seem to hang on the edge of the world, ready to fall into the void. In relation to Patmos, the islands of Samos and Kos evoke for me ferry schedules, disembarking at deserted ports in the middle of the night, postponed and even canceled crossings because of storms—to which you have to add, as far as Kos is concerned, the archaeological bureau, where decisions are made as to what can be built or restored on these islands, and where the bureaucrats get a perverse pleasure (if you ask them at least to let you know what they decide) in saying that you'll hear in two weeks, and then once the two weeks have elapsed, in a month, and once the month has gone by, in another month, and so on. Anyway. From Miletus they go on to Kos, and from there they cross over to Rhodes—that's the route of the Blue Star Ferry, which we take each summer—then from Rhodes to Patara, where they change ships and set sail for Judea.

•

Some historians credit Luke with good navigating experience, because he uses a couple of technical terms in the Acts. But I think that before this big voyage his experience was limited to the occasional sail along the Aegean coast. The Mediterranean is treacherous; you sail as much as possible within view of the shore. To get to Judea, unfortunately, there's no alternative: you have to cross the high seas. The voyage takes eight days without touching land. The merchant ships have a couple of cabins for the rich passengers, and mats on the deck covered with tent canvas for the rest. Of course, Luke and his companions are among the rest. Maybe they go all green during the trip, and maybe they throw up overboard. But, be that as it may, they must all take themselves for Odysseus.

They know *The Odyssey*, of course. Everyone back then knew *The Iliad* and *The Odyssey*. Those who know how to read learned it by reading Homer, and those who don't were told the story. Since they were written almost eight centuries before Paul's day, the Homeric poems have turned their innumerable readers more or less into amateur historians. At school everyone wrote essays, and as adults they engaged in heated discussions about what is true and what is legend in the tales of the Trojan War, and where exactly Odysseus went. When Luke and his traveling companions see an island in the mist, alone on their nutshell in the middle of the sea, they must wonder if it's not the island of the lotus-eaters, or of the Cyclops Polyphemus, or of the sorceress Circe, who turns men into swine, or of the nymph Calypso, who—if she feels like it—can open the doors to eternal life.

43

The story takes place in book V of *The Odyssey*. Odysseus ran aground on Calypso's island seven years ago and hasn't budged since. The island is full of the fragrance of cedar and juniper fires. There are garden vines, four springs of clear water, and soft meadows full of violets and wild celery all year round. Above all, the nymph is beautiful and Odysseus shares her bed. Life in this walled garden is delightful, and every bit enticing enough to make the traveler forget his goal, which as we know is to get back home to the rocky island of Ithaca, to his wife, Penelope, and his son, Telemachus—in short, the world he comes from and that he had to leave long ago to take part in the siege of Troy. But he doesn't forget. He's seized by nostalgia. During two ecstatic nights he lies motionless on the shore, lost in thought. He weeps. On Mount Olympus, Athena argues his case: as voluptuous as it is, his punishment has lasted long enough. Zeus, convinced, sends Hermes to inform Calypso that she has to let the hero go. "Because it is not his destiny to die on this island, far from his loved ones. In fact, his fate is to see his family, to regain the roof of his high house, in the land of his fathers." (I'm quoting Robert Fagles's translation, in verse.) At these words, Calypso shudders. She's horribly sad. But she submits. That night, Odysseus and Calypso get together. They both know that he'll leave the next morning. In the grotto where they so loved to make love, she serves him food and drink, in the silent affliction of pending separation. Finally, Calypso can't bear it any longer. She tries her last chance:

"So then, royal son of Laertes, Odysseus, man of exploits, still eager to leave at once and hurry back to your own home, your beloved native land? Good luck to you, even so. Farewell! But if you only knew, down deep, what pains are fated to fill your cup before you reach that shore, you'd stay right here, preside in our house with me and be immortal. Much as you long to see your wife, the one you pine for all your days . . . and yet I just might claim to be nothing less than she, neither in face nor figure. Hardly right, is it, for mortal woman to rival immortal goddess? How, in build? in beauty?"

Odysseus replies:

"Ah, great goddess, don't be angry with me, please. All that you say is true, how well I know. Look at my wise Penelope. She falls far short of you, your beauty, stature. She is mortal after all and you, you never age or die . . . Nevertheless I long—I pine, all my days—to travel home and see the dawn of my return. And if a god will wreck me yet again on the wine-dark sea, I can bear that too, with a spirit tempered to endure. Much have I suffered, labored long and hard by now in the waves and wars. Add this to the total—bring the trial on!"

•

Let's transpose and flesh out the scene, without being afraid to hammer the point home. Calypso—the prototype lover whom all men would like to have but not necessarily marry, the type to turn on the gas or swallow pills on New Year's Eve while her lover is celebrating with his family—has a trump in her hand that's more powerful than her tears, her tenderness, and even the curly fleece between her legs. She can offer him the stuff of everyone's dreams. What? Eternity. No less. If he stays with her, he'll never die. He'll never get old. They'll never get sick. Forever, she will retain the miraculous body of a very young woman, and he the robust frame of a forty-year-old man at the height of his seductiveness. They'll spend eternity making love, taking naps in the sun, swimming in the blue water, drinking wine without getting a hangover, making love again, never getting tired of it, reading poetry if they feel like it, and, why not, writing poetry as well. It's tempting, Odysseus says, but I have to return home. You know what's waiting for you at home? A woman who's already getting on in years, with stretch marks and cellulite, and who's not going to get any better with menopause. A son whom you remember as an adorable little boy, but who's become a problem adolescent while you've been gone, and who stands a good chance of becoming a druggie, an Islamist, a psychotic, obese, everything fathers worry will happen to their sons. If you leave, you too will soon be old, you'll ache all over, your life will be nothing more than a dark corridor that shrinks with time. And dreadful though it may be to make your way down this corridor with your walker and your drip, you'll wake up in the night gripped with terror because you're going to die. That's the life of a man. I am offering you the life of a god. Think about it.

"I have thought about it," says Odysseus. And he leaves.

•

Many commentators see in Odysseus' choice the height of ancient wisdom, and perhaps of wisdom altogether. The life of a man is better than that of a god, for the simple reason that it's real. Authentic suffering is better than deceptive bliss. Eternity is not desirable because it's not part of our common lot. This imperfect, short-lived, deceptive lot is the only one for us to cherish, to it we must always return, and the entire story of Odysseus, the entire history of men who consent to be no more than men so as to be men to the full, is the story of this return.

We moderns have little merit in claiming this wisdom for our own, because there's no longer anyone to make us an offer like Calypso's. Luke, Sopater, and the others, however, have enthusiastically accepted the offer made to them, and I wonder if, sailing by an island and smelling the odor of olive trees, cypress, and honeysuckle on the breeze, that is what Luke is thinking about.

•

I don't know anything about his childhood or his adolescence, but I imagine that he dreamed of being a hero like Achilles (brave to the point of madness, preferring a glorious death to an ordinary life) or an accomplished man such as Odysseus (able to get out of any predicament, seducing women and winning over men, marvelously acclimatized to life). And then in growing up he stopped identifying with the Homeric heroes because it didn't work. Because he wasn't like them. Because he had to face the fact that he didn't belong to the happy family of men who like life on earth, to whom life is good and who want no other. He belonged to the other family, the family of the worriers, the melancholic, those who believe that real life is taking place elsewhere. You can imagine that they were in the minority in antiquity, that they kept undercover and were reduced to silence, and that it was thanks to our morose friend Paul that they took power and kept it until today. But even so, they had glorious spokesmen: Plato to start with, the man who held that all our lives take place in a dark cave where we see nothing but vague reflections of the real world. Luke must have read Plato: four centuries after he died he was still very widely known, everyone who had a taste for elevated thoughts went through a Platonic period. Like many of his contemporaries, Luke then went on to become interested in Judaism via Philo, the Jewish Platonist from Alexandria, and wasn't disoriented. The soul was in exile. In Egypt, it pined for Jerusalem. In Babylonia, it pined for Jerusalem. And in Jerusalem, it pined for the *true* Jerusalem.

And then he met Paul, who promises nothing other than eternal life. Paul says what Plato said before him, that life on earth is bad because man is flawed and his flesh corruptible. He says that the only thing to expect from this life is to be delivered from it, and to go to where Christ reigns. Of course, where Christ reigns is less sexy than where Calypso reigns. Those bodies that were once corruptible will come back to life incorruptible, that is to say, they will no longer grow old, no longer suffer, no longer desire anything but the glory of God—and it's easier to imagine them hidden under long robes and singing endless hymns than caressing each other while swimming naked in the sea. That would put me off, but I have to admit that it most likely didn't put Luke off. Moreover, I don't want to ridicule him: the extinction of desire isn't just the ideal of puritan bigots but also of people who have profoundly reflected on the human condition, like the Buddhists. The real issue lies elsewhere: in the troubling resemblance between what Paul promises and what Calypso promises: being delivered from life—or, as Hervé would say, "getting out of this mess"—and in the unsolvable difference between Paul's ideal and that of Odysseus. Each one calls the only true good what the other condemns as a baneful illusion. Odysseus says that wisdom always consists in turning your attention to the human condition and life on earth, Paul says it consists in tearing yourself away. Odysseus says that regardless how beautiful it is, paradise is a fiction, and Paul says that it's the only reality. Paul, carried away, goes as far as congratulating God for having chosen *what is not* to invalidate what is. That's what Luke chose, that's what he embarked on—quite literally—and I wonder if, once on board, he doesn't ask himself whether he's making a huge mistake. Whether he's dedicating his entire life to something that simply does not exist, and is turning his back on what really does exist: the warmth of human bodies, the bittersweet taste of life, the marvelous imperfection of the real.

III

THE INVESTIGATION

(JUDEA, 58–60)

I

After eight days at sea, Paul and his delegation disembark in Syria. They are met by several followers of the Way, as the Christian cult is known locally. In Caesarea, the region's major port, they stay at the home of a preacher named Philip, the father of four virgin daughters gifted with prophecy. A friend of the family, who also has a reputation as a prophet, wants to talk Paul out of visiting Jerusalem. Miming the scene by binding his own feet and hands, he predicts that the Jews there will arrest him and hand him over to the Romans, who will kill him. In vain. Paul remains firm. If he has to die for the cause, he'll die. His hosts bid him a teary farewell, and it's tempting to think that Luke, writing these scenes thirty years later, deliberately echoes the scenes in his Gospel when Jesus is also determined to travel to Jerusalem despite the repeated warnings of his disciples.

•

Despite the warnings of his own followers, Paul enters the holy city with his entourage. There they stay with Mnason, a Cypriot disciple, and the very next day they pay their respects to James. And now it's time to ask why the latter headed the followers of the Way in Jerusalem.

It should have been Peter, Jesus' most senior companion. It could have been John, who by his own admission was Jesus' favorite. The two of them had all the necessary legitimacy. In the same way, Trotsky and Bukharin were well suited to take over from Lenin, in spite of which a sinister-looking Georgian, Joseph Dzhugashvili—a.k.a. Stalin, against whom Lenin had expressly warned—took over by eliminating all his other rivals.

What Jesus had said about his brother James, and about his family in general, was no more encouraging. When asked about his mother and brothers, he shook his head and pointed to the strangers who followed him, saying, "Here are my mother and my brothers." To a woman who gushed, "Blessed is the womb that bore you, and the breasts at which you nursed!" he replied curtly, "Blessed rather are those who hear the word of God and obey it." You have to admit, Jesus didn't seem overly thrilled about breasts or wombs. He didn't make much fuss about his family either, and his family made even less about him. The evangelist Mark relates a scene where Jesus' family even considers having him arrested because they think he's out of his mind. If James had been the only one to stand up for his brother, we would certainly have heard about it. Like the rest, James must have taken Jesus for a freak who discredited his modest but honorable family. The fact that this visionary, this rebel, this rabble-rouser was finally executed like a common criminal should have convinced everyone that his virtuous brother was perfectly right, but then something strange happened: despite—or because of—this shocking execution, the dishonorable brother became the object of a veritable cult after his death, a little of his posthumous glory started to rub off on James, and James didn't object. More through his blood ties than through his merit, thanks to a purely dynastic principle, he became one of the major figures of the early Church: equal and even superior to the historic disciples Peter and John, something like the first pope. A strange career path, indeed.

2

When he met James for the first time, Luke knew nothing about his brother Jesus. Neither his untraditional morals, nor the bad company he kept, nor his contempt for sanctimonious behavior. Maybe he imagined that when he was alive he was like James, of whom tradition—that is to say, Eusebius, the Bishop of Caesarea who wrote a history of the Church in the fourth century—left us this engaging portrait: "He was holy from his mother's womb; and he drank no wine nor strong drink, nor did he eat flesh. No razor came upon his head; he did not anoint himself with oil, and he did not use the bath. He wore not woolen but linen garments. He was in the habit of entering alone into the Temple, and was frequently found upon his knees in prayer, so that his knees became hard like those of a camel."

It's in front of this intimidating character and the council of elders of the Way that Paul undergoes a sort of oral exam. After the usual civilities, he gives a detailed report on the works that the Lord has carried out among the Gentiles through his ministry. Always positive, always careful to play down any tensions, Luke says that Paul's listeners "praised God for what they heard," but is strangely silent about what was in fact the main reason for Paul's visit: bringing the collection money to the church of Jerusalem. From here it's only a short step to thinking that James rejected Paul's offering, as God rejected Cain's . . . Both of our two sources are silent here, but if you think about it, accepting Paul's gift would come down to granting him the status of a Church father, and there's no reason to think that James was ready to do that.

As positive as he is, Luke can't hide the fact that once God has been praised, the elders—that is to say, James—address Paul as follows: "You see, brother, how many thousands of Jews have believed, and all of them are zealous for the Law. You must know that they are worried about the rumors that circulate about you. It's said that you teach all the Jews who live among the Gentiles to turn away from Moses, telling them not to circumcise their children or live according to our customs." (One assumes Paul listens to this in silence: all of it is true.) "What shall we do? They will certainly hear that you have come, so do what we tell you, to calm them down and show that you have been slandered." (Here Paul has a hard time swallowing.) "There are four men with us who have made a vow. Take them to the Temple, join in their purification rites, and pay their expenses, so that they can have their heads shaved. Then everyone will know there is no truth in these rumors about you."

•

In demanding that Paul act in a way so contrary to everything he professed, James wanted to show that he was the boss, and no doubt humiliate his enemy. Paul submitted. Not out of a lack of courage, I'm sure, but because it made no difference to him. Because it was only a blow to his pride, and he was able to stomach such slights. That's what you want? Fine. He did everything he was asked. He accompanied the four pious men to the Temple, and performed the ritual purifications with them. He spent money—quite a bit of money—on offerings and sacrifices, and, at the end of a seven-day fast, he gave notice of the ceremony in which they would have their heads shaved. One wonders how the four pious men treated Paul. In his relations with them, Paul most certainly made it a point of honor of remembering that love is soft and patient, showing patience to his God and not getting upset.

3

While Paul endures this week of hazing, Luke and his comrades from Asia and Macedonia are left to themselves, and have nothing better to do, I imagine, than take a look around Jerusalem. Subjects of the Roman Empire, they're used to Roman cities, whose straight, white streets are all more or less the same. The Jewish holy city is unlike anything they've seen. What's more, they arrive during Pesach—Passover— which commemorates the people of Israel's coming out of Egypt. Crowds of pilgrims, merchants, and caravan drivers jostle in the narrow streets and converge around the Temple, which is also completely new to them. Of course, Luke has heard about it, but before seeing it with his own eyes he had no idea what to expect—and I'm not at all certain it was really to his liking. What is to his liking are the synagogues, the discreet, welcoming little houses that exist everywhere there are Jews, in which he first got his taste for Judaism. Synagogues aren't temples: they're places of study and prayer, not of worship—to say nothing of sacrifice. Luke likes the idea that unlike other people, the Jews have no temple, or that their temple is in their hearts. But the truth is that, in fact, they do have a Temple, a single Temple, the way they have a single God, and, as they think that this God is the greatest of the gods and that all of their neighbors' gods are puny imposters, their Temple must be worthy of him. Instead of wasting their time and money dedicating little temples to him wherever they live, Jews all over the world send an offering each year to maintain and embellish the big, the true, the only Temple. The richest and most pious go there on a pilgrimage three times a year for the biggest celebrations, Pesach, Shavuot, and Sukkot, and the others go when they can. During these celebrations, the population increases tenfold. From the four corners of the earth, everyone converges on the Temple.

•

You can see it from everywhere, crowned with marble and gold, and, depending on the time of day, shining like the sun or glittering like a mountain covered with snow. It's absolutely gigantic, thirty-seven acres in surface area—or six times the Acropolis—and almost brand spanking new. Destroyed by the Babylonians long ago when the Jews were led into exile, it was rebuilt at the start of the Roman occupation under the reign of King Herod the Great, a refined, ultrarich megalomaniac who made it one of the wonders of the Hellenistic world. The English historian Simon Sebag Montefiore, who after two highly engaging books on Stalin wrote a sweeping history on Jerusalem down the ages, assures his readers that the Herculean stones in the foundations, which still today make up the Western Wall and in whose cracks devout believers slip their prayers written on small bits of paper, weigh six hundred tons. That seems like a lot to me, but the same Simon Sebag Montefiore cites among the exploits of King Ptolemy Philadelphus II of Egypt—the one who in the third century B.C. commissioned the Greek translation of the Jewish Scriptures known as the Septuagint—the organization of a celebration in honor of Dionysus featuring a giant leopard-pelt wineskin that contained no less than two hundred thousand gallons of wine. The reconstruction of the Temple took so much time that in Jesus' day, thirty years before Luke strolled through its courtyards, it was still considered brand-new. At the time I'm discussing, Luke doesn't yet know the response Jesus gave to his provincial disciples when they arrived at Jerusalem and were filled with wonder at so much grandeur: "Do you see all these buildings? Truly I tell you, not one stone here will be left on another; every one will be toppled." And he still doesn't know the story of the merchants Jesus chased from the immense forecourt where business was transacted. But, accustomed as he is to the gentle ardor of the synagogues, I imagine him shocked by the crowds, the pushing and shoving, the shouting, the haggling, the animals led in a din of frightened bleating while the horns sound for prayer: animals that are cut up and laid steaming on the altars for the pleasure of the great God, although, speaking through the prophet Hosea, that same God was perfectly clear about his distaste for burnt offerings. Because what he likes is purity of spirit, and Luke doesn't find anything he sees within the Temple to be very pure at all.

•

I say "the Temple": in fact, there are several enclosures, one within the next, each more sacred than the last. The center of the vortex is the Holy of Holies, the space reserved for God, which only the high priest has the right to enter once a year. When the Roman conqueror Pompey heard that, he shrugged his shoulders: I'd like to see who's going to stop me. He went in, and was surprised to see that there was nothing in the innermost sanctuary. Not a thing. He was expecting statues, or a donkey's head, because he'd been told that's what the mysterious God of the Jews was, but the room was empty. He shrugged once more, perhaps he was uncomfortable. He never spoke about it again. He suffered a cruel fate: after executing him, the Egyptians sent his head to Caesar, preserved in brine; the Jews rejoiced. Moving outward, we come to the inner courtyards, in which only the circumcised are allowed. Outside that is what's called the Court of the Gentiles, where tourists are free to enter. It's more or less like that today, except that the Temple of the Jews has become the Esplanade of the Mosques, but the Palestinians refuse to recognize that. I mean: they refuse to recognize that the Temple of the Jews once occupied the place where their mosques are situated. This is in fact one of the greatest obstacles to resolving the Israeli-Palestinian conflict, and an example of the religious craziness rampant in this city where Jews, Muslims, and Christians fight over the tiniest strip of wall or underground conduit, all affirming that they've been there the longest, which makes archaeology an extremely delicate business. In any case, it's here, in these inner courtyards and on the Court of the Gentiles, that Jesus taught and argued with the Pharisees in the last days of his life. It's here that James and the elders of the Way, although marginalized by their strange belief in the resurrection of a common criminal, continue to pray until their knees become hard like those of camels. It's here that Paul, as a very young man freshly arrived from Tarsus, followed the teaching of the Pharisee teacher Gamaliel with a fervor bordering on fanaticism. It's here that he swore to eradicate the blasphemous sect that professed the resurrection of the common criminal. And it's here that we find him twenty years later with four pious men of the sort you still run across on every corner in Jerusalem—except that today they're dressed like eighteenth-century Polish country squires—observing prescriptions that no longer have any value in his eyes but that he would no doubt have staunchly continued to observe if the incredible thing that happened to him hadn't happened. Maybe that's what he thinks about while observing these rites: the life he would have lived if that incredible thing hadn't happened, a life centered around the Temple, a pious life with camel's knees. Instead of which, stripped from himself by Christ, no more than the semblance of Paul, inhabited by Christ and giving thanks to Christ for this staggering metamorphosis, he has traveled the world for twenty years, faced a thousand dangers, converted a thousand men to this mad belief he had so abhorred, and now he once more finds himself back in the Temple, among the circumcised like himself, but at the head of a gang of uncircumcised men who, of course, aren't allowed to enter the inner courtyards and so remain in the immense Court of the Gentiles, where people arrange to meet, and where they open their eyes and ears wide.

4

Unlike the rest of the group, Timothy has become a seasoned traveler since he's been tagging along behind Paul. In his capacity as a traveling doctor, Luke has toured around Philippi and even been as far as the Asian frontier. As for the others, Sopater, Trophimus, and Aristarchus, they must not have spent much time away from home. They wander around Jerusalem like a group of tourists, not speaking the language, knowing nothing about the local customs, and there's no point counting on the local followers of the Way to serve as guides. During the meeting at James's place, none of the bearded devotees addressed so much as a word to them, or even offered them a glass of water. If someone did help them find their footing, it was the Cypriot sympathizer Mnason, on whose roof they sleep, rolled up in their flea-ridden blankets and asking themselves what on earth they're doing there.

In a film or TV series, I'd try to cast this part like the sexually ambiguous dwarf photographer who welcomes the young journalist played by Mel Gibson to Jakarta in *The Year of Living Dangerously*, filling him in on the forces that make the political situation so explosive. The Cypriot Mnason might have done Luke the same favor. That said, what I know about the political situation in Judea, and what all historians know, didn't come down to us from Mnason but from a key witness of events known as Joseph ben Matityahu to the Jews, Titus Flavius Josephus to the Romans, and to posterity merely as Josephus.

•

He, too, was in Jerusalem in A.D. 58. But there's no chance of his having rubbed shoulders with the humble Cypriot Mnason, or with Luke, or even with Paul. A Jewish aristocrat from a grand priestly family, he had done the rounds of the diverse sects of Judea—which he considered as just many philosophical schools—by the age of sixteen. After that, he'd rounded off this education with a stint in the desert. He was seen as a sort of rabbinical wunderkind, destined for a brilliant career as a religious apparatchik. He was anything but a mystic, rather someone with power and networks, a diplomat whose writings show him to be intelligent, vain, and extremely class-conscious. Later in this book I'll give an account of the tragic revolt of the Jews and the part played by Josephus. For now, it's enough to know that after the fall of Jerusalem in A.D. 70, he wrote a book called *The Jewish War*, thanks to which we know more about the history of first-century Judea than we do about that of any other people in the Empire, apart from Rome. Totally independent of the Gospels, this chronicle is in a way the reverse-angle shot, the only source with which we can cross-check them, which explains the passionate attention paid to it by specialists on the origins of Christianity. In fact, when you start working on the period, it doesn't take long to see that everyone exploits the same very limited terrain. First the Christian writings of the New Testament. Then the apocryphal writings, which were written somewhat later. The Dead Sea Scrolls. Some pagan authors, always the same: Tacitus, Suetonius, Pliny the Younger. And finally, Josephus. That's all. If there were other sources we'd know it, and what can be got out of the above texts is limited as well. With a little practice you recognize the standard explanations, spot useful perspectives, and skip over what you've read ten times before. Reading a historian, whatever his obedience, you see how he goes about his work, you identify the ingredients he's obliged to use in the taste they give to his sauce—making me think that I no longer need a cookbook, and can start cooking on my own.

5

What Josephus describes in the first chapters of *The Jewish War*, and what Mnason may have explained to Paul's disciples as they tried to make sense of Jerusalem, is a complex powder keg of colonial forces and religious nationalism. For us that's a perfectly familiar political tableau, but it wasn't at all for Luke and his companions. Asia Minor and Macedonia—where they're from—are pacified countries that have gracefully accepted the Roman yoke and adopted the Roman culture and way of life. That's true of practically all the countries in the Empire, but it's not true of Judea, because Judea is a theocracy, a religious state that places its Law above the laws imposed on it unquestioningly by the dominant world civilization. In the same way, Islamic Sharia law today runs counter to the freedom of thought and human rights that we consider acceptable, and even desirable, to everyone.

As I've already said, the Romans were proud of their tolerance. They had nothing against the gods of others. They were ready to try them the way you try exotic food, and if they liked them, to adopt them as their own. It would never have occurred to them to call them false. At worst they found them a bit rustic and provincial, and in any case the equivalent of their own with other names. Just because there are hundreds of languages, and so hundreds of words for an oak tree, that doesn't change the fact that an oak tree is an oak tree wherever you go. Everyone, the Romans thought in good faith, would agree that Yahweh was the Jewish name for Jupiter, just as Jupiter was the Roman name for Zeus.

Everyone, but not the Jews. In any case not the Jews of Judea. Those of the Diaspora were another story: they spoke Greek, read their own Scriptures in Greek, mixed with the Greeks, didn't cause trouble. But the Jews of Judea thought that only their God was the real God, and that other people's gods were idols that it was wrong, and stupid, to worship. This type of *superstitio* was inconceivable for the Romans. They would have been filled with indignation if the Jews had had the power to impose it on them. But since they didn't, the Empire tolerated their intolerance for a long time and, all things considered, showed a fair amount of tact in their regard. Just as the Egyptians could marry between brothers and sisters if they wanted, the Jews could use their own coins without Caesar's image or even without a human figure. They were exempt from military service, and the whim of Caligula, who announced in the year 40 that he would have his statue erected in the Temple, remained an isolated provocation that was taken as proof of the tyrant's madness. And in any event, he was murdered before he could follow through.

Despite these concessions, the Jews refused to be placated. They rose up on a regular basis, and kept alive the heroic memory of a bygone uprising: that of a clan of guerrilla fighters named the Maccabees. And they nurtured hopes for a revolt that would change everything. The Roman Empire believed it was eternal, but the Jews of the first century A.D. were convinced that eternity was on their side. One day, they believed, a second David would appear. He would be the Caesar of the Jews, and his reign would really be eternal. He would restore to glory those who had patiently endured offense, topple the proud and vain from their thrones, and to start with, drive out the Romans. "The main cause that had incited them to the war," wrote Josephus—himself a Jew, but one who wrote for the Romans and who, like Paul, was inclined to talk about the Jews as if he weren't Jewish himself—"was an ambiguous prophecy also found in the sacred scriptures which announced that in those days a man from their land would become master of the universe." This man would be the Messiah, the Lord's anointed, both an invincible warrior and an impassive judge. Little attention was paid to this figure in the Diaspora, and proselytes like Luke listened absentmindedly when talk came around to him. But the Jews of Judea were obsessed with him, all the more so as Rome had sent mediocre and corrupted governors who had only made things worse for the last thirty years.

•

The long second chapter of *The Jewish War* covers these thirty years that stretch, in world-historic terms, from the reign of Tiberius to that of Nero, and, in terms of the then-still-obscure story we're dealing with, from the death of Jesus to Paul's visit to Jerusalem that I'm now relating. On the local level, it covers the governorships of Pontius Pilate and his successors Felix, Festus, Albinus, and Florus. Each of these gauleiters was worse than his predecessor and, as Tacitus says with disdain, "wielded the power of a king with the soul of a slave." There were kings as well: the infamous Herodian dynasty. But they were minor, indigenous kinglets, like the maharajas in the days of the British Raj, which the colonial power liked to leave on the throne to please the population, provided they were at their beck and call. And there was a whole priestly order around the Temple. The members of this Brahman-like class were called the Sadducees. They succeeded each other from father to son, built up huge fortunes, and lent their support to the Roman authorities. Josephus hailed from an eminent Sadducee family.

Under such conditions, the chronicle of the three decades that led up to the major rebellion of the sixties is a tedious series of revolts and reprisals, corruption and blunders. Pilate distinguished himself here, Josephus tells us, by misappropriating funds intended for the Temple to finance an aqueduct, introducing military standards bearing the image of the emperor into the holy city, and covering up for a Roman soldier who had lifted his frock and shown his bare ass on the Temple court-yard during Pesach. It would be provocative, but not wrong, to say that Pilate treated the Jews the way Ariel Sharon treated the Palestinians of the territories. When the Jews protested, throwing themselves face downward in front of his residence in Caesarea and remaining there stretched out for five days and five nights, his only thought was to send in the troops. At the same time, he and his successors didn't stop raising the taxes and helping themselves to the money they gathered. And when you read in the Gospels that Jesus created a scandal by associating with publicans—that is, with tax collectors—you have to understand that these tax collectors, poor Jews paid by the Roman occupiers to extort money from Jews who were even poorer than they were, aroused far more ire than the principled hostility with which tax employees are treated the world over. They were collaborators backed up by militiamen: the scum of the earth, really.

Excessive taxes, corrupt officials, a brutal, edgy occupying force that doesn't understand the occupied country's traditions and doesn't want to either; it's a familiar scenario, and it's not hard to imagine the upshot: peasant revolts, banditry, clandestine attacks, uncontrolled national liberation movements, and—the local touch—messianic fervor. It's almost surprising that despite its relative obscurity, the Jesus affair escaped the notice of Josephus, who draws up an endless list of all the agitators, guerrillas, and false kings, the last of whom—right when Paul and his gang arrive in Judea—was a certain Egyptian who gathered together a couple of thousand peasants in a training camp in the middle of the desert. Overburdened with taxes, crushed with debt, and crazed with anger, they got it into their heads to march on Jerusalem with the Egyptian at their head. They were all massacred.

•

I can well imagine the Cypriot Mnason telling Luke this story, which had just been in the news and later made it into the Acts—the only disagreement between the Jewish historian and the Greek evangelist being the number of rebels: thirty thousand according to the first and four thousand according to the second, which tallies with the ratio that traditionally separates police estimates and those of the organizers of a demonstration, and I wonder why Luke, otherwise so willing to believe what he hears and himself not afraid to stretch the truth, was so modest on this point. I can well imagine Mnason, too, putting the unhappy tourists on their guard against the Sicarii, trendsetters in the art of urban terrorism. "They murdered people in broad daylight and in the middle of the city; especially at festivals they mixed with the crowd and struck down their opponents with small daggers, which they had hidden under their clothes," Josephus writes. "When their victims fell, the assassins melted into the indignant crowd, and entirely defied detection. Every man hourly expected death, as in war. They watched at a distance for their enemies, and not even when their friends came near did they trust them."

Oh, and then there were the zealots. One could confuse them with the Sicarii, but Josephus wants to be precise, commenting: "So these miscreants called themselves, as though they were zealous in the cause of virtue and not for vice in its basest and most extravagant form." Josephus is biased, it's true. He sees himself as a moderate, while objectively he's a collaborator who tends to present any resistance movement as a gang of thugs. That said, when he cites as an example of "zeal"—that is, the love for his God—that of the high priest Phinehas, who, having surprised an Israelite sleeping with a Midianite woman, took a spear in his hand and drove it into both of them, one tends to agree with Josephus, and with Pierre Vidal-Naquet, who, in his long and brilliant preface to the French edition of *The Jewish War*, defines the zealot "not as one who adopts a lifestyle in conformity with the Law, but one who imposes that lifestyle on everyone with every means at his disposal."

•

And there were a lot of people like that. There was at least one, named Simon, among Jesus' twelve historic disciples. These men had their reasons for being violent. They felt they'd been offended, and, in fact, they had been. None of that is new to us.

6

In getting Paul to do things that were unacceptable to him, were James and the others hoping he would rebel and break with the sect, allowing them to exclude him in turn? Were they disappointed by his good grace? Or did it make them all the more furious? These questions hide another, more serious one: Paul was denounced. And Luke—our only source on these events that none of Paul's letters otherwise document—remains hazy about the identity of those who denounced him. He talks of "Jews from the province of Asia," but you have to ask if his worst enemies weren't in reality friends of James's, and maybe even Jesus' brother himself.

Giving James the benefit of the doubt, we'll go with the "Jews from the province of Asia." The seven days of purification are reaching their end when, seeing Paul in the Temple, they point at him and shout: "Men of Israel! This is the man who preaches to all men everywhere against our people and the Law and this place; and besides he has even brought Greeks into the Temple and has defiled this holy place."

They were talking, Luke specifies, about Trophimus the Ephesian, whom they'd seen walking around the city with Paul. Luke doesn't explicitly deny the accusation, which Renan finds totally implausible: to bring an uncircumcised Greek into the sacred courtyards you'd either have to be completely oblivious to the risk or intentionally provocative, and Paul was neither. In any case, "the whole city was aroused, and the people came running from all directions. Seizing Paul, they dragged him from the temple, and immediately the gates were shut. They were trying to kill him."

In the absence of Governor Felix, who lives in Caesarea, the civil and military authority in the holy city is in the hands of the garrison commander, Claudius Lysias. Alerted to the situation, he sends in soldiers who barely manage to stop the lynching. Paul is arrested and bound in chains. He's asked who he is, what he's done, what he's accused of. But some in the mob shout one thing, others something else. Unable to question him satisfactorily because of the uproar, Lysias orders that Paul be taken to Antonia Fortress, very near the Temple, where the garrison is located. The crowd follows, shouting, "Kill him!" The soldiers have to carry the prisoner to protect him from the rabble.

"May I say something?" Paul asks the commander, who is taken aback:

"You speak Greek?" (Quite evidently Paul doesn't look like he speaks Greek.) "Then you're not the Egyptian who stirred up a revolt and led four thousand Assassins into the desert?" (The question doesn't seem very plausible: the Egyptian was executed six months earlier. I suspect Luke of dropping this information to show off his knowledge of the local situation.)

"No," Paul answers, "I'm a Jew of Tarsus, in Cilicia. Please allow me to speak to the people."

•

The scene is very lively. Reading it, you don't doubt that Luke was there. That said, those describing the Passion are lively too, and he wasn't there. The speech that follows, by contrast, is one of the long rhetorical farragoes that he loved to write—though it must be said, the same goes for all the historians of antiquity, from Thucydides to Polybius right through to Josephus, who, in his *Antiquities of the Jews*, a digest of the Bible for Roman readers, can't resist the pleasure of quoting the exact words pronounced by Abraham to his son Isaac in a famous but more soberly treated passage of Genesis—and I, too, won't resist the pleasure of quoting this deadpan comment by the English historian James H. Charlesworth: "Before sacrificing Isaac on Yahweh's command, Abraham subjects him to a long harangue, showing him that this sacrifice will hurt him a lot more than it will hurt Isaac. Isaac then responds with noble sentiments. At this point the reader is terrified that the ram, caught in the burning bush, will also hold forth with a speech of his own."

But to continue. Standing in front of the entrance to the fortress, Paul goes on to tell the angry mob everything that readers of the Acts know already—but he does it in Aramaic, not Greek, and is careful to portray himself as the most Jewish of Jews. He reminds the crowd that he studied in Jerusalem and received the strictest education on the Law from the grand Pharisee Gamaliel. That he had every bit as much love for the God of his fathers as those who want to lynch him today. That this zeal made him persecute the followers of the Way, have them chained and thrown into prison, and travel as far as Damascus to arrest them on behalf of the high priest. But then something happened to him on the road to Damascus—something that Luke has already told once and that he will tell once again after this: in all, there are three versions of the story in the Acts, with slight differences that pious exegetes have spent their entire lives shedding light on. The core version is the flash of white light, the fall, the voice that murmurs in his ear: "Saul, Saul, why are you persecuting me?" Saul, who asks, "Who are you?" and the voice that answers, "I am Jesus of Nazareth, whom you are persecuting." But in the second version, clearly destined for an audience of Orthodox Jews, instead of going into the desert alone for three years to reflect on his experience—as he tells the Greeks, to convince them that he depends on no one—this time Paul says that he had nothing more pressing to do than to return to Jerusalem and pray in the Temple. It's in the Temple, he says, within the most hallowed walls of Jewish piety, that the Lord again appeared to him and ordered him to announce the good news to the Gentiles.

"They listened to him until he said this," Luke continues, "but then they raised their voices and shouted," again demanding that the blasphemer be put to death. The commander orders that Paul be taken into the fortress, both to protect him and to question him on why they were making such an outcry against him. In line with his stubborn habit, Paul waits until he's been bound and even beaten a few times before politely asking if it's lawful to flog a Roman citizen like that. Very put out, the centurion charged with interrogating Paul informs the commander, who comes back to see the prisoner. "You're a Roman citizen?" "Yes," Paul answers, thoroughly enjoying the trouble he's got the commander into.

7

The next day the commander has done some thinking. What his troublesome prisoner has been accused of does not fall within the scope of Rome's responsibilities. So he has him freed so he can appear before the Sanhedrin: the Jews' religious tribunal. When he witnessed the events, Luke must not have had a very clear idea of just what the Sanhedrin was, but by the time he gets around to telling the story twenty or thirty years later, he's much better informed. He knows that in an identical situation Pilate sent Jesus before the Sanhedrin, and doesn't lose an occasion to bring the parallel to his readers' attention. Paul, in any event, does a better job of defending himself than Jesus did. He knows that the Sanhedrin is composed of Sadducees and Pharisees—also a distinction that Luke knew little about at the time, but that he will quickly learn to make: the Sadducees are the hereditary sacerdotal elite— powerful, corrupt, arrogant—on whom the Romans rely; the Pharisees virtuous scholars, devoted to commenting on the Law, who remain above politics and can at best be reproached for their propensity to split hairs. Paul decides to play the second off against the first. "My brothers," he says, "I am a Pharisee, the son of Pharisees; I am on trial for my hope in the resurrection of the dead." It's not true at all: he's on trial for having brought the impure Trophimus into the Temple, but he knows that the Pharisees believe in the resurrection of the dead and the Sadducees don't, and that they'll start to bicker. They do, and, unable to pass the buck, the commander has no choice but to put Paul in prison.

•

Following which, Luke tells us, forty bloodthirsty Jews swear they will neither eat nor drink until they have killed the blasphemer. To make him leave the fortress, they persuade the Sanhedrin to request that Paul be brought before the assembly again so that it may examine his case more closely—planning on murdering him on his way to the tribunal. Then who should show up but a son of Paul's sister, about whom we've heard nothing until now and will hear no more in what follows. Having caught wind of the ambush, he manages to get the news to his uncle in prison. Paul tells the centurion, who then tells the commander, and the commander, who is increasingly alarmed at the whole situation, decides to send the prisoner to Governor Felix in Caesarea. By night, well guarded (Luke counts two hundred soldiers, seventy horsemen, and two hundred spearmen, and, whatever the difference between soldiers and spearmen, that seems like a lot), along with a letter testifying to the same secular scruples as those of Proconsul Gallio in Corinth and even of Pontius Pilate: "Wanting to know the charge they were accusing him of, I brought him down before their Sanhedrin. I found out that the accusations were about disputed matters in their law, and that there was no charge that merited death or chains. When I was informed that there would be a plot against the man, I sent him to you at once, also instructing his accusers to bring charges against him before you." Nothing wrong with that: good riddance. In his presentation of the events, Luke insists on the Romans' impartiality, the Jews' fanaticism, and Paul's cleverness. As to what James is up to: total silence.

•

Felix is the governor that Tacitus described as "wielding the power of a king with the soul of a slave." He was considered corrupt and debauched, but on the other hand his wife Drusilla was Jewish and Luke says he was "well acquainted with the Way." Such curiosity in a totally marginal cult is surprising to say the least. It testifies to open-mindedness that other high state officials like Gallio did not possess, and reminds me of certain lazy, rather unreliable, low-rated diplomats I met when I was a Peace Corps worker in Indonesia, who despite all their faults were the only ones to take a real interest in the country where they'd been posted by the luck of the Foreign Service draw. Hoping to gain some time and let things calm down, Felix wisely starts by adjourning Paul's trial. He keeps him prisoner, but "lets him have some liberties." Meaning that Paul lives in one wing of his vast residence, is free to walk around guarded by a soldier, and can receive visits from friends. From time to time Felix and his wife send for him and get him to tell them about his faith and the Lord Jesus Christ. Sometimes the apostle's discourses on justice, chastity, and the coming judgment frighten the governor, and he sends Paul back to his quarters, which I imagine modest but comfortable. Luke says that Felix was hoping to squeeze a bribe out of Paul, but mentions nothing about what happened to the offerings that Paul had brought from Greece and Asia Minor. Did Paul still have them? Couldn't Felix have got his hands on them anytime he wanted?

8

These questions remain unanswered, because at this point Luke interrupts his story. More exactly, he leaves out a huge chunk of time that, after the sudden appearance of the "we" in the Acts, gave me a second door into this book.

This door too is little. You have to be attentive, or else you can walk by without seeing it. Luke writes: "Felix was also hoping that money would be given to him by Paul. For this reason he sent for him quite often and conversed with him." Then: "After two years had passed, Felix was succeeded by Porcius Festus."

Modern editions of the Bible separate these two sentences with a line, but ancient manuscripts didn't separate sentences at all; the text flowed smoothly without punctuation or even spaces between the words. Two untold years reside in this lack of spaces, and in these two untold years resides the heart of what I would like to tell.

9

Everything I've told until now is known and more or less accepted. In my own way I've done what all historians of Christianity have done for almost two thousand years: read the letters of Paul and the Acts, cross-referenced them, and corroborated what can be corroborated using the small number of non-Christian sources. I believe I've carried out this work honestly, and not misled the reader as to the likelihood of what I'm telling. For the two years Paul spent in Caesarea I've got nothing. Not a single source. I'm free—and forced—to invent.

•

Twenty years later, here is how Luke will open the tale we call his Gospel:

> Since many have undertaken to compile a narrative of the events that have been fulfilled among us, just as those who were eye-witnesses from the beginning and ministers of the word have handed them down to us, I too have decided, having carefully investigated everything from the beginning, to write it down in an orderly sequence for you, most excellent Theophilus, so that you may know the truth of the things you have been taught.

A single, winding sentence that doesn't leave out a thing and that I'm told is written in elegant Greek. It is instructive to compare it with the terse introduction of Luke's contemporary, the evangelist Mark: "The beginning of the good news about Jesus the Messiah, the Son of God" (the case is clear: if you don't agree, read something else). And then with that of the great ancient historian Thucydides in his account of the Peloponnesian War: "With reference to the narrative of events, far from permitting myself to derive it from the first source that came to hand, I did not even trust my own impressions, but it rests partly on what I saw myself, partly on what others saw for me, the accuracy of the report being always tried by the most severe and detailed tests possible. My conclusions have cost me some labor from the want of coincidence among accounts of the same occurrences by different eye-witnesses, arising sometimes from imperfect memory, sometimes from undue partiality for one side or the other."

Between Mark and Thucydides, you can see where Luke's sympathies lie. Even if he admits honestly that he is also working as a propagandist (Theophilus must know the truth about the things he has been taught), his project is that of a historian—or a reporter. He says he has "carefully investigated everything from the beginning." He says that he has conducted a thorough investigation. I see no reason not to believe him, and my project is to investigate what his investigation may have been like.

10

To recapitulate: Luke is a learned Greek attracted by the Jewish religion. Since meeting Paul, a controversial rabbi who keeps his followers in a state of exaltation, he has become a fellow traveler of this new cult, a Hellenized variant of Judaism that is not yet known by the name of Christianity. In his little Macedonian city he is one of the pillars of the group converted by Paul. When the collection takes place, he volunteers to accompany the delegation to Jerusalem. This is the voyage of his life. Paul warned his companions: The visit to the head office won't be easy. But Luke never thought it was going to be this hard, or that his mentor was as hated as he is in the holy city of the Jews. He has seen Paul accused, not by Orthodox rabbis as he expected, but by the leaders of his own sect. Subject to a humiliating ordeal, denounced, almost lynched, Paul escaped by a hairsbreadth, and now, on top of everything, he's been imprisoned by the Romans.

Luke will later tell the story in a clear and lively account in the Acts, but for now he's been tossed into the thick of things without understanding anything much at all. During these confusing, nerve-racking days, the little group of Greeks from Macedonia and Asia Minor remains holed up at Mnason the Cypriot's place. Perhaps through his nephew— the one who appears for a single sentence and never resurfaces again— they learn that Paul was secretly removed to Caesarea, the seat of the

Roman administration situated seventy-five miles from Jerusalem. His disciples follow him at a distance. I imagine they stay once again with Philip, the follower of the Way who put them up just two weeks ago—but so much has happened during those two weeks that Luke feels like it was two months ago. They wander around the ancient palace of King Herod, where the governor has now set up residence. Sparkling white, bounded by the sea on one side and by beautiful gardens with palm trees standing out against the blue sky on the other, it looks like the residences of all colonial administrators or Indian viceroys. Only a select group of locals are welcome there: Jews from the upper crust of society like Josephus, but not the likes of Luke and his comrades. Another week of uncertainty and rumors, and then things settle down. Paul remains under house arrest, with a status that's both comfortable and uncertain, less a prisoner than a political refugee to whom the authorities grant asylum and protection without overly compromising their relations with his enemies. Trotsky enjoyed exactly the same status in the various places he stayed while in exile, and Paul's life in Caesarea must have been much like that of the former generalissimo of the Red Army in Norway, Turkey, or Mexico, his last abode. Frequent walks in a restricted perimeter. Access to a limited number of people: close acquaintances who must have had to clear security; Governor Felix and his wife when the whim took them to invite him; and, from morning to night, soldiers who didn't know very well themselves if they were bodyguards or jailers, whether they should respect him like a bigwig or bully him like a prisoner. No end of reading, letter writing, and book projects to stave off the boredom, which must have weighed heavily on a man of action.

•

Paul didn't imagine that this life would last for two years. How many of his companions remained with him for the length of his stay? Who went home? Nothing is known. Luke doesn't say anything about that. But given that he resumes his tale in the first person at the end of the two years and continues to say "we," I think that he at least remained. If, as tradition tells us, he was unmarried, then no one was waiting for him at home in Philippi. He was free to prolong his stay abroad, and perhaps what he was learning, what he was beginning to understand, and the excitement he felt when two pieces of information fit together made him sense that his place was here: that a little by accident he was caught up in something major, the most important event of his time, and that it would be a shame to leave now. Maybe he kept working as a doctor in Caesarea. What I'd like to believe is that, at least at the start of his visit, he lived at the home of Philip and his four virgin daughters, and that they became friends.

11

Although the list of the twelve apostles includes one Philip, this particular Philip was not part of Jesus' immediate entourage. Did he know Jesus during his lifetime, or hear him speak? If yes, it was from afar: as an anonymous listener, lost in the crowd. By contrast, he played a vital role in the first community, the one that, against all odds, developed around the twelve in Jerusalem after their master's execution. I believe that when, in the first eight chapters of the Acts, Luke tells the story of this community up to and including Paul's entry on the scene, he will base his narrative on this Philip's testimony.

•

Its founding act is the mysterious episode at Pentecost. In fact, like many Christian celebrations, the feast the Christians celebrate under this name is a Jewish festival, Shavuot, which takes place forty-nine days after Passover. So it's less than two months after the death and—they believe—the resurrection of Jesus that his twelve companions get together on the upper floor of a friend's house, in the same room where he ate his last meal with them. Judas—who betrayed him and paid dearly for it, because according to Luke, "he bought a parcel of land with the reward for his treachery, and falling headlong, he burst open in the middle, and all his insides spilled out" (others say he hanged himself)—was replaced by a certain Matthias. They hope, they pray. Suddenly a violent gust of wind fills the house and slams the doors. Flames appear and play in the air, part, and come to rest on each of them. To their own surprise, they start speaking languages they don't know. When they walk out onto the street, the foreigners they address each hear them speak in their own language. First case of glossolalia, which as we've seen will become a common occurrence in Paul's churches.

Some of those who witness the scene will put it down to drunkenness. Others are impressed enough to convert to the strange belief held by the twelve. From this moment on Luke keeps count of the new recruits: one hundred and twenty, three thousand, five thousand—maybe he's exaggerating a little. Soon the group organizes itself into a communist microsociety. "All the believers were one in heart and mind," Luke will write about the heroic period that the Church still looks back on with nostalgia. "No one claimed that any of their possessions was their own, but they shared everything they had. There were no needy persons among them. For from time to time those who owned land or houses sold them, brought the money from the sales, and laid them at the feet of the apostles. And they were distributed to each according to need. And every day with one accord they broke their bread, with joy and sincerity of heart."

One accord, joy, and sincerity of heart are the rewards of those who join the sect without looking back or leaving themselves a way out. The *a contrario* proof is the story of Ananias and his wife, Sapphira. They sold their house and laid the money at the feet of the apostles, but kept part of it for themselves, just in case. Informed of their fraud by the Holy Spirit, Peter becomes so cross that first Ananias and then Sapphira fall down dead in front of him—which fills the whole church with fear. Luke goes on: "Many signs and wonders [healings, and not just killings] were done among the people at the hands of the apostles. As a result, people brought the sick into the streets and laid them on beds and mats so that at least Peter's shadow might fall on some of them as he passed by."

•

Good Jews as they are, the twelve remain in the Temple and pray most of the time. No one really dares to join them in public, because the healings they bring about and the belief they profess cause them, like their master before them, to have regular brushes with the religious authorities. What's most surprising is that they do all of that even though they're neither educated nor cultured, just a group of Galilean peasants who don't even speak Greek.

That said, with time, their converts include a growing number of Hellenists, as the socially and culturally higher-placed Jews are called, some of whom have lived abroad and, back in Jerusalem, attend synagogues where the Scriptures are read in Greek. The first quarrels oppose

Hebrews and Hellenistic Jews. The first community is still composed only of Jews—at the time there is still no question of Gentiles joining the movement. But the conflict, classic among all parties that start to become successful, is already visible between the founders, who benefit from the legitimacy that comes from their having been there from the start, and those who arrived later but are more educated, more dynamic, more in touch with the affairs of the world. They tend to want to take matters into their own hands and, according to the founders, believe they can do anything they want. The Hebrews start to gripe because their widows—old, illiterate women who don't dare to protest—are being neglected in the daily distribution of food. The affair is brought before the twelve, who say they've got better things to do than look after the cafeteria, and order seven men of good repute to be designated for this task. Thus is created the group of seven men, also called the deacons, who take charge of logistics—a key position, as revolutionaries know. The twelve are all Hebrews, the seven all Hellenists. Philip is one of them.

•

Another of the Hellenists is Stephen. "Filled with grace and power, performing great wonders," he's the rising star of the sect. Like Jesus in the past, and after him Paul, he's accused of blaspheming against the Temple and the Law, and brought before the Sanhedrin. He, in turn, accuses his accusers of welcoming the Holy Spirit the way their fathers welcomed the prophets throughout the history of Israel: by killing them. Hisses of anger, gnashing of teeth. Hands close around stones. His eyes lifted skyward, enraptured, Stephen sees the heavens open and the Son of Man standing at the right hand of God. With a literary skill that has all of my admiration, Luke slips this sentence into the particularly realistic account of Stephen's stoning: "The witnesses laid down their cloaks at the feet of a young man named Saul." Then, a few lines later, once Stephen had breathed his last: "Saul approved of his execution."

•

Enter the hero. A few lines later we meet him again, no longer an onlooker but an actor in his own right: "Swearing menaces and carnage, ravaging the Church, he entered house after house, dragged off men and women, and put them in prison." The violence reaches such a climax that most Hellenists flee Jerusalem and are scattered across Judea and Samaria. Only the twelve remain in the holy city, probably out of attachment to the Temple. And it's probably also during this trying time, as the ranks dwindle and only the pillars remain, that James, the brother of the Lord, begins his ascent.

Philip finds himself in Samaria, alone, obliged to start over from scratch. Samaria is a very special place. Although its inhabitants are descendants of Abraham and followers of the Law, they worship God not in the Temple but on their hillsides. The Jews in Jerusalem consider them unworthy to be called Jews, and mix with them even less than they do with the Gentiles. Philip must feel a natural affinity with these schismatic people who are used to being despised, and his teaching works wonders. It's accompanied by the usual signs and miracles: healing the crippled and casting out unclean spirits, which "screamed as they left their victims."

All of chapter 8 of the Acts is dedicated to Philip's exploits in Samaria. Whether it's because starting his missionary career among these schismatics makes him particularly open-minded or because Luke credited him with this innovation after the fact, he's the first Christian of the New Testament to take the leap and convert a Gentile. Not a Greek, but an Ethiopian eunuch: a high dignitary in his country, interested enough in Judaism to have come on a pilgrimage to Jerusalem. Philip sees him on the road to Gaza, sitting in his chariot and reading Isaiah the prophet. Inspired by the Spirit, Philip proposes to help him understand what he is reading. The passage is about the mysterious character the prophet calls "a man of suffering." "Like a lamb he was led to the slaughter," and through him God wants to accomplish the salvation of the world. Philip explains that this "man of suffering" is Jesus, whose story he outlines broadly. At the first water they come to, he baptizes the new convert.

•

Philip must have been a bit of a maverick, one of those men of action who prefer to work alone without having to answer to the head office. He must have been wary of people like James—and James of people like him—which explains why he gave a good welcome to the black sheep Paul in Caesarea, where he had set up shop. He must have been one of the rare first members of the movement who, twenty years after

Paul watched over the clothes of those who had stripped down in order to stone Stephen, were aware of the apostle's past and were inspired by his having become what he had become.

12

Luke must have learned all of the stories about the early Church, which he will tell in the first part of the Acts little by little, during his conversations with Philip. But I think that very early on he must have felt a sense of shock in Philip's company, and that, with him, he first realized that this Christ about whom Paul was continually talking—this Christ who lived in Paul and whom Paul nurtured inside everyone he converted, this Christ whose death and resurrection would save the world and at the same time bring about its end—had been a man of flesh and blood, who had lived on this earth and trodden these paths not even twenty-five years earlier.

In a way he'd always known it. Paul had never denied it. But what he said about it was so immense, so abstract, that all the while believing that of course Jesus had existed, Luke couldn't help thinking that he'd existed like Hercules or Alexander the Great, in a space and time that were not those of the people who lived today. Already, Luke must have only made a hazy distinction between Hercules and Alexander the Great. I think it would have been asking too much of him—and of most of his contemporaries—to differentiate clearly between mythology and history. More common were the notions of near and far, human and divine, day-to-day and supernatural, and when Luke listened to Philip, everything about Jesus suddenly went from the second order to the first, which made a huge difference.

·

I try to imagine their conversations. Philip, older and wizened, was curious to know about the path that led a Macedonian doctor as far as the fig tree in front of his little house in Caesarea. Luke, more timid, is full of questions that he doesn't dare ask at the start, and becomes bolder bit by bit. An idea occurs to me. What if the first story he heard was the last one in the book he'll later write: the meeting at Emmaus? He only names one of the two travelers. What if the other was Philip? What if Philip told it to him under the fig tree?

13

The text speaks of two disciples. Philip isn't a disciple in a strict sense. He's not one of the Galileans. He's just a young man who heard Jesus talk in Jerusalem. What Jesus said, which was unlike anything that was known at the time, filled him with enthusiasm. Each day he returned to the Temple to hear him speak. He thought of undergoing the rite of baptism by which you really became one of his disciples, but he didn't have time. Everything took place in a couple of hours: arrest, trial, sentencing, punishment. Philip wasn't there, he only heard rumors that shocked him profoundly. The day of Passover, which marks for Israel the flight out of Egypt, the liberation of the soul, and the greatest rejoicing, he spends shut away at home steeped in fear and shame. Philip and his friend Cleopas, another sympathizer, decide to leave Jerusalem for their hometown, Emmaus, on the first day of the week—the one the Christians will call Sunday—to get away for a couple of days. It's on the road that leads to the sea, two hours' walk. They leave in the afternoon, planning on arriving for dinner.

On the way, a traveler draws near. He could speed up and pass them, or slow down so they can overtake him, but no, he walks alongside them, close enough so that it's difficult not to strike up a conversation. He asks them why they look so sad. "You must be the only person in Jerusalem who doesn't know about the things that happened there in the last few days," Cleopas says. "What sort of things?" the stranger asks. He must be a foreigner visiting Jerusalem for Passover, they think. "About Jesus of Nazareth," they replied. "He was a prophet, powerful in word and deed before God and all the people. We thought he was the one who would deliver Israel. But our high priests handed him over to the Romans to be sentenced to death. He was crucified the day before yesterday."

The three walk on in silence. Then Cleopas repeats something he heard before setting out. In the alley where he lives, one neighbor said to another: Some women who had come from Galilee with Jesus wanted to cleanse his body that morning. They went to the tomb with perfume and herbs, and he was gone. The only thing that remained was the bloodstained sheet on which he'd been carried. The women ran to tell the news to the other Galileans. At first they said they were crazy, then they took a look for themselves, and sure enough, the body was no longer there. "Maybe other disciples took it and buried it," Philip suggests. "Maybe . . ." At which point the traveler who seemed so uninformed starts quoting passages of the Law and the Prophets, proving that in fact he knows very well who Jesus was, and that he even knows more about him than they do.

At Emmaus, he wants to continue on his way. Philip and Cleopas detain him. "Stay with us," they insist, "it's getting dark." It's not just that they're hospitable. They don't want the stranger to go, they're almost afraid that he will. Although obscure, his words comfort them. As he talks, they start to feel that this horrible, disheartening disaster could be seen as something other than a horrible, disheartening disaster. The man sits down to eat with them. He takes the bread, and says a few words of benediction when breaking it. He gives a piece to each, and when he does, Philip understands. He looks at Cleopas. He sees that Cleopas has understood as well.

•

Did the three stay there for a minute, or for an hour? Philip can't remember. He also can't remember if they ate. What he does remember is that they didn't speak, that he and Cleopas didn't stop looking at the stranger, in the light of the candle that had been lit because they could hardly see a thing. Finally he got up, thanked them, and left, and for a long time Cleopas and Philip didn't exchange a word. They felt good, they'd never felt so good. After that, they talked all night. They compared what they had felt, and whereas each one thought that his experience was unique, they were astonished to learn that they had felt the same thing at the same moment. It had started on the road when the traveler had quoted the Scriptures, and spoken of the Son of Man who must have suffered greatly before he could enter into his glory. It rose up softly within them, this sensation that something extraordinary was taking place. However, neither of them had thought that it was *him*. That didn't occur to them. And there was no reason why it should have, because physically he didn't look at all like him. It was only when he gave them the bread that it all became clear. They were no longer sad, not at all. And although it was strange, they admitted to each other that they thought they'd never be sad again. That sadness was over.

And it's true, Philip said to Luke under the fig tree: I've never been sad again.

14

Just as there was necessarily a first encounter between Luke and Paul, a meeting whose details I imagined but that is not imaginary, there was definitely one between Luke and a direct witness of the life of Jesus. I call this witness Philip, because in reading the Acts attentively it seems plausible to me, and I imagine how overwhelming this meeting must have been for Luke. Until now, he thought that Paul knew everything. In any case, that no one knew more about Jesus. And now he's just spent an evening with a man who's not even very old, who talks about him familiarly, and who's honest enough to say that he didn't know him very well—but that of course there were people who did. "Could I meet some?" Luke asks. "Of course," Philip answers. "I can introduce you, if you like. You have to be careful, because as a goy and Paul's traveling companion many people won't trust you. What's more, my word won't open all the doors: I don't have a very good reputation, you know. But you look like someone who knows how to listen. You don't spend your time thinking about what you're going to say when other people are talking: it should be all right."

•

I imagine the night that Luke spent after this conversation. The insomnia, the elation, the hours spent walking through Caesarea's regular, white streets. What allows me to imagine this are the moments when I've been struck by an idea for a book. I think of the night that followed the death of my sister-in-law Juliette and our visit to her friend Étienne, which became my book *Lives Other Than My Own*. An impression of utter self-evidence. I had witnessed something that had to be told, it was up to me and no one else to tell it. Then this self-evidence fades, often you lose it altogether, but if it doesn't appear for at least a moment, nothing can be done at all. I know you have to beware of projections and anachronisms, but I'm certain that there was a moment when Luke said to himself that this story had to be told, and that he would tell it. That fate had put him in the right place to gather the statements of the witnesses: first of all Philip, then others to whom Philip would introduce him. And that he would conduct research of his own.

•

He must have asked himself a thousand questions. For years he had taken part in ritual meals commemorating the Lord's Last Supper. By eating bread and drinking wine, those present had entered a mysterious communion with him. But this last meal, which he had always imagined taking place in a sort of Olympus suspended between the earth and the sky, or more likely that he had never imagined at all, had taken place twenty-five years earlier, he suddenly realized, in a real room in a real house, in the presence of real people. He, Luke, would have to enter this room and speak with these people. In the same way, he knew that before being resurrected, the Lord had been crucified. Hung on a tree, in Paul's words. Luke knew perfectly well what crucifixion was; it was practiced all across the Roman Empire. He had seen crucified bodies on the side of the road. He knew that there was something strange and even scandalous about worshipping a god whose body had been subjected to this shameful torture. But he had never asked himself why he had been condemned, under what circumstances, and by whom. Paul didn't dwell on the subject, he said "by the Jews," and, as all of Paul's troubles had to do with the Jews, Luke didn't linger on the subject either, or ask any more specific questions.

•

Maybe I'm on thin ice here, but I imagine that in the course of this night when his project came to him, still vague but dazzlingly self-evident, he thought about Paul, and that, without really knowing why, he felt somewhat guilty. As if, following the trace of the real Christ who had lived in Galilee and Judea, and seeking out those who had known him, he was betraying the announcement that Paul guarded so jealously. If there was one thing Paul could not stand, it was when people listened to preachers other than him, particularly if they were Jews. To make him happy, you had to put in earplugs and only take them out again when he opened his mouth. Luke liked listening to Paul, and if it made Paul happy, he was ready to plug his ears when an Athenian educator or an Alexandrian rabbi like Apollos started to talk. But he wasn't going to stop listening to Philip for anything in the world. And he knew very well that, even if the two men respected each other, even if Paul praised Philip's open-mindedness, he would not like to find out that Luke had turned to Philip to discover more about Jesus.

•

Luke really didn't have a head for abstract ideas. He was interested in quarrels between real people with real names, people he knew. And he was even more interested when they buried the hatchet, because he liked it when people made up. But big theological developments were over his head. What he liked was when someone forgave someone else's offenses, or when a simple Samaritan behaved better than a Pharisee who was full of his own virtue. But he couldn't suppress a yawn when talk came around to atoning or forgiving sins—or, in any case, to what is translated as that. Of course you can always say it's the fault of the translations, but in Greek too, it's abstract and unconnected to everyday life. What he liked most about what Philip told him were the concrete details: the two guys returning home with heavy hearts, the dust on the road, the exact distance between Jerusalem and their village, and the gate they left by. It was the idea that this Philip standing in front of him had himself stood in front of Jesus. I imagine that before falling asleep, as day broke on his night of insomnia and clairvoyance, Luke asked himself: What did he look like?

•

He had a face: the people who had known him could describe it. If Luke asked Philip about it, he'd be glad to answer. Did he ask him? If he did, why does his Gospel bear no trace of the answer? I know, I know: because such concerns are completely foreign to the literary genre Luke had adopted, and to the sensitivities of his time. In the same way, there are no physical descriptions of emperors, consuls, or governors in the works of Tacitus or Josephus. Sure, there were busts, but that's something else. So I won't push the issue, lest I commit an anachronism. But still: I have a hard time imagining that Luke, who had a love for detail and was passionately interested in Jesus the person, never asked himself if Jesus was big or small, handsome or ugly, bearded or smooth-chinned, and that he didn't ask others in turn. Maybe it's the answer that's difficult to understand.

15

The tales of Jesus' appearance on the day after the Sabbath that the Christians will call Sunday differ from evangelist to evangelist, but even while differing they tally with one another. First one woman, or group of women, arrives early in the morning at the tomb to anoint the body. John says it was Mary Magdalene alone, Matthew says that Mary Magdalene was accompanied by another woman also named Mary, Mark and Luke add a third. All four agree that they are very astonished because the body is no longer there.

Starting from here, John is the most precise—so precise and rich in details that you want to believe he was there, that what you're reading really is the testimony of the "disciple whom Jesus loved." Mary Magdalene runs to find Peter and "the other disciple"—the one Jesus loved—and says to them: "They have taken the Lord from the tomb, and we don't know where they put him." The two men decide to go look. They also run, the other disciple faster than Peter. He arrives first at the tomb—which is described as a cave dug into the rock. But he doesn't go in. He waits for Peter, who goes in and sees the burial clothes. Then when he goes in, the other disciple "sees and believes," which you have to admit is a little hasty, because all there is to see is the absence of a body—an intriguing absence that called for an explanation, but not one that would immediately prompt people to think that the body had risen from the dead. What's more, he must have kept the idea to himself, because the two men return home puzzled, but no more than that.

•

Mary Magdalene remains near the tomb, weeping. In John, she sees two angels in white robes sitting there calmly, one where Jesus' head had been, and the other in the place of his feet. In Matthew, there's just one angel but he descends from heaven in a peal of thunder. His appearance is like lightning and his clothing white as snow, and at the sight of him the guards shake for fear and fall like dead men. In Luke, there are two men clothed in dazzling garments. And in Mark, as always the most understated, there's a young man dressed in a white robe. In John, the angels stick to asking Mary why she's weeping. In the other three, they announce to the women that Jesus has risen from the dead.

As beautiful as the words of these angels are (according to Luke: "Why do you seek the living among the dead?"), I find them less beautiful than the scene that follows, and in which, according to John, they don't take part. Having told the angels why she's weeping, Mary Magdalene turns around and sees Jesus standing there, but she doesn't know it's Jesus. "Why are you crying?" he asks her in turn. "Who are you looking for?" Thinking he's the gardener, she answers: "If you have taken my Lord away, tell me where you have put him, and I will go and get him." Jesus then says: "Mary." Because he says her name, and because he says it in a certain way, she opens her eyes wide and murmurs in Aramaic: "Rabboni," which, John explains to his Greek readers, means "Teacher." She throws himself at his feet. Jesus says: "Do not hold on to me, for I have not yet ascended to the Father. Go instead to my brothers and tell them."

Mark says that Mary and the others said nothing to anyone, "because they were afraid"—these are the last words of his account. Luke says that they went to see the others, who didn't believe their story because they thought it was nonsense. Matthew says that the guards who fell down as if dead rose up to tell the chief priests "everything that had happened"—without our learning if that meant simply the disappearance of the body, the angel's passage, or, already, a resurrection. In any event, the chief priests were troubled by the news, and, after taking counsel, they gave money to the guards to say that after the agitator was crucified, his partisans came at night and stole his body. This urban legend, Matthew adds, "has circulated among the Jews to the present day"—and not just among the Jews: Renan, too, does not exclude it from his hypotheses.

•

It's late afternoon on the same Sunday when the meeting at Emmaus—told only by Luke—takes place. After the mysterious traveler has left them, Cleopas and the person I think was Philip decide to go back to Jerusalem. That very evening they take the same road in the opposite direction and find the eleven in the upper room. There, writes John, who also relates the scene, they hole up "for fear of the Jews." All of a sudden Jesus appears in their midst and says, Shalom, peace be with you. They are frightened, and think they're seeing a spirit. Luke says that Jesus invites them to touch him, and that after letting himself be touched he asks them something a spirit would never ask: if there's anything to eat. Yes, a little fish, which they share with him.

•

This fish meal also comes in the final scene of John, the one that brought about my conversion when read by Father Xavier in his chalet in Le Levron: the apostles fishing on the Sea of Tiberias, the stranger who calls out to the fishermen from the shore and tells them to cast their nets, and Peter, who tucks in his garment, jumps into the sea to greet the stranger, whom he has recognized, and then makes a fire with twigs to grill the fish.

•

The most striking thing about these stories is that no one recognizes him at first. At the tomb, he's the gardener. On the road, a traveler. On the shore, a stranger who asks the fishermen, "Any bites?" It's not him, and, strangely, that's what makes him recognizable. He's what they had always wanted to see, hear, and touch, but not the way they thought they would see, hear, and touch him. He's everyone, he's no one. He's the first to come along and the last to draw attention to himself. The very person he was talking about when he said this sentence that they must have remembered: "I was hungry and you gave me no food, I was thirsty and you gave me no drink, in prison and you did not care for me." Maybe they also remembered this striking statement, which was preserved not in the Gospels but in an apocryphal text: "Cleave the wood: I am there. Lift the stone, and you will find me there. Look at your brother: you see your god."

•

What if that's why no one described his face?

16

All of this is confused, but I find this confusion realistic. If you question the witnesses of a crime, you always find the same sort of inconsistencies, contradictions, and exaggerations, which only get larger the farther you are from the source. And a good example of someone who's far from the source is Paul. In his First Letter to the Corinthians, Paul draws up a list of the people Jesus appeared to after his death. The list is personal, to say the least, and includes Jesus' own brother James, although the two had their differences, and even "more than five hundred brothers at once." Some have died since, Paul specifies, others are still alive. Subtext: You can go see them yourselves, and ask them what you like. Luke was close to Paul and certainly aware of this testimony, and he could have done just that. He didn't. Either that, or he did and it came to nothing, the five hundred brothers boiled down to ten or so—which is neither more nor less convincing.

•

Luke wasn't a modern investigator. Even if he insists that he has "carefully investigated everything from the beginning," I have to resist the temptation to put into his mouth questions I would ask myself, and which I would try to put to others if I visited the place where such strange things had happened twenty-five years earlier and a good number of witnesses were still alive: How many women discovered that Jesus' body was gone? One, two, three? Were they believed on the spot? And just what did people believe? Once it became clear that the body was no longer in the tomb, why was the realistic hypothesis that it had been removed dropped so soon in favor of the extravagant one of Jesus' resurrection? And who could have removed it? The Roman authorities, to stop a cult from forming around his body, like the U.S. Navy commandos who eliminated Osama bin Laden? A group of pious disciples, to pay a last tribute to their teacher, who then provoked the whole fuss by forgetting to let the others know? A group of scheming disciples, who knowingly organized the colossal imposture that later prospered under the name of Christianity?

17

"No one can know what happened to Horselover Fat," Philip K. Dick said about his alter ego, "but one thing that is certain is that something happened to him."

No one knows what happened on that day of Passover, but one thing that is certain is that something happened.

•

When I say that no one knows what happened, I'm wrong. What happened is very well known, only: it's one of two different and incompatible things according to what you believe. If you're a Christian, you know that Jesus was raised from the dead: that's what being a Christian means. Or you believe what Renan believed, and what reasonable people believe. That a small group of women and men—the women first—deeply stricken by the loss of their guru, started spreading the word that he'd been resurrected, and that what happened next was not at all supernatural but astonishing enough to be worth telling in detail: their naïve, bizarre belief that should normally have withered and died with them went on to conquer the world, and is still shared by roughly one-quarter of the earth's population.

•

I suspect that when this book appears I'll be asked: "Okay, but really, are you Christian or aren't you?" I could beat around the bush, and say that if I put so much work into this book it was precisely so as not to have to answer the question. To leave it open, and let everyone decide for themselves. That would be just like me. But I prefer to answer.

No.

No, I don't believe that Jesus was resurrected. I don't believe that a man came back from the dead. But the fact that people do believe it— and that I believed it myself—intrigues, fascinates, troubles, and moves me—I don't know which verb is the most appropriate. I'm writing this book to avoid thinking that now that I no longer believe, I know better than those who do, and better than my former self when I believed. I'm writing this book to avoid coming down too firmly in my favor.

18

Another thing must have bugged Luke. A respectful subject of the Empire, he approved of its administration and the peace it provided. And although he wasn't Roman himself, he was proud of Rome's power. Neither he nor his Macedonian compatriots had the slightest nationalistic aspirations or indulgence for rebels. These they lumped together with highway robbers, and applauded when they were crucified for stirring up trouble. It had been all the easier for Paul to win them over in that he never spoke of revolt. On the contrary, he invited everyone to remain where they were and strictly abide by the laws. Each time he had fallen afoul of the Jews, the Roman authorities had bailed him out. That had been the case in Corinth with the wise Governor Gallio, and again in Jerusalem when the soldiers from the garrison saved him from being lynched. Even if Governor Felix was a bit of a shady character, it was to him that Paul owed his safe abode in Caesarea.

To believe Philip, however, those who followed Jesus during his lifetime had hoped he would deliver Israel from the Romans, and it's for this reason that the Romans had sentenced him. He said that as if it were common knowledge. He didn't seem to find it at all surprising that while Jesus was the Son of Man and the savior awaited by all men—including those who didn't know it—on the one hand, on the other he was the leader of a rebel movement, comparable to other leaders and other groups whose names and exploits he cited: the Maccabees, Theudas, Judas of Galilee, the Egyptian, in short all those who had taken up arms and harassed and ambushed the Roman cohorts—all of whom, incidentally, came to a bad end.

Luke had heard Mnason the Cypriot name some of these names that we know thanks to Josephus. He got them mixed up: for him they were all part of an exotic, somewhat menacing folklore. Aghast, he said: "You're talking about Jesus? Jesus Christ?" Philip answered: "Yes, that is, Christ is what you Greeks call him. That's what they call him in Antioch. Here we call him the *Mashiah*, or Messiah, and the Messiah is the king of the Jews. The one who will deliver the Jews from their bondage, as Moses delivered them from their slavery to the Pharaoh."

On the cross where Jesus died, the centurion charged with the execution had nailed a sign exposing the victim to the mockery of passersby as "Jesus, king of the Jews." A miscalculation: the passersby didn't mock him. Apart from a few of the high priest's accomplices, most of the people in Jerusalem sympathized with the resistance, even if they didn't have the courage to take part in it themselves. Those who had believed that Jesus was the Messiah were cruelly disappointed. Those who hadn't believed were filled with pity. None had the heart to mock him. He had tried and failed. The horror and injustice of his torture confirmed that the revolt had been justified. All that was proved by the sign, and the cross, and the poor man suffering on the cross, was the arrogance of the Romans.

•

This question of whether the Jews or the Romans were responsible for the death of Jesus is a minefield. It comes up regularly, for example in Mel Gibson's strange naturalist film *The Passion of the Christ*. Nevertheless, the Gospel narratives—and the reasons for the hostility Jesus elicits—seem perfectly coherent on this point. Not content to be an extremely popular healer, he provokes the official religion and its representatives time and again. He shrugs his shoulders at their rites and rituals. He takes a lax attitude to the Law. He scoffs at the hypocrisy of the virtuous.

He doesn't condemn eating pork, but he does condemn those who bad-mouth their neighbors. To this already extensive record he adds a major scandal in the Temple as soon as he gets to Jerusalem, overturning tables, harassing the merchants, and, as we'd say today, holding the customers hostage. As a result it's no longer just his previous enemies, the Pharisees, but also the Sadducee high priests who, on hearing of this new provocation, decide that its author must die. As he's charged with blasphemy, Jesus is to be stoned. Since the Sanhedrin doesn't have the power to pronounce a death sentence, it takes the matter before the Roman authorities, being careful to present it not as a religious dispute—like Gallio in Corinth, Pontius Pilate would send them packing—but as a political one. Although he never explicitly claimed he was the Messiah, Jesus never denied it either. At the very least he didn't stop people from addressing him as such. Messiah means king of the Jews, and that means rebel. This crime requires the death penalty, and Pilate will drag his feet but he won't have any choice. He has no doubt that, at worst, Jesus is no more than an enemy of the Law, but his file was put together in such a way as to convincingly portray him as an enemy of Rome.

The Gospels disagree on the details about what was said before the Sanhedrin, and then before Pilate, but in the main their accounts of the trials before the Jewish and Roman tribunals coincide. Most historians, Christian or not, go along with this version, which is also that of the Church and Mel Gibson's film. On the Jewish side, incidentally, the Talmud substantiates it as well. Certain rabbis whose opinions it compiles go as far as saying that the death sentence was pronounced by the Sanhedrin, and don't even mention the role played by Pilate: in short, the Jews not only condemned Jesus, they boast about it too.

•

However there's another, relatively recent version of the story, whose most radical proponent is a professor named Hyam Maccoby. This counter-version seeks to denounce the fiction according to which the Jewish authorities had Jesus sentenced, and, by extension, to condemn the Christian anti-Semitism it has relatively little difficulty identifying in the New Testament. It's in the name of this version that Mel Gibson's film is accused of anti-Semitism. I find it stimulating, if not convincing, and I'd like to take the time to sum up its arguments.

The Pharisees, Hyam Maccoby starts by explaining, were not at all the hypocritical mandarins that the Gospels make them out to be—that is, the adversaries and ultimately the accusers of Jesus—but pious and wise men, reputed for their ability to see how each person is different, their flexibility in adapting the Torah to everyday problems, and their tolerance for divergent opinions. More peaceful than Jesus, whom Maccoby portrays as an anticolonialist agitator, they nonetheless took a sympathetic view of his political struggle. On the spiritual and moral level, they pretty much agreed with him, and when small differences did arise, they talked them through without animosity, as is shown by a scene imprudently preserved by Mark before Matthew rewrote it in conformity with what had by then become the dominant ideology, that is, as an acrimonious quarrel. In fact, Jesus and the Pharisees got along fine together, because they all loved and observed the Law. And their mutual enemies, after the Romans, were the Sadducee collaborators, those arrogant, sold-out priests, traitors to the Jewish nation and religion.

Each time the word "Pharisee" designates a bad guy in the Gospels, according to Maccoby, you have to read "Sadducee," more or less the way you use the search-and-replace function of a word-processing program. Why such deceit? Because, flying in the face of historical reality, the evangelists decided to paint Jesus as rebelling against the Jewish religion, and not against the Roman occupation. The historical reality is that he was a sort of Che Guevara whom the Romans—seconded by their Sadducee straw men and not by the good Pharisees—arrested and executed with their customary brutality as soon as the public order was threatened. In short: on this account, what the evangelists present as a travesty of the truth is in fact the truth.

There's an easy explanation for why they pushed through this revisionist version. Paul's churches wanted to please the Romans, and the fact that their Christ was crucified on the orders of a Roman governor posed a serious problem. They couldn't deny the brute facts, but they did all they could to reduce their significance. Forty years later they explained that Pilate's hand had been forced, and that even if the formal sentencing and execution had been carried out by the Romans, the instigation and the true responsibility lay with the Jews, who were from then on all lumped together. "The Pharisees and the Sadducees," say Matthew, Mark, and Luke, as if they walked around hand in hand the whole time. John simply says "The Jews." The enemy camp. The birth of Christian anti-Semitism.

19

Behind this counter-version hides a counter-portrait of Paul, about whom Hyam Maccoby wrote a book called *The Mythmaker.* The key idea is as follows: if Jesus, whom the Gospels present as the sworn enemy of the Pharisees, in fact sympathized with them, Paul, who says he was a Pharisee and the son of Pharisees, was no such thing. Not only was he not a Pharisee, he wasn't even Jewish.

Paul? Not Jewish? Let's take a closer look.

•

Born into a pagan family in Syria, the young Saul, according to Maccoby, was influenced both by Oriental mystery religions and Judaism, which fascinated him. Ambitious and tormented, he dreamed of being a prophet, or at least a high-profile Pharisee—a major intellectual like Hillel, Shammai, or Gamaliel. It's possible, Maccoby concedes, that he did go to a Pharisee school in Jerusalem, as he never missed a chance to point this out. But it certainly wasn't Gamaliel's, because they took only very highly placed students, and that wasn't Paul's case. Maccoby dedicates an entire chapter to showing that the rabbinical character of Paul's argumentation in his letters, on which all commentators agree, is a pure invention: in fact, Paul was a lousy rabbi who would have flunked the first year of any yeshiva.

Vexed and resentful—still according to Maccoby—the young Saul saw that he wouldn't get very far in this way, so he turned to the Sadducees. He even entered the service of the high priest as a mercenary, or hatchet man. Only such a version can explain the fact that he had the power to persecute the partisans of this guerrilla fighter who, according to a strange rumor, came back to life after the Romans killed him on the cross. A clandestine resistance movement, a charismatic, martyred leader who could be dead and could be alive: according to this scenario, the morose Paul is an auxiliary on the payroll of the occupying force. Now, all of a sudden, we have no problem understanding how he could have people chained, put them in prison, and even hunt them down in Damascus, a nonoccupied zone—which would have been simply impossible for the Pharisee he subsequently pretended to have been: the Pharisees had no policing powers, and if they did, they would never have used them against people with whom they were so closely allied. And patently, these reprehensible activities clashed with the high idea this young man, who liked to see himself as a prophet among the Jews and now winds up doing the dirty work of a local gauleiter, had of himself. As he will say very much to the point later on: "What I do, I do not understand. For I do not do what I want, but I do what I hate."

Nothing is more foreign to Judaism, Maccoby rightly observes, than this sense of guilt and despair based on the experience that human effort is useless and that there is an unbridgeable gap between what the Law demands and what the sinner can achieve. The Torah is made for man, it's scaled to him, and all of the Pharisees' interpretative work aimed at tailoring it to each person's possibilities. By contrast, Paul's famous statement perfectly describes a man who has tried to become Jewish without success: a failed convert, covered in shame. This horrible distress and interior conflict are resolved on the road to Damascus. The divided ego, an enemy to itself, experiences a deep and radical transformation after which a totally new life begins. Totally new, but rooted in the superstitions of his childhood, in mystery religions in which gods like Osiris or Baal-Taraz—who gave his name to Saul's native city, Tarsus—die and are reborn. Such a belief circulated about the rebel whose partisans Saul persecuted. And it's over this belief that Paul came to hold sway.

Strictly speaking, according to Maccoby, Paul wasn't a convert. For him to convert it would have been necessary for Christianity to exist, which wasn't the case. Like Moses, whom he could not have failed to think of, Paul withdrew into the Arabian Desert after his incredible experience and came back with *his* religion. The strange thing in all of this is that he broke neither with the small Galilean sect, nor with Judaism: to construct his edifice he continued to refer to this obscure, rustic Jew whom everyone would certainly have forgotten without him, and ran the risk—which was nothing less than suicidal when you think about it—of returning to Jerusalem and presenting himself alone and unarmed to the members of the resistance network whose comrades he had had arrested, tortured, and executed. Maybe he ran this crazy risk because, despite everything, he remained sentimentally attached to Israel.

Maybe it was because he understood that rather than basing his mutant religion on nothing more than his own personality, it was better to give it a historical foundation going back to the dawn of time. And maybe, finally (here I'm doing the talking, not Hyam Maccoby), because he wanted to test whether his former victims had learned Jesus' lesson that you should love your enemies and pray for those who persecute you.

That exercise must have been difficult. In the following years (back to Maccoby now) Paul's duplicity is extreme. On the one hand, he tries to promote *his* Gospel, as he says, in a pagan environment. The proselytes provide favorable terrain for an increasingly extravagant theological invention, with Jesus becoming a cosmic divinity, a universal redeemer, a sort of myth, and a ritual focusing on a completely pagan ceremony that was totally foreign and even repugnant to the disciples of the real Jesus: the Eucharist. On the other hand, Paul's obsession with not breaking with the headquarters forces him to demonstrate his orthodoxy by prevaricating, lying, and pretending—all evidence to the contrary—that he is very attached to the Law. That goes wrong the first time, and even more wrong the second. The rupture is consummated. Nonetheless, it's Paul who wins out, because, as we'll soon see, the Temple is destroyed, Israel as a nation is annihilated, and the church of Jerusalem dispersed. Its traditions will only survive in little lost sects in the desert; nevertheless, Hyam Maccoby affirms that they are more reliable than anything written in the New Testament.

•

That's because the New Testament—he says—is nothing more than history written by the victors, the result of a huge falsification aimed at having people believe that Paul and his new religion are the inheritors of Judaism and not its detractors. That despite minor differences of opinion, Paul was accepted, appreciated, and adopted as a minister by the church of Jerusalem. That although Jesus didn't like the Pharisees, like Paul he respected the Romans. That Jesus didn't engage in politics, that his kingdom was not of this world, and that like Paul he taught the respect for authority and the pointlessness of all revolt. That in calling himself the Messiah, Jesus wasn't at all talking about a worldly kingdom, but about a nebulous identification with God, or with the Logos. That the only good Jews are those who believe they are no longer subject to the Law. And, finally, that Paul is the only one who knows the real Jesus' deepest thoughts, precisely because he never knew him in his earthly, imperfect, muddled incarnation, but as the Son of God, and because all historical facts that risked compromising this dogma must not only be declared wrong but also—which is more surefire—erased altogether.

This, Maccoby holds, is the lie that established itself two thousand years ago, with the success that we know. The few dissenting voices were silenced: whether they belonged to the little sects descended from the church of Jerusalem—the only ones to know what really happened and to uphold it in their traditions—or, within the dominant Church, to an honest and logical-minded Pauline like Marcion, who in the second century wanted to put an end to the fiction according to which Christianity is the continuation of Judaism, and sought to rid the Bible of the Jewish Scriptures. Then, finally, after two thousand years of darkness, Professor Maccoby appeared.

•

I've summed up these views, I don't subscribe to them. Passing off two thousand years of Church history as complete revisionism strikes me as the height of revisionism. I think that Maccoby is right to insist that the Pharisees were very wise, virtuous people, but that he's wrong to conclude that Jesus couldn't have clashed with them. If he did, it's *precisely because they were wise and virtuous*, and because his heart went out to sinners, losers, those who were disappointed in themselves, and not to the wise and virtuous. I also think Maccoby is right—a thousand times over—to denounce Christian anti-Semitism, but that he's wrong to claim, all testimony to the contrary and in a purely ideological way, that Jesus was sentenced by the Romans without the Jews having anything to do with it. That's as absurd as accusing Plato of being anti-Athenian or anti-democratic because he shows Socrates being sentenced by the Athenian democracy. Both cases involve free, paradoxical, uncontrollable men who clash with the major institutions of their day: the one with the Greek city, the other with the Jewish theocracy. Affirming that is neither anti-democratic nor anti-Semitic. As to the portrait of Paul as a goy informer to the secret police, I find it picturesque, but all things considered less rich, less complex, less Dostoyevskian than the one that emerges from his letters if you approach them simply on the basis that he's telling the truth.

•

What is true, however, is that this type of rumor circulated about Paul among James's entourage: that he wasn't even Jewish; that he had himself circumcised out of love for the daughter of the high priest in Jerusalem; that this operation, performed by an amateur, was botched and left him impotent; that the high priest's daughter mocked him cruelly; and that out of spite he started writing furious pamphlets against circumcision, the Sabbath, and the Law. And, finally—the height of villainy— that he embezzled the money collected by his churches to buy the favor of Governor Felix—something Hyam Maccoby doesn't fail to accuse him of as well.

Yes, everything Hyam Maccoby says was also said in a less elaborate way in the church of Jerusalem. Luke must have got wind of it and been troubled by what he heard.

20

Luke retained a painful memory of the week he spent in Jerusalem, but after everything Philip told him, he must have dreamed of nothing but going back. Not knowing what to look for, he hadn't seen anything. Now he wanted to see with his own eyes the site of the crucifixion, the tomb the women had found empty, and above all the mysterious upper room where Philip and Cleopas, after returning hastily from Emmaus, had found the eleven assembled, troubled by the rumor that Jesus had been seen alive. It's in this room that he appeared to them all that night, and asked them for food. It's in this room that the flames came to rest on each of them a little later on, after which they started speaking in tongues they didn't even know existed. It's in this room, above all, that Jesus shared the Last Supper with his twelve, during which he announced his coming death and initiated the strange ritual based on bread and wine that Luke and his friends have practiced for years without really knowing its origin.

•

That first day the disciples weren't yet familiar with the house. Having come down from their native Galilee with their master, they hadn't been in Jerusalem for long. During the day, Jesus taught in the Temple courtyard, attracting ever more listeners—among them Philip. At night the whole group slept under the stars on the Mount of Olives, on the edge of town. Passover was approaching and Jesus sensed that it would be his last. He wanted to celebrate it in a dignified way, that is, to eat spring lamb with a roof over his head. "Fine," Peter and John said, "but where?" Like the others, they were penniless countrymen who didn't know a soul in Jerusalem, didn't know their way around, and were embarrassed by their accents. Jesus told them: "Take such and such a gate into town. When you meet a man carrying a jug of water, follow him. Don't talk to him in the street. When he goes into a house, follow him. Say the master sent you. You'll be taken upstairs, where there's a big room full of cushions. You'll find all you need to prepare Passover. Prepare it, and I'll come eat with you tonight."

•

These instructions resemble those of all clandestine movements: paper chases, passwords, covert sympathizers who must not be compromised under any circumstances. This friendly house, which subsequently served alternately as a headquarters and a hideout, was owned by a certain Mary. She had a son named John Mark. She must have been dead when Luke arrived in Judea, because the location is generally referred to as "John Mark's house" in the Acts.

I imagine this John Mark as the second witness whom Luke meets during his investigation, and I also imagine that he met him through Philip, because that's what happens in an investigation: you meet one person, who introduces you to a second, who tells you about a third, and so on. Like in *Citizen Kane* or *Rashomon*, these people say things that contradict each other, things you have to come to terms with by telling yourself not that there is no truth, but that although it's out of your reach you must grope around for it nonetheless.

•

(Kafka: "Yes, I'm ignorant. The truth exists nonetheless.")

21

To our ears John Mark's double name has a particularly non-Jewish, and not very ancient, ring to it. But just as his mother, Mary, like all the other Marys in the New Testament, was in fact named Mariam—the most common female name in the region—and as Peter was called Shimon; Paul, Shaoul; and James, Yaacob, like all the Johns in the New Testament John Mark was in fact named Yohanan—the most common male name—to which he himself added, because such things were done, the Roman name Marcus.

Tradition holds that this Yohanan-Marcus was the author of the Gospel known as the Gospel of Mark. It also says something so moving about him that for once I don't want to hold it back. It's a simple detail in the story of Jesus' arrest. The evangelist says that it took place at night, on the Mount of Olives. After the famous meal in the large, cushion-filled room, the entire group went back there to sleep. The exact spot of their bivouac was known as Gethsemane. Jesus, seized by a mortal fear of what awaits him, says to his favorite disciples: "My soul is deeply grieved, even to the point of death. Remain here and stay awake with me." He prays, they go to sleep. He tries to wake them up three times, in vain. Judas arrives, at the head of a death squad sent by the high priest. Lanterns, swords, clubs. The scene is violent and confused, perfect for Rembrandt or Caravaggio. The disciples all run off. Only, adds Mark and only Mark: "A young man followed him wearing nothing but a linen sheet over his body. They seized him, but he left the sheet behind and ran away naked."

•

This detail is so strange, so gratuitous, that it's hard to believe it's not true. And what tradition says is that this young man is Mark himself. He was the boy of the house, about thirteen or fourteen years old. As with Eutycus—that other adolescent who would later listen to Paul and his companions talking all night at his parents' house in Troas, nod off to sleep on the windowsill, and fall into the courtyard—you imagine him burning with curiosity for this group of strangers his mother is putting up. He saw them arrive one by one, so cautiously that you'd think their meeting was dangerous. He was told not to bother them, not to go up to the upper room. He was sent off to bed, but he can't get to sleep. Later, much later, he hears them leave. The sound of steps on the stairs, hushed murmurs on the doorstep. They're already in the street. The boy can't hold himself back any longer, he gets up. It's warm, he's naked, all he has on him is his sheet, he wraps it around himself like a toga. He follows the strangers at a distance. When he sees them leave the city, he hesitates. It would be more sensible to turn back, but he keeps following them. They get to the Mount of Olives, the Garden of Gethsemane, and all of a sudden the torches in the night, the group of armed men who come to arrest the leader. The boy watches all of that from behind a bush. When the men lead their prisoner away, he follows them. Now that he's started he'll follow through to the end, it's too thrilling. No one has seen him yet, but now a soldier does. "What are you doing there?" The boy turns away, the soldier runs after him and grabs the sheet, which remains in his hand. The boy runs home naked, across the country-side and then through the streets, under the moon. He goes back to bed. The next day he doesn't tell a soul. He wonders if it wasn't all a dream.

22

Whether he was the boy in the sheet or not: as the boy of the house where the sect gathered, John Mark never needed to convert. He grew up in the new religion, it was his family. Like a little Mormon or Amish boy, he was steeped in this strange cult and its exalted atmosphere, among this community of people who went into trances, started talking unknown languages, and cured the sick with their hands.

He had a cousin named Barnabas, also a frequent visitor to the house. The Acts relates a surprising fact about him. Paul had just come back to Jerusalem after the road to Damascus and his retreat in the des-ert. "He tried to join the disciples," says Luke, "but they were all afraid of him, not believing that he really was a disciple." You can understand them: looked at objectively, they have excellent reasons for not believing him. Paul is taking a huge risk, but there's one man in the group who is ready to trust him. This man is Barnabas. Back on page 124 I said that there were no episodes in the Acts of the Apostles that compared to the one in *Quo Vadis* when a Christian frees his persecutor, embraces him, and welcomes him into the sect instead of taking revenge. That's not quite true: it's exactly what Barnabas does.

Barnabas will team up with Paul in Antioch, and John Mark will join them there. All three will start to evangelize the pagans. Apparently they all get along fine. Soon they extend their activity to Cyprus, and from there they leave for Pamphylia, that is, the south coast of Turkey. But there they have a falling-out. Why they do isn't known, most probably it's because John Mark has a hard time with Paul's growing disrespect for the Law. He leaves his two companions and goes back to Jerusalem alone.

After a year or two, Paul and Barnabas return from their first long voyage—the one where they're taken for gods by the Lycaonians. While they're getting ready for a second trip a new quarrel breaks out, because, Luke tells us, "Barnabas wanted to take John Mark with them as well, but Paul insisted that they should not take with them someone who had deserted them once before. So sharp was their quarrel that they separated."

For the pacifist Luke to say they quarreled, it has to be a big blowup indeed, and from that point on, both Barnabas and John Mark disappear from the Acts. They go their way, Paul goes his, and from then on we follow Paul. Having gotten rid of Barnabas, Paul puts as much distance between himself and Jerusalem as he can; penetrates deep into distant, isolated, virgin territories; evangelizes the Pamphylians, the Lydians, and the Galatians one after the next; and recruits the young Timothy, who will advantageously replace John Mark in the role of the zealous apprentice. A few years later we run into him again in the port of Troas, where he meets Luke. The rest we know.

•

Tradition has it that after separating from Paul, Barnabas returned to Cyprus, where he lived a long and virtuous life. As for John Mark, he went on to become the secretary and interpreter of Peter, who didn't speak Greek. It seems plausible to me that Philip introduced him to Luke, while telling the latter that he should be diplomatic: John Mark had worked together with Paul, things didn't pan out, after which he came back and joined Paul's adversaries. Luke was diplomatic. He didn't use Paul's peremptory tone. He didn't think he knew everything. All he wanted was to listen to people who had known Jesus.

John Mark didn't say he knew Jesus, and he never will. If it's true that he was the boy in the sheet, and if in writing his Gospel later on he slipped in this mysterious detail that he alone could understand, the way a painter shows himself in the corner of a painting, I don't think he spoke about it with anyone. No, I think he considered his secret more like a dream, and that he kept it hidden deep inside him. If Luke managed to gain his confidence, however, what is possible is that John Mark introduced him to people in the church of Jerusalem, maybe even Peter himself, and that he invited him to his mother's house.

•

I've tried to write this scene several times. The house has a narrow façade, the two men walk through the low door that opens onto the alleyway. Once inside, they enter a little inner courtyard. There's a fountain, some washing on a line. The people who live there—brothers, sisters, cousins—aren't at all surprised to see John Mark bring home a visitor: it's his house, he can invite anyone he likes. Maybe they're offered a glass of water and some dates, maybe they sit down and talk with the others before John Mark takes the visitor over to the stone steps, which they mount one after the next to the door of the upper room where everyone gathered, where they still gather, where everything happened. There's nothing particular in the room. Cushions on the floor, a carpet. Nevertheless, I imagine Luke seized by a fit of dizziness before going in. Maybe he doesn't even dare to enter.

In any case, I don't dare.

2 3

I take a step back. John Mark seemed perfect, but he takes me too far—or too near—so I look for other witnesses Luke can question. I go over his Gospel with a fine-tooth comb as if it were a casting, closely examining the smaller roles and bit parts. I note their names. There are people who crossed paths with Jesus, and who happen to be named. It could have been different. Luke could have simply written "a leper," "a tax collector," "a centurion," "a woman who had bled for twelve years and whom no one could cure." In fact, most often that's what he does write, but he gives some people's names, and I think that if he gives them it's because they're real. Of course, he must have recopied most of them, but perhaps some of these names, those he's the only one to mention, belonged to people he really met.

•

It could be that in Jericho, Luke knocked at the door of an old tax collector at whose place Jesus was reputed to have slept thirty years earlier. There are still people in French villages who once put up General de Gaulle for a night, and who love to tell stories of how the bed was too small, and how the great man's feet stuck out the end. It could be that this old tax collector, Zacchaeus, told Luke what Luke will relate in chapter 19 of his Gospel. On the road to Jerusalem, Jesus passed through Jericho. Zacchaeus was curious to see him, but unlike General de Gaulle he was short in stature and there was a crowd around Jesus. So he climbed a sycamore tree. Jesus saw him, and asked him to climb down and invite him to his house, because he wanted to rest. Delighted, Zacchaeus opened his house to him, the same house where Luke comes to see him. He promised to give half his belongings to the poor, and to repay fourfold those he had wronged. I'm fully aware how subjective it is to say that something "rings true," but if you asked me for an example of a detail that does ring true, a detail that I would swear was witnessed firsthand, I'd say it's the short Zacchaeus who climbs up the sycamore tree. Or, in similar circumstances, the paralytic who's taken to see Jesus. Since there are too many pushing to get in the door of the house where he's teaching, the men carrying him climb onto the roof, make a hole, and let him down on his stretcher.

•

It could be that in Bethany, Luke knocked on the door of two sisters named Martha and Mary. John the Evangelist mentions them as well, and above all their brother Lazarus, whom Jesus is said to have brought back from the dead. Luke says nothing about Lazarus or his resurrection—which, however, if it happened, must have been quite a significant event. By contrast, he tells a little story very much drawn from daily life. Jesus has stopped at the two sisters' place to rest. While resting, he speaks in a way one imagines to be particularly intimate and familiar. Sitting at his feet, Mary never tires of listening. During this time Martha busies herself in the kitchen. Finally, she's had enough of this division of labor: "Lord," she says, "do you not care that my sister has left me by myself to do the serving? Tell her to help me." Jesus' response: "Martha, Martha, you are anxious and worried about many things. There is need of only one thing. Mary has chosen the better part and it will not be taken from her."

For me, this scene also rings true, like an anecdote that was experienced firsthand. At the same time, for twenty centuries it has served to illustrate the opposition between active and contemplative lives, and I have to admit that this theme of the "better part," according to which

Hervé leads his daily life, gets on my nerves: his wife does everything, while he reads the *Bhagavad Gita*. It seems to me that the same elements could just as well give you the opposite moral: in praise of the good girl who slaves away so the meal can be served while her snotty sister sips tea in the living room, holding her pinky finger in the air. But, as Hervé gently points out, that's not what Luke wrote. What Luke wrote is no doubt what Mary, or Martha, or both, remembered thirty years later, and it's no doubt what Jesus said, he who also said: "Seek the kingdom, and the rest will be given to you in abundance."

•

Now that we're talking about the women in Jesus' entourage, there's a whole cluster of them who followed Jesus and the twelve, Luke tells us, and "provided for them out of their own means." He names these fellow travelers: "Mary Magdalene, from whom seven demons had gone out, Joanna, the wife of Herod's steward Chuza, Susanna, and many others."

Of course, Mary Magdalene, from whom seven demons had gone out, would be the biggest catch. All the accounts agree: this hysteric who had been healed by Jesus was the first to talk of his resurrection, the first to spread the rumor, and perhaps, seen like that, the one who invented Christianity. But everyone knows Mary Magdalene. When he discusses her, Luke merely repeats what Mark wrote. He doesn't say a word more, doesn't add any of his own *Sondergut*—his own "special material," as the German exegetes say to describe what occurs in one and only one Gospel.

Susanna is nothing but a name. That leaves Joanna, the wife of Herod's steward Chuza.

24

I've had my share of dreams about this Joanna, the wife of Chuza. At one point I was convinced that there was a novel to be written about her. At another I thought she would be my third door into this book.

She's sixty when Luke meets her. Maybe she and Chuza are still living in a wing of Herod's former palace, where Paul is now under house arrest. Being Herod's steward is no small thing: Chuza must have been quite important, and Joanna a sort of upper-class housewife. A bored upper-class housewife, a Jewish Madame Bovary, the ideal follower for a guru. There was a lot of talk at the time about this healer who traveled throughout Galilee, but he tended to be confused with another man: a hothead who ate grasshoppers, led his disciples into the desert, and dunked them in the Jordan River while telling them to repent because the end of time was near. The hothead even told Herod to repent. He told him it was wrong to sleep with Herodiade, his brother's wife, and in the end Herod took it badly, put the hothead in prison, and had his head cut off. It's not the hothead but the other guru Joanna goes to see, and he makes her feel good. She returns, starts to follow him. His followers are an odd bunch: tax collectors, prostitutes, many who've had a tough time in life. Chuza can't be happy about that. He says it's inappropriate, people are talking. But Joanna can't help it. She makes up stories to justify her absences. She lies. She takes money from her dowry, then from Chuza's finances, to give to the healer and his followers. For several months it's as if she had a lover. Then the healer leaves for Jerusalem and Joanna finds out a little later that things went wrong there, that like the other hothead he came to a bad end. Not decapitated, worse: on the cross. That's sad, but at the same time it's not surprising. These are troubled times. Chuza shrugs his shoulders: Don't say I didn't warn you. Thirty years later, Joanna thinks back from time to time. She's happy to talk with this nice Greek doctor who asks her question after question, and, what's more, listens to her answers. What did he look like? What did he say? What did he do? She doesn't remember too well what he said: beautiful things, but things that lacked common sense. What impressed her most were his powers. And above all: his way of looking. As if he knew everything about her.

·

Stop. It's all very well for me to say there's a novel in there: it simply doesn't inspire me. And, if that's the case, maybe it's because it's a novel. And apart from that, while some people are fully able to put on a straight face and get characters from antiquity dressed in togas and skirts to say things like "Salve Paulus, come with me to the atrium," I can't. That's the problem with historical novels, and even more with those set in ancient Rome: I can't help being reminded of *A Funny Thing Happened on the Way to the Forum*.

2 5

Despite several attempts, I've never made it to the end of Marguerite Yourcenar's *Memoirs of Hadrian*. What I like a lot, however, are the notebooks she published as an annex to the novel that occupied her for twenty years. Good modern that I am, I prefer the sketch to the grand tableau—which should serve me as a warning, as I've never envisaged my own book as anything other than one of those sweeping, finely balanced architectural compositions, a masterpiece of artisanship at the end of which I'll finally be able to take a deep breath and relax, but that won't be for a while yet. For now I'm going to great lengths to fit into this majestic edifice the thousands of notes I've jotted down day by day, reading by reading, mood by mood. Sometimes I suspect that these notes, just as they are, frolicking freely in their notebooks or mismatched files, are far more lively and pleasant to read than they are once they've been ordered, unified, and interconnected by skillful transitions, but it's stronger than I am: what I love, what reassures me and gives me the illusion of not wasting my time on earth, is sweating blood and water to blend everything that goes through my head into the same homogeneous, smooth, richly superimposed material. And, good obsessive that I am, I never have enough layers, I'm always planning to add another, and over that a glazing, a varnish, and who knows what else, anything rather than letting things breathe, unfinished, transitory, beyond my control. Anyway. Here's how Yourcenar says she wrote *Memoirs of Hadrian*:

> The rules of the game: learn everything, read everything, inquire into everything, while at the same time adapting to one's ends the *Spiritual Exercises* of Ignatius of Loyola, or the method of Hindu ascetics, who for years, and to the point of exhaustion, try to visualize ever more exactly the images which they create beneath their closed eyelids. Through hundreds of card notes pursue each incident to the very moment that it occurred; endeavor to restore the mobility and suppleness of life to those visages known only to us in stone. When two texts, or two assertions, or perhaps two ideas, are in contradiction, be ready to reconcile them rather than cancel one by the other; regard them as two different facets, or two successive stages, of the

same reality, a reality convincingly human just because it is complex. Strive to read a text of the second century with the eyes, soul, and feelings of the second century; let it steep in that mother solution which the facts of its own time provide; set aside, if possible, all beliefs and sentiments which have accumulated in successive strata between those persons and us. And nevertheless take advantage (though prudently, and solely by way of preparatory study) of all possibilities for comparison and cross-checking, and of new perspectives slowly developed by the many centuries and events separating us from a given text, a fact, a man; make use of such aids more or less as guide-marks along the road of return toward one particular point in time. Keep one's own shadow out of the picture; leave the mirror clean of the mist of one's own breath; take only what is most essential and durable in us, in the emotions aroused by the senses or in the operations of the mind, as our point of contact with those men who, like us, nibbled olives and drank wine, or gummed their fingers with honey, who fought bitter winds and blinding rain, or in summer sought the plane tree's shade; who took their pleasures, thought their own thoughts, grew old, and died.

Recopying this passage, I find it beautiful. I approve of its proud, humble method. The poetic list of invariants leaves me pensive, because it touches on a huge question: What is eternal, unchanging, "in the emotions aroused by the senses or in the operations of the mind"? And what, as a consequence, is not part of history? The sky, the rain, thirst, the desire that pushes men and women to mate: fine, but in our perception of things, in the opinions we form of them, history—that is, the changing nature of things—quickly creeps in and never stops occupying places we thought were beyond reach. But what I can't go along with has to do with keeping your shadow out of the picture and leaving the mirror clean of your breath. For me that's something you can't avoid. I think that shadows—and the tricks with which you try to remove them—will always be visible, and that in that case it's much better to accept them and work them into the narrative. It's like shooting a documentary. Either you try to pretend that you're seeing people "for real"— that is, as they are when you're not there to film them—or you admit

that by filming them you change the givens, and that what you're filming is a new situation. Personally, I'm not bothered by what's known in
technical jargon as the "direct gaze": when people look straight into the
camera. On the contrary, I work it in, and even draw attention to it. I
show what this gaze is interacting with, the things that are supposed to
remain offscreen in classical documentaries: the team during the shoot,
me directing the team, our quarrels, our doubts, our complex relations
with the people we're filming. I'm not saying this approach is better.
There are two schools, and all you can say in favor of mine is that it's
more in tune with modern sensitivities, with their penchant for suspicion, making-ofs and looking behind the scenes, than Marguerite Yourcenar's lofty and somewhat naïve claim to step aside and show things as
they are in their true essence.

What's amusing is that unlike more modern painters like Ingres,
Delacroix, or Chassériau, who were careful to depict Livy's Romans or
biblical Jews realistically, the old masters naïvely applied the modernist
credo and Brechtian-style detachment. If they'd been asked, many of
them would no doubt have admitted that Galilee in A.D. 30 probably
didn't look much like Flanders or Tuscany in their day, but the question
never occurred to most of them. The desire for historical realism wasn't
part of their intellectual framework, and I think that basically they
were right. They were truly realist, to the extent that what they represented was truly real. It was them, it was the world they lived in. The
Blessed Virgin's home was the home of the painter or his funder. Her
clothes that were painted with such care and love for detail were those
worn by their wives or lovers. As for the faces . . . Oh, the faces!

26

Luke was a doctor, but one tradition, which is better preserved in the
Orthodox world, has it that he was also a painter, and that he painted
the portrait of the Virgin Mary. Eudocia, the ravishing wife of Emperor
Theodosius II, who ruled over the Byzantine Empire in the fifth century,
claimed to possess this portrait, painted on wood. As the story goes, it
was destroyed in 1453 during the Turkish conquest of Constantinople.

Eighteen years earlier, in 1435, the Brussels painters' guild ordered a
painting from Rogier van der Weyden for the Cathedral of St. Michael

and St. Gudula, a work representing Saint Luke, the patron saint of their corporation, painting the Virgin. Rogier van der Weyden is one of the great masters of the Flemish School and one of my favorite painters, but I've never seen this painting because it's kept at the Museum of Fine Arts in Boston—where I've never been.

However, I have a very good friend in Moscow whose name is Emmanuel Durand. He's a big guy with a full beard and a saturnine temperament. He's serious and tender, his shirt sticks out from under his sweater, and he's got a wide philosopher's forehead—he wrote his doctorate on Wittgenstein. Over the last fifteen years we've shared quite a few adventures in Russia. In train compartments and empty restaurants from Krasnoyarsk to Rostov-on-Don, I've often talked with him about this book I was writing. Emmanuel's wife, Irina, is Orthodox and paints icons, and he himself is one of my few Christian friends. After a couple of vodkas, he loves launching into interminable sentences about the angels and the communion of saints. One evening I tried to describe the painting by Rogier van der Weyden, and complained to him about how difficult it was to find good reproductions of it. What I'd really like, I said, is to have one with me in my studio, watching over my work the way the Madonnas with which my godmother covered the shelves of her study watched over her. Back in Paris, I found a huge package in the mail containing the only monograph then available on van der Weyden. But in fact "available" is saying too much: it was out of print, unobtainable; nevertheless, Emmanuel found it, and it's magnificent.

Despite its weight, I took it to Le Levron, where I went walking with Hervé that fall. I was planning to work for a few hours a day on a chapter that was still hazy in my mind but that was supposed to revolve around the painting representing Luke and the Virgin. Delving into the book that Emmanuel had given me, I learned that the figure of Luke is generally considered a self-portrait of the artist. And I thought: That suits me fine. For me that long, serious, meditative face suits both van der Weyden and Luke. The fact that the former painted the latter with his own features is all the more pleasing in that I'm doing the same thing in another way.

•

I like landscape paintings, still lifes, and nonfigurative works, but above all else I love portraits, and in my domain I consider myself a sort of portrait artist. One thing that has always intrigued me on this subject is the difference that people instinctively make, without necessarily formulating it, between portraits done using a model and those based solely on the imagination. I recently saw a striking example of both types: the fresco by Benozzo Gozolli representing the *Journey of the Magi to Bethlehem*, which covers all four walls of a chapel in the Medici Riccardi Palace in Florence. If you look closely at the procession of magi and their entourage, it's clear that the noble faces are those of personalities at the Medici court, and the masses behind them those of people picked randomly in the street. But there can be no doubt that they were all painted from nature. Even if you don't know the models, you could swear that they looked just like that. Once you reach the holy infant, however, the faces change to those of angels, saints, and a host of heavenly figures. All of a sudden they become regular, more idealized. What they gain in spirituality they lose in vitality: you can be sure they were no longer painted using real models.

The same phenomenon is visible in the painting by Rogier van der Weyden. Even if you didn't know that Saint Luke is a self-portrait, you'd still be certain that it's modeled on someone who actually existed. But it's not the same with the Madonna. She's marvelously painted—above all, her clothes—but she's modeled on other Madonnas, according to the conventional, ethereal, slightly insipid idea of a Madonna. There are exceptions, including Caravaggio's incredibly sexy Madonna in the Basilica of Sant'Agostino in Rome. It's known that the model was the painter's mistress, a courtesan named Lena. Van der Weyden could also paint sexy women—witness the extraordinary portrait that adorns the book Emmanuel Durand gave me: one of the most expressive and sensual women's faces I know. But van der Weyden wasn't a lout like Caravaggio: he would never have allowed himself to portray the Holy Virgin like that.

27

Saying that evenings are quiet in a mountain village in the Valais region is an understatement, and I dedicate some—in fact almost all—of them to watching pornography on the Internet. Most of what's on offer leaves me indifferent, not to say disgusts me: extreme gang bangs, pussies getting fucked by machines, pregnant women screwed by horses . . . My most persistent inclination is toward female masturbation. One night, consequently, I type "girls masturbating," and among dozens of pretty similar videos I see "brunette masturbates and has 2 orgasms"—that's the title—and it's incredibly exciting. So much so, in fact, that I add it to the favorites on my computer, after which it seriously disrupts and then ultimately stimulates my daytime work on the painting by Rogier van der Weyden. At first I thought the two subjects had nothing to do with each other, but it's like in analysis: it's enough to insist that two things that are always on your mind have nothing to do with each other to be sure that, on the contrary, they're intimately linked.

•

For me the question of whether a portrait is painted using a model corresponds in pornography to the question of whether a video is amateur or professional. In other words, whether the girl filmed herself, or was filmed, for the pleasure, or if she's more or less a professional porn actress. Of course, the sites prefer to say that the girls are cheeky students who are in it for the fun, but most of the time you have your doubts. One pretty surefire clue: Does she show her face? If she doesn't, I'm more inclined to think she's an amateur who's turned on by public masturbating but careful to avoid being recognized by her friends, her family, and her colleagues at work. Because after all, you run quite the social risk exposing yourself like that, and I wonder how many people are liberated enough to do it in a carefree way. Maybe many, in fact, and maybe that's one of the major civilizational changes brought about by the Internet. But that said, other things can also give the actress away: her body, the setting, a certain number of clues that would allow her close acquaintances to recognize her. And there's her pussy. All the professionals, and no doubt a lot of amateurs, shave theirs, but a hairy bush is a strong—compelling, even—sign of authenticity, which of course hasn't escaped the webmasters' attention: among the search options are "hairy," and even "super hairy."

•

The video that turns me on so much has a still frame. The camera doesn't move and doesn't zoom, which suggests to me that the girl is alone. Maybe she's shooting it for someone, but he's not there now. She lies on her bed, in jeans and a little bustier top. She's pretty but not stunning, and nothing about her, neither her body nor her expression, suggests that she's a porn actress. In her early thirties, brunette, with an intelligent face, she seems pensive, far away. After a minute she starts touching her breasts—small, pretty, not redone. She licks the tips of her fingers and runs them over her nipples. She straightens up a bit to remove her top, hesitates a moment, then unbuttons her jeans and slips a hand into her underpants. She could caress herself like that, but now that she's come this far she might as well go all the way, it's more comfortable to take off her jeans, then her panties, to get completely naked, and if it weren't for the camera that must have been placed at the end of the bed with some intention in mind, you'd think that the idea just occurred to her. Her pubes are also brown, not too long, for me very attractive. She runs her fingers through them, starts to touch herself, her legs wide, nonetheless it's nothing at all like what the girls on the porn sites generally do: no taunting winks, no emphatic, slutty smiles, no overdone panting—just her slightly accentuated breathing, her half-closed eyes, the lapping of her fingers between her lips. Nothing that's directed at a viewer. You'd really think she was alone, you could swear no one was watching her, and that there's no camera. At first unmindful, almost careless, she gets excited little by little, throws her head back, pants (but not too much, again without making a thing of it), arches her back and her legs, has a violent orgasm. She trembles, takes some time to calm down. A pause. You have the feeling that it's over, but no, her fingers linger and she starts over, she comes again, even stronger this time. After a few convulsions that I find absolutely magnificent, she lies there for a moment catching her breath, her smooth stomach rising softly. She opens her eyes, sighs, like someone who's coming back to earth. Then, with extreme grace, she reaches over for her panties, lifts her legs and slips them on, puts on her jeans, her top, and leaves the frame. It's over.

•

I could watch this video twenty times over. In fact, I have watched it twenty times over, and I'll watch it again. The girl turns me on completely, sexually speaking she's quintessentially "my type." Unlike everyone else you see on this sort of site—more or less carefully shaved girls with breast implants, tattoos, and pierced belly buttons, who strip down to nothing but stiletto heels or more often huge running shoes—she looks like women I know, women I could love, whom I could live with.

There's something serious about her; I even get the impression that she takes this break because she's got things on her mind, that she's a little sad, and needs to come back to the source of comfort between her legs that has never let her down. That, too, is clear: her body is her friend.

So I wonder. Could it be that despite appearances the hero of this video is, if not a professional porn actress, then at least a part-time porn worker, who for the equivalent of two hundred or five hundred dollars—I have no idea what it pays—is ready to strip down and masturbate the way she would no doubt be ready to do a trick now and then to pay the rent? The two are not incompatible. Well, I may be naïve, but I don't think so. This girl has class, you can tell, even if she has a bohemian side to her. I imagine that she's a translator, for example, or a freelance journalist, who doesn't know what to do with herself in the middle of the afternoon. So if she doesn't go out for coffee with a friend who lives nearby, she lies down on her bed and whacks off. Her plain, gray-brown sheets resemble the ones Hélène and I sleep in, whereas the bedding in porn videos is usually outrageous, ranging anywhere from flowery quilts to a plush version of what you'd associate with an orgy-going dentist: black satin and animal skins. From what you can see of her apartment it could be ours. There must be books, boxes of tea, maybe a piano. It's more likely that her name is Claire or Elizabeth than Cindy or Loana. I imagine that she has a pretty voice and a certain cultivation when she speaks. She has a sort of style and composure when she lets herself go that you never see in pornography. She's incongruous on this site. She shouldn't be there. But she is.

What was it that led this woman to set a video camera at the foot of her bed before letting herself go in such a totally intimate moment? First off, the desire to offer this display to a man—or a woman, though I'd say it's more likely to be a man—she loves. It's the kind of present I'd love to be given, one that Hélène could give me. Fine, but how to explain that once it was done she put it on the Internet? A very unpleasant idea comes to mind: it wasn't her but the man she made it for. That kind of thing happens. There are even whole sites dedicated to nothing but that. Your girlfriend dumped you? Fooled around behind your back? Take revenge, upload all the amateur porn videos you filmed with her. But what if that's not it? What if it was her? Why? What overcame her to want to show that to anyone who wants to watch? What can make a girl like her—I mean a girl whom, rightly or wrongly, I put on the same sociocultural level as Hélène, Sandra, Emmie, Sarah, Ève, and Toni, our delightful friends from our yoga class—exhibit herself masturbating on the Internet? Unless I'm completely wrong with my above comments, there's something enigmatic about it that goes a long way in explaining my infatuation, and makes me want to know more—in fact, it makes me want to meet her.

28

Since we enjoy sharing our erotic reveries, I send the link of the site to Hélène, along with an e-mail that's more or less the chapter you've just read—I've made a few changes, but not many. She answers:

> Well, it took a bit of time, but I found her, your brunette who has two orgasms. I searched for brunettes and masturbation, excluding lesbians, couples, sodomy, mature, and so on. While I was at it I saw some real vintage pearls: role plays, 1970s bell-bottoms, I'll show you when you get back. When the thumbnail and caption appeared it was a bit like meeting someone people have told you a lot of nice things about, hoping you'll become friends.
>
> I agree: she's a very pretty young woman. Above all she moves prettily. She puts elegance into masturbating: that's what you like about her. As to whether she's a professional, it's a hard call to make. Like you, I don't think so, but above all it's clear that she really comes. If she's faking it, she does it so well that she must be remembering moments of intense pleasure, which is itself a form of pleasure (and the secret of all women who've faked it at one time or another). It's very rare to find such convincing orgasms in porn videos. Nevertheless, I can't help thinking that she's extremely recognizable in the film, and that these eight minutes of her life on the Internet are a kind of social suicide, or assassination if the video is a present she gave to a lover who put it online. As charming as it is to watch, there's something very cruel about it.

I also wondered about what you wrote in this text about your desire. The first thing—and the funny thing is that I get the feeling you don't even notice—is that it's completely sociological. If you like this girl so much, it's because in your fantasies she's someone from your own social background, lost among the commoners of the porn industry. I'm not going to hold that against you: that's what you're like, and I love you just as you are. What's more, when you describe the effect her shuddering has on you, the subtext is that what really turns you on is the pleasure women have. I'm lucky.

Ah, Saint Luke, Saint Luke . . .

29

Three things occurred to me when I got this e-mail. First, that I was also lucky. Then, that if I were an artist commissioned to paint the Madonna with clasped hands and chastely lowered eyes, following Caravaggio, I would have taken great pleasure in using the brunette who has two orgasms as a model. Finally, that the difference between portraits done from real life and those done from the imagination that jumps out at you in painting also exists in literature, and that you can see it in the Gospel of Luke.

Once again: I know it's subjective; nevertheless, you can feel this difference between characters, quotes, and anecdotes that, even if they've been changed, still correspond to something real, and others that have their origin in mythology or pious imagery. Some things simply ring true, and make you think that they're not related to edify or show that some distant verse of Scripture has been fulfilled, but simply because they happened: the short tax collector Zacchaeus in his sycamore tree, the men who make a hole in the roof to lower their paralyzed friend into the house where Jesus is staying, the wife of Herod's steward who steals away to help the guru and his group. But the Holy Virgin and the Archangel Gabriel? I'm sorry, but no. I'm not just saying that there's no such thing as a virgin who gives birth to a baby, but that the faces have become ethereal, celestial, too regular. That, just as clearly as in the Magi Chapel in Florence, we've passed from portraits based on models to those based on the imagination.

•

Yet she did exist. Not the Holy Virgin, I mean—honestly, I don't think so—but the mother of Jesus. Since he existed, was born, and died—facts only a few screwball atheists contest—he must have had a mother, and this mother must have been born and died. If she was still living at the end of the fifth decade, when I believe Luke was traveling in Judea, she must have been a very old woman: seventeen when her son was born, fifty when he died, pushing eighty three decades later. I'm not saying Luke met her, and even less that he painted her portrait as legend has it—or that she told him her secrets. I'm just saying that this meeting is possible because they were both in the same little country at the same time, and because they both belonged to the same order of reality. It wasn't as if—as you see in the painting by Rogier van der Weyden and in most religious paintings, and as you read in the Gospel that Luke will later write—there was a human being with a human expression, human wrinkles, and a human sex organ under his garment on one side, and on the other a creature devoid of sex, wrinkles, and any expression apart from a boundless and conventional indulgence. There were two human beings, each as human as the other, and one of them must have been a very old woman dressed in black, like you see in all the medinas of the Mediterranean region, sitting outside her door. One of her sons—because she had several—died a violent and shameful death many years ago. She didn't like to talk about it; either that or she never stopped talking about it. In a way she was lucky: people who had known her son, as well as others who hadn't, venerated his memory and showed her a huge amount of respect. She didn't really understand much of what they said. Neither she nor anyone else had so much as imagined the possibility of her being a virgin when her son was born. Paul's Mariology can be summed up in a couple of words: Jesus was "born of a woman," period. At the time I'm discussing, that's as far as things have come. This woman knew a man in her youth. She had sex. She might have come, let's hope so for her, maybe she even masturbated. Probably not with as much abandon as the brunette who has two orgasms, but whatever else is true she had a clitoris between her legs. Now, all wrinkled, a little deaf, and somewhat soft in the head, she was a very old woman whom you could go visit, and maybe Luke did go to see her after all.

•

The Gospel he will write later is filled with magnificent scenes about Jesus' childhood, each more ethereal and edifying than the last, but it also contains one that's very different, which takes place when the young savior is twelve. His parents have brought him to the Temple to celebrate Passover. They leave after the festival, in the confusion they think their son is with the other travelers, and at the end of the day's journey they discover that he's not, they've left him in Jerusalem. Panic-stricken, they go back, look for him for three days, and finally find him in the Temple courtyard, where all those listening to him are amazed at his understanding. Relief blends with rebuke. "We looked everywhere for you," his mother says. "Your father and I have been worried sick." "Why were you looking for me? Did you not know that I must be about my father's business?" They don't understand what he meant. Back in Nazareth, his mother kept all these things to herself.

Apart from the boy Jesus' solemn words, everything in this scene rings true. The margins of the ETB, where references to the Scriptures are noted, remain exceptionally silent here. Rather than referencing verses of the Prophets or the Psalms to demonstrate that they have now come true, the details give the impression that they're there simply because they happened. Stories like that are told in all families: the child who gets lost at the supermarket or on the beach, who everyone thought was in the back of the car but who was in fact left at the gas station, and when he's found again he's talking calmly with a couple of truckers he's befriended. You can just imagine an old woman telling the story, and the keen journalist who keeps her talking and writes it all down, thrilled because it all rings so true . . .

30

There's no doubt about it: I'm turning in circles. And since I started this book it's always been at the same point. As long as I'm comparing the quarrels between Paul and James with those between Trotsky and Stalin, everything's okay. Discussing the times when I thought I was Christian is even better—I can always be counted on to talk about myself. But as soon as it's time to turn my attention to the Gospel, I'm speechless. Because too much of it is imagined, because there is too much piety, because there are too many faces without real-life models? Or because if I'm not seized with fear and trembling when I approach it there's no point?

•

In May of 2010, Hervé and I replaced our ritual stay in Le Levron with a trip to the part of the Turkish coastline that used to be called Asia. We both wanted to see Ephesus, which was so touristy and dusty that we left right away. We rented a car and drove to the Bozburun Peninsula. At its tip is the site of Cnidus, which was long famous because it hosted the first life-size representation of the nude female form in ancient statuary art. Everyone wanted to touch it, come on it, steal it, and it's no surprise that today only copies of it remain. None of these copies is located in the National Archaeological Museum of Athens, where I encounter the same enigma each time I visit: for centuries the Greeks represented men naked, and women dressed. As soon as it was time to depict a woman, the same sculptors who never stopped glorifying the male anatomy put all their talent into rendering not the curve of the model's breasts or the contours of her thighs, but the folds of her dress. That changed in the fourth century B.C., and I've yet to run across an explanation for this radical development. Of course, you can always say, as historians often do, that this shift was the fruit of a slow and subterranean maturation. Nevertheless, no matter how slow and subterranean the development is, the moment when the fruit falls is a precise moment in time. One fine day, whose date we don't know but which was that particular day and no other, a sculptor who was that particular sculptor and no other was audacious enough to let the garments fall and represent a woman in the raw. That sculptor was Praxiteles, and the model of his Aphrodite was his mistress, a courtesan named Phryne. For I don't know what reason, she had been on trial, and her lawyer had defended her by asking her to pull down her robe: could the tribunal sentence a woman with such lovely breasts? It seems the argument won out. The inhabitants of Kos, who had ordered the statue, found it scandalous and refused it. The people of Cnidus then snatched it up, and it made their fortune for several centuries. Luke mentions Cnidus in the Acts, but he is silent about its main attraction, and I'm sorry to say that during their trip to Jerusalem the wind didn't allow the apostle and his party to stop on the peninsula. Too bad: Paul and Aphrodite face-to-face would have been a scene not to be missed.

•

Hervé and I stopped in a pretty seaside village named Selimiye, where we spent two weeks swimming, eating honey yogurt, working on our separate balconies, and getting together for meals. All you could hear was the lapping of water, the clucking of chickens, the braying of donkeys, and the soothing sound of a rake dragged across the pebbles by a beach attendant who busied himself as best he could in the lull before the tourist season. We were the only guests in the hotel. The staff must have taken us for a couple of aging gays who sleep in separate bedrooms because they've pretty much stopped having sex, but who enjoy each other's company even though they hardly talk at all.

The closer the end of the holiday came, the more excited I got, because right after that I was going to go to the Cannes Film Festival as a member of the jury. First the retreat with Hervé, then the whirlwind of Cannes: I liked that huge contrast. What was new was that I was happy with my life. I said to myself that as long as I was vigilant, I could have it both ways. I could be a serious artist, a friend of the nether regions, and at the same time enjoy success and the benefits of my art, despising neither glamour nor fame. As Seneca said when he was reproached for preaching asceticism while wallowing in his millions: As long as you're not attached to what you own, where's the problem? Hervé shook his head: You be careful all the same. While I would be taking the plane back to Paris, where Hélène was waiting for me with suitcases packed with formal wear, he was thinking of heading southeast, exploring the Lycian coast and then taking a boat for Patmos, where during his difficult adolescence he had experienced a moment of appeasement, ecstasy even. He was finishing *Les choses comme elles sont*—things as they are—his book on ordinary Buddhism whose manuscript he gave me to read that fall in Le Levron. As for me, I spent the holiday filling a whole notebook with jottings on the Gospel of Luke.

31

Three years later, I read over these notes. They're the exact opposite of the ones I took on the Gospel of John, twenty years earlier. I no longer believe that what I'm reading is the word of God. I no longer wonder, in any event not first and foremost, how each word can guide me in life. Instead, I ask myself verse after verse: Where does Luke get his information?

Three possibilities. Either he's read it and recopies it—most often from the Gospel of Mark, whose anteriority is generally admitted and more than half of which finds its way into his own. Or someone told it to him, but then who? Here we enter the tangle of hypotheses: first-hand, secondhand, thirdhand accounts, people who saw the man who saw the bear . . . Or, finally, simply, he's making it up. For many Christians, saying that is sacrilege, but I'm no longer a Christian. I'm a writer who's looking to understand how another writer went about writing, and it strikes me as self-evident to say that he often made things up. Each time I have good reason to believe that a passage belongs in that category, I'm happy, all the more so in that some of what ends up here is pretty big game: the Magnificat, the Good Samaritan, the sublime story of the Prodigal Son. I appreciate these bits from the point of view of a fellow tradesman; I'd like to congratulate my colleague.

•

Today I approach as an agnostic this text that I used to approach as a believer. In the past I wanted to immerse myself in its truth, in the Truth, now I try to lay bare its literary apparatus. Pascal would say that once a dogmatic, I'm now a Pyrrhonian. He rightly adds that you can't remain neutral on the subject. It's like people who say they're apolitical: all it means is that they're conservative. The problem is that in not believing, you can't help being conservative, that is, feeling superior to those who believe. All the more so in that you believed, or wanted to believe, yourself. You've been there, you've heard it all before—like reformed communists. The result: this strong-headed reading to which I devoted myself during our stay in Selimiye while thoroughly enjoying seeing myself both as this serious, peaceful man who spends his time annotating the Gospel of Luke in a village on the Turkish coast in the off-season, and as a big shot who ten days later would walk up the steps of the Cannes Film Festival with Hélène in the most flattering of roles. Because let's face it, apart from being president of the jury, few situations are as socially gratifying as being a jury member at Cannes. In this spectacle of perpetual humiliation where everything revolves around making everyone know that other people are more important than they are, you're beyond reach, out of the running, aboveground, in a celestial realm filled with demigods where, since you're not allowed to utter a word about the films in the competition, each of your evasive comments and even expressions is received like an oracle. It's a strange experience, which luckily only lasts two weeks, but it gives you an insight into why very famous or very powerful people, the ones who never open a door themselves, so often go out of their minds.

•

I don't want to come across as more stupid or more vain than I am. While I was engaging in my clever little interpretation, part of me remained aware that there's no better way of missing the Gospel, and that one of the things Jesus repeats in the clearest terms is that the kingdom is closed to the rich and the intelligent. And just in case I forgot, there was always Hervé to remind me. We met for lunch and dinner, always in the same restaurant in the port, because, in addition to the fact that not many others were open, when we go somewhere we like to create habits and then stick to them. Each time I indulged in irony or skepticism when talking about my work, I could count on him to say, for example:

"You say you don't believe in resurrection. But in fact you don't have any idea what resurrection means. What's more, in establishing your lack of faith from the start and making it clear that you know more and are superior to the people you're talking about, you ban all access to what they were, and what they believed. Be careful of such knowledge. Don't start by saying that you know more than they do. Rather than lecturing to them, try to learn from them. That has nothing to do with trying to believe something you don't believe. Open yourself up to the mystery, instead of ruling it out from the start."

I protested for form's sake. But even without believing in God, I always gave thanks to him—and our godmother—for blessing me with Hervé's presence.

32

Our conversations always come back to a confrontation between his version of things, which I call metaphysical, and mine, which is historical, agnostic, fiction-oriented. My position, basically, is that the search for a meaning to life, for a glimpse behind the scenes, for this ultimate reality often referred to as "God," is, if not an illusion ("You can't know that,"

Hervé objects, and I agree), at best an aspiration to which certain people are disposed, and others aren't. The first are no more in the right or more advanced along the path of wisdom than those who spend their lives writing books or generating economic growth. It's like being blond or brown-haired, liking spinach or not. There are two families of beliefs: the one that believes in heaven, the one that doesn't; the one that thinks we're in this life of change and suffering to find the exit, and the one that grants that although life consists of change and suffering, that doesn't mean there is an exit.

"Maybe not," Hervé answers, "but if you admit that this world consists of change and suffering, which is the first of the Buddhist noble truths, if you admit that life is being trapped in this state, then the question of whether there's an exit or not is important enough to justify looking into it. You want to call your book *Luke's Investigation* (that was my title at the time). It would be too bad to act as if you knew from the start that this investigation has no object, or to try to get yourself off the hook by saying that it doesn't concern you. If it does have an object, it concerns everyone, you can't disagree with that."

No, I can't disagree with that, and I admit it with the good grace of Socrates' discussion partners, who in Plato's dialogues never stop saying things like "That's true, Socrates," "I must agree, Socrates," and "You are right again, Socrates" . . .

"So you admit," Hervé goes on, "that if there's a reason, even a tenuous one, to believe that it's possible to pass from ignorance to knowledge, from illusion to reality, this voyage justifies devoting yourself to it, and that to turn away from it, to believe that it's futile without having taken a look, is a mistake or a sign of laziness. All the more so in that some people *have* taken a look. They came back with a detailed report, and maps that let you follow in their footsteps."

•

When he talks about these pathfinders, Hervé's thinking about the Buddha, about whom he's writing, but also about Jesus, whom I have forced myself to write about, because when you write about Luke and Paul, at one moment or another you have to turn your attention to the person they were both discussing. Of course, you can always say with Nietzsche that any philosophical or religious doctrine can never be anything but an outgrowth of the ego and a particular way some people have of keeping busy while waiting for death to strike. But even I, who am supposed to defend this view in our discussions, am obliged to admit that it's rather shortsighted. Okay, that doesn't stop it from being right, but the problem is that no one knows. Besides, I have to be honest: For more than twenty years Hervé's been my best friend, I've been doing meditation, reading mystic texts, and continually coming back to the Gospels. And although, of course, there's no guarantee that this path will lead me to the desired end—knowledge, freedom, love, which I believe are all the same thing—and although I play the role of the relativist in our discussions, come across as narcissistic and vain and strut my stuff at the Cannes Film Festival, I can't deny that I'm on it.

•

The huge difference between Hervé and me isn't just that I live in perpetual worship of and worry about my person, but also that I strongly believe in this person. I know nothing other than my own ego, and I believe that this ego exists. Hervé less. Or rather, he doesn't attach so much importance to the little guy named Hervé Clerc, who wasn't around some time ago and will no longer be around some time from now, and who in the meantime, of course, keeps him busy with worries, desires, and a chronic sinusitis. He knows that all of that is transitory, volatile, a vapor, as Ecclesiastes says. In *Les choses comme elles sont*, Hervé writes with a good dose of humor that the advantage of having a not particularly resilient ego, one on the strength of which you haven't accomplished much, is that you don't get overly attached to it.

During our last trip to Le Levron, which was already two years after Selimiye, we were drinking our habitual *ristretto* coffees at our habitual Café d'Orsières before going for a walk in Val Ferret. He was pensive, and at one moment he blurted out: "You know, all things considered, I'm disappointed. When I was young I thought I was going to escape the human condition. But I've just turned sixty and I have to face the fact that—at least for this life—I can forget it."

I laughed affectionately, and said that one of the reasons I liked him so much is that he's the only person I know who can calmly say something like: "I hoped to escape the human condition."

My amazement amazed Hervé. The desire to escape the human condition seemed to him something quite normal, and certainly not uncommon, even if it's true that people don't talk about it that much. "Why do yoga otherwise?"

I could answer: to get in shape, or as Hélène, who so gracefully plays the role of materialist in our couple, says, "to have a nice ass." But Hervé's right; the truth is that I more or less expect to receive—and admit it more or less, depending on whom I'm talking to—what these exercises explicitly promise to those who make the effort: the expansion of awareness, illumination, the *samadhi*, based on which, if you believe the tales of travelers, you see what you've been calling "reality" in a completely different way.

•

Or rather: whether it's completely different is up for discussion. At the start of the path, according to a Buddhist text that Hervé quotes in *Les choses comme elles sont*, a mountain looks like a mountain. A little farther down the path it doesn't look like a mountain at all. And then at the end it looks like a mountain again: it *is* a mountain. You can see it. Being wise is seeing a mountain, and nothing else, when you're in front of it. In general one life is not enough.

33

At Selimiye I drew up a list of the miracles Luke relates in his Gospel.

The first one is an exorcism, and takes place in the synagogue of Capernaum. Feeling menaced by Jesus' words and above all by his mysterious authority, a man possessed by a demon begins shouting at him. Jesus orders the demon to come out of the man and the demon obeys, without doing the man any harm. Leaving the synagogue, Jesus goes to the house of Simon, who has recently become a follower. Simon's mother-in-law is sick with a high fever. Jesus touches her forehead with his hand and the fever leaves her. After that, he cures a leper, a paralytic, and a man with a withered hand. I don't know what a withered hand is, but one day I shook hands with a man in the initial stages of Lou Gehrig's disease. His hand was cold, inert. With a sad smile he said: "That's just the beginning. In a year I'll be like that all over, and in two years I'll be dead."

I mentioned the paralytic when I dealt with the details you can't make up: he's the one four men lower through the roof on his stretcher because so many people are trying to get into the house where Jesus is staying. But Jesus doesn't heal him right off the bat. At first he simply tells him that his sins are forgiven. General disappointment, but also murmurs of outrage among those present: "What did he say? Blasphemy! Only God can forgive sins." When he hears that, Jesus provokes them: "Which is easier: to say 'Your sins are forgiven' or to say 'Rise and walk'? So that you may know that the Son of Man has authority to forgive sins, I say to you, get up, and pick up your stretcher and walk." The paralytic obeys, everyone is amazed. Lacan would say: the cure comes as a side effect.

•

Then there's the Roman centurion whose little servant is gravely ill, on death's door. This centurion loves Jews: he donated money for the construction of a synagogue, he must be a proselyte like Luke. He shows exemplary faith by sending word to Jesus, saying that he isn't worthy to receive him: a simple word from Jesus will suffice. Jesus does not say the word, but when the centurion's messengers return to the house they find the little servant in perfect health.

What I like about this story is above all the sentence: "Lord, I am not worthy to have you come under my roof, but say the word and my servant will be healed," which becomes at Mass: "Lord, I am not worthy to receive you, but say the word and *I* will be healed."

A very similar story is the one about Jairus, the head of a synagogue whose twelve-year-old daughter is dying. Like the centurion, Jairus requests Jesus' help. Jesus is about to go with him when a parenthesis opens in the story. He feels someone touch the fringe of his cloak. He stops and asks: "Who touched me?" "No one in particular," says Peter, "the people are crowding and pressing in on you." "No," Jesus says. "Someone has touched me. For I know that power has gone out from me." A woman throws herself at his feet. She has long suffered from constant bleeding, in the place where women bleed. But with her it never stops, and this perpetual impurity makes her life hell. "Daughter," Jesus says to her, "your faith has healed you. Go in peace." The parenthesis closes, he's about to head off again when a servant arrives from Jairus' house with the horrible news: the girl is dead. Her father collapses. "Do not be afraid," Jesus says. "Just believe, and she will be healed." And although he's told what I would also say, that it's too late, that if she's dead she's dead, he goes anyway. Entering the house with the father and the mother, Jesus says to them: "Do not weep any longer, for she is not dead, but sleeping." Then he wakes up the girl, who starts playing right away.

•

As soon as Jesus arrives somewhere, the blind regain their sight, the deaf hear, the lame walk, the lepers are healed, and the dead come back to life. (They come back to life: okay—I've already said what I thought about all these resurrections when I discussed the adolescent Eutycus, no need to say more.) Although Luke is a doctor, you feel he loves these scenes. I like them less, and Ernest Renan likes them even less than I do. "For vulgar audiences," he wrote, "the miracle proves the doctrine; for us the doctrine makes us forget the miracle." And, he adds, very unwisely in my view: "If the miracle has any reality, this book is but a tissue of errors."

It's true, Renan and we moderns prefer to forget miracles and sweep them under the rug. We like Meister Eckhart, Saint Teresa of Ávila, and Saint Thérèse of Lisieux, the grand mystics, but we prefer to look the other way when it comes to Lourdes or Medjugorje, the village in Herzegovina that so fascinated my godmother and where—according to the description given by my friend Jean Rolin, who spent a lot of time in the area during the Balkan Wars—"at fixed dates the Holy Virgin accomplishes miracles such as spreading rose perfume in the air, setting crosses on fire, or making the sun spin, attracting hundreds of thousands of pilgrims and earning enough money for the inhabitants to build all kinds of blasphemously ugly commercial buildings around the sanctuary, which is hideous in itself."

The only resource open to us purportedly nonvulgar audiences that avoids throwing out the baby with the bathwater is to give a more refined sense to what displeases us. To consider Jesus not as a miracle-maker who impresses a naïve audience with his supernatural powers, but as a sort of psychoanalyst, able to heal secret, buried physical and mental wounds simply by listening and speaking. Twenty years ago a lot of people were talking about the ideas of the German priest Eugen Drewermann, whose license to preach had been revoked by the Vatican and who had written a book called *Word of Salvation—Word of Healing.* Françoise Dolto expressed similar ideas that I'm only too happy to go along with, with the caveat that while it pleases me to read the Bible in this way, I'm fully aware that this is not at all the spirit in which it was written. The argument isn't new: Philo of Alexandria, already, was very good at giving new spiritual and moral meaning to texts that, when read literally, shocked both him and his audiences. In the book of Joshua, for example, when the Israelites slaughter every last Canaanite so that they can take their place—and pride themselves on it—I want nothing better than to buy into Philo's explanation according to which the text deals with something as respectable as the soul's struggle with the passions that inhabit it. Nevertheless, I fear that what the author of Joshua really had in mind was more like the cleansing of Bosnia by Serbian troops. In a nutshell: I'm all for reading the Bible as it suits me, as long as I bear in mind that I'm doing just that. And I'm all for projecting myself onto the figure of Luke, as long as I'm aware that I'm projecting.

•

In any event, Jesus didn't have a monopoly on such miracles. Luke tells us without embarrassment that Philip did as much in Samaria, as did Peter, Paul, and all kinds of pagan magi with whom the apostles engaged in superpower competitions. If he'd done no more than that, Jesus' name would have been forgotten a couple of years after his death. But that's not all he did. He *said* something, in a certain way, and it's to this something, and this way of saying it, that after many detours I now want to return.

34

Speculating on the sources of the Gospels is not a modern sport. Christian scholars have been devoting themselves to the activity ever since the second century, with the prevailing opinion having long been that of Eusebius of Caesarea (when you say "the tradition," in general it's him you're talking about), according to which Matthew wrote the first one. It was only in the nineteenth century that German exegetes established the anteriority of Mark and what's known as the "two source" hypothesis, which almost no one contests nowadays.

According to this hypothesis, both Matthew and Luke had independent access to Mark's text, and, each on their own, they recopied large parts of it: it's the first source. But they also had access to a second source, whose existence Mark ignored and which was even older than his Gospel, and which must have been lost very early. Even though there is no material trace of it, everyone admits (well, *almost* everyone, but I'm starting to tire of qualifying every sentence with an "almost") that this document must have existed, and must have been very much like the reconstitution proposed in 1907 by the liberal exegete Adolf von Harnack under the name of *Q*—for *Quelle*, which means "source" in German.

The principle that allowed this reconstitution is simple: all the passages that are common to Matthew and Luke and that don't appear in Mark are presumed to belong to *Q*. These passages are numerous, and, which makes the hypothesis even more solid, they occur in the same order in the two Gospels. Well then, one could say, if both Matthew and Luke used these two sources in the same order, shouldn't their texts be identical? No, because in addition each one had a third source that belonged to him alone. German exegesis gives this third source the name I've already mentioned and that I like a lot: *Sondergut*, or "special material." To sum up, one can say very roughly that the Gospel of Luke is composed half of Mark, a quarter of *Q*, and a quarter of *Sondergut*.

There: now you know what you have to know about *Q*.

This proto-Gospel must have served as a memory aid for Judeo-Christian missionaries in Palestine and Syria—people like Philip, through whom Luke must have had access to it. It's a short text of about ten pages, 250 verses, and the first thing that strikes you is that nine-tenths of these 250 verses aren't *tales about Jesus*, but his *words*. Earlier on in this book I wrote: "We'll never know who Jesus really was or what he really said, but we do know who Paul was and what he said." I stand by that. You have to resist the temptation to read this virtual document, the result of a philological hypothesis, as a verbatim transcription. Nonetheless, nowhere are we closer to the original. Nowhere do we hear *his voice* so clearly.

Listen.

35

Raising his eyes toward his disciples, he said:

Blessed are you who are poor, for the kingdom of God is yours.

Blessed are you who are now hungry, for you will be satisfied.

Blessed are you who are now weeping, for you will laugh.

•

Bless those who curse you, pray for those who mistreat you.

Whoever hits you on the cheek, offer him the other also.

Whoever takes away your coat, do not withhold your shirt from him either.

Give to everyone who asks you, and if anyone takes what belongs to you, do not demand it back.

If you love those who love you, what credit is that to you? If you lend money to those from whom you expect repayment, what credit is that to you?

•

Do not judge lest you be judged. For in the way you judge, you will be judged. And by your standard of measure, it will be measured to you.

Why do you notice the splinter in your brother's eye, but do not perceive the wooden beam in your own? How can you say to your brother, "Let me remove that splinter in your eye"? Remove the wooden beam from your eye first.

•

A good tree does not bear rotten fruit, nor does a rotten tree bear good fruit. For every tree is known by its own fruit.

•

Why do you call me "Lord, Lord," but not do what I command?

Everyone who listens to these words of mine and acts on them will be like a wise man who built his house on rock. The rain fell, the floods came, and the winds blew and buffeted the house. But it did not collapse; it had been set solidly on rock. And everyone who listens to these words of mine but does not act on them will be like a fool who built his house on sand. The rain fell, the floods came, and the winds blew and buffeted the house. And it collapsed and was completely ruined.

And I tell you, ask and you will receive; seek and you will find; knock and the door will be opened to you. For everyone who asks, receives; and the one who seeks, finds; and to the one who knocks, the door will be opened. Which one of you would hand his son a stone when he asks for a loaf of bread? If you then, who are wicked, know how to give good gifts to your children, how much more will your heavenly Father give good things to those who ask him?

I praise you, Father, Lord of heaven and earth, because you have hidden these things from the wise and learned, and revealed them to little children.

•

Whoever is not with me is against me. Whoever does not gather with me scatters.

•

Woe to you, scribes and Pharisees, you hypocrites. You pay tithes of mint and dill and cumin, and have neglected the weightier things of the Law: judgment and mercy and fidelity. You cleanse the outside of cup and dish, but inside they are full of plunder and self-indulgence. Woe to you, who impose on people burdens hard to carry, but you yourselves do not lift one finger to touch them.

•

Do not store up for yourselves treasures on earth, where moth and decay destroy, and thieves break in and steal. Store up treasures in heaven. For where your treasure is, there also will your heart be.

Therefore I tell you, do not worry about your life, what you will eat, or what you will wear. Look at the birds in the sky; they do not sow or reap, they gather nothing into barns, yet your heavenly Father feeds them. Are not you more important than they? So do not worry and say, "What are we to eat?" or "What are we to drink?" or "What are we to wear?" All these things the pagans seek. Your heavenly Father knows that you need them all. Seek first the kingdom, and all these things will be given you besides.

•

What is the kingdom of God like? To what can I compare it? It is like a mustard seed that a person took and planted in the garden. When it was fully grown, it became a large bush and the birds of the sky dwelt in its branches.

You ask me: "When will this kingdom come?" You can't seize it, you can't say: "Here it is! Here it is!" It is among you, it is in you. To enter you must pass through the narrow door.

The last will be first, and the first will be last. Those who exalt themselves will be humbled, and those who humble themselves will be exalted.

•

Stay awake. If they knew when the thief would come, no one would be robbed. The kingdom is like a thief, it comes when you don't expect it. Do not go to sleep.

If a man has a hundred sheep and one of them goes astray, will he not leave the ninety-nine in the hills and go in search of the stray? And if he finds it, will he not rejoice more over it than over the ninety-nine that did not stray?

36

In selecting, I've chosen the passages that speak to me the most. And this little evangelical digest still seems to me to justify the words of the guards who came to arrest Jesus: "No one ever spoke like this man."

•

He doesn't call himself the Christ, or the Messiah, or the Son of God, or the son of a virgin. Just "the Son of Man." And, biblical scholars tell us, this expression, which seems shrouded in mystery when translated into Greek and then into any other language, simply meant "man" in Aramaic. The one who speaks in _Q_ is a man, just a man, who never asks us to _believe_ in him, just to put his words into practice.

Let's imagine that neither Paul nor Christianity ever existed, and that all that remains of Jesus, a Galilean preacher who lived during the reign of Tiberius, is this little compendium. Let's imagine that it was added to the Hebrew Bible as the words of a late prophet, or that it was discovered two thousand years later among the Dead Sea Scrolls. I think that we would be staggered by its originality, its poetry, its authoritative, self-evident tone, and that outside of any church it would take its place among the grand texts of human wisdom, beside the words of Buddha and Lao-tze.

Is it possible that he was read like this, and _only_ like this? From the fact that _Q_ deals neither with the life nor with the death of Jesus, but only with his teaching, the exegete who wrote the preface to my edition boldly concludes that in the first Judeo-Christian circles, Jesus was venerated for his wisdom and not for his resurrection. I'm not convinced. I don't think readers of *Q* didn't know or care that Jesus rose from the dead. On the contrary, I'm certain that they read or listened to it *because* they believed in his resurrection. Nevertheless, you don't have to twist my arm too far for me to say that even if I don't believe that Jesus rose from the dead, this compendium contains what the second-century Christian apologist Saint Justin called the only philosophy that is "safe and profitable." That is, if there is such a thing as a compass that can tell you at every moment in life whether you're heading in the wrong direction, this is it.

<h1 style="text-align:center">37</h1>

The scene takes place in Jerusalem, or Caesarea. Philip holds out the roll of papyrus to Luke, telling him to be very careful with it because there's only one copy. I say Philip, but it could be someone else. All we know is that it's not John Mark, because the roll contains everything that's not in his Gospel. Luke reads the words. For the first time, he's exposed to their force.

•

If you stick to their message, there's no reason for him to be disoriented. He's known Paul for the past ten years, he's familiar with the systematic inversion of all values: wisdom and foolishness, strength and weakness, grandeur and pettiness. He can hear without batting an eyelid that it's better to be poor, hungry, suffering, and hated than rich, well fed, cheerful, and respected. None of that is new to him. What is new—totally new—is the voice, the words, which are like none he's ever heard. It's the little stories, drawn from the most day-to-day experience—and from a rustic experience at that, whereas Paul and Luke are men of the city and have no idea what a mustard seed is like or how a shepherd treats his sheep. It's also the striking way of not saying: "Do this, don't do this," but rather: "If you do this, this will happen." These aren't moral prescriptions but laws of life, karmic laws. Of course Luke doesn't know what karma is, but I'm certain that he feels intuitively that there is an enormous difference between saying "Do to others as you would have them do to you" (the Golden Rule, which the rabbi Hillel said sums up the Law and the Prophets) and "What you do to others you do to yourself." What you say to someone else you say to yourself. Calling someone an idiot is saying "I'm an idiot," writing it on a Post-it and sticking it on your forehead.

•

The Gospel of Luke and the Acts of the Apostles are written in exactly the same way—the same language, the same narrative processes. That's one of the many reasons for thinking they stem from the same author. But there is nothing similar between the words of Jesus in the former and the speeches that the characters in the latter declaim every chance they get. Long, rhetorical, and interchangeable, these speeches are written by Luke, who thinks he's doing the right thing and has a soft spot for such pleas. Josephus and all the historians of his time wrote similar ones. Jesus' words are the exact opposite: natural, terse, both totally identifiable and totally unpredictable. This way of using language has no historical equivalent. It's a sort of hapax legomenon that stops anyone with a good ear from doubting that this man actually existed and spoke in this way.

38

The man who speaks in the papyrus roll speaks continuously about the kingdom. He compares it to a seed that germinates in the ground, in the dark, undetected. But he also compares it to an immense tree in which birds will make their nests. The kingdom is both the tree and the seed, that which will come about and that which is already there. It's not a hereafter but a dimension of reality that is for the most part invisible but sometimes, mysteriously, appears. And in this dimension there is perhaps a reason to believe, against all evidence, that the last are the first, and vice versa.

That's what touched Luke the most, I think. The poor, the humiliated, the Good Samaritans, the pettiest of the petty, people who considered themselves not much to speak of: the kingdom is theirs, and the biggest obstacle to entering it is being rich, important, virtuous, intelligent, and proud of your intelligence.

•

Two men are at the Temple: a Pharisee and a publican. A publican, let's remember, is a tax collector, meaning a collaborator, meaning a poor schmo—a goon even. The Pharisee stands and prays: "O God, I thank you that I am not like the rest of humanity—greedy, dishonest, adulterous—or even like this tax collector. I fast twice a week, and I pay tithes on my whole income." A little farther back the tax collector doesn't even dare to raise his eyes to heaven. He beats his breast and says: "O God, be merciful to me, a sinner." I tell you, Jesus concludes, it's the latter and not the former whose prayer is of value, for everyone who exalts himself will be humbled, and the one who humbles himself will be exalted.

A rich young man comes to see Jesus. He wants to know what he must do to inherit eternal life. "You know the commandments," Jesus tells him. "You shall not commit adultery; you shall not kill; you shall not steal; you shall not bear false witness; honor your father and your mother." The young man replies, "All of these I have observed from my youth." "Fine," says Jesus, "then there is still one thing left for you: sell all that you have and distribute it to the poor, and you will have a treasure in the kingdom of heaven." When the young man hears this, he is saddened, for he has great wealth. He walks away.

•

Reading these stories that Luke will go on to write, I wonder who he identifies with: the tax collector or the Pharisee? Did he see himself more as a poor man who delights at the good news? Or as a rich man who takes it as a warning?

I have no idea, I can only talk about myself here.

I identify with the rich young man. I have great wealth. For a long time I was so unhappy that I didn't know it. The fact that I grew up on the good side of society, blessed with a talent that allowed me to live more or less as I pleased, seemed little to me in view of the anxiety, the fox that devoured my entrails, and the inability to love. I was living in hell, really. And I was seriously angry when people reproached me for being born with a silver spoon in my mouth. Then something changed. I touch wood and don't want to tempt the devil: I know that nothing can be taken for granted and that you can fall back into hell at any moment; nevertheless, experience has taught me that you can put neurosis behind you. I met Hélène and wrote *My Life as a Russian Novel*, which was my release. Two years later when *Lives Other Than My Own* appeared, many readers told me that it had made them cry, that it had helped them, that it had done them good, but some told me something else: that it had hurt them. The book deals with nothing but couples—Jérôme and

Delphine, Ruth and Tom, Patrice and Juliette, Étienne and Nathalie, and, in extremis, Hélène and me—who love each other truly and can count on that love despite their terrible ordeals. A friend commented bitterly: It's a book written by someone who's privileged in love, meaning privileged, period. She was right.

I've just had a quick read-through of the notebooks I've filled since I started writing on Luke and the first Christians. I found this sentence, copied from a second-century Apocryphal Gospel: "If you bring forth what is within you, what you bring forth will save you. If you do not bring forth what is within you, what you do not bring forth will destroy you." It's not as well-known as Nietzsche's saying "What doesn't kill you makes you stronger" or Hölderlin's "Where the danger is, also grows the saving power," but in my view it deserves to join them in the more upmarket personal-development books, and what is certain is that I copied it to con-gratulate myself for having brought forth what is within me. In a general way, each time I've stopped to take stock of my life for the past seven years, it's been to congratulate myself on defying all odds and becoming a happy man: to marvel at what I've accomplished, to imagine what I'll still accomplish, and to repeat to myself that I'm on the right track. A lot of my daydreams follow this pattern—and when I give myself up to them I invoke the fundamental rule of both meditation and psychoanal-ysis: consent to think what you think, to have what comes to mind come to mind. Don't say that it's good or bad, but that it *is*, and that you can only root yourself in what is.

Nevertheless, a stubborn little voice persistently interrupts these moments of pharisaical smugness. It says that all the riches I enjoy—the wisdom I pride myself on, the confident hope I have of being on the right track—are what prevent real accomplishment. I never stop winning, although to really win I'd have to lose. I'm rich, gifted, praised, deserv-ing, and conscious that I deserve: for all of that, woe to me!

When this little voice makes itself heard, the voices of psychoanalysis and meditation try to drown it out: Please! No glorification of suffering, no misplaced guilt, no self-flagellation. Start by being kind to yourself. All of that is cooler and suits me better. Nevertheless, I think that the little voice of the Gospel is right. And like the rich young man, I walk away, sad and pensive, for I have great wealth.

•

This book I'm writing on the Gospel is part of that. I feel enriched by its scope, I see it as my crowning achievement, I dream it will be a global success. Like Perrette, the milkmaid in the fable by Jean de la Fontaine, I imagine it will bring me calves, cows, pigs, and chickens . . . And then I think about the coat of Mrs. Daniel-Rops.

Her husband, Henri Daniel-Rops, a Catholic scholar, wrote a bestselling book about Jesus in the 1950s. At the coat check of a theater, his wife finds herself beside the author François Mauriac. She's given her sumptuous mink coat. Mauriac strokes the fur and chuckles: "Sweet Jesus . . ."

39

It would be out of place for me to complain: no one forced me to write *The Adversary*. Nevertheless, I can't shake the memory of the years I spent working on it as a long, drawn-out nightmare. I was ashamed of my fascination with the story of this monstrous criminal Jean-Claude Romand. In hindsight, I believe that what I was so frightened of sharing with him I share—we both share—with most people, even if, luckily, most people don't go as far as lying for twenty years and then killing their whole family. Even the most self-assured of us, I think, are fraught with worry at the discrepancy between the image they try their best to portray to others and the one they have of themselves when they're dogged by insomnia or depression, when nothing is for sure and they sit on the toilet holding their head in their hands. Within each of us there is a window onto hell that we avoid as best we can, and of my own free will I spent seven years rooted to the spot in front of it.

•

The Adversary is one of the names the Bible gives to the devil. When I named my book I never thought of the term as referring to poor Jean-Claude Romand, but to that evil essence that exists in him as it does in each one of us—except that in him it took over completely. We're used to associating evil with cruelty, with the desire to cause harm, with the pleasure of seeing others suffer. Jean-Claude Romand wasn't like that at all. Everyone concurs that he was a nice guy, eager to please, afraid of hurting people's feelings: so afraid that he preferred to kill his whole family rather than hurt their feelings. He converted in prison. He spent much of his time praying, and for all I know still does. He thanks Christ for flooding his darkened soul with light. When we started corresponding he asked me if I was also a Christian, and I said yes. At times I've felt guilty about giving him this answer, because at that time I could just as well have said no. Two years had gone by since the end of what I was by then calling "my Christian period," I no longer had the slightest idea of where I stood on that score, and it was a bit to win him over that, given the choice of yes or no, I said yes.

A bit: but not only.

•

His neurosis, the void that deepened within him, all of the dark, sad forces that I call the Adversary led Jean-Claude Romand to lie for his whole life, to others and above all to himself. He killed the others, at least those who counted for him: his wife, children, parents, dog. His lie was exposed. He tried to kill himself, without too much conviction. He survived in a hostile desert, alone and naked. But he found refuge in the love of Christ, who never hid the fact that it was for people like Romand that he had come: collaborators, tax collectors, psychopaths, pedophiles, hit-and-run drivers, people who talk to themselves in the street, alcoholics, vagrants, skinheads capable of setting vagrants on fire, child abusers, abused children who abuse children in turn when they're adults . . . I know, it's shocking to jumble together torturers and victims, but it's essential to bear in mind that Christ's lambs are both: torturers just as much as victims. And if that rubs you the wrong way, no one is forcing you to listen to Christ. His customers aren't just the humble— as worthy and pleasant as they may be to cite as examples—but also, and above all, those who are hated and disdained, and who rightly hate and disdain themselves. With Christ, you can have killed your whole family, you can have been the worst low-life scum, nothing is lost. As low as you have fallen, he will come to get you, or else he's not the Christ.

•

Worldly wisdom says: that's convenient. A guy like Romand, who fraudulently claims to be a doctor, will inevitably end up being exposed. But you try telling a guy, still like Romand, who claims to have casual discussions with the Lord Jesus that he's telling tales or lying to himself. That type of lie, if it is one—and psychiatrists, journalists, and honest people have every reason to believe it is—is an impregnable fortress. No one can force him to come out of it. He's in prison for life, yes, but beyond reach.

I heard that a lot, during and after Romand's trial. It was repeated with indignation, irony, disgust. And goodness knows, I had nothing to say against it. Apart from this: everything that worldly wisdom and honest people say about Romand, he also says himself. He is horribly, continually afraid, not of lying to us—I think that's no longer his problem—but of lying to himself. Of once again being toyed with by that thing that tells lies deep within him, that thing that has always lied, which I call the Adversary and which now takes the image of Christ.

So in that case, what I call being Christian, and which made me answer that yes, I was a Christian, consists simply in saying, faced with a dogging, abysmal doubt: Who knows? Strictly speaking, that consists in being agnostic. In recognizing that you don't know, that you can't know. And, because you can't know, because the matter can't be decided, it consists in not totally rejecting the possibility that, in the depths of his soul, Jean-Claude Romand is at grips with something other than the liar who inhabits him. This possibility is what is called the Christ, and it's not out of a sense of diplomacy that I told him I believed in it, or tried. If that's the Christ, I can still say I believe in it today.

IV

LUKE

(ROME, 60–90)

I

Two years go by, the two years about which nothing is known and that I've tried to imagine. Luke picks up his story again in August of the year 60, when Felix is replaced by another governor, Porcius Festus. In the mass of files Festus discovers when he takes up office there's the one on Paul, the rabbi under house arrest in a distant wing of the palace, who's had some disputes with the Jews "about their own religion and about a dead man named Jesus who Paul claimed was alive." Festus shrugs it off: not a hanging offense. But he's reminded that this is Judea and that everything is complicated in Judea: the most innocent discussion can quickly blow up into a riot. On the one hand, the high priests are calling for Paul's head, and to ensure peace it's a good idea to get along with the high priests. On the other hand, Paul has appealed to none other than the emperor, which as a Roman citizen he's entitled to do. In short, it's a tangled, unresolved affair that Felix knowingly passed on to his successor.

•

A couple of days after his arrival, the Judean king Herod Agrippa and his sister Bernice pay a visit to the new governor. The fact that it's the local sovereign who offers his respects to the Roman envoy and not the other way around makes it clear just where the power lies. Great-grandson of the cruel and hedonistic Herod the Great, Agrippa is a thoroughly Hellenized—and Romanized—Jewish playboy, like the maharajas brought up in Cambridge in the days of the Raj. In his youth he partied it up in Capri with the emperor Caligula. Back in his country he's a bit bored. Bernice is pretty, intelligent. She lives with her brother, word has it they sleep together. As the conversation unfolds, Festus tells the two about the awkward situation Paul has got him into. Agrippa is intrigued. "I'd like to hear the man myself." Fair enough: Paul is sent for. He appears, chained between two soldiers, and doesn't need to be asked twice to tell his story again. It's the third version given by the Acts, clearly Luke never tires of telling it. As usual, those present are captivated by the fury with which Saul persecutes the new sect, by the road to Damascus, and by his great turnaround, but they balk at the resurrection. When Paul gets there, Festus interrupts: "You're mad, Paul; much learning is driving you mad." "I'm not mad," Paul replies, "I'm speaking words of truth and reason." (Of truth, perhaps; of reason, okay, if you say it quickly.) He turns to Agrippa: "Do you believe the prophets, King Agrippa?" Subtext: If you do, what stops you from also believing what I'm saying? Amused, Agrippa answers: "Oh no. Do you think that in such a short time you can persuade me to be a Christian?" Paul fires back: "Short time or long—I pray to God that not only you but all who are listening to me today may become what I am, except for these chains!" Bravo!

Paul's in good company, it's a conversation between tolerant, witty people, and Agrippa and Festus draw the same conclusion: he can't be charged with anything serious. If he hadn't got it into his head to appeal to Caesar, the easiest thing would have been just to set him free. But he appealed to Caesar. More power to him, Agrippa says with a dubious look. Because he's been a courtier to three Caesars, and when Nero, the last of the three, was named emperor, he even pushed brownnosing to the point of renaming a city in his little kingdom after him. Paul wants to be judged in Rome? Fine, let him be judged in Rome.

•

For lovers of maritime tales like *Two Years Before the Mast*, the chapter that follows is no doubt a treat: sailing along the coast, then navigating the high seas, storms, a shipwreck, wintering in Malta, mutiny, hunger, thirst . . . Honestly, I find it boring, and will be content with noting that the voyage was long and perilous, that Paul's courage was matched only by his pretension to teach the hardened seamen how to sail, and that Luke shows an impressive knowledge of nautical vocabulary. The whole chapter is filled with descriptions of maritime gear, drift anchors, jettisoned tackle, and even an artemon, or foresail—which a note in the ETB tells me was a little sail rigged at the bow of the ship, the ancestor of the jib, except that the jib is triangular and the artemon was square.

Under the heading of parallel lives we should also note that around the same time, the twenty-six-year-old Sadducee aristocrat Joseph ben Matityahu, who was not yet known as Flavius Josephus, undertook the same voyage, which he describes in a narrative that is almost every bit as eventful. Josephus, however, must have traveled in much more comfortable circumstances than Paul did, because he wasn't a prisoner but a diplomat—or rather a lobbyist—at the head of a delegation of Temple priests on their way to Rome to defend their corporative interests before Emperor Nero.

2

It's hard to bear in mind because of what ensued, but Nero made a rather favorable impression when he donned the imperial purple after Tiberius, who was paranoid; Caligula, who was simply crazy; and Claudius, who was a stammerer, a drunkard, a cuckold, and dominated by women whose names have gone down in history as synonymous with debauchery (Messalina) and intrigues (Agrippina). Once she was rid of Claudius, thanks to a plate of poisoned mushrooms, Agrippina maneuvered to eliminate the legitimate heir, Britannicus, from the line of succession, in favor of her own son, Nero. He was just seventeen, she was planning on ruling through him. To this end she recalled someone we've already crossed paths with from his exile in Corsica, where, disgraced by Claudius, he'd been languishing for the past eight years: the celebrated, fantastically wealthy, ambitious, disillusioned philosopher and politician Seneca, the official voice of Stoicism, who now made his big comeback as the young prince's tutor and counselor. The result: At first, Nero gained a reputation as a philosopher and philanthropist. The first time he had to sign a death sentence, he's said to have exclaimed "How I wish I had never learned to write . . ." But more than philosophy Nero loved the arts: poetry, singing, as well as the games. He took to climbing onto the stage to recite his own verses while accompanying himself on the lyre, and going into the arena to drive the chariots. That shocked the Senate but pleased the people. Nero was the most popular emperor of the entire Julio-Claudian dynasty, and when he realized that, this snide, chubby-cheeked boy whom his mother thought she'd always be able to control started to break free. She became worried. To bring him to heel, she brought her disinherited stepson Britannicus out from the wings. Threatened by his mother, Nero did exactly what his mother would have done in his place: like Claudius, Britannicus was poisoned. After the assassination, Seneca went on praising his student's virtue, clemency, and indulgence, and even declared in one particularly cheesy tribute that for the grace of his features and the beauty of his singing, Nero was every bit the equal of Apollo.

Seneca will soon be disgraced in turn, and Agrippina assassinated in circumstances that, like everything in this chapter, we know thanks to two major historians of the epoch, Tacitus and Suetonius. But things haven't quite come that far when Josephus and his delegation of Jewish priests arrive at the imperial court. Nero hasn't yet rid himself of his mother and his mentor, but he's in the process of shaking off their yoke. He leaves Octavia, the daughter of Claudius whom Agrippina made him marry in a bid to tighten her hold over this vipers' nest, for a courtesan named Poppaea. Fifteen centuries later, Claudio Monteverdi will make her the heroine of *The Coronation of Poppaea*, the most immoral and explicitly erotic opera in all of the Western repertoire. Poppaea must have been great in bed, but what interests us above all here is that she was Jewish—or half Jewish, or at least a proselyte. Nero's favorite mime was also Jewish, and the old Roman senators were alarmed at this twin influence over the emperor. Like the satirist Juvenal—the Roman version of that universal character the caustic, talented, and charming reactionary—they deplored the fact that the mud of the Orontes River flowed into the Tiber. By that you have to understand that the eternal city was overflowing with Eastern immigrants whose tenacious, conquering religions were more successful among the younger generations than were the bloodless celebrations of the city's gods. Nero's idea of Judaism must have been vague at best: if he'd been told it was customary to sacrifice young virgins on the Sabbath, I think he would have believed it and approved. Regardless: during his mission, Josephus, who had planned on being more Roman than the Romans, was surprised and almost embarrassed to discover an emperor who was a friend of the Jews—and even, in the words of the anti-Semites of another epoch, *Jewified.*

•

Of course, Paul knows nothing at all about these imperial customs and whims. Accustomed to the restricted world of his churches, he must hardly know that the new Caesar is named Nero. Like Josephus, he disembarks at Puteoli, near Naples. Only whereas Josephus leaves a first-class cabin, Paul emerges from the hold. And while the high priests' lobbyist travels to Rome amid much pomp, Paul not only goes on foot as usual but, what's more, in chains. In a film version it would be hard to resist showing the wheels of the official convoy splashing mud on a gang of prisoners, among them Paul. Bearded, his face lined, wearing the same grimy coat he's worn for the last six months, he lifts his head and watches the procession as it heads off into the distance. And, beside him, we also recognize Luke, Timothy, and, his wrist bound to the apostle's by a yard-long chain, the centurion charged with escorting Paul to Rome. This centurion is little more than a bit part. The Book of Acts tells us that he was named Julius, and that, having developed a high esteem for his prisoner, he did all he could to make life easy for him—which was also in his own interest, because the two couldn't even get away from each other to go take a piss.

It's in this company that we reach Rome.

3

In his *Daily Life in Ancient Rome*, the French historian Jérôme Carcopino investigates the city's population in the first and second centuries and, after devoting three long pages to exposing, opposing, and finally demolishing the estimations of his colleagues, finally concludes on the basis of all available evidence that the city must have counted between 1,215,000 and 1,727,000 inhabitants. Whether the truth lies at the top or the bottom end of this surprising tally, Rome was the largest city in the world: a modern metropolis, a true tower of Babel. And when I say tower, you have to understand it literally, because under the incessant pressure of these immigrants whose numbers—and morals—saddened Juvenal, it was the only city in antiquity to have pushed skyward. The historian Livy tells the story of a bull that escaped from the cattle market and climbed as high as the third story of a building before leaping to its death, much to the fright of the inhabitants. He mentions this third floor in passing as if it were nothing special, whereas everywhere besides Rome it would seem as strange as science fiction. For the last century, buildings had risen so high and become so unsafe that Emperor Augustus had had to prohibit them from having more than *eight* floors—a decree that promoters excelled at circumventing any way they could.

If I'm telling this, it's to bring home to readers that when the Acts says that Paul was authorized to rent a small apartment when he arrived in Rome, they shouldn't imagine this apartment like one of the single-story houses he'd always lived in in the medinas of the Mediterranean, but rather like a studio or two-room apartment in one of those low-rises on the outskirts of our own cities that we know only too well: run-down no sooner than they've gone up, unsanitary, crammed with poor people and illegal workers, run by penny-pinching slumlords, with walls that are as thin as paper so that no space is wasted and staircases where the tenants shit and piss and no one cleans up afterward. In those days only the beautiful, horizontal manors of the wealthy had bathrooms: large, sumptuously decorated rooms equipped with a circle of seats allowing family members to engage in conversation while relieving themselves. The poor people living in the tenement housing had to make do with public latrines, and the public latrines were a long way off. The streets became dangerous as soon as night fell: it was the sign of a fool, Juvenal wrote, to go out to dinner without having made your will.

•

Paul had no taste for comfort, he was anything but a hedonist. This new dwelling, which would be his last, must have disoriented him without overly depressing him. I also think that he saw in these living conditions, so frightening for newcomers, the comforting confirmation that the end of the world was near. As he was still a prisoner awaiting trial, he had to share his dwelling with a soldier charged with guarding him. Whether this soldier was as good-tempered as the centurion Julius, Luke doesn't say. He also doesn't say where he and Timothy lived. I imagine near their master, on the same upper floor—because the higher you lived, the less you paid: you had to walk up the stairs, it was more dangerous in the frequent case of fires, and a good view had yet to be seen as an asset. To conclude this overview of Roman real estate, let it be said that even on the upper floors the question of what constituted cheap was entirely relative, and that the soaring rents were just as much of a recurring topic in writing under the Roman Empire as the congested traffic. The poet Martial, a typical representative of the poor middle class who lived on the third floor of a pretty decent building near Quirinal Hill, regularly sighs that for the price he pays for his garret he could live in a comfy little country estate. Nothing is stopping him, in fact, but it's in Rome that things are happening, and sigh as he might he wouldn't leave the city for anything in the world.

•

Paul must have been chained when he went out, but at home he could do what he wanted and receive whomever he liked, and three days after he arrived, he invited—or rather convened—the notable Jews of Rome. One might find it surprising that he first addressed himself to them, and not to the Christian Church that already existed in the capital. The explanation, to my mind, is that he was even more afraid of being rejected by members of this Christian-Jewish church, who had been warned against Paul and his entourage by James's envoys, than by the Jews pure and simple. What Luke reports is a true dialogue of the deaf. Speaking to a couple of puzzled rabbis who climbed the stairs without really knowing what to expect, Paul vehemently defends himself against accusations his guests have never even heard of. They show their goodwill, nod their heads, try to understand. Apart from the fact that Paul is preaching at home and not in the synagogue, this meeting with the Jews of Rome makes readers feel like they're back at the start of the Acts, although they're almost at the end. Paul gives the standard pitch for beginners, starting from the Law and the Prophets and ending with the birth and divinity of Jesus. Some of those present believe what he says, most remain skeptical. That evening, they go their separate ways, and here's what Luke writes: "Paul remained for two full years in his lodgings. He received all who came to him, and with complete assurance and without hindrance he proclaimed the kingdom of God and taught about the Lord Jesus Christ."

•

With these words ends the Acts of the Apostles.

4

This abrupt ending leaves a strange impression, and much has been written about it. The exegetes advance two hypotheses for why Luke gives his readers the slip in this way: either it was an accident, or it was on purpose.

The hypothesis that it was an accident holds that the end of the book existed, but has disappeared. That's entirely possible; remember that the last quarter of Seneca's *Moral Letters to Lucilius*, at the time a veritable bestseller, was lost somewhere between the first and the fifth centuries. But it's a bit of a letdown.

The hypothesis that it was on purpose maintains that the text hasn't been cut short: its author *wanted* it to end just like that. Rome, say its proponents, was the center of the world. Getting to Rome was the crowning of Paul's apostolic career, and once this goal had been reached, the story can be seen as having reached its conclusion: Paul teaches with complete assurance and without hindrance, all's well that ends well.

Bearing in mind that what happened next is the burning of Rome, the persecution under Nero, the likely martyrdom of Paul and Peter, followed six years later by the destruction of the Temple and the sacking of Jerusalem, and also bearing in mind that the Acts was written in A.D. 84 or 85 and that its author witnessed all of these events, I admit that I have a bit of a hard time accepting the explanation according to which Luke had said all he had to say and preferred to end with a highlight.

A more appealing variant would be that he *didn't want* to tell these events because they do nothing to honor Rome. But on the one hand, he couldn't have hoped to keep them secret, and on the other, by the 80s of the first century the Romans were certainly ready to agree that Nero's rule was a dark period in their history, and it wouldn't have shocked them for it to be described as precisely that.

And so?

And so I don't know. All things considered, I tend to favor the theory that it was an accident, and that part of the manuscript was lost. Now, if that's true, why didn't the second- or third-century Church bring this clearly unfinished text to an end, like it did, as we'll see, with the Gospel of Mark? Why didn't it attribute Luke with an orthodox account of the last days of Peter and Paul, in conformity with tradition? Maybe for the same reasons—motivated by the same, strange textual honesty—that made it preserve four accounts of the life of Jesus, full of embarrassing contradictions, rather than unifying them into a single, coherent, homogenous story that tallies with its dogmas and councils.

I'm trying in this book to tell how one Gospel can have been written. How the canon was constituted is another story, albeit one that's every bit as mysterious.

5

The Acts bows out of the story starting with Paul's arrival in Rome, but a handful of letters attributed to the apostle bear witness to this period. I say "attributed" because the exegetes disagree both about their authenticity and about their dates—a discussion I prefer not to enter into. These "prison epistles," as they're called, are striking for their mystical, tenebrous tone. Paul describes himself as loaded with chains, decrepit, exhausted, healed of the dreary illusion of life on earth, no longer wanting anything but to go over to the other shore. In his letter to the church of Philippi, he affirms that he is indifferent to whether he lives or dies, or rather that departing this life and joining Christ would be far better for him. Only it would be such a loss for his disciples that he resolves to go on living for their sake. A similar argument, a bit later on, makes him accept the money that the faithful Philippians have sent him, explaining that he's doing it for their good: he himself could do without it, but he would not like to deny them the joy of giving.

·

It's in the Letter to the Philippians that we find the hymn that Jacqueline read me so long ago. I can still hear her voice resonating in the living room of her apartment on Rue Vaneau, and I think of her as I recopy it. I repeat it to myself in a low voice, unable to turn it into a prayer but nevertheless saying to myself that it would be good to hear in it a little, just a little, of what she heard in it:

> He who, though he was in the form of God,
> did not regard equality with God
> something to be grasped.
> Rather, he emptied himself,
> taking the form of a slave,
> coming in human likeness;
> and found human in appearance,
> he humbled himself,

becoming obedient to death,
even death on a cross!
Because of this, God greatly exalted him
and bestowed on him the name
that is above every name,
that at the name of Jesus
every knee should bend,
of those in heaven and on earth
and under the earth.

In my youth I was a declared enemy of pages filled with exclamation marks, ellipses, and capital letters. That saddened Jacqueline, who saw such aesthetic puritanism as a sign of spiritual tepidness. "What are you going to use to praise the Lord, my boy?" None of these emphatic signs existed in the language Paul wrote in. What bothered me, and still bothers me, is how difficult it is not to make use of them when you translate his later letters, which are so solemn, so abstract, so far from the brilliant flashes that illuminate each line of the letters to the Galatians or the Corinthians.

The Letter to the Colossians and the Letter to the Ephesians deal only with things like the mystery of His will, praise for His grace, the benevolent design that He formed in advance to realize when the fullness of time had come. "He," of course, is God, and Paul prays night and day for God to show those he is writing to the hope that His calling gives them, the riches of His glorious inheritance, the greatness of His power . . . He deployed this power in Jesus Christ, raising Him from the dead and seating Him at His right in heaven, far above any principality and authority, and He put everything at the feet of Jesus Christ, who is the head of the Church, which is His body, and we, the believers, are its members. He rose up; Paul wonders: What does that mean if not that He came down? And why did He come down? To live in us and to allow us to understand what is the Breadth and Length and Height and Depth, so that we can know the Love that surpasses knowledge and that, standing with the belt of Truth, the shield of Faith, and as shoes the Readiness to spread the Word, we will enter through His Fullness into the Fullness of God.

•

The older Paul got, the more his preaching took on this sort of character. He had never talked about Jesus as the guide to life whose words Luke had started to read in secret. Talking about him as the Messiah only concerned the Jews, and with the Jews, even if they were interested a priori, you invariably came back to tedious topics like circumcision. Whereas talk about a god who had taken on human form to visit earth didn't faze the pagans at all. Although it was blasphemy for the Jews, the incarnation—or God made human—was a perfectly acceptable myth for the Asian and Macedonian hicks whom Paul was addressing. Targeting this audience, his Christ became increasingly Greek, increasingly divine, and his name became more or less synonymous with that of God. For the simpleminded he was a mythological figure; for the more subtle, a divine hypostasis: something like the Logos of the Alexandrian Neo-Platonists. This theosophy was all the more necessary in Paul's eyes in that the announced end of the world was long in coming. So, little by little, he started to say that in fact it had come, along with the resurrection, and that coming to terms with this immense and blinding secret that was so opposed to the testimony of the senses was a sign that one was dying in the world and living in Christ, that is to say that, like Paul, one was *truly* alive.

I wonder what Luke must have thought of the later Paul's overblown prophesizing. When he visited Paul in his little apartment and heard him dictating these letters to Timothy in his raspy voice, maintaining that the entire world, past, present, and future, was not enough to contain the grandeur of Jesus Christ, how would Luke have put this Jesus Christ together with the man he researched in Galilee: the man who had eaten, drunk, shit, walked on stony paths with a group of naïve, illiterate men to whom he told stories about quarrelsome neighbors and repentant tax collectors? Luke hadn't dared to say any of this to Paul while they were there: he felt guilty about this curiosity, which the apostle must have seen as siding with the Jews against him. But in Rome? Later on? Wasn't he tempted to talk about that Jesus? To edify their little group by reading them some of the sayings he'd recopied from Philip's papyrus?

•

I imagine him testing the waters, behaving like the narrator's aunts in Marcel Proust's *In Search of Lost Time*, who, wanting to thank Swann for sending them a present without being too obsequious, lose themselves in such tortuous allusions that no one, and certainly not Swann, understood a thing. I imagine him meekly dropping phrases about seeds, harvests, and herds to the hard-boiled city dweller Paul, trying to fit in the story he likes so much about the shepherd with a hundred sheep who loses one, leaves the ninety-nine others to go look for it, and is happier when he finds it than he is with the ninety-nine he hasn't lost. And if he did manage to fit it in, I imagine Paul scowling and knitting his bushy black eyebrows. He doesn't like it when people start quoting stories he doesn't know, and even less when they tell him—supposing that Luke went that far—that these stories came straight from Jesus' mouth. He's got no time for such rustic anecdotes. What he cares about is Breadth and Length and Height and Depth. Luke rolls up his papyrus: you might as well try to charm Emmanuel Kant by reading him Winnie-the-Pooh stories.

6

Paul must have been as isolated in Rome as he'd been in Caesarea. When Luke says that he received all who came to him, it could only have been a couple of Jews, very few, and even fewer Christians, because the Christians of Rome, for the most part also Jews, followed instructions from Jerusalem. A couple of years earlier, Paul had sent them a long letter from Corinth explaining that the Law was over and done with. But although he'd hoped it would be received like a revelation, this letter was viewed as a sectarian text and its author as dubious, to say the least, and once the waves had settled it had been quickly forgotten. This marginal, uncomfortable position caused him to sorely miss the authority he'd enjoyed among the churches of Asia and Macedonia.

Things must not have gotten any better in the year 62, when Peter arrived in Rome together with several members of the church of Jerusalem, among them Mark, who served as interpreter, and perhaps John—although we know little about John, the most mysterious of the group. No doubt none of them stooped to visiting Paul. And proud as he was, Paul wasn't the type to take the first step. Luke was, though. Maybe he didn't know Peter, and he certainly didn't know John, but he knew Mark, and with him he must have renewed the type of friendship that exists between the sherpas of rival politicians. Thanks to Mark, Luke was invited to the agapes presided over by Peter. He didn't tell Paul, but he was on familiar ground and, all in all, very comfortable—he the Greek—in this milieu of good Jews who, all the while believing in the resurrection of Jesus, continued to observe the Sabbath and the ritual prescriptions.

•

No doubt it was Mark who told him about James's death. In the last two years things in Judea had been getting worse and worse. Zealots, Sicarii, guerrillas, and false prophets abounded in a country where tensions were rife. Governor Festus, whom the Acts describes as a man of the world, turned out to be violent and unjust, systematically bleeding the country and encouraging all manner of theft provided he got his share. With his benediction, his friend the client king Agrippa had installed an immense and luxurious apartment right at the top of his palace with a terrace that looked out over the inside of the Temple. Rumors circulated that Agrippa and his sister Bernice committed acts of lust while looking down on what was happening in the sanctuary. The faithful were outraged. It's in this explosive context that James, who defended the humble and scorned the powerful, drew upon himself the anger of the high priest, Ananias the Younger, who brought him before the Sanhedrin and, after a speedy trial, had him stoned to death.

•

Stoned to death, James! Luke is troubled and perhaps devastated by the news. James was his master's sworn enemy, and all of his missionary activity came down to running after Paul and undoing everything that he had done. Nevertheless, I think that in learning of his death, Luke realizes that deep down he loved this old man with a stiff neck and camel's knees. Of course the world needs people like Paul, spiritual heroes who break down all barriers and throw off all yokes, but it also needs men who submit to something grander than themselves, who observe rites whose meaning they would consider sacrilegious to question because their fathers observed them before them, and their grandfathers before their fathers. All of the complicated prescriptions in Leviticus—not to eat hoofed animals that are not cloven-footed or do not chew the cud, not to eat a cooked mixture of milk and meat, not to do this, not to do that—aren't very important for Luke. They may have been in the early days of his curiosity about Judaism, but Paul taught him not to worry about them because the only thing that counts is love.

Nevertheless, Luke vaguely suspects that they serve a purpose—namely, to separate those who respect them from other people, and to assign to them a unique destiny. All the while gaping in admiration when he hears Paul proclaim that as of now, in the Lord Jesus Christ there will no longer be Jews or Greeks, nor slaves nor free men, nor men nor women, he's not entirely certain he agrees that there should no longer be Jews—or women, for that matter—or that the lights of the Sabbath should no longer be lit, or that the *Shema Yisrael* should no longer be read out twice a day.

Yes, I think that Luke mourned James and everything he stood for, although his master declared it obsolete. And perhaps, while mourning, he got an idea. In any event, I'm getting one.

7

No historian thinks that Peter, James, or even John actually wrote the letters that the New Testament has preserved under their names. But no one doubts that Paul did, and his letters were influential enough for the other pillars of the early Church to feel obliged to imitate him. Starting from the 60s or 70s, each of them had to have *his own* circular, articulating his doctrine and demonstrating his authority. James and Peter couldn't write in Greek, and probably didn't know how to write at all. Supposing that the letters that were being circulated in their names were composed during their lifetime and under their control, at best they would have been co-written by scribes, who could have had the apostles say pretty much anything they wanted. Who were these scribes? At the end of his First Letter, Peter stipulates that he dictated it to a certain Silvanus. But he also mentions Mark, whom he calls "my son," and it would be surprising if the future evangelist didn't lend a hand himself. James's letter doesn't even mention a name. It must have had a ghostwriter, but whoever he was he did nothing to make his identity known. It's said that the letter is written in a very refined Greek, and that it quotes the Scriptures from the Septuagint. Which brings me to my hypothesis: the ghostwriter is Luke. Learning of James's death, he thought to himself: Why not a letter in his memory? He listened to Mark and the others who'd come from Jerusalem and who'd known the old man, and, without anyone asking him, of his own initiative, Luke, who until now had written nothing in his own name, took the plunge.

•

This is a bold hypothesis, and reflects no more than my own personal opinion. Let's read a few lines and see how far it takes us.

If any of you lacks wisdom, you should ask God, who gives generously to all without finding fault, and it will be given to you. But when you ask, you must believe and not doubt, because the one who doubts is like a wave of the sea, blown and tossed by the wind. That person should not expect to receive anything from the Lord.

Do not merely listen to the word, do what it says. Anyone who listens to the word but does not do what it says is like someone who looks at his face in a mirror and, after looking at himself, goes away and immediately forgets what he looks like. But whoever looks intently into the perfect Law that gives freedom, and continues in it—not forgetting what they have heard, but doing it—they will be blessed in what they do.

Those who consider themselves religious and yet do not keep a tight rein on their tongues deceive themselves, and their religion is worthless. The one who speaks against a brother or judges his brother speaks evil against the Law and judges the Law. Do not swear, either by heaven or by earth or with any other oath. Let your yes be yes, and let your no be no.

If a man wearing a gold ring and fine clothing comes into your assembly, and a poor man in shabby clothing also comes in, and if you pay attention to the one who wears the fine clothing and say, "You sit here in a good place," while you say to the poor man, "You stand over there," you are acting badly. Has not God chosen those who are poor in the world to be rich in faith and heirs of the kingdom? And now, you rich, weep and wail for the miseries that are coming upon you. Your gold and silver have corroded, and their corrosion will be evidence against you and will eat your flesh like fire.

Now listen, you who say, "Today or tomorrow we will go to this or that city, carry on business and make money." Why, you do not even know what will happen tomorrow. What is your life? You are a mist that appears for a little while and then vanishes. Instead, you ought to say, "If it is the Lord's will, we will live and do this or that." As it is, you boast in your arrogant schemes.

What good is it, my brothers, if someone says he has faith but does not have works? Can that faith save him? If a brother or sister has nothing to wear and has no food for the day, and one of you says to them, "Go in peace, keep warm, and eat well," but you do not give them the necessities of the body, what good is it? So also faith of itself, if it does not have works, is dead.

Martin Luther, who considered Paul's letters, and in particular the Letter to the Romans, as the "heart and marrow" of faith, believed the Letter of James was an "epistle of straw," unworthy to be part of the New Testament. Still today, everyone looks down on James, the brother of the Lord: the Christians because he was Jewish, the Jews because he was Christian, and the ETB sums up the general mood when it speaks of "his often banal teaching, without a doctrinal message comparable to those that make up the charm of the epistles of Paul or John." If you excuse me, however: While I agree completely that this letter does not contain a "doctrinal message comparable to those that make up the charm of the epistles of Paul or John," nevertheless, this "often banal teaching" is that of Jesus. The style, the voice, in fact everything is reminiscent of Q, the oldest compilation of Jesus' sayings. If James wrote these words, we would have to revise our prejudices against him and admit that he was the most faithful of his brother's disciples. But he couldn't have written them. Who could have written them is a learned Greek, one with a subtle grip of his language, who knew Q and was able to imagine convincing variations of the topics given by Jesus, an able and particularly inspired imitator as soon as it came down to raising the humble, telling the righteous to take a hike, and delighting in lost sheep. Apart from Luke, I see no one else among the authors of the New Testament who fits this profile.

8

The important thing, Paul tirelessly repeated, is to believe in the resurrection of Christ: the rest will come. No, James answers—or Luke, speaking for James—the important thing is to be compassionate, to help the poor, to avoid shrugging and turning away. And someone who does all of that without believing in the resurrection of Christ will still be a thousand times closer to him than someone who believes and is content to stand back with his arms folded and delight in the Breadth and Length and Height and Depth. The kingdom belongs to the Good Samaritans, the loving whores, the prodigal sons, not to the masters of thinking or the men who believe themselves above everyone else—or below, but it's all the same, as is illustrated by this Jewish story that I can't resist the pleasure of telling. Two rabbis go to New York for a rabbinical conference. At the airport they decide to share a taxi, and in the taxi they outdo each other with modesty. The first says: "It's true, I've studied the Talmud a bit, but I know very little compared to you." "Little?" says the second. "You must be joking. I'm simply no match for you." "Oh no," says the first. "Compared to you I'm less than nothing." "Less than nothing? I'm the one who's less than nothing." And so on, until the driver turns around and says, "For ten minutes I've been listening to you two grand rabbis claiming to be less than nothing. But if you are less than nothing, what does that make me? Less than less than nothing!" The two rabbis look at the driver, then at each other, and say: "Just who does he think he is?"

I see Luke in the role of the taxi driver, and Paul in the role of the rabbis.

9

Let's be serious. Is it possible that Luke, our "dear doctor" and Paul's faithful companion, wrote this letter—each sentence of which seems to come straight from Jesus' mouth but has the effect of raking Paul over the coals—behind Paul's back, all the while attributing it to Paul's worst enemy?

Yes, I think it is.

When he heard Paul bad-mouthing James, the Luke that I imagine—because, of course, he's a fictional character, all I'm saying is that this fiction is plausible—couldn't stop himself from thinking that James was right in a way. Or from thinking that Paul was right when James bad-mouthed him. Does that make him a hypocrite? One of those divided men to whom the Lord does not give himself? A man whose yes tends toward no, and whose no tends toward yes? I don't know. But I do think he's a man for whom the truth always has one foot in the opposite camp. For whom both the drama and the interest of life resides in the fact that, as one character in Jean Renoir's film *The Rules of the Game* says, everyone has his reasons and none of them are wrong. The very opposite of a sectarian, and as such the opposite of Paul—which didn't prevent him from loving and admiring Paul, remaining true to him, and making him the hero of his book.

•

Perhaps it's time to admit that Luke doesn't have particularly good press among the people who are interested in such questions. Modern historians reproach him for smoothing the rough edges and putting his skill, elegant language, and storytelling ability in the service of an official, propagandist, deceitful tale. In presenting him as a falsifier on top of everything else, I don't hope to make his case any less incriminating. But it's not just the modern historians who rebuke him in this way: it's also the demanding souls.

If there's one person you can call a demanding soul, a soul on fire, in comparison to whom you can't help feeling second-rate, conservative, fainthearted, and lukewarm, it's Pier Paolo Pasolini. He had been planning on making a film on Saint Paul set in the twentieth century. I've read the screenplay, which was published posthumously. The Romans are played by Nazis, the Christians by members of the resistance, and Paul is presented as a sort of Jean Moulin, the French resistance leader: all very fine and good. I was unpleasantly surprised, however, when I discovered that Luke's role is that of the double-dealing conniver who lives in the shadow of the hero and ultimately betrays him. Once I'd gotten over my surprise—my stupefaction, even—I came to understand, I believe, why Pasolini so hated Luke. In Pasolini's eyes—and in the eyes of everyone who, like the God of Revelation, spit out the lukewarm—the sentence from *The Rules of the Game* maintaining that everyone has his reasons and that the drama of life is that none of them is wrong is the gospel of relativists and, let's not be afraid to say it: of collaborators all down the ages. Because Luke is everyone's friend, he is the enemy of the Son of Man. But Pasolini doesn't stop there: He shows us Luke at his desk, writing, and I quote, "in a deceitful, euphemistic, officious style, inspired by Satan." He even goes as far as saying that under his modest air, Luke is Satan.

•

Satan? Is that all?

•

In one of the notebooks in which I wrote down comments on the Gospel
of John twenty years ago, I copied a passage by Lanza del Vasto, denouncing "he who makes the truth a subject of curiosity, holy things a
matter of enjoyment, and the ascetic exercise an interesting experience; he who knows how to divide himself, rebound, and live a mul-
tiple life; he who loves the for as much as the against, who takes as much
pleasure in truth as in lies, who lies so much he forgets he is lying, and
fools himself; the man of today, in short, who touches everything, over-
turns everything, comes back from everything; he who is closest to us
and best known to us. Is it I, Lord?"

The disciples murmur these words "Is it I, Lord?" after Jesus tells
them that one of them had betrayed him. In tracing this portrait, Lanza
del Vasto is targeting Judas, not Luke. But when I recopied it, I felt like
I was the one who was being targeted.

IO

Now that we're on the subject of apocryphal letters, let's talk about the
ones that Paul and Seneca are said to have exchanged. They were written in the fourth century by a Christian forger who wanted to prove
that the two men knew each other and that Paul's sermons made a big
impression on Seneca, who purportedly admired the "lofty speech and
majestic thoughts" of Paul's letters to the Corinthians. As for Paul, he
purportedly declares in the letters to the philosopher that he is "happy
to deserve, O Seneca, the admiration of a man like you," and invites him
to dedicate his talent to the service of the Lord Jesus Christ. Seneca
doesn't seem at all opposed to the idea. In addition to being faked, this
correspondence between men of letters is rather insipid, but Saint Augustine thought highly of it, and I think it could sell quite well today if
you gave it a snappy title like *The Apostle and the Philosopher*. In fact it's
completely out of the question that Seneca ever read a line of what Paul
wrote, and it's doubtful whether Paul even took a remote interest in
Seneca. But what is possible is that Luke read him, and that, at least in
his imagination, a dialogue took place between these two great men.

•

Already the most famous author of his day, Seneca became something even better late in life: one of those people who inspire respect because they say what they do and do what they say. As a counselor of Nero he had put up with one thing after the next without batting an eye: first Britannicus' assassination, then Agrippina's—which was particularly muddled because it started with the sabotage of the boat that took her from a festival in Baiae to the imperial villa at Bauli, and then, after she miraculously survived, continued with a hastily thrown-together suicide that no one believed. But the more he saw his pupil make a fool of himself on the stage and in the arena, the more Seneca felt his dignity as a philosopher was compromised. Using his age as an excuse, he asked Nero's permission to retire from his service. Nero took it badly: he liked to be the one who let people go, not for them to up and leave. Seneca had the courage to leave anyway. He knew the price he would pay for this conscientious objection. While waiting, he shut himself away in his villa, neglected his countless business affairs, closed his door to his countless clients, and wrote his *Moral Letters to Lucilius*.

•

Each time I've brought up Seneca in the previous chapters I haven't been able to help making fun of him a bit. True to a high school prejudice (dating back to days when high school students had prejudices against Seneca), I saw him as the archetypical sermonizer. But then I spent an entire winter reading the *Moral Letters to Lucilius*, one or two every morning in the café on Place Franz-Liszt, after taking Jeanne to school and before coming home to get down to work. I can't find any other word for it: the book is sublime. Together with the works of Plutarch, it was Michel de Montaigne's favorite reading, and you can see why. In this long, mulling, sumptuous meditation on the art of living, wisdom is no longer a pretext for verbal sallies. Death is approaching, Seneca puts his all into his last incarnation: He wants to outlive his vices. He wants his thoughts to finally match his acts. To the classic objection that he's heard only too often, "Do you practice what you preach?" he answers, "I'm sick and I'm not going to play the doctor. We're sharing the same hospital room, so let me tell you about the ills we suffer from and the cures I propose, for what they're worth."

This exchange of diagnoses and remedies—for what they're worth— reminds me of my friendship with Hervé. And the more I read Seneca and apply his teachings, the more similarities I find between his Stoicism and Buddhism. Seneca uses indifferently the words "nature," "providence," "fate," and "god"—or "gods"—to designate what the Chinese call "tao" and the Hindus "dharma": the root of things. He believes in karma. He believes that our fate is the fruit of our actions, that each action produces good or bad karma, and he even believes, more originally, that the effect is immediate: "No man, if he be ungrateful, will be unhappy in the future. I allow him no day of grace; he is unhappy forthwith." He doesn't believe in the hereafter, but he does believe in reincarnation: "Death, which we fear and shrink from, merely interrupts life, but does not steal it away; the time will return when we shall be restored to the light of day. And many men would object to this, were they not brought back in forgetfulness of the past." Happiness interests him less than peace, and he believes that the royal road to attain it is attention. Constantly exercising it, always being present to what you do, to what you are, to what comes to mind, is what Stoicism calls *meditatio*. In his book Hervé describes it as "the patient and scrupulous espionage of oneself by oneself." Paul Veyne puts it another way, very funnily: "A Stoic does three things when he eats: he eats, he observes himself eating, and he composes a little epic poem about it." The more he engages in *meditatio*, the more the accomplished Stoic, like the accomplished Buddhist, no longer deliberates on what he's doing. He escapes the necessity, because he wants what it compels him to do. With his habitual modesty, Seneca writes: "I don't obey God, I agree with him."

•

Paul Veyne wrote a very long, very erudite, very charming preface for the French edition of the letters. While not hiding his admiration for Seneca, he pokes gentle fun at the Stoic ideal. It's an ideal for self-help freaks, he says, an obsessive ideal, extremely reassuring for those who suffer from their inner drives and rifts. Its only fault: it misses out on what makes life interesting. The Stoic tends to turn himself into something like a temperature controller, whose function is to keep the heating at a constant level when the temperature varies. An even temper, tranquillity, a well-ordered soul. I remember when Hervé and his wife, Pascale, moved to Nice, where they hardly knew anyone, and Pascale said it would be nice to invite some people for dinner one day. Hervé's response: "Why?" He said it calmly, without the slightest aggressiveness.

Pascale took it with her usual indulgence: "You see, that's what Hervé's like." But it drove me mad. What is this wisdom that consists in purging life of all novelty, emotion, curiosity, desire? That's the major objection you can also put to Buddhism: that it considers desire an enemy. Desire and suffering go hand in hand: remove desire, and you also remove suffering. Even if it's true, is it worth it? Isn't that turning your back on life? Well, who said life was that good, anyway? Like Hervé, Seneca thinks that dying is being let off the hook.

•

Moral Letters to Lucilius, published between A.D. 62 and 65, was hugely successful. At that time Luke was living in Rome. If he read it, he must have liked it. Inclined to believing that all men of good faith are Christian without knowing it, he must have delighted in sentences like: "God is within you, Lucilius. A holy spirit indwells within us, who marks our good and bad deeds. As we treat this spirit, so are we treated by it." He must have thought: He's one of us. Paul, who was far more intelligent than Luke, would never have thought anything of the sort. Paul didn't believe in wisdom. He disdained it, and he said it to the Corinthians in unforgettable terms. As for me, I agree with Nietzsche when he compares Christianity and Buddhism, and congratulates the second on being "colder, more truthful, more objective," but it seems to me that like Stoicism, Buddhism lacks something essential and tragic that's at the heart of Christianity, something this borderline lunatic Paul understood better than anyone. Stoics and Buddhists believe in the power of reason, and ignore or play down our deepest inner conflicts. They think that human misfortunes stem from ignorance and that if you have the recipe for a happy life, well then, all you have to do is apply it. When, flying in the face of wisdom, Paul dictates the dazzling sentence "I do not do the good I want, but the evil I hate," whose depths Freud and Dostoyevsky never tired of exploring and which has not stopped irking petty Nietzscheans of all stripes, he completely leaves the sphere of ancient thought.

•

Seneca was at home with a few friends when a centurion came to deliver Nero's order that he should die. He invited his friends to show courage in adversity and to take the only thing he could leave to them: the exemplary image of his life. He asked his young wife, Pauline, to find honorable consolation at losing him. Pauline said she preferred to die with him. If that was her wish, he would consent, Seneca said. The two of them opened the veins in their wrists, and on top of that, Seneca had the veins in the hollows of his knees slit as well, as his old man's blood flowed too slowly. For an hour or so he continued to discuss wisdom, then, as death was taking its time coming, he took poison that he kept in reserve. But he had lost too much blood and his body was too cold for the poison to take effect quickly. He had himself carried to the steam room. As he was finally giving up the ghost, the order came from on high that Pauline should be saved: Nero had nothing against her personally, and didn't want to make himself more unpopular than he already was. Her wrists were bandaged, and she survived. And there was no shortage of people, Tacitus snidely concludes, who believed that once she was assured of the glory attached to her noble sacrifice, she would allow herself to be conquered by the charms of life.

I I

As I've already said, the Romans opposed *religio* and *superstitio*, the rites that bind people and the beliefs that separate them. These rites were formalist and contractual, not anything to get excited about, but that was exactly their strong point. Just think of us twenty-first-century Westerners. Secular democracy is our *religio*. We don't ask it to be triumphant or to fulfill our innermost aspirations, just to provide a context in which each person's freedom may unfold. Taught by experience, we dread first and foremost those who say they have a formula for happiness, or justice, or personal accomplishment, and impose it on others. In the past the truly fatal *superstitio* was communism, today it's Islamism.

Most Romans found the Jews bizarre and their God unlikable for his refusal to mix with the gods of others. But as long as they kept it to themselves there was no reason to pick a fight with them. They were given special exemptions—the way that in today's France, Jewish or Muslim children aren't obliged to eat pork in school lunches. Christians, as far as we know, were another thing altogether. I say "as far as we know" because in the early 60s the best informed considered them Jews of a sort: followers of a minority current characterized by a far more menacing trait that Tacitus went as far as calling "hatred against mankind."

One characteristic that must have seemed particularly suspect was their disgust for sexual life. Roman sexuality was very free, in many respects freer than ours, but certain of its principles seem strange to us. A free man could screw other men but not be screwed himself, that was reserved for slaves. Fellatio, cunnilingus, and women riding men were all obscene practices. (Paul Veyne, from whom I borrow these observations, concludes that "the historian's job is to give the society in which he lives the feeling that its values are relative." I agree.) You could sleep with whomever you wanted, men, women, children, animals. You started very young, divorced often, walked around naked at the drop of a hat. Although certain texts evoke the weariness of the debauched, none mention their sense of guilt. The pleasures of the flesh were no more problematic than those of the table: you had to control them, and to be no more a slave to your desire than to your appetite, that's all.

The Jews were more puritanical. Enemies of frivolity, pederasty, nudity, they embedded all of their acts in a web of ritual prescriptions. That didn't stop them from considering the act of the flesh as pleasing to God and to themselves, procreation as commendable and a large family as an ideal. Being happy meant growing and prospering, becoming rich enough to be generous, welcoming friends under your fig tree, growing old alongside your wife, and dying at a ripe old age without having lost a child. This ideal—which I share—was serious, unfrivolous, but not at all inimical to the real world, or to the desires that stir the hearts and the bodies of men. It took account of their weaknesses. The Law was there to guide men, and demanded nothing that was above them or that jarred with their nature. It could ban its adherents from eating this or that animal, command them to give this or that much of their revenue to the poor. It could even enjoin them not to do to others what they would not want done to themselves. Never, however, would it have said: "Love your enemies." Treat them with indulgence, yes, show them grace when you could harm them, if necessary. But love them, no, that's a contradiction, and a good father doesn't give his son contradictory orders.

Jesus broke with all of that. While telling nothing but stories taken from daily life, and showing that he knew it well and took pleasure in it, he drew conclusions that contradicted everything that was known about it, and ran counter to everything that had always been considered natural and human. Love your enemies, take joy in being unhappy, prefer being small to being big, poor to rich, sick to healthy. And whereas the Torah posits the elementary, evident, and verifiable truth that it's not good for men to be alone, Jesus said: Don't desire women, don't take a wife, if you have one, keep her so as not to harm her, but it would be better if you didn't have one. Don't have children either. Let them come to you, take inspiration from their innocence, but don't have any. Love children in general, not in particular, not like men have loved their children since time began: more than those of others, because they're their own. And even—no, above all—don't love yourselves. It is human to want one's own good: don't. Beware of everything that it is normal and natural to desire: family, wealth, respect, self-esteem. Prefer bereavement, distress, solitude, humiliation. Hold everything that is considered good for bad, and vice versa.

•

For a certain type of mind there's something extraordinarily attractive in such a radical doctrine. The more opposed it is to common sense, the more that proves its truth. The harder it is to believe, the more deserving you are. Paul personified this type of mind—which could be called fanaticism. Luke, as I imagine him, didn't. He came from a province with gentle, patriarchal customs. Roman liberty, when it deteriorated as far as the bloody games in the circus and the no-holds-barred feasts recounted in the book *Satyricon*, could only have alarmed him, but what he had seen of Judaism suited him well: the serious, fervent life, the way of taking the human condition seriously. At the same time, he had embarked on a journey with Paul and wasn't about to start backtracking. And he was overwhelmed by the words of Jesus he had read without Paul's knowing: the lost sheep, the forgiving of sins, all of that spoke to him. But when he expounded his sect's doctrines to his Roman acquaintances, wasn't he embarrassed by the belief's basic dislike for the world? Did he feel comfortable drawing up an indictment of worldly life and human aspirations? Did he not try to attenuate them—both because you don't use a sledgehammer to crack a nut and also because even if he had no family, it seemed normal to him to love your wife and children?

•

One would like to say: This condemnation of the life of the flesh is a diversion. It's Paul the puritan who misrepresented Jesus' message. As they say: the Gulag is Stalin, not Lenin. But things aren't that easy: after all, it was Lenin who invented the term "concentration camp," and while you can imagine that a lot of things are distorted in the image the Gospels give of Jesus, this condemnation is definitive, absolute. You'd like to believe those who maintain that he slept with Mary Magdalene or with the disciple he loved, but you can't. He didn't sleep with anyone. You could even say he loved no one, in the sense that loving someone means showing them a preference, and thus being unjust to others. It's not a small flaw: it's a huge shortcoming, justifying the indifference— or hostility—of people like Hélène, for example, for whom life is love, and not charity.

12

Strangely, there is no talk in the contemporaneous Christian sources either of the burning of Rome in A.D. 64 or of the subsequent persecution. As far as the Roman sources go, there are two that all historians cite. Suetonius says that among other punitive measures, "the Christians, a sort of men holding a new and noxious superstition, were put to torture," for which he gives most credit to Nero. Tacitus writes in more detail: "All human efforts, all the lavish gifts of the emperor, and the propitiations of the gods, did not banish the sinister belief that the conflagration was the result of an order. Consequently, to get rid of the rumor, Nero fastened the guilt and inflicted the most exquisite tortures on a class hated for their abominations, called Christians by the populace. Christ, from whom the name had its origin, suffered the extreme penalty during the reign of Tiberius at the hands of one of our procurators, Pontius Pilatus, and a most mischievous superstition, thus checked for the moment, again broke out not only in Judaea, the first source of the evil, but even in Rome, where all things hideous and shameful from every part of the world find their center and become popular. Accordingly, an arrest was first made of all who pleaded guilty; then, upon their information, an immense multitude was convicted, not so much of the crime of firing the city, as of hatred against mankind."

Odium humani generis: Here we are.

•

Did Nero burn Rome to copy the burning of Troy? To rebuild the city to his taste? Or simply to show, as Suetonius says, that "until him no one knew the extent of what a prince could do"? Above all, did he burn Rome at all? Did he really come back from his villa in Antium, as shown so graphically in the film version of *Quo Vadis*, and play the lyre while looking down on the blazing city? Historians have their doubts, all the more so in that he himself lost collections to which he attached great importance. They believe the fire was accidental: many Roman houses were made of wood, they were lit with torches, oil lamps, fire pits; fires broke out everywhere, incessantly. Nevertheless, rumors circulated that he did just that—like the ones implicating Putin's FSB in the bloody attacks in Moscow in 1999.

If Nero was looking for scapegoats to neutralize this rumor, the question remains: Why the Christians? Why not the Jews *and* the Christians, groups the Romans had a hard time distinguishing and held in equal disdain? Perhaps because, precisely, they were starting to tell them apart, and, for reasons I brought up in the last chapter, to believe that the Christians were worse: even more inimical to mankind. This is a preliminary explanation, and personally I'm happy with it, but I'm obliged to say a word about another, more unpleasant one, which held that Nero's new wife, Poppaea; his mime, Aliturus; and the relatively large number of Jews who Josephus says made up his entourage suggested the idea to the emperor. It was suggested to them, in turn, or so the theory goes, by the Great Synagogue of Rome, exasperated by this competition that was robbing it of its clients and harming its image. To back up this hypothesis, it's said the district that is now Trastevere, which was a sort of Christian ghetto, was one of the few neighborhoods spared by the flames—and it's not my fault if that sounds a lot like the rumors about the Jews who didn't go to work in the Twin Towers on September 11, 2001. Both of these hypotheses are equally unpleasant, but that said, there's one that's never tendered: that the Christians really could have done it. Not Peter or Paul, of course, nor those closest to them, but, as the expression goes, uncontrolled elements, who understood wrong—or not so wrong, as the case may be—the words of the Lord like those that the gentle Luke, and Luke alone, committed to writing later on: "I have come to set the earth on fire, and how I wish it were already blazing!"

After all, they were all waiting for the end of the world. They summoned it with their prayers. Although they may not have lit—and probably didn't light—the fires that consumed this hated Babylonia, they must have wanted to, and must have expressed their joy more or less openly. Add to that the legends that were starting to spread about them, the same ones that would later circulate about the Jews: kidnapped children, ritual murders, poisoned wells. All of that made ideal culprits.

•

What follows is a grand moment of gore. The Christians were mostly people of modest means, and could not demand noble deaths such as decapitation or Stoic suicide. Public executions in Rome were the stuff of celebration. Those who weren't sewn into animals' skins and thrown into the arena to be devoured by hounds in the morning were kept for the evening, dressed in coats soaked in pine tar and transformed into living torches that lit up the parties in Nero's gardens. Women were attached by their hair to the horns of raging bulls. Others were smeared with the secretions of female donkeys and raped by excited jackasses. Suetonius describes Nero having himself covered with the skin of a wild animal and attacking the private parts of condemned men and women—especially women, who were attached naked to stakes. In this way he became the Antichrist, the Beast, for all Christians.

13

Tradition, that is, the unavoidable Eusebius, tells us that Peter and Paul died in the grand persecution of August A.D. 64. As a Roman citizen, Paul is said to have been beheaded and Peter crucified upside down, because he didn't consider himself worthy to suffer the same fate as Jesus. And there were very good reasons for uniting in martyrdom the two leaders whose rivalry was the infant malady of Christianity, even if that meant inventing the whole story. On the face of it, no one was more suited to be the first spokesman of such unity than Luke. After all, in his own narrative he never stops rewriting history and imposing the idea of an atmosphere of understanding among the apostles with at the very most a few minor, quickly resolved disputes marring the mutual concord. But he didn't. He must have known what happened, but he didn't tell it. The mystery of the abrupt end of the Acts of the Apostles is joined by another: that of the end of Paul.

•

Flipping through a life of Saint Paul written by a Dominican whose
name figures in most recent bibliographies, I went straight to the end to
see how he would deal with the obscurity shrouding the last years of the
apostle's life. Imagine my surprise to find them told in minute detail.
Paul didn't die in Rome in A.D. 64. He appeared before Nero, who had
him released. He fulfilled his dream and traveled as far as Spain, but
Spain disappointed him, and he recrossed the entire Mediterranean to
take solace in the company of his dear churches of Greece and Asia.
Then he had the bad idea of going back to Rome, where he was once
again arrested, imprisoned, and, this time, executed, in A.D. 67. The
author gives the exact date. None of this is impossible, and I have
nothing at all against such conjectures; the only astonishing thing is that
at no moment does it so much as cross the mind of this professor of exegesis, in a work that is respectfully cited by his peers and put out by a
serious publishing house, that he should mention to his readers that he
simply has no way of knowing what he is affirming. That, for lack of
documents like the letters or the Acts, he has nothing more to back him
up in piecing together the last years of Paul's life than his imagination
and the "conviction," alluded to in a footnote and not substantiated in
the least, that the Second Letter to Timothy is authentic—which almost
no one has thought for the last two centuries. In saying this I'm not trying to bad-mouth the author of this biography, but to remind myself
that I, too, am free to invent provided I say that I'm inventing, and set out
as scrupulously as Renan does the degrees of the certain, the probable,
the possible, and—right before the completely excluded—the not entirely impossible: the realm in which a good part of this book is based.

•

The Second Letter to Timothy, then. The general opinion is that it wasn't
written by Paul, but that it's a sort of portrait of him, written not long
after his death, for people who knew what went down, full of details—
gripes and reproaches, mostly—that make it sound authentic:

> You know that everyone in Asia deserted me, including Phygelus
> and Hermogenes. Demas, enamored of the present world, de-
> serted me and went to Thessalonica, Crescens to Galatia, and
> Titus to Dalmatia. Luke is the only one with me. Alexander the
> coppersmith did me a great deal of harm. You too be on guard

against him. Everyone deserted me, they are ashamed of my chains . . . Hymenaeus and Philetus have become more and more godless, their teaching will spread like gangrene . . . I have sent Tychicus to Ephesus. When you come, bring the cloak I left with Carpus in Troas, the papyrus rolls, and especially the parchments . . .

This letter too could have been written by Luke. You can recognize his taste for the down-to-earth, and the preference for people over ideas that made him the first ancient author to present a religious movement by expounding not its doctrine but its history. In my mind it is very much like Luke to have painted the tired fighter, who dictated to Timothy letters that deal with nothing but divine thrones and the principle of all things, in a Rembrandtesque half-light: bitter, crotchety, going on and on about how Phygelus, Hermogenes, and Demas have deserted him, Hymenaeus and Philetus are shooting their mouths off, Alexander the coppersmith did him no end of harm, and finally asking that the no doubt moth-eaten coat that he left at the home of a certain Carpos the last time he was in Troas be brought to him. It's just like Luke to want to quote this name, Carpos, and to choose Timothy as the addressee of the letter—because, it's true, he was Paul's favorite disciple—but also to slip in that he, Luke, stayed with the old moaner right up until the end. Tiny lives on the one hand, a grand theology on the other. Paul was a genius, soaring high above the common run of mortals, Luke a simple chronicler of events who never sought to escape his lot. The question isn't whom I prefer, but it doesn't harm anyone for me to attribute this letter to him.

•

It's the last trace we have of Paul. A ghostly palpitation, a tired flicker before everything is engulfed in darkness. At this point in the story, all of the main characters disappear.

14

All except John.

•

I've almost not talked about him at all until now. I'm working my way up to him, but it scares me, because John is the most mysterious charac-

ter in the first Christian generation. The most elusive, the most multi-
faceted. He'll soon be credited with authoring the fourth Gospel and
the Book of Revelation. But thinking that the same man wrote the
fourth Gospel and Revelation would be like thinking, if all of the references concerning twentieth-century French literature were lost, that the
same person wrote *In Search of Lost Time* and *Journey to the End of
the Night*.

There are several Johns in the New Testament, and they're almost
impossible to distinguish from one another: John the son of Zebedee,
John the disciple Jesus loved, John of Patmos, John the Evangelist. The
oldest of them all, the one whose seniority all the others would like to
usurp, is unquestionably John, son of Zebedee, who was one of the first
four disciples. These four were Simon, who would become Peter; his
brother Andrew; John; and his brother James, who, as he was the elder
of the two, was called James the Greater: all four fishermen on the Sea
of Tiberias who dropped everything to follow Jesus.

Jesus nicknamed James and John Boanerges, sons of thunder,
because of their fiery tempers. Later Luke gives two examples. One
day, John lashes out at a man who casts out demons in the name of Jesus,
because he is not part of their group. He wants to have him denounced,
neutralized. Jesus shrugs his shoulders and tells him to leave the guy
alone: "Whoever is not against you is for you." Another day, the group
is poorly received in a Samaritan village. James and John go all out and
want Jesus to punish the inhabitants by calling down fire from heaven.
Jesus shrugs again. Still another day (now it's Mark who tells the story),
James and John come to Jesus because they have something to request.
"Yes?" says Jesus. Like children, they first want him to promise that
he'll do whatever they ask him. "What do you wish?" Jesus replies. You
can imagine these brothers, two big oafs squirming and egging each
other on: "You say it." "No, you." One of them finally blurts out: "When
you sit on your glorious throne, we want to sit in places of honor next to
you, one on your right and the other on your left." Jesus said to them,
"You do not know what you are asking. Can you drink the cup that I
drink or be baptized with the baptism with which I am baptized?" Yes,
sure, say the two oafs. "Fair enough," Jesus replies, "granted. But to sit at
my right or at my left, that is up to God, not me."

•

Mark and Luke, as we see, show neither John nor his brother in a particularly glorious light. It's only in the fourth Gospel that John becomes "the disciple that Jesus loved," his closest confidant, the one who reclines on his bosom during the Last Supper, and whom Jesus, on the cross, chooses to care for his mother. It's hard to imagine that a young, irascible, somewhat ditzy, and no doubt illiterate Galilean fisherman could have become, forty or sixty years later, the prophet of Patmos, the author of the obscure and dazzling book called Revelation. But who knows? Such metamorphoses aren't unheard of. Marcel Proust tells one that I love in his *In Search of Lost Time*: near the start of the work, Octave, the fun-loving young idler nicknamed "I'm a wash-out," is involved with several of the little band of Balbec girls. Everyone thinks he'll spend the rest of his life concerned with nothing weightier than ties and flashy cars, and we lose sight of him. Then, near the end, we learn in passing that he has become the greatest, deepest, and most innovative artist of his time. One can imagine John undergoing a similar evolution: age, responsibilities, and the respect shown to him have knocked some sense into him. Thirty years after Jesus' death he's fifty or sixty, and like Peter and James he has become one of the pillars of the church of Jerusalem, which Paul alternately woos and defies. He's often a bit dreamy, he doesn't speak much and doesn't smile. He's considered unsociable. The agitated youth has become a grand old man.

•

The Church father Tertullian affirms that John was also in Rome at the time of Nero's persecution. That he too was tortured—plunged into a vat of boiling oil—and miraculously survived. He had already fled from Jerusalem, which had become too dangerous for Christians since James's death. Now he had to flee from Rome. According to tradition, in his travels John never left the side of Mary, Jesus' old mother. It's with her and several dozen survivors of the decimated Roman Church that he is said to have left for Asia. There he ended up in Ephesus, the way fortunate German Jews left for America in the 1930s and wound up in New York. It suits my purposes to imagine that Luke made the voyage as well.

15

All he knew of Ephesus, and more generally of the seven churches of Asia, Luke learned from Paul, who had founded them and—knowing how they could be influenced—never stopped worrying that they might be led astray. Before leaving for Jerusalem, the apostle had put the Ephesians on their guard against savage wolves, who, in his absence, would not spare the flock. He wasn't wrong: when he got there, Luke discovered that in the ten years of Paul's absence, what the master had considered his most solid stronghold had passed heart and soul into the enemy camp.

Well, enemy . . . Luke didn't really see these Judeo-Christians who followed James as enemies. He understood them, and as always he felt that a little goodwill would get you a long way. But since the death of James and Peter and the horrors of the summer of 64 in Rome, and above all since John had become their leader, their faith had hardened. When Luke joined the Ephesian Christians' agape not long after arriving, he hoped to find Timothy, or Philip and his four virgin daughters, who he'd been told were also in the region, or at least a few familiar faces, a couple of Greeks like him. But there were only Jews, or Greeks disguised as Jews: serious, bearded types who celebrated the memory of the Lord not just as if they were in a synagogue but also as if it were the Temple of Jerusalem. John, whom he'd seen from a distance but steered clear of, also had a thick beard, was surrounded by followers, and wore the petalon, a golden plate fixed on the forehead and traditionally worn by the high priests of Israel. Thanks to the catastrophe in Rome, the church of circumcision had won out, and the church of the foreskin was in disarray.

•

In the days that followed, Luke realized that John was literally venerated by the Christians of Ephesus. Paul had been venerated as well, but not in the same way: you could go visit him in his workshop whenever you liked, he'd be there behind his loom, smiling or grumpy, grumpy more often than not, but always bristling with life, passionate, and willing to talk to you about Christ. Not John. When you saw him, you bowed as if he were a supreme pontiff: intimidating, inaccessible, floating on a cloud of incense. That said, he was hardly seen. People furtively pointed out the house where the disciple whom Jesus loved lived with Jesus' mother, who was seen even less, who never left the house—gone were the days when she could be found sitting outside her door. Was it even their house? No one was sure, it was said they changed houses often for fear of being arrested by the Romans. People lowered their voices when talking about them. Everything about them was solemn, charged with mystery.

•

Luke must have felt very alone at Ephesus. Paul's disciples were nowhere to be found. And if he did run across one or the other, they avoided his gaze and turned away. Some were named in Paul's letters, they must have been hugely proud of that at the time, but when Luke mentioned the apostle's name to them now they said they'd never met him. Those who hadn't fled had gone over to the other side and were careful not to meet anyone or do anything that could risk evoking their deviationist past. In the agapes everyone outdid each other in observing the Jewish rituals, insisting on the purity of the meat, and denouncing the enemy. The enemy, of course, was Nero, guilty of the massacres of A.D. 64, but also Paul, who was seen as Nero's toady. It was considered good form to rejoice loudly at his death. He was called the gravedigger of the Law, Balaam, or even Nicolas, and those who remained faithful to him the Nicolaitans.

16

The four evangelists, unanimous for once, tell that after his arrest, Jesus was taken to the residence of the high priest to be interrogated. The scene takes place at night. Peter, who has managed to slip into the courtyard, spends the night waiting near a fire where some soldiers and servants of the high priest warm themselves, half-asleep. It's cold, the way it can be cold in April in Jerusalem—and in passing I realize that this detail does not at all tally with the story I like so much about the young boy who, on this same night, slept naked and wrapped himself in his sheet to follow the group to the Mount of Olives. Too bad. At one moment, a servant girl looks at Peter and says: "You were with the one they arrested." Peter becomes afraid and answers: "No, I don't know him." Another insists: "Yes you were, I saw you, you were part of the group." "You must be mistaken," Peter says. A third puts in: "And you've got a Galilean accent, like the others. Go on, admit it." "I've got nothing to admit," Peter answers, "you're talking nonsense." At this moment a cock crows, and Peter remembers what Jesus said the previous night: "You will betray me." "Never, Lord," Peter said, and Jesus answered: "Peter, I

say to you, tomorrow morning the cock will not yet have crowed, and
you will have three times sworn that you do not know me." So Peter
leaves the courtyard and, in the dirty morning light, starts to cry.

•

Mark was the first to tell this story, and we know that Mark was Peter's
secretary and that Peter called him "my son." He could have kept quiet
about an event that on first sight doesn't show Peter in a good light. But
he had it from Peter; Peter must have told it himself, insisted on it, and
this honesty makes him infinitely likable. It's more than honesty, even.
If you're a Christian, you spend your life denying Christ. You do it
morning and night, a hundred times a day, that's all you do. So when
the most faithful of the faithful says: I've done it too, I've denied him,
I've betrayed him, and at the most terrible moment, it's extraordinarily
comforting. And it has to do with the pure goodness that makes you
want to throw out the bathwater but not this misshapen baby, this child
with Down syndrome named Christianity.

I wonder—and this is really what I'm getting at—if, pressured
from all sides in Ephesus by enemies of Paul and summoned to give his
record of service, Luke also denied his master. Maybe: as I imagine him
he wasn't particularly courageous. But when he recopied the story of
Peter's denial years later, it must have made him cry as well, and at the
same time consoled him.

•

(While we're on the subject of Peter: When he hears Jesus say that the
Son of Man will soon suffer and die, he cries out: "God forbid, Lord!
No such thing shall ever happen to you!" Jesus replies violently: "Get
behind me, Satan! You are an obstacle to me." That being said, the
Greek word we translate as "obstacle"—*skandalon*, which will become
"scandal"—literally means "the stone you trip over." Thus, Peter isn't
only the rock on which Jesus will build his church, as everyone knows,
but also the pebble in his shoe. He's both: the unshakable rock, and the
pebble that makes his life miserable. All of us are both, for ourselves
and for God, if we believe in God. That, too, makes Peter very likable,
and makes me feel very close to him.)

17

It's at this time that the Jewish War starts in Judea. It was simmering for ten years, and breaks out in earnest in A.D. 66, partly through the fault of the new governor, Florus, who makes his predecessors Felix and Festus look like upstanding officials. All the governors feathered their nests, but there were limits: Cicero cited himself as an example because during the year he spent in Sicily he pocketed no more than two million sestertii. Florus had no such scruples, and apparently came to consider a nice little war a way of hiding any misappropriations that the Jews could accuse him of in front of Caesar. Each time the troubles run the risk of dying down, he's there to pour oil on the fire: at least that's what Josephus maintains, a bit like the way my cousin Paul Klebnikov explained the First Chechen War by citing the interest the Russian General Staff had in passing off the huge quantity of military material that had been misappropriated and sold on the black market, notably in the Balkans, as combat losses.

The starting point, Joseph relates, is a new tax that Florus decrees off the cuff, because he's continually in need of money, which sparks a sort of Intifada in Jerusalem. The people are under pressure, loaded down by debts, they can't go on. The question put to Jesus—"Is it right to pay taxes?"—was already highly charged thirty years earlier; now it's dynamite. As a sign of derision young Jews shower Florus' cortege with copper coins, which they soon follow with stones. The retaliation is immediate: legionnaires force their way into houses, slit the throats of hundreds of residents, and put up crosses to execute hundreds more on the orders of the governor. The situation is serious enough for King Agrippa and his sister Bernice to feel they should intervene. The elegant princess shaves her head in a sign of mourning and, barefoot and dressed in a coarse shirt, begs the governor to pardon the condemned. Florus refuses. Agrippa the playboy, the king of the Roman dolce vita in the days of Caligula, does what he can to convince his compatriots that rebellion is hopeless. Josephus, who has as much of a soft spot as Luke does for long speeches he himself would have liked to deliver, fills seven large pages with Agrippa's address:

> As to the desire of recovering your liberty, it is unseasonable to
> indulge it so late; whereas you ought to have labored earnestly

in old time that you might never have lost it. You say it is hard to endure slavery. Yes; but how much harder is this to the Greeks, who were esteemed the noblest of all people under the sun? [The argument is clumsy: it wouldn't occur to the Jews to think that the Greeks outdo them in noblesse.] But certainly no one can imagine that you can enter into a war as by agreement, or that when the Romans have got you under their power, they will use you with moderation, or will not rather, for an example to other nations, burn your holy city, and utterly destroy your whole nation. And the danger concerns not those Jews that dwell here only, but those of them which dwell in other cities also. For there is no people upon the habitable earth which have not some portion of you among them. In case you go to war, every city which hath Jews in it will be filled with slaughter for the sake of a few men.

This warning is as lucid as it is post factum, but it's heeded all the less as Agrippa is a friend of Rome: the archetypical collaborator. He barely escapes being lynched, and Jerusalem is up in arms. The Roman garrison is besieged in Antonia Fortress, the one where Paul was held captive, next to the Temple. The cohort leader tries to negotiate with the newly formed provisional government. This provisional government is a blend of moderates—including Josephus—and radicals, for the most part zealots. The moderates promise the commanding officer that his soldiers' lives will be spared if they surrender. They surrender, but the radicals didn't promise a thing and immediately slaughter them. The worst-case scenario sets in. The high priest, the head of the moderates, is assassinated, his palace and the building where the debt registers are kept—let's not forget that overindebtedness is a key factor in the rebellion—are burned. While awaiting reinforcements, a first legion that has arrived from Caesarea, where the governor resides, encircles Jerusalem, where not only the inhabitants but also thousands of pilgrims are present. At the last minute Josephus manages to escape. No one imagines that the siege will last more than three years.

18

No people had revolted against the Roman Empire since the Gauls, way back in the days of Julius Caesar. The emperor should take matters under his control, but the emperor has other things on his mind. Since the death of Seneca, Nero has freed himself of any form of superego and given free rein to his artistic instincts. He thinks of nothing but his career, his voice, his poetry, the genuineness of the applause. How to be certain your audience is sincere when you can have any insufficiently enthusiastic spectators put to death? He's tormented by the question. In A.D. 66, he goes on a grand tour of Greece, a country of refined connoisseurs, whose approval means everything to him. His entire court goes along. It's all very well to tell him that leaving Rome vacant like an unlocked house is dangerous; he couldn't care less. He's participating in the chariot races at the Olympic Games—he wins first prize although he fell on the first turn—when he receives the news that the Roman legion has suffered a defeat and retreated from Jerusalem. The news is grave, but that doesn't stop Nero from going on with his triumphant tour. He contents himself with appointing a general of common extraction to head the punitive campaign, someone considered full of good sense, who distinguished himself during the conquest of Brittany. This general is named Vespasian, nicknamed the mule dealer because he got rich selling mules to the army. The mule dealer sets off for Judea with an army of sixty thousand men. The reconquest—that is, the systematic massacre of the rebels and anyone suspected of being in league with them—commences. Villages are set on fire, men crucified, women raped, and the children who manage to hide will become terrorists when they grow up. A familiar story. The revolt spreads to the entire region, and the steamroller gets moving in Galilee. That's where we meet up with Josephus once again. Promoted by the provisional government to the rank of general, he has been commander of the Jewish forces for the last two months.

•

When he describes himself in the third person in *The Jewish War*, Josephus says that Josephus courageously defended his positions against the inexorable advance of the Roman legions, and that after fierce fighting, he found himself encircled with forty or so fighters in a cave on the hillside near Jotapata. You can just imagine this man so familiar with embassies, roundtables, and smooth-tongued negotiations surrounded by a horde of bearded, sweaty, fiery-eyed Jewish jihadists, all ready to die a hero's death. Josephus is for surrender, of course: We were courageous, now it's time to be reasonable. His companions say that's not an option, and give him a choice: either he can kill himself as a general, or he can be killed by them as a traitor. Josephus is disheartened for a moment, but doesn't give up. He gets them to agree that instead of committing suicide, they should slit each other's throats, and draw lots to determine the order. Luckily, he's the second to last; he cuts a deal with the other guy and leaves the cave with his hands in the air, shouting that he's giving himself up.

Now he risks being executed by the other camp. As a Jewish general, he points out that he's entitled to speak with the Roman general, and his authority is such that instead of being crucified on the spot, he's received by Vespasian himself. Solemnly he tells the general that he's had a vision: Israel will be defeated and he, Vespasian, will become the emperor of Rome. It's very unlikely on the face of it: the imperial succession of Caesars obeys a more or less dynastic principle, and Vespasian is no more than a simple career soldier. Nevertheless, the announcement gets him thinking, and makes his prisoner interesting. Josephus is saved. He remains a prisoner of the Romans and doesn't complain, because if they freed him he'd be killed straightaway by the Jews. He enjoys special treatment. Soon he meets Vespasian's son Titus, a friendly boy for whom a day is lost if he hasn't given a present to a friend. Josephus becomes Titus' friend, and receives presents from him. His career as a turncoat begins.

•

With Galilee pacified—that is to say, almost flattened—it's time to occupy Jerusalem, the hotbed of the insurrection. Vespasian discovers that this bleak wasp's nest, perched on a steep hill, is in fact very well defended. No problem, he'll take his time and let the rebels kill each other off, and too bad for their hostages, the inhabitants, and pilgrims. The calculation is correct: they kill each other off. All that's known about the three years of the siege comes down to us from Josephus, who followed events from Vespasian's camp, and gathered the statements of prisoners and deserters. These accounts are terrifying, in a way that is unfortunately all too familiar to us. Rival warlords at the head of militias that terrorize the poor souls who are simply trying to survive. Famine, mothers who lose their minds after eating their children. Deserters who swallow all their money before they leave, hoping to shit it out once they reach safety, and Roman soldiers, forewarned, who make a habit of disemboweling their prisoners at the barricades and searching through their guts. Forests of crosses on the hillsides. Naked, tortured bodies decomposing under the scorching sun. Pricks hacked off in a mood of merriment: circumcision was always a cause for amusement among the legionnaires. Packs of dogs and jackals feed on the corpses, and that's nothing, Josephus says, compared with what's happening inside the walls of the city, which is like "a wild animal that's made crazy with hunger and feeds on its own flesh."

•

Without being overly hurried, Vespasian gets ready to launch the final assault when news arrives in June of A.D. 68 that the emperor has died. Back in Rome after his triumphant tour of Greece, having won all the prizes at all the games and on all the stages, Nero faced hostile armies, a senate that declared him an enemy of the city, and a conspiracy in the palace. Things went so wrong for him so fast that he had no choice but to kill himself, at age thirty-one. "What an artist dies in me!" he is said to have sighed before having a slave thrust his knife into his throat.

History will side with the aristocrats and senators against Nero, but the people will remain faithful to him long after his death: Suetonius says that his grave was always covered with flowers by anonymous, loving hands. His death ushers in a year of continuous and unprecedented crises, border uprisings, and *pronunciamientos.* No fewer than four emperors follow in short succession, put in power by, and sometimes emerging from, the ranks of the army. One will commit suicide, two others will be murdered, soon we'll come to the fourth. The year 68 is one of convulsions and terror, signs and extraordinary events. Nothing but monstrous births, babies with several heads, sows giving birth to clawed monsters, a plague epidemic in Rome, famine in Alexandria, adventurers showing up in the four corners of the Empire and claiming to be Nero, eclipses, meteors, shooting stars, earthquakes. Too bad for my story: the major eruption of Mount Vesuvius, the one that covered Pompeii and Herculaneum with ash, will happen only ten years later, but it's preceded by smaller ones. The entire region around Naples seems on fire, the mouth of hell opens. Add to that the pogroms in Egypt and Syria, with the peaceful Jews of the diaspora paying for the rebels of Judea, as

Agrippa predicted. Is this not what the prophets announced, the "beginning of the birth pains," and maybe more than the beginning: the height of evil before the end of ends?

19

For Renan it jumps out: the Book of Revelation was written during this year of planetary chaos. Its flamboyant images are just so many more or less coded allusions to Nero and the brewing catastrophe in Jerusalem. Other historians tend to date it thirty years later, during the reign of Domitian. Although the second school is in the majority, I sympathize with the first, because otherwise the Book of Revelation would fall outside the temporal scope of my book, and that doesn't suit me because I want to discuss it. It's not that I'm all that wild about it, but it was written on Patmos, and it's there that, after a year of searching and several disappointments, Hélène and I finally found the house where I'm writing this chapter, in November 2012.

•

It's the first trip I've made here alone, this is the first time I've used the house as a writing base. The weather has been good for a week, and every day I've gone swimming at Psili Ammos, our favorite beach, where, alone in the company of a couple of goats, I could have taken myself for Odysseus. I often think of Odysseus when I'm on this island, which I consider my own private Ithaca: the place you return to, the place of calm after the storms, where you renew contact with the real. I think of him all the more in that the first thing we did after we bought the house was to replace the sad twin beds in our bedroom with a *matrimoniale*—as the Italians say—worthy of the name. That didn't involve going to IKEA and buying a big box spring. No, our room now boasts a traditional Patmian-style bed consisting of a platform with steps and cupboards underneath, and a sculpted railing all around. Getting it just as we wanted involved quite a complex—and expensive—bit of woodwork. As it is, we love this bed. Even when I'm alone, as I am now, I can feel Hélène's presence in it. And this is what you find in book 23 of *The Odyssey*:

Odysseus finally reaches Ithaca. Twenty years after he left—ten years of war, ten of wandering—Penelope is waiting for him. She's older, but every bit as faithful. Cleverly she staves off the suitors who would like to have Odysseus declared dead so they can share her bed. Odysseus prowls around his own palace. Disguised as a beggar, he observes this world that is his own, without him. He's recognized by the maid Eurycleia, the swineherd Eumaeus, his dog Argos, then he massacres the suitors, and after this exploit the time seems right to reveal himself to Penelope. He appears before her, she looks at him. She should throw herself in his arms, but she doesn't budge. She doesn't say a word. Telemachus, their son, who has also recognized Odysseus, says his mother has a heart of stone. Penelope doesn't have a heart of stone: she's cautious, and she knows her mythology. She knows that to deceive men, and especially women, the gods are able to take on any appearance they want.

"If he is truly Odysseus," she says, "home at last, make no mistake: we two will know each other, even better—we two have secret signs, known to us both but hidden from the world." These secret signs, so decisive in fairy tales and science fiction stories where the hero, changed into a toad or prisoner of a time loop, must be recognized by someone who *can't* recognize him—in his place, the hero wouldn't recognize himself either—are of an entirely different order than the scar on Odysseus' thigh, which the maid Eurycleia sees when he approaches the fire. It could be something they say while making love, something they murmur the moment they come. What's more, when Penelope talks of secret signs, Odysseus smiles. Maybe it's not the only time that he smiles, but in all of *The Odyssey* it's the only time that Homer underscores the fact that he does, and it's certainly not for nothing. He goes to bathe, to have himself cleaned, oiled, made ready, and discovers when he's done that Penelope has prepared a bed for him.

Their bed.

So Odysseus tells the story of this solid, welcoming bed that he himself built from the trunk of an olive tree. He tells how he squared the wood, how he cut it, planed it, put it together, pegged it, polished it, inlaid it with ivory, fitted it with gold and silver, wove the straps across it with gleaming red oxhide, and the more he talks about the bed, which is the locus of their desire, their potency, and their rest, the more Penelope feels her knees—and her heart—melting. When he's finished she really does embrace him. Odysseus holds his wife in his arms, and maybe he remembers, in any case the reader remembers, his promise to the young and beautiful Princess Nausicaa, who fell in love with him when she first set eyes on him, and what he sincerely wished her: "And may the good gods give you all your heart desires: husband, and house, and lasting harmony too. No finer, greater gift in the world than that when man and woman possess their home, two minds, two hearts that work as one."

20

All of a sudden the weather has changed. The temperature has dropped by almost twenty degrees, the wind has picked up, the clouds burst in sudden deluges, and I'm pleased to discover that even in these conditions the house is more than livable. Protected by thick walls, you feel good in it. In the evenings, lying on the couch, I read Roman history while watching the rain running down the windows that reflect the reassuring light cast by the red lampshade. I go to bed early, sleep through the night, and get up at dawn to sit down with a cup of tea behind this desk, which I liked the first time we walked into the living room. I take advantage of sunny spells to do yoga on the terrace, facing the hill topped by a little monastery dedicated to the prophet Elijah. Our house is nestled into the hillside below Chora, at the foot of the far more commanding Monastery of Saint John the Theologian. From there I ride my scooter to Skala, the port down below. I eat lunch in one of the two taverns that are still open at this time of the year, then go into the kitchen to choose my dinner—they pack it up for me in a Tupperware container that I bring back the next day—and ride back up the winding road on which, about halfway, you pass the Cave of the Apocalypse. The bus station is called Apokalipsi. In the summer there are always two or three tourist buses and a souvenir shop, but not in the off-season. I've visited it, of course. The cave houses an Orthodox chapel, a wall of icons, and chandeliers bristling with candles. Above all, it contains the rock wall with the holes circled with silver where the visionary rested his head and hands. Meaning that the house where I'm writing this, our house, is on the same hillside and less than half a mile from this cave where the mysterious John, a Jew from Galilee, son of thunder, companion and witness to the Lord, the last living pillar of the community of the poor and the saints of Jerusalem, the hidden imam of the churches of the Lord in Asia, is said to have heard behind him, almost two thousand years ago, the voice as powerful as a trumpet of someone who wanted to give him a message for the seven churches of Asia: Ephesus, Smyrna, Pergamum, Thyatira, Sardis, Philadelphia, and Laodicea.

He turned around.

Before him, surrounded by seven golden chandeliers, was the Son of Man.

21

He was wearing a long robe, a gold sash around his chest. His hair was white as snow, his eyes a fiery flame, his feet like polished brass, his voice like the roaring of the oceans. His right hand held seven stars, his words were like a two-edged sword. Seized with fear, John fell at his feet. Placing a hand on his shoulder, the Son of Man said to him: "Do not be afraid. I am the first and the last, the one who lives. Once I was dead, but now I am alive forever and ever. Write down, therefore, what you have seen, and what is happening, and what will happen afterward."

•

After that it's no longer John who speaks but the Son of Man himself, through John. That's why the title of the book isn't the Revelation *about* Jesus Christ (Apocalypse means "revelation"), but the Revelation *of* Jesus Christ.

This revelation starts with separate, personalized messages to the angels charged with watching over each of the churches of Asia.

The angel of the church in Ephesus, first of all, the Son of Man congratulates because, he says, "you have tested those who call themselves apostles but are not, and discovered that they are impostors. You hate the works of the Nicolaitans, which I also hate." All of that is good. However: "Yet I hold this against you: you have lost the love you had at first. Mend your ways. Otherwise I will do it for you."

Now to the angel of Smyrna. He too affronts "the slander of those who claim to be Jews and are not, but rather are members of the assembly of Satan," and is told that "the devil will throw some of those he cares for into prison, that they may be tested, and they will face an ordeal for ten days." That will separate the wheat from the chaff.

Then it's Pergamum's turn: "I have a few things against you. You have some people there who hold to the teaching of Balaam, who wants to put a stumbling block before the Israelites: to eat meat sacrificed to idols and to play the harlot."

The angel of Thyatira, now, is reprimanded for tolerating "the woman Jezebel, who calls herself a prophetess, who—also—teaches and misleads my servants to play the harlot and to eat food sacrificed to idols. I have given her time to repent, but she refuses. So I will cast her on a sickbed and put her children to death. Thus shall all the churches come to know that I am the searcher of hearts and minds."

Sardis: "I know you: you have the reputation of being alive, but you are dead. If you are not watchful, I will come like a thief, and you will never know at what hour."

Philadelphia, despite its limited strength, has not denied the Lord's name, so that "those of the assembly of Satan who claim to be Jews and are not will prostrate at your feet, and realize that I love you."

It's Laodicea, finally, that he calls lukewarm, a reproach the most vehement Christians have hurled at people like Luke and me for two thousand years: "I know your works; I know that you are neither cold nor hot. So, because you are lukewarm, neither hot nor cold, I will spit you out of my mouth. Those whom I love, I reprove and chastise. I stand at the door and knock. If anyone opens the door, I will enter his house and dine with him, and he with me." (Of all the verses in the last book of the Bible, this is the only one that I really like. Right after that, things go sour again, in a familiar way:) "I will give the victor the right to sit with me on my throne, as I myself first won the victory and sit with my Father on his throne. Whoever has ears ought to hear."

•

A question: Who is being targeted by these terrible maledictions listed in the Book of Revelation against the assembly of Satan, the Nicolaitans, the Jews who are not Jews and who eat meat sacrificed to the idols? Without batting an eye the ETB says: "The Jews who don't accept Christ." If you've read the above with a minimum of attention, you'll be speechless, as I am. Who does the ETB think it's kidding? Where have we seen first-century Christians reproaching Jews for their lack of respect for ritual prescriptions? I'm sorry, that doesn't wash. Those who are accused of eating meat sacrificed to idols, or of letting others eat such food, or of saying that it's not bad to eat such food because nothing is impure in itself and that while the words that come out of our mouths may be impure, the food that goes in is not, are of course Paul and his disciples. They are the assembly of Satan, the Nicolaitans, the false prophet Jezebel. And the one who casts these aspersions on them can only be a Judeo-Christian from the most fundamentalist fringe of the church of Jerusalem, someone who makes the late James, brother of the Lord, look like a model of tolerance and openness.

•

Is it being an unbeliever to say that this photofit does not resemble the Son of Man? That this was neither how he thought nor how he spoke, and that in the Book of Revelation it's John the son of thunder who is speaking, and not the Lord Jesus through his mouth? I don't know. What is certain is that the man who is speaking addresses the seven churches in a way that suggests that he knows them well. His allusions to their internal conflicts are incomprehensible for today's readers—and even for today's exegetes—but must have been very clear to the churches themselves. He hands out good and bad marks like a teacher who's got every right to do so. Even if their styles are diametrically opposed— Paul calls a spade a spade, while John prefers to call it a beast with ten horns and seven heads—John's tone of jealous, irascible authority re- calls the one adopted by Paul in his most polemic letters.

For the Christians of Asia, the author of the Book of Revelation must have been both an almost mystical figure and someone who had lived among them, someone they knew quite well. He had always trav- eled, one day here, another there. He hadn't been seen in Ephesus for some time. No one knew where he'd gone, and no one knew where the mother of the Lord, whom he took with him everywhere, was either. Like Osama bin Laden, he was an elusive, mysterious leader, who pitted every last ounce of his faith and cunning against the Empire that had it out for his fold: suddenly appearing where he wasn't expected, miracu- lously escaping the traps that had been set for him by police all over the world. Messages came from him out of the blue. Rumors said he was dead, or halfway around the globe, or exiled on a barbaric, hostile island—that's how Patmos was viewed at the time, and on certain days in the winter you can understand why. And as with bin Laden's videos, when a message from him was disseminated for the community of the faithful, no one could say for sure that it wasn't two years old, or that it was really from him at all.

•

So it happened that one day there was a huge commotion in the church of Ephesus. They'd received a letter from John! A very long letter, recording not only his words but those of the Lord himself! If Luke was still around, he must have been there when it was read aloud. I imagine the reading punctuated by fainting, fits of tears, and above all cursing at these imposters and Nicolaitans whom the Lord spits out of his mouth and casts on a sickbed, before putting their children to death. As Luke did not benefit from the wisdom of the ETB, I imagine that hearing these afflictions, as a disciple of Paul he felt directly targeted and in danger of getting lynched if he were identified. Finally I imagine that, not at the moment but later, he took a certain pleasure in painting John, in his youth, as a whippersnapper who was constantly put in his place by Jesus because he wanted—already!—to have the fire of heaven descend on those who weren't to his liking, to neutralize those who healed without carrying the party card, and to reserve his place in heaven at the boss's right hand.

•

After the addresses to the churches comes the interminable procession of the seven seals, the seven angels, the seven trumpets, the four horsemen, the beasts that rise up from the depths—the best known, the one that most fired people's imagination, being the beast with two horns like a lamb but the voice of a dragon, whose number is 666. "This calls for wisdom," the text states. "Let the person who has insight calculate the number of the beast, for it is the number of a man." There has been no lack of people willing to calculate, and the man they found is Nero. The explanation: if you transcribe the Greek letters of Nero Caesar into Hebrew consonants, replace these letters by their corresponding numerals, and then add these together, you get 666. It's crystal clear, yes, but I have to add that in playing around with the same numbers in his period of religious delirium, Philip K. Dick came up with his sworn enemy Richard Milhous Nixon, and found that no less clear.

After that, to cut to the quick, there's Babylon the Great, the mother of prostitutes, destruction on earth, the feast in heaven, the thousand-year reign, the Last Judgment, the new heaven and the new earth, the new Jerusalem, the wife of the lamb, this whole potpourri that the Church, extremely uncomfortable at having allowed it into the canon, had no idea what to do with for the longest time. It was only in the twelfth century with the prodigious Calabrian scholar Joachim of Flora that this obscure piece of writing was deemed to contain all the secrets of the past, present, and future and, on a par with the prophesies of Nostradamus, became the favorite playground of all manner of esoteric screwballs, Philip Dick among the best of them and Dan Brown among the worst. Saying this, I'm aware that in many people's eyes I am only admitting my dismaying impermeability to mystery and poetry. Too bad, that's just not my thing, and I'm convinced that it wasn't Luke's thing either. After a couple of months, the air in Ephesus must have seemed to him just as unbreathable as the air in Moscow to partisans of Trotsky or Bukharin during the 1936 show trials. I don't know what Luke did, but in his place I would have gone back home to Philippi, where I could breathe easily again.

22

Like Odysseus, whom he resembles so little, Luke undertook a long voyage, far longer than he imagined it would be when he set sail at Troas with Paul and the Church delegates. He traveled to Jerusalem and Rome. He saw his master imprisoned in Jerusalem and Rome. He witnessed the anger of the Jews and the brutality of the Romans. He saw the burning of Rome and he saw his own companions transformed into human torches. He crossed the Mediterranean at least three times, encountered storms and shipwrecks. And now, after seven years, he comes home.

He doesn't have Odysseus' luck: no one's waiting for him. If it were up to me, I'd give him a wife. Unfortunately tradition has it that, like Paul, he was a bachelor, and even, also like Paul, that he remained a virgin his whole life. Although I'm not thrilled at the thought, I'd feel like I was cheating if I bucked tradition on this point: there's something delicate about Luke, something ordered and a bit sad, a way of standing on the sidelines of life that makes me think this celibacy is more plausible than a large family.

So no Penelope, no secret signs or bed of olive wood. But there is one point of reference: Lydia's house. It's still there and so is Lydia, as busy, generous, and tyrannical as ever. And the old acquaintances are there as well: Syntyche, Euodia, Epaphroditus, and the others. They haven't changed, it's Luke who's changed. For me his face was a bit soft before he left, still childlike in a way. Now he's thinner, tanned, his features have become sharper. Maybe they don't recognize him at first, maybe the maid makes him wait at the door, but once they've recognized him, there's no doubt they welcome him with open arms. They kill the fatted calf in his honor and flood him with questions, their eyes sparkling. And to his own astonishment he slips easily into a role he never thought or so much as dreamed he'd occupy one day: that of the seasoned traveler, the adventurer who arrives from afar, his duffel bag slung over his shoulder, who knows more about the wide world than all of them together will ever know. Maybe there's one of his former school friends in the group, someone he looked up to when they were children, someone he considered a real tough nut. And now the tough nut is still selling sandals in his stall while everyone sees him, Luke—the good little boy who walked around with his nose in a book, the melancholic adolescent who was afraid of girls—as a hero, and hangs on his every word.

•

These years that for him were full of sound and fury passed relatively peacefully in Philippi. The Philippians suffered no persecutions, either from the Romans, whom they never gave any reason to complain, or from the local Jews, who were few in number and finally ended up viewing the sect across the way as good neighbors who'll lend you salt when you're out. There weren't many new recruits: the group counted twenty or so when Luke left, now there were thirty at most. They kept out of harm's way, among themselves, waiting for Jesus and above all for Paul. They read and reread his letters. I know that the one to the Philippians is contested, but when I imagine how happy the members of the small church must have been to receive a letter addressed to them personally, I want to declare it authentic. From time to time, at Lydia's initiative, everyone pitched in and sent money to Paul, and Luke didn't need to have his arm twisted to tell them that these were the only donations Paul was willing to accept, which he did gladly while sending his blessings in return. They were far from Jerusalem: none of James's emissaries had made it to Macedonia to denounce Paul as an imposter, and if one had knocked on Lydia's door you can be certain he would have got a good roasting. And they were far from Rome: of course they'd heard about the fire and the persecution, they knew that for several months one Caesar had followed the next in bloody succession, but it was like the catastrophes or wars you see on TV. Their agapes, meanwhile, were like pastry competitions. They didn't get drunk. No one cursed anyone. They sang: "Come, Lord Jesus," then walked each other home and went to bed. They spoke quietly so as not to disturb the neighbors, their voices echoed softly in the silent streets, they said good night on the doorstep. Luke must have realized that he'd missed this rustic friendliness, this nonhysterical fervor—Paul was no longer there to get them all fired up. After seven years of living in perpetual tension, where a threat lurked behind every encounter and every instant held a life-or-death choice, he was charmed by this lack of stress. Macedonia was his Switzerland, his Le Levron, his *querencia*: he relaxed.

23

Every evening, the group assembled to listen to him. They formed a circle and waited for him to come down from his room—I suppose that, at least at first, he lived at Lydia's place. The story of what he had personally experienced at Paul's side must have occupied many evenings and got many children dreaming, if they weren't sent off to bed. I think that they weren't, and that Luke was better than I am at telling stories about storms at sea and shipwrecks. It strikes me as entirely plausible that that's when he started writing it all down. The passages of the Acts that are told in the first person would then date from this time, and only later, much later, would he get the idea of making them part of a much larger story dealing with all the information he'd gathered on the history of the young Church. I think, because it's straightforward and plausible, that he started writing the Acts well before his Gospel, and I also think—this is just my own opinion—that while Luke could speak volumes about Paul, Peter, James, Philip, and the first community in Jerusalem, he said nothing, or next to nothing, about Jesus.

Because his listeners were more interested in Paul, but not only. He'd gotten into the habit of not talking to Paul about the investigation he'd led in Judea, and I think that at Lydia's place he stuck to it. He wouldn't have known how to tell it. He wasn't sure what it related. The face he'd tried to approach shied away. The words he'd copied from Philip's scroll remained hidden in the bottom of the trunk with all his things, and that's where they stayed. He didn't dare read them to the others or even to read them himself, because he was afraid they wouldn't be understood, and maybe that even he wouldn't understand them.

•

How old was Luke in A.D. 70? If he met Paul when he was twenty or thirty, he'd now be between forty and fifty. He'd spent almost half his life in a campaign that he'd joined as a fellow traveler and continued to wage as a sort of veteran, yet whose meaning now escaped him. He could no longer tell if it was a victory or a defeat. On the defeat side were the catastrophe of Rome, Paul's bitterness at the end of his life and his tragic death, the hostility with which the churches of Asia now remembered him, their transformation under John's authority into a fanatical sect. On the other side were the faith of Lydia and her little group in Philippi, and, despite everything, this scroll that he kept like a treasure at the bottom of his trunk but never unraveled—for fear of discovering that in fact it wasn't a treasure, that he'd been given a false diamond, but also out of an intuition that the time was not yet right.

•

Two times when telling the story of Jesus' childhood, Luke says "Mary kept all these things in her heart." He must have done the same. He didn't quite know what to think of "all these things" that concerned Jesus. Maybe he didn't think of them often, maybe they didn't take up much room in his mind. But he kept them in his heart.

24

I imagine that he stayed in Philippi for a year, two years, three years. That he went back to his trade as a doctor, and took up his old habits. Agapes at Lydia's place, the old circle of friends, patients, walks in the mountains, maybe a small glass at the tavern in the evening. Early dinner, early to bed, early to rise: Switzerland. A couple of hours writing his memoirs in the morning, like a pensioner who's seen the world. Things could go on like that in a slow and easy way until the end of his days.

From Philippi, however, he must have followed the events in Judea with more attention than the average retiree. Good Christian though he was, he no doubt frequented the synagogues of Berea or Thessaloniki, the ones that had practically tarred and feathered Paul fifteen years earlier. Although these Jews grew up far from Israel and had mostly never set foot there, he could talk with them about Jerusalem, the Temple, Agrippa. He knew more than they did, he had trodden the courtyards of the Temple, but they got regular news and he listened to them with the discerning look of one who's spent time in a global hot spot and knows the terrain.

This news was increasingly distressing. Like Luke, the Jews of Macedonia respected the Romans. It would never have occurred to them to rebel, and they were very alive to the risk Agrippa had pointed out: if things worsened in Judea, they would suffer here. Certainly, Macedonia was quiet, as far as you could get from the theater of operations, but it had already happened that the authorities had turned against Jews living outside of Judea who had had nothing whatsoever to do with the revolt. To test their loyalty to the Empire, the authorities in Antioch had got the idea of obliging them to worship pagan gods, eat pork, and work on the Sabbath. The number of checks and inspections was redoubled, those who were found lighting their lamps and refusing to work were whipped, sometimes executed. Old men's pants were pulled down to see if they were circumcised. That's why, apart from a few enthusiasts like the ones in John's entourage in Ephesus, most of the Jews in the Empire hoped the rebels would be defeated and order restored. But right up to the last moment, none hoped for or even imagined the absolutely monstrous event the news of which would reach them at the end of the summer in A.D. 70: the sack of Jerusalem, the destruction of the Temple.

25

It could be that I was unjust with Josephus when I insinuated that his vision of the defeat of Israel and Vespasian's accession to the imperial throne was a fiction invented to gain the general's favor. Maybe he did have a vision, like John in Patmos. But whereas people are still trying to figure out just what John's vision referred to, Josephus' vision came true in almost no time at all, on both points. And, at least as far as the second was concerned, he must have felt a divine surprise: in July of 69, after a year of chaos, three Caesars crowned and killed one after another, the legions of Syria and Egypt proclaimed Vespasian emperor.

As I've said, two years earlier that was all highly improbable, but in the meantime people had gotten used to the army proclaiming the Caesars. Thanks to Josephus, Vespasian had prepared himself for the role. He assumed it like someone who wasn't particularly keen on the job, but hey: you have to do what you have to do, and if someone has to do it, he might as well be the one. He was in no more of a hurry to return to Rome than he was to attack Jerusalem. Like General Kutuzov in *War and Peace*, Vespasian didn't like to rush, preferring to take his time. Knowing that that was a quality people liked about him, he played it up. He was counted on to reestablish order, and he went about it at his own speed with the wily good nature of a mule dealer. He put off the journey for several months, then finally departed, leaving his son Titus to finish the job in Jerusalem.

Josephus had backed the right horse. It's at this time that, as a tribute to the new Caesar who descended from the Flavia family, he exchanged his Jewish name, Joseph ben Matityahu, for the Latin name we know him by, and his status as prisoner of war for that of a sort of commissioner for Jewish affairs reporting to Titus, who had become generalissimo for the Orient. In Titus' entourage Josephus met up with two old acquaintances: the client king Agrippa and his sister, Bernice—now Titus' lover. You could say that, like Josephus, Bernice and Agrippa were collaborators, but they weren't cynical rogues. What was happening before their eyes horrified them. They did all they could to argue their people's case with the Romans, and to argue the Romans' case with their people. Apart from that they had a good time of things, always in the lap of luxury, always on the side of those in power. When he joined this group of goodwilled, well-heeled turncoats, Josephus— who in addition was very worried about several family members trapped in Jerusalem—did not want to be outdone. Having obtained from Titus the promise that all those who surrendered before the onslaught would be spared, he left the Roman camp to offer the besieged a last chance. In his book he describes how he circled the ramparts, seeking the right distance to be within earshot but out of arrowshot, and beseeched the rebels to think of their lives, the Temple, and the future of the Jewish people. He just had enough time to say a few words before a stone hit him in the face. Bloody and sorrowful, he beat a retreat.

•

Very much in love with Bernice, Titus would have liked to please her and show a willingness to compromise, but on the one hand it's difficult to show a willingness to compromise when you're faced with a frenzied mob—which the besieged Jerusalemites had now become—and on the other, when he left for Rome his father had given him an unambiguous road map: the new emperor's rule was to be inaugurated with a grand and significant victory, showing that you can't defy Rome and get away with it. As Vladimir Putin said in the rather similar context of Chechnya, he would waste the terrorists in their shithouses.

And he did.

•

Writing in praise of Titus, Josephus says that the general had recommended moderate bloodshed and forbidden that the temple be destroyed. But he couldn't keep an eye on everything: the Temple was set ablaze, and the women and children who had taken refuge inside it were burned alive. The dead numbered in the hundreds of thousands, rebels, inhabitants, and pilgrims taken together, and so did the survivors, herded into camps to be sent to the mines in Egypt, sold as slaves, or—for the most attractive—set aside with an eye to the triumphal procession being prepared in Rome.

Jerusalem is a city of tunnels and underground passages. In the archaeological zone known as the City of David, my friend Olivier Rubinstein once showed me the gigantic paving stones, each of which is split neatly in two. It's a very strange sight, you don't understand what could have happened, what natural cataclysm could have caused such regular cracks. Olivier gave me the answer: it's not a natural cataclysm but the work of Roman legionnaires. Using mallets, they methodically split the stones to flush out the last insurgents who had hidden themselves away like rats underground. Simon bar Giora, one of the rebel leaders who kept the besieged city under a reign of terror, was captured at the end of a subterranean passage, his face covered by a thick beard, half-crazed, like Saddam Hussein. When there was no one left to kill, kind Titus had the city destroyed, its walls knocked down, the Temple razed. In engineering terms that was no mean feat. The huge blocks had to be put somewhere, and, once the ravine that separated the Temple from the upper city in those days had been filled to the brim, the rest were just left in heaps here and there. The various Roman, Arab, Crusader, and Ottoman conquerors who captured and recaptured Jerusalem down the centuries helped themselves to these stones to rebuild the city as they saw fit, each one claiming that it was their work. In this gigantic Lego construction, the only wall that has never collapsed is the Western Wall of the Temple, to which even today the Jews address their prayers. Josephus concludes from all of this that "the rebellion destroyed the city, and Rome destroyed the rebellion." The idea being that the Jews started it, and that in order to reestablish peace, the Romans didn't have a choice. Or you can say, like the Caledonian chieftain Galgacus, whose strong words are related by Tacitus: "Where they make a desert, the Romans call it peace."

2 6

Masada, one of the most impressive sites you can visit in Israel, is a citadel built by the luxury-loving King Herod on a rocky spur overlooking the Dead Sea. In this eagle's nest reminiscent of the Cathar Castles in southern France or the fort in Dino Buzzati's novel *The Tartar Steppe*, a last group of Zealots held out for several months after the fall of Jerusalem before ending their days in a mass suicide. Today, schoolchildren are taken there once a year, the young people called up for military service go there to take an oath, and political scientists use the term "Masada complex" to describe Israel's tendency to see itself as a besieged fortress to be defended if need be to the bitter end. Whether it's right to hold the Zealots of Masada up as an example to younger generations is a debate in which historians are invited to participate, because the answer isn't the same if the besieged committed suicide, which is forbidden by the Law, or if they cut each other's throats, which is allowed. Josephus, whom this tragedy must have reminded of a crucial episode in his own life, gives it particular emphasis in *The Jewish Wars*. It's the subject of his last chapter, and reading it, you realize that in his mind what he's describing is much more than the last chapter of his book: it's the last chapter in the history of the Jewish people.

As usual he can't stop himself from giving a long speech, which he credits to the leader of the Zealots, Eleazar. This man, who will die a hero's death under the same circumstances in which he, Josephus, survived as a traitor, is quoted as follows:

> Perhaps we should have thought about this long ago when we were defending our liberty. It seems that the same God, who had long ago taken the Jewish nation into his favor, has now condemned them to destruction. If he had continued to be favorable toward us or at least been a little less displeased with us, maybe there wouldn't have been so many men killed, and his most holy city would not have been burnt and demolished by our enemies . . . For it now appears that God has made a decree against the whole Jewish nation, that we are to be deprived of this life which he knew we would not make a due use of . . . Let us not receive the punishment from the Romans, but from God himself, as executed by our own hands.

The entire history of Israel is a series of warnings given by God to his people. Threats, exhortations, condemnations that he always ends up repealing, loving father that he is. At the last minute, he stops Abraham's knife and saves Isaac. Later, he lets the Babylonians take Jerusalem and destroy the Temple, but he allows the Jews to return from exile and build a second Temple. Not this time: it's the last condemnation, and this one is irrevocable.

There will be no third Temple.

•

In principle, the Romans didn't destroy sanctuaries. They didn't humiliate the gods of their defeated enemies. Through a specific ritual, the *evocatio*, a place could be made for these gods in the pantheon. But there had never been any question of that for the god of Israel, and even less of the reconstruction of his Temple. It was decided that the Jews of the Diaspora would continue to pay the offering of two denarii that they had made a point of sending to Jerusalem each year for the upkeep of the Temple, and that the money would now be used for the maintenance of Capitoline Hill, that is, in the service of pagan gods. This welcome revenue, which was given the name *fiscus Judaicus*, was the idea of

Vespasian himself, an emperor appreciated for his good sense, fatherly management, and imaginative taxation. Legend wrongly credits him with the invention of public urinals. They already existed, but it is true that he literally taxed urine: wool producers used it as a grease remover, and, to be sure they had enough at their disposal, they placed jars in front of their workshops where the locals were encouraged to empty their chamber pots. Fine, said Vespasian, carry on, provided you pay a small levy, prompting the saying, so the story goes, that money has no smell.

Sixty years later, the good emperor Hadrian, who like all "good" emperors was anti-Semitic and anti-Christian, had a modern Roman city named Aelia Capitolina built on the site of Jerusalem, with a temple to Jupiter where the Temple had stood. This provocation caused a last burst of rebellion among the Jews still living in the region, and this uprising was also drowned in blood. Circumcision was banned, Jews were encouraged to abandon their faith. The region was renamed Palestine, in reference to the most ancient enemies of the Jews, the Philistines— inhabitants of the Gaza Strip whom the Jews, in fact, had driven from their homeland. Destroyed and then profaned, Jerusalem became synonymous with mourning and desolation. "He who repaints his house," says the Mishnah, "should leave one corner of the wall unpainted, in memory of Jerusalem. He who prepares a meal should leave out one ingredient, in memory of Jerusalem. She who dresses herself in fine garments should remove one, in memory of Jerusalem."

•

Nevertheless . . .

27

Nevertheless, says the Talmud, there was a very pious rabbi in Jerusalem named Johanan ben Zakkai. A student of the great Hillel, he was a Pharisee who had dedicated his life to studying the Law. During the siege, he argued in vain for peace. When he realized that the situation was desperate, he managed to get himself smuggled out of the city in a coffin, lying with a rotting carcass so that the odor of decaying flesh would fool the soldiers on the barricades. His disciples carried him right to Vespasian's tent, and Jewish tradition has it that, like Josephus, Rabbi ben Zakkai announced to the general that Israel would be defeated and that he, Vespasian, would become emperor. (As narrator I would have liked to avoid this redundancy, but there you go, two different sources attest to these parallel predictions: if it's true, it must have given Vespasian enough to chew on.) After which, the story has it, the rabbi obtained from the future emperor that a small enclave should be preserved from the imminent destruction of everything Jewish, and that there a handful of pious men could continue to study the Law in peace.

•

The Temple of the Jews no longer existed. The city of the Jews no longer existed. The country of the Jews no longer existed. Normally the Jewish people should have ceased to exist, like so many peoples before and after them that have disappeared or melted into others. That's not what happened. In the history of humanity, there is no other example of a people that persisted in their existence as a people for so long, after being deprived of their territory and worldly power. This new, absolutely unparalleled way of being started in Yavne, near Jaffa, where Rabbi ben Zakkai's small Pharisee reserve was set up after the sack of Jerusalem. It's there that in secret, in silence, what became rabbinical Judaism took seed. It's there that the Mishnah was born. It's there that the Jews stopped living in a country and started living in the Law. From now on there will be no high priests but wise men, no glorious Temple but humble synagogues, no sacrifices but prayers, no sacred place but a day, the Sabbath, which, as it had become necessary to forget about space, unfolded the most impregnable of sanctuaries in the realm of time, dedicated to attention, solicitude, and everyday gestures sanctified by the love of God.

The Talmud describes the rabbi walking with one of his disciples over the field of ruins that Jerusalem had become. The disciple laments: *Oy vavoy.* "Don't be sad," the rabbi says to him. "We have another way of worshipping God the way he likes." "What?" "Acts of kindness."

28

And the poor? The saints? The family of Jesus, the Judeo-Christians of James's obedience? It's said that they, too, or at least some of them, were able to flee the besieged city and find refuge on the other side of the Jordan River, in the desert region of Batanaea.

They were the last to have known Jesus. They spoke of him as a prophet who had come to summon Israel to follow the Law more purely. Now Israel had gone down in flames and they no longer knew what to think. That had already been the case when Jesus, who was supposed to drive out the Romans, ended up being crucified by them. Now, absolutely stunned, they no longer understood a thing. They weren't what you'd call wizards of interpretation.

They reminded each other of anecdotes and things that he'd said. They could have described his face if anyone had asked them. They drew up genealogies to show that he really did descend from David—that was very important for them, to the point that the very essence of their faith resided in such questions of genealogy. They had seen his brother James stoned to death, they'd been told that Peter had died in Rome, John, too, perhaps. They thought that "the man enemy" had denounced them. "The man enemy" is what they called Paul. They didn't know much about him, but they knew enough to curse him. They spread stories about him engaging in black magic. They said that he wasn't even Jewish, that he'd wanted to seduce the high priest's daughter— we know a little about all of this thanks to Professor Maccoby, who gathered his information from their patchy, frayed traditions and persuaded himself that it was the truth hidden by the deft storytellers of the New Testament. At the same time, the Jews told stories of the same kind about the mother of Jesus: that she had fooled around with a Roman soldier named Panthera. Or even, no holds barred: with a panther.

Rejected both by the Jews and by the Christians, the Judeo-Christians became heretics in the church that they had founded. Not very annoying heretics, granted, as no one paid them any heed or even knew they existed, alone in the desert with their genealogies. If, half a millennium later, Muhammad hadn't formed his idea of Jesus on the basis of what remained of their sects, you could say that all trace of them would have been lost in the sand.

29

Until the year A.D. 70, a Christian was a sort of Jew. This kind of conflation was useful, because the Jews were identified and—by and large— accepted by the Empire. The first time when the distinction was made, it didn't benefit the Christians: they, and not the Jews, were burned in revenge for the burning of Rome. But when the Jews found themselves in the position of being outcasts after their revolt was crushed, viewed as potential terrorists and deprived of all their pleasant dispensations, it started to be in the interest of the Christians to distinguish themselves from them. Until A.D. 70 the pillars of their church were James, Peter, and John: good Hebrews. Paul was nothing but a deviationist troublemaker whom no one had talked about since his death. After A.D. 70, everything changed. James's church gets lost in the sand, John's group turns into a sect of paranoid esotericists: the time is ripe for Paul and his de-Hebrewed church. Paul himself is no longer around, but his partisans are dispersed here and there throughout the known world. Luke is one such Paulist. Back in his native land, he thought he'd retired for good. He thought the tale was told, the game was up, but now his former companions are telling him that everything's starting up again, and they need him.

•

Now that I'm bringing Luke back to Rome, we may as well make it June of A.D. 71, so that he can witness Titus' return from Jerusalem together with the rest of the population. A triumphal procession is never anything more than a military parade, but the Romans didn't do things by halves. If they built a stadium they put in 250,000 seats, and their military parades looked like the Rio Carnival. Back in Rome as part of the victorious general's entourage, Josephus observed this ceremony celebrating the victory of Roman civilization over Oriental fanaticism from the stand reserved for high officials. He described it with a wealth of detail worthy of Gustave Flaubert's *Salammbô* and a sense of marvel that one could easily find out of place, given that the defeated enemy was his own people.

The most surprising things are the moving structures. As high as four-story buildings, they advance with the parade, carrying whole clusters of prisoners and representing, for the edification of the masses, I quote: "the strongest fortifications taken, as also every place full of slaughter, and supplications of the enemies, when they were no longer able to lift up their hands in opposition. Houses were overthrown and falling upon their owners, rivers also ran down, not into a land cultivated, but through a land still on fire upon every side. On the top of every one of these pageants was placed the commander of the city that was taken, and the manner wherein he was taken. Moreover, there followed a great number of ships." I have to admit I have a bit of difficulty imagining the scene, but you can be sure it was spectacular.

One of the generals placed in "the manner wherein he was taken" is Simon bar Giora. After being captured in the ruins of Jerusalem, he is transported to the place of his execution with a rope around his neck and whipped by soldiers. Josephus must think that if he hadn't changed sides when he did he could have shared the same fate. After the prisoners comes the plunder, in particular everything that had been taken from the Temple: lampstands with seven branches, liturgical costumes worn by service boys like in Federico Fellini's *Roma*, purple veils from the Holy of Holies. The scrolls of the Law end the parade of spoils. After that come porters bearing statues representing the victory, all made of ivory and gold, and behind them, finally, on his chariot, Vespasian himself. Very simple, very natural, flanked on both sides by his two sons, Titus and Domitian. The latter, Josephus notes, "on a horse that was worthy of admiration."

•

Vespasian will reign for ten years, Titus two, Domitian fifteen. The first two reigns will be peaceful, prosperous, a sort of Restoration that puts the madness of Tiberius, Caligula, Claudius, and Nero behind it as quickly as possible. With Domitian, things will take a turn for the worse once again, but we're not there yet. For now everyone is breathing easy. Rome rests and recuperates. The defeat of the Jews makes people feel like they're back in the good old days when there weren't too many foreigners, and when the Romans weren't softened by city life, excessive banquets, exotic influences, and long hours at the thermal baths: when they were rugged warriors who smelled of man and sweat, and not of Oriental perfumes. Vespasian rules the Empire like a family father. While waiting to succeed him, Titus acts as his efficient second.

Suetonius nicknamed Titus "the darling of the human race"—a reputation that posterity has ratified. Renan insists that the goodness he is attributed with is not natural: that Titus forced himself. I don't know where Renan derives such acute psychological insights, but this trait touches me because goodness isn't natural to me either: I also force myself, knowing that goodness is all that counts, and I believe that does me all the more credit. The only fault that Titus is charged with is having come back from his two-year campaign in Judea with a whole group of Jews who are out of place at court: his great friends Agrippa and Josephus, and above all his mistress Bernice. He never goes anywhere without her, rumors of an impending marriage do the rounds. The old Romans don't approve. Vespasian asks his son to put things in order. Titus submits. Suetonius sums things up in one sentence: "Titus had Queen Bernice removed from Rome, against his will and hers." So Bernice returns to the deserted Orient. She will come back to Rome after Vespasian's death and see Titus once again, but too late. After a reign unanimously judged too short, he dies of a mysterious illness that will make people ask whether he was poisoned by his horrible brother Domitian, or—as the Babylon Talmud has it—if his brain was eaten away by a gnat as punishment for destroying Jerusalem. Suetonius, once again, tells us that on his deathbed Titus complained that life was being taken from him despite his innocence, for, he says, "I have only done one thing wrong." What that was, however, remains anyone's guess.

30

Through Tacitus and Suetonius we have full knowledge of the grand history of Rome in the first century: emperors, senate, border wars, and palace intrigues; but we are no less well informed about daily life, thanks to Juvenal and Martial. The first, as I've said an incarnation of the charming reactionary, wrote caustic, angry satires, and the second minimalist epigrams, half of which are dirty and all of which hit the nail on the head. If you think, as I do, that Luke went back to Rome at the start of the 70s, and if you try to imagine his life there, it's better to read Martial than *Quo Vadis*.

Of course there's a huge difference between Martial and Luke: one is Christian, the other isn't, but both—for Martial it's certain, for Luke it's just my opinion—belong to the lower middle class. Both were rootless city dwellers, the one from Spain, the other from Macedonia, not at all poor in that they don't have to worry about where their next meal will come from, but far, very far, from being rich in a city where staggering fortunes are accumulated with the help of private banks and speculation. The nice thing about Martial, and the reason I bring him in here, is that he tells everything, with a predilection for trivial details that the noble authors disdain. Like Georges Perec and Sophie Calle, he's able to turn his shopping lists or his address book into literature. He lives in a two-room apartment on the third floor of an investment property. He's constantly complaining about the noise, which prevents him from sleeping because the convoys carrying merchandise are only allowed to enter the city at night, so that no sooner has the din of swerving chariots and shouting drivers subsided than the hubbub of the storekeepers opening their shops and hollering to each other starts at the crack of dawn. Martial's a bachelor, his household is limited to two or three slaves—that's the minimum: if you don't have at least that many you're a slave yourself. He himself sleeps in a bed, his slaves on mats in the next room. They're not high-class, expensive slaves, but he likes them a lot, treats them kindly, sleeps with them kindly. His real extravagance is his personal library, comprising old-fashioned papyrus rolls as well as codices: sheaves of pages with words on both sides, which, apart from the fact that the text isn't printed but copied by hand, are books in the modern sense. This new format was starting to replace the old one, like the e-book today: the change was taking place but not entirely finished. The major classics were published in this format: Homer, Virgil, but also contemporary bestsellers like the *Moral Letters to Lucilius*, and when Martial himself is honored in this way for his last collections of epigrams, he's as proud as a French author today when he's published in the Bibliothèque de la Pléiade collection in his lifetime. Martial is a man of letters, vain like all men of letters, but aside from that a likable lazybones, more worried about his pleasures than his career. His ideal day consists of strolling through the city in the morning, hanging around in bookstores, going to the market and picking out the dinner—asparagus, quail's eggs, arugula, sow's teats—to which he'll treat two or three friends that evening. Together they'll talk shop and finish off a jar of Falernian wine—late-harvested, his favorite. The afternoons he spends in the baths. There's nothing better: you bathe, you sweat, you talk, you play, you doze off, you read, you dream. Some prefer the theater or the circus; not Martial. He could spend his entire life in the baths. And in fact that's pretty much what he does. But these pleasures are paid for with an unpleasant task, which is the lot—and the nightmare—of most Romans: the morning visit to the patron.

•

You have to understand this: in the Empire, as in any preindustrial society, the productive work was agriculture, and agriculture, as we know, takes place in the countryside. So what did the city dwellers do? That's just the point: not much. They received support. The rich, who owned the land and drew immense revenues from it, furnished the poor with bread and games—*panem et circenses*, according to Juvenal's formula—so that neither hunger nor idleness would give them the idea of rebelling. Two days out of every three were public holidays. The baths were free. Finally, as everyone needs a little money to live, urban society was divided not into employers and employees, with the first paying the second for their work, but into patrons and clients, the first supporting the second to do nothing apart from express their gratitude. In addition to land and slaves, a rich man had clients. That is to say, a small number of individuals less rich than he was showed up at his door every morning to receive a modest sum called the sportula. At worst six sestertii, the equivalent of a minimum wage. Poor Romans lived on that—and the less poor lived on the same thing one or two notches up: their patrons were richer, and were themselves clients to even richer patrons. Martial was a well-known poet, more or less happy with his life, but that didn't exempt him from complying with this ritual every morning for the forty years he lived in Rome, and goodness knows he complained about it. One thing he hates is getting up early. Another is dressing in a toga: it's stiff, heavy, inpractical, plus it runs up a huge cleaning bill. But you have to put on a toga to greet your patron, the way you put on a tie to go to work at the office. You rush—on foot because there's not enough money to pay for a litter—through the narrow, poorly paved, muddy streets where you always risk adversity, or at least dirtying your toga. Then you stand out in the hallway at the patron's place with a group of other parasites whom you view with disdain and distrust. When the patron finally deigns to appear—as put out by the whole thing as his clients are—you wait your turn to whisper a few words to him in an appropriately flattering voice. This tone was known as the *obsequium*, which needs no explaining. Once that's over with it's checkout time, and the cashier is a sort of steward. Then and only then, armed with your meager sportula, you start your day of more or less productive idleness. You could say the whole ritual is not too high a price to pay for the right to laziness, but you could also say the same thing about unemployment benefits, which few jobless people receive without hoping for better days. This morning ritual was servitude, humiliation, and that's one of the reasons why, pushing sixty, Martial preferred to return to his native Spain, where he died of boredom. He loved Rome, but he could no longer stand the sportula, the congested streets, the vain talk: he believed he was too old for all that.

3 I

Luke was the opposite of a pleasure-seeker like Martial. He only went to the baths to bathe. If he had slaves, he didn't sleep with them. A meal was an occasion to give thanks, not to peddle gossip. But outwardly, his life as an old lettered bachelor must have been much like Martial's. It was the life of an average Roman; in those days the Christians in Rome had understood Paul's lesson: they acted like average Romans. No waves, no strange behavior, no long prophet's beards, let alone secret meetings in the city's catacombs. They met for the agape in the houses of respectable families. These were increasingly pagan families who had converted discreetly or were in the process of converting. Even if he earned his living by working as a doctor, that didn't stop Luke from having a patron like everyone else. Luke's Gospel and the Acts are dedicated to a certain Theophilus. We don't know if this is a symbolic figure—his name means "friend of God"—or if he really existed. From the way Luke addresses him in the prologues to these two books, it's clear in any case that he's a pagan, curious about Christianity, and that the idea is to convince him with arguments that are within his grasp. As for me, I find it entirely plausible that this Theophilus was Luke's patron, that Luke gradually went from being a morning parasite to a frequent visitor, and eventually to family doctor, and that it was with him in mind that Luke phrased the language of his Gospel.

•

For starters, he had to bear in mind Theophilus' extreme distrust—and in general the distrust of respectable Romans—for the Jews. Even those who had previously been attracted by their religious fervor had since lost their enthusiasm and now just considered them dangerous terrorists. This is where Luke worked wonders, by demonstrating by means of his own person that Christians were not Jews, that in fact they had nothing to do with the Jews. Some of them were Jewish by birth, there was no denying that, but not many, fewer and fewer in fact, and they had renounced Jewish Law. Christians observed none of the rituals that people had considered picturesque for so long and now saw as a threat. They weren't affiliated with any foreign party. They respected Rome, its officials, its institutions, its emperor. They paid their taxes and claimed no exemptions.

Nevertheless, as some people who were better informed than the rest challenged Luke from time to time: This master whom you invoke, and who you claim was raised from the dead, he was Jewish, right? He was crucified on the orders of the Roman governor for rebelling against the emperor, right? It's more complex than that, Luke answered. He was Jewish, yes, but his loyalty to the Empire made him unbearable to the Jews: in fact, that's why they had him put to death. The Roman governor merely applied a Jewish sentence—the good man's hands were tied, and he did it reluctantly, believe me.

•

His propaganda proved successful. Once the obstacle of Jewishness had been removed, what Luke had to say was pleasing to Theophilus, his family, and his friends. They were proud to adhere to such an elevated doctrine, which at the same time was so respectful of their social status. They started to give to the poor, which wasn't done in Rome. You gave to your clients, not to people who were too impoverished to have a patron. They considered receiving baptism. As for Luke, he increasingly thought about putting everything he said to Theophilus down in writing. It's at this time that a short account of the life of Jesus that was said to be the work of Mark, Peter's former secretary, started to circulate among the Christians of Rome.

32

Frédéric Boyer is a writer my age who, in 1995, convinced the Catholic publishing house Bayard to undertake a huge project: a new translation of the Bible. Each book would be entrusted to one writer and one exegete, who would work together closely. Most of the exegetes were representatives of the Church, most of the writers atheists. When I was contacted, the editorial board at Bayard still hadn't given the green light, the project was in the testing phase. "There's a biblical scholar who's started to work on Mark," Frédéric told me. "How'd you like to team up with him?"

Of course I said yes: How often do you get to translate the Bible? At best, once in a lifetime. And, all things considered, I was happy that I'd been spared the trouble of having to choose. Some years earlier, alone in my study, I'd commented on the Gospel of John and believed, or wanted to believe, in the resurrection of Christ. But I didn't say anything about that to Frédéric, or to anyone on the team that was gradually forming. Some people are embarrassed by pornography, not me. What embarrasses me, and seems far more delicate a matter to deal with, far more indecent than sexual secrets, has to do with "those things": the things of the soul, the things involving God. Deep down, I liked to believe I was more familiar with them than my colleagues in the little world of literature, as I spent a significant part of my life holding them in my heart and turning them over in my mind. That was my secret, which I'm discussing here for the first time.

•

Hugues Cousin, the exegete who had started to work on the Gospel of Mark, was a short, gentle man with a quick smile: a fount of knowledge and modesty. He had been a priest but didn't take to celibacy: he wanted a wife, children, a family. If the Church had let him, he'd have gotten married and remained a priest. He would have liked that, because for him the two vocations were perfectly compatible. But it didn't, so he made his choice. Without protesting or even so much as entertaining the thought of lying, as so many priests do at the cost of inner torment and other terrible collateral damage, he left the priesthood, got married, and raised three children. But he never broke with the Church, he didn't even distance himself from it. When I met him, on top of his scholarly research and publications he was the chief collaborator of the archbishop of Sens-Auxerre in Burgundy, and lived with his family just a stone's throw from the Diocesan House. That's where I went to see him for our sessions. Other times he came down to visit me in Paris, in my study on Rue du Temple. He commented on each verse word by word, so that I could appreciate the plethora of associations that arose from each Greek term. I risked a translation, which he criticized, qualified, enriched. We met dozens of times, and it took us just under a year to come up with a first version of these thirty or so pages.

Hugues was thrilled by what he saw as the revolutionary side of our undertaking, and pushed me to be more and more audacious. I remember, one day, how disappointed he was at the timidity of one of my attempts: "Sounds like the Jerusalem Bible, your stuff. If it were Luke, okay, but Mark . . ." He put a lot of stress on Mark's poor Greek—like the English spoken by a Singapore taxi driver, he said. He would have liked me to remain faithful to it, and deliberately translate the text into incorrect French. We talked about that a lot. I said that the mistakes weren't intended by the author. Maybe, Hugues answered, but they're there. The two positions can be defended, we agreed on that much—we both liked to agree—and I finally opted for a style that was correct but awkward and somewhat disjointed: with the sentences placed one after another without transition. The opposite of the "flowing style so admired by the *bourgeois*" that Baudelaire could churn out hand over fist and that I, too, spontaneously tend to adopt: always connect one sentence with the next, always look for a smooth transition.

•

Two major ideas inspired the group of writers and scholars involved in Frédéric's project. The first was that the books of the Bible constituted a heterogeneous ensemble written over a thousand years, comprising such diverse literary styles as prophesy, historical chronicles, poetry, jurisprudence, and philosophical aphorisms, involving hundreds of different authors. The major translations, whether they're the work of a single man such as Martin Luther or Lemaistre de Sacy, as they were in the past, or of a group of scholars, like today's Jerusalem Bible or New American Standard Version, tend to flatten this concert of discordant voices with an artificial harmony: everything sounds a bit the same, the Psalms are written like the Chronicles, the Chronicles like the Proverbs, and the Proverbs like Leviticus. The advantage of entrusting the translations to different writers, each of whom has, or purports to have, a style of his or her own, is that they won't be the same. And it's true: You don't at all feel like you're reading the same book when you go from the Psalms according to Olivier Cadiot to Ecclesiastes according to Jacques Roubaud, which is refreshing. The disadvantages are, first of all, that the same Greek or Hebrew words aren't translated the same from one book to the next, so anything goes, whim rules the day; and second, that the writers aren't really all that different, all of them belonging not only to the same day and age and the same country but also to the same literary school—namely, the rarefied milieu of the two publishers P.O.L and Les Éditions de Minuit. I'd have liked it if they'd asked, I don't know, Michel Houellebecq or Amélie Nothomb. But there you go, nobody's perfect, it was worth the shot and this project enriched our lives for a few years.

Behind the other major idea is the dream of a return to the roots, and to the days when the words weren't worn out by two millennia of pious use. Gospel, apostle, baptism, conversion, Eucharist: these words that rang out with such brilliance have become emptied of significance or filled with another, humdrum and inoffensive, meaning. "Salt is good," says Jesus, "but if salt loses its taste, how can its flavor be restored?" We spent dozens of hours seeking ways of saying "Gospel" in today's language. Already, the French word *évangile* is just the transcription of the Koine Greek *evangelion*. "Apostle," likewise, is just the lazy, pedantic transcription of the Greek *apostolos*, which means "emissary"; *église*—or church—the transcription of the Greek *ekklesia*, meaning "assembly"; "disciple" the transcription of the Latin *discipulus*, which means "student"; and "Messiah" the transcription of the Hebrew *Mashiah*, which means "anointed." That's right, anointed: rubbed with oil. The fact is that neither the word nor the thing itself is very appetizing, and I remember one joker in our group who suggested translating the word "Messiah" as "the Oiled One."

•

Most people today think that "Gospel" designates a literary genre, the story of Jesus' life, and that Matthew, Mark, Luke, and John wrote Gospels the way Racine wrote tragedies or Ronsard sonnets. But that meaning only established itself around the second century. The word that Mark wrote at the start of his narrative meant "good news." When Paul wrote to the Galatians and Corinthians thirty years earlier about "my Gospel," it meant: what I preached to you, my personal version of this good news. The problem is that while it's true that "Gospel" has lost its original sense and, in fact, now has no meaning at all, writing "good news" in its place is a cure that's worse than the disease: it has a "nice Catholic" ring to it, you instantly imagine the priest's syrupy smile and voice. Finally, after I don't know how many dismaying attempts like "the happy message" or "joyful announcement," I backtracked and stuck with "Gospel."

It's the very first word Mark writes, and before there's any time to recover, a few lines later you hit the minefield: "John appeared in the wilderness, proclaiming . . ." Proclaiming what? What the ETB calls "a baptism of penance for the remission of sins," the JB "a baptism of repentance for the forgiveness of sins," and old Lemaître de Sacy "a baptism of penitence for the remission of sins." Baptism, penance, repentance, penitence, remission, and, worst of all, sin: to us, who believed we could give a more pure meaning to the words of the tribe, each of these terms was burdened with ecclesiastical unction and guilt-inducing terror, and inspired a sacred horror. It was necessary to get out of this sacristy and find something else. But what? I ended up writing: "John appeared in the desert, baptizing. He proclaimed that with this immersion one came full circle, and was freed of one's faults." All I can say in my defense is that I went to huge lengths to come up with this result. But it's clear to me that it's not good, and that fifteen years later this modernism is already outdated. Sin and repentance will bury us all, I fear.

33

One day, at the start of our cooperation, Hugues asked me: "By the way, do you know how the Gospel of Mark ends?" I looked at him, taken aback. Of course I knew how it ends, I'd read it and reread it enough times over the past months: Jesus is resurrected, he appears to his disciples and tells them to go out into the world and proclaim the Gospel to all creation. Think again, Hugues said, happy with the effect his words were having. That's not the real ending. The last chapter was added much later. It's not in the *Codex Vaticanus* or the *Codex Sinaiticus*, the two oldest preserved manuscripts of the New Testament, which date from the fourth century. That was before the Church put things in order, and the Gospel of Mark still ended with the three women, Mary Magdalene, Mary the mother of James, and a third woman called Salome, who go to anoint Jesus' body the day after his death. They find that the stone blocking the entrance to the tomb has been moved, and, inside, a young man dressed in a white robe, who tells them not to be afraid: Jesus is no longer there, he has risen from the dead. The young man orders them to announce the news to the disciples. The women run away. "They said nothing to anyone, because they were afraid."

•

"They were afraid": these are Mark's last words.

I remember my amazement and, I have to admit, my delight, when Hugues told me that. I pleaded, in vain, to be able to end my translation after this passage. Not many people know that the oldest of the four Gospels doesn't show Jesus resurrected, but ends with the image of three women terrified in front of an empty tomb.

•

The collection of texts known as *Q* tells us how Jesus spoke. Mark tells us what he did, the impression he made, and this impression is characterized by strangeness, coarse manners, and a sense of menace, rather than by gentleness or elevated philosophical thoughts. When I was in Turkey with Hervé, I drew up a list of exorcisms and healings in the Gospel of Luke. With just two exceptions, Luke copied them all from Mark, but if you look back at the original version, you realize that he sugarcoated them. In Mark they're more rustic, more trivial, slightly disgusting: Jesus sticks his fingers in the ears of a deaf person, wets the tongue of a stammerer with his saliva, rubs the eyes of a blind man. Above all, they take up far more space. If you only knew Jesus from this testimony, the image you would take away would be less that of a wise man or spiritual master than of a shaman with uncanny powers.

No pretty stories in Mark's Gospel, no Sermon on the Mount, and no more than a handful of parables. The famous one about the sower. The one about the seed that, once in the ground, sprouts and grows on its own, without our knowing how it does it. The one about the mustard seed that's tiny when it's sown, and grows into the largest of plants, becoming a tree. All three use the same agricultural metaphor, but say different things about the word of Jesus and its effect on those who hear it: that it's infinitely small at the start but destined to become immense; that it grows in us, unbeknownst to us and independently of our will; finally, that it's productive for some and not for others, because some of those who hear it are rooted in good, fertile soil, and all power to them, but others are rooted in thorns and rocky ground, and too bad, that's just how things are: "To the one who has, more will be given; from the one who has not, even what he has will be taken away."

I think that this saying is profoundly true, that it's proven every day, but that it's anything but pleasant to hear. And Jesus isn't any nicer when his disciples ask him to be a little clearer. He answers: "The mystery of the kingdom of God has been granted to you. But to those outside everything comes in parables, *so that* they may look and see but not perceive, and hear and listen but not understand, lest perhaps they should be converted and their sins should be forgiven." I remember my unease when I was translating this verse, and how I pulled in the direction of basic pedagogical notions—with classes of different levels—something that is in fact more like a lesson in esotericism reserved for the guru's inner circle, and that relegates the profane to the darkness outside. This approach was the opposite of Paul's, and Luke must also have had his difficulties with it. The proof: When he recopied this passage he left out the terrible words "lest perhaps they should be converted and their sins should be forgiven." Jesus could not be that harsh.

•

Another thing that must have bothered Luke, but also pleased him at times, is Mark's way of treating the disciples. As word of Jesus' healings spreads, more and more people follow him, and from among this group of cripples, marginals, and unemployed laborers, Jesus chooses twelve who will work for him full-time. He sends them to nearby villages, in groups of two, with a minimum of supplies—no provisions, no bags, no spare clothes—charged with rubbing the sick with oil and casting out demons. All of that could be told as the birth of an elite unit, a legion of glorious soldiers of Christ, but Mark doesn't lose a chance to show the disciples under the least flattering light. They're supposed to cast out demons, but as soon as they have their backs to the wall they go running for their master. They're obtuse, quarrelsome, and envious, as shown by the story of how John and James want to have the best seats to the left and right of Jesus on Judgment Day. Jesus puts them in their place, but just a few pages later they find another pretext for bickering, and want to know which of them is the greatest. Jesus repeats to them, less patiently this time, that he who wants to be first will be the last of all: that's the law, and it's much grander than the Law. When he tells them that he will soon be rejected, persecuted, and killed, Peter protests: You shouldn't say such things, they bring bad luck—drawing on himself the response I cited above, "Get behind me, Satan!" Jesus knows Satan: he says he spent forty days in the desert in his company, with wild animals that served him.

After the Last Supper, in the Garden of Gethsemane, he goes off to pray with Peter, John, and James. He asks them to remain awake, but after a minute they're snoring like troopers. When the soldiers come to arrest him, one of the disciples resists and cuts off the ear of the high priest's servant, but after that it's turmoil. None of them are at the foot of the cross when Jesus is dying and moans: "My God, why have you forsaken me?" Just a few women look on from afar. A distant sympathizer, Joseph of Arimathea, takes down the body and places it in a tomb. Still no disciples far and wide. In the end there's no one but the three haggard women, the ones who looked on from afar, and they don't say anything to anyone because they're afraid.

•

To sum up: Mark's account is the story of a rural healer who drives out spirits and is taken for a sorcerer. He speaks with the devil in the desert. His family would like to have him put away. He surrounds himself with a group of losers whom he terrifies with predictions that are as sinister as they are mysterious; all of them save their own skins when he's arrested. His adventure, which lasted less than three years, ends with a hasty trial and a sordid execution, all steeped in an atmosphere of discouragement, abandonment, and fear. Nothing is done to enhance the story or make the characters more likable. Reading about this brutal incident, you feel as if you're the closest you can get to this horizon that is forever out of reach: what really happened.

34

I know, I'm projecting. In any event, I think that when he discovered Mark's account, Luke couldn't help feeling bitter. Ah, okay, someone's beaten me to it . . . Because he himself had wanted to do just that, because he may have started doing it. And then, once he'd read Mark, he must have thought: I can do better. I'm more educated, I can write. This book is a draft, written by a Jew for Jews. If Theophilus read it, he'd be bored stiff. It's up to me to write the definitive version, the one that will be read by cultivated pagans.

•

Modern scholars reject top-down versions of history. They prefer the evolution of the land registry and three-year crop rotation to treaties, battles, or the coronation of Napoleon. On biblical matters, their key concern is to play down individual contributions in favor of a disembodied, collective tradition. They say: a Gospel is composed of strata, it's the product of such and such a community, let's not succumb to the naïve idea that it was written by one person. I don't agree. Of course it's the product of a community, of course it's also the work of copyists, and copyists of copyists, but no matter how you look at it, at one point or another someone had to write it—and this someone, in the story I'm telling, is Luke. They also say: Let us beware of the anachronism of imagining an Evangelist working with several documents that he keeps at arm's reach, spread out on his writing table—as I have a couple of Bibles, Renan not far away, and, on my right, shelves that just get fuller and fuller. I'm childishly proud of this biblical library, in my study I feel like Saint Augustine busy writing in Carpaccio's marvelous painting, the one with the little dog, in the Scuola di San Giorgio degli Schiavoni in Venice, and in fact I don't see what's so implausible about this image, at least as far as it applies to Luke.

Luke was a man of letters, and although his quarters in Rome were even more modest than Martial's, that doesn't rule out his having a little bookcase like the one Martial had. The anachronism, if you want to find one, is the table: a piece of furniture that the Romans had little use for. They did everything lying down: sleeping, eating, screwing, writing. Let's suppose that, like Marcel Proust, Luke wrote his book in bed. Spread out on the quilt, we discover first of all the Septuagint Bible, then Mark's Gospel copied by him, and finally the collection, also copied by him, of the words of Jesus that Philip first lent to him in Caesarea. This small roll that he's always kept in the bottom of his trunk is his treasure. It's also, now, his edge over Mark, who, as he had no access to it, says little about Jesus' teaching. The Septuagint, Mark, and Q: these are his three reference documents, to which I believe must also be added Josephus.

•

As a friend of Titus', Josephus did not suffer from the anti-Jewish backlash that followed the fall of Jerusalem. The Jewish prisoners of war mostly became slaves in Rome. Josephus settled comfortably in a fine house on Palatine Hill with a lifetime pension and the gold ring of the equestrian class. And, like many diplomats who are obliged to take premature retirement, he reinvented himself as a historian. First in Aramaic, then in a Greek that is refined to the point of archaism, he wrote the story that I have made abundant use of, in which he seeks to flatter Titus, put himself in a good light, and defend his people whose ruin has been brought about by a gang of irresponsible thugs. *The Jewish War* appeared in A.D. 79. A cultivated Roman who was interested in Judaism could not have not heard about it. It's a big book—five hundred dense pages in my French version. It must have cost a lot. Luke might have read it in a public library—Rome had excellent libraries, like the one in the Temple of Apollo—but I tend to see him tightening his belt to buy a copy in one of the bookstores on the Argiletum where Martial also bought his books. As I am also no stranger to this pleasure, I imagine him bringing home his booty, this bubbling spring of words, names, and customs, and scouring it for details. In his Gospel and above all in the Acts, he will speak of the Pharisee teacher Gamaliel, the rebel Theudas, the Egyptian, and many other people completely unknown to the Roman world with all the relish of the journalist who's just discovered the document that will give his story clout and allow readers to situate it in terms of verifiable events. That's why we too read Josephus alongside the New Testament, and why Arnauld d'Andilly, the Jansenist who translated him into French in the seventeenth century, called him the "fifth Evangelist."

35

There: we're in Rome, near the end of the 70s in the first century A.D. Luke starts to write his Gospel.

I now invite you to turn back to page 196 to reread the first lines: the address to Theophilus. Go on, I'll wait here.

•

You've read it? We agree? The program Luke sets himself is that of a historian. He promises Theophilus a field investigation, a report that can be trusted. But then what does he write no sooner than he's stated this intention, starting the very next line?

Fiction. Pure fiction.

36

"In the days of Herod, King of Judea, there was a priest named Zechariah of the priestly division of Abijah; his wife was from the daughters of Aaron, and her name was Elizabeth."

The reader has no idea who Zechariah and Elizabeth are. No one has ever heard of them, but King Herod is known, and it's like in *The Three Musketeers*, where characters like King Louis XIII and Cardinal Richelieu lend their credibility to Athos, Porthos, Aramis, and d'Artagnan. Zechariah and Elizabeth, Luke goes on, are righteous, they love God and observe his Law. Unfortunately, they have not been blessed with children. One day, as Zechariah prays in the Temple, an angel appears to him. Elizabeth will bear him a son, the angel announces, and the son must be named John. Zechariah asks how he can be sure: he and Elizabeth are already old . . . To teach him to believe, the angel removes his power of speech. Zechariah leaves the Temple mute, and stays that way. Soon, Elizabeth is pregnant.

The big difference between the Old and the New Testament, said the German philosopher Jacob Taubes, is that the Old Testament is filled with stories of barren women whom God graces with children, while there's not a single such story in the New Testament. It's no longer a question of growing, multiplying, and prospering, but of becoming eunuchs for the kingdom of heaven. The story of Elizabeth seems to disprove this penetrating remark, but in fact it doesn't: in Luke's mind we're still in the Old Testament. Zechariah and Elizabeth stand on the threshold of the Gospel as representatives of old Israel, and one of my hero's traits that touches me the most is his tenderness in painting their portraits.

It's true, this painting is a bit of a pastiche. When the angel in the Temple announces to Zechariah that the child "will be great in the sight of the Lord, will drink neither wine nor strong drink, will be filled with the Holy Spirit even from his mother's womb, and he will go before the Lord in the spirit and power of Elijah . . ." you have to remember that this flow of emphatically Jewish words and abundance of local color are the invention of a Gentile who saw the Temple for the first time just a few years earlier, without the slightest understanding of the hoops that his master Paul was being obliged to jump through. But he went back. He had a look around. All the while having a vested interest in a movement that was irresistibly freeing itself from Judaism, he wanted to become familiar with Judaism. And in the process he came to love it.

At the time he's writing, the party line demands that fault should be found with Israel. That's what the other Evangelists, who are Jewish, do. Not Luke. Luke, the only goy in the gang of four, opens his Gospel with this little historical mini-novel, full of Semitisms he's pinched from the Septuagint, in the hope of letting Theophilus appreciate the beauty of this vanished world, this piety expressed less in the vast colonnades of the Temple than in the contemplative, principled spirits of righteous souls like Zechariah and Elizabeth. As if, before he starts his tale, he wants to remind us that these people know better than any others the meaning of Job's words: "From my flesh I will see God."

37

Elizabeth hides her pregnancy for five months. In the sixth, the same angel, Gabriel, goes to see Elizabeth's cousin Mary, who lives in Nazareth, in Galilee. She too will become pregnant, he announces: she will give birth to a son. She will name him Jesus, but he will be known as the Son of God. This announcement troubles Mary: she's engaged to a certain Joseph, but only engaged, that is to say, still a virgin. How will she conceive if she has never known a man? "Don't worry," the angel responds. "Nothing is impossible for God. Even your cousin Elizabeth has also conceived a son in her old age; and she who was called barren is now in her sixth month." Mary could point out that a late pregnancy and a virgin pregnancy aren't exactly the same thing, but she contents herself with answering: "I am the handmaid of the Lord. May it be done to me according to your word."

•

Paul and Mark, the earliest witnesses to Christianity, don't know this story of the virgin conception. Ten or twenty years later it shows up in two Gospels whose authors don't know each other. Luke writes in Rome, Matthew in Syria, they both tell the story of the birth of Jesus, and aside from this point their stories have nothing in common. Matthew says that magi came from the Orient, guided by a star, to adore the future king of the Jews. He says that on hearing this, Herod, the real king of the Jews, fears he'll be dethroned one day and has all of the children in the region under two years old massacred. He says that Joseph, forewarned by the angel, saved his family by taking them to Egypt. Luke doesn't tell any of that, although it's anything but insignificant. But like Matthew he says that Jesus is born of a virgin. Where does this story come from? Who circulated it? No one knows. Its birth is mysterious, even if you don't believe Jesus' is. I don't have any particular theory on the subject.

But I do have a theory about the way in which Luke wrote his story, and on this topic I feel considerably more competent. Because this scene of the Annunciation contains a stroke of creativity worthy of a novelist or screenwriter, as extraordinary as Paul's entry on the scene in the Acts. You remember: Luke relates the stoning of Stephen and adds in passing that to be more at ease, the murderers gave their coats to a young man named Saul. And it's just as incidentally that we discover, in the words of the angel Gabriel, that this Elizabeth, who seems to have been introduced into the start of the Gospel for no apparent reason, is Mary's cousin—meaning that the two children who would be born, John and Jesus, will be cousins as well.

•

My reader may have noticed: at times I don't hesitate to follow tradition against skeptical historians. For example, I don't find the hypothesis that Luke obtained some of his information from Mary in person all that absurd, even though it's associated with the crassest fundamentalism. But I'm ready to bet my place in the kingdom of heaven that this family relationship between Jesus and John the Baptist that's found nowhere else but here is simply an invention. And not, like the visit of the angel Gabriel, an invention inherited from one of the nebulous "primitive communities" that wrote the Gospels according to Bible scholars. No: an invention by Luke, pure and simple.

Luke had a bill of specifications that demanded that he should deal first with Jesus' virgin birth, and second with the figure of John the Baptist, which he didn't really know how to treat. He was in his bed, or in the baths, or walking on the Campus Martius when the idea struck him: What if Jesus and John were cousins? That would solve his narration problems! Having encountered similar ones, I can well imagine Luke's excitement, and I imagine that the entire structure of his two first chapters fell into place in the wake of this idea, as majestic and pure as a fresco by Piero della Francesca.

38

After the Annunciation comes the Visitation. That is, Mary leaves her Galilean village to go visit her cousin in Judea. When Mary enters, the child that Elizabeth is bearing leaps in her womb. The two women, the one pregnant with Jesus and the other with John, stand facing each other. Inspired by the Holy Spirit, Elizabeth tells Mary that she is the most blessed among women because she is the mother of the Lord, and Mary intones what one is tempted to call her grand aria, as it has been—sumptuously—rendered in music so many times. In the Latin Bible this giving of thanks starts with the words *Magnificat anima mea Dominum*, "my soul exalts the Lord," which explains why it's called the Magnificat.

•

More than ten years ago, I did some tentative research into my maternal grandfather, Georges Zurabishvili, which led to my book *My Life as a Russian Novel*. Eternally doomed to unhappiness, this brilliant but shadowy figure who died tragically at the end of the Second World War looked to the Christian faith for answers to the questions that tormented him. As I would do fifty years later, he went to Mass every day, confessed, and took Communion. Reading the documents he left behind, I recognized what I also experienced: the desire for certainty as a cure for anguish; the paradoxical argument according to which submission to a dogma is an act of supreme freedom; the way of giving meaning to an unlivable life by viewing it as a succession of ordeals imposed by God. In his papers, I found a long commentary on the Magnificat. What is the Gospel? he asks. His answer: the Word of God, revealed to men and infinitely greater than them. And what is the Magnificat? The best response one can give to the Word of God. Proud docility, joyous submission. It's what every soul should strive for: being the servant of the Lord.

Like my grandfather, I recited these verses while seeking to infuse myself with their fervor. Jacqueline said that devotion to the Virgin was the surest path to the mysteries of faith: I wanted to give myself up to it, and for several months I kept a rosary she'd given me in my pocket and recited Hail Mary twenty, thirty times a day. Today I'm sketching the portrait of an Evangelist cum man of letters, story writer, and imitator, and I note that this sublime poem, the Magnificat, is a patchwork of Bible quotes from start to finish. The margins of the ETB cite two per line, most are taken from the Psalms, and, strangely, the emotion I'd have liked to feel and didn't when saying the rosary, I now feel when I imagine Luke scouring the Septuagint, choosing these fragments of old Jewish prayers, and setting them into his narrative with meticulous care, like a jeweler making a necklace of precious stones, to give Theophilus an idea of what the love of God was to these Jews whom God was supposed to have forsaken.

Mary stays with her cousin for three months, then returns home. Elizabeth gives birth. The plan is to call the child Zechariah after his father, but the latter, who had remained silent since his vision in the Temple, writes on a tablet that no, he must be called John. Once he has written it, his tongue loosens and he, in turn, recites a canticle on God's designs and the role his son would play: "You, child, will be called prophet of the Most High, for you will go before the Lord to prepare his ways, to guide those who sit in darkness and death's shadow into the path of peace." The ETB says very vaguely that this song, called the Benedictus, must "stem from the Palestinian community"—an affirmation that runs no risks and dispenses with the need to admit that, like the Magnificat, it's a sumptuous collage put together by Luke. My son Jean Baptiste was baptized to the words of this Benedictus.

•

And now Caesar Augustus' decree comes out, with the aim of conducting a census of no less than the entire world. Quirinius, then governor of Syria, is charged with applying it in Palestine. At least that's according to Luke, who wants to come across as a historian and a supplier of reliable and verifiable facts. But historians two thousand years later are a little put out by this, because this census, which really was supervised in Palestine by Governor Quirinius, took place ten years after the death of Herod, under whose reign both Matthew and Luke say Jesus was born. In Luke's account, this whole census serves one purpose: having Jesus born in Bethlehem and thus fulfilling a completely marginal, convoluted prophesy that nothing forced him to play up. It's a classic screenwriter's mistake: trying to solve a contradiction that all your efforts only serve to highlight. The result: In the end it's glaringly obvious, whereas if you hadn't mentioned it, no one would have noticed it at all. But as it's part of Luke's bill of specifications to have Jesus born in Bethlehem, he feels obliged to explain why Joseph and Mary, who are from Nazareth, come to Bethlehem for Jesus to be born there. The answer: because around that time there was a census, you have to be registered in your hometown, and Joseph, although he wasn't born in Bethlehem himself, was a member of the family of David, which had its roots there.

O-kay . . .

The fact is, however, that what makes a good film a good film isn't the plausibility of its script but the force of the scenes, and on that front Luke is unbeatable: the crowded inn, the manger, the newborn child wrapped in swaddling cloths and laid in a feeding trough, the shepherds in the fields nearby who, informed by an angel, come in a procession to admire the infant . . . The three kings come from Matthew, the ox and the donkey are much later additions, but everything else was invented by Luke, and in the name of the brotherhood of writers I say: Respect.

•

At this point it comes as no surprise that Luke is the only one of the four Evangelists to remind his readers that Jesus was circumcised. At a time when old men were having their pants pulled down in the middle of the street to see if they belonged to the accursed race, it would have been tempting to pass over this detail, but Luke doesn't pass over it. He draws attention to it, like he insists on the presentation of the child in the Temple. A very old man named Simeon is there. He is righteous and devout, he is awaiting the consolation of Israel, and the Holy Spirit has revealed to him that he will not die before he has seen the Messiah. This Simeon is a lot like Zechariah. Above all, both of them are like James, the brother of the Lord. Just as, in my opinion, Luke wrote the New Testament letter attributed to James, so too I'm convinced that he was thinking of James when he composed the third of the magnificent canticles that punctuate his prologue. The old man holds the child in his arms: "Now, Master," he says, "you may let your servant go in peace, for my eyes have seen the salvation of Israel." One imagines he lulls the baby while murmuring this, and the sublime cantata that Bach based on it, *Ich habe genug,* lulls our souls as well.

•

The two boys, John and Jesus, grow and become strong and wise, and are blessed with the favor of God. Mary keeps all of these things in her heart. Thus ends this prologue of gold, frankincense, and myrrh, after which the two heroes come back on the scene as adults, like the heroes in *Once Upon a Time in America*, who are now played by Robert De Niro and James Woods, and no longer by little tykes who look like them.

39

Since Plutarch, the parallel lives of illustrious men had been a fashionable genre. Luke constructed a magnificent prologue along these lines, but he's soon in a bind because he's got lots to tell about one of his two protagonists and not very much at all about the other. And while he gave free reign to his talent as a novelist when telling the story of Jesus' and John's childhoods, he's content to be a scrupulous copyist when it comes to fleshing out the adult life of John the Baptist, limiting his narrative to the information provided in his sources and refraining from giving his own opinion. I think that's because he doesn't have one. Because this part of the story doesn't speak to him. He finds ascetics intimidating: you can feel his relief when Herod throws the Baptist in prison, where he'll languish until he's decapitated. It's as if he were trying to get done with this part of the story. And you get the same impression when, between the baptism of Jesus and his forty days with the devil in the desert, he squeezes in a genealogy of the savior that is totally different from the one given by Matthew except in one respect: both of them make a point of showing that Jesus descends from David through Joseph, although they've clearly said that Joseph was not his father. Evidently he can't wait to get straight to the heart of the matter, and the same goes for me. And to show how he goes about it, I would like to propose a short exercise in textual analysis.

•

Let's start with Mark: "He departed from there and came to his native place, accompanied by his disciples. When the Sabbath came he began to teach in the synagogue, and many who heard him were astonished. They said, 'What kind of wisdom has been given him? What mighty deeds are wrought by his hands! Is he not the carpenter, the son of Mary, and the brother of James and Joses and Judas and Simon? And are not his sisters here with us?' And they took offense at him. Jesus said to them, 'A prophet is not without honor except in his native place and among his own kin and in his own house.' So he was not able to perform any miracles there."

Now let's look at what Luke does with this synopsis.

Jesus "came to Nazareth, where he had grown up, and went according to his custom into the synagogue on the Sabbath day. He stood up to read."

(Remember: that's what Paul did as well.)

"He was handed a scroll of the prophet Isaiah. He unrolled the scroll and found the passage where it was written:

The Spirit of the Lord is upon me,
because he has anointed me
to bring glad tidings to the poor.
He has sent me to proclaim liberty to captives
and recovery of sight to the blind,
to let the oppressed go free,
and to proclaim a year acceptable to the Lord."

(You can be sure that Luke carefully selected this text in the Septuagint. He must have hesitated between several, I'd be curious to know which.)

"Rolling up the scroll, he handed it back to the attendant and sat down, and the eyes of all in the synagogue looked intently at him."

(Our old friend the Church historian Eusebius says that Mark wrote his Gospel according to Peter's "didascalia": meaning his instructions. But in French the word is also used to denote a playwright's scenic instructions, and we can say that the master of such didascalia is Luke.)

"He said to them, 'Today this scripture passage is fulfilled in your hearing.'"

(In other words: This is about me. This too is typical Paul, and in fact I used this scene as a guideline to describe Paul's speech in the synagogue in Troas.)

"All were amazed. They asked, 'Isn't this the son of Joseph?'"

(Luke finds a place for Joseph, whom Mark doesn't know. But he leaves the brothers and sisters right out of it.)

"Jesus said to them, 'Surely you will quote me this proverb, Physician, cure yourself, and say, Do here in your native place the things that we heard were done in Capernaum. Amen, I say to you, no prophet is accepted in his own native place. Indeed, I tell you, there were many widows in Israel in the days of Elijah when the sky was closed for three and a half years and a severe famine spread over the entire land. It was to none of these that Elijah was sent, but only to a widow in Zarephath in the land of Sidon. Again, there were many lepers in Israel during the time of Elisha the prophet; yet not one of them was cleansed, but only Naaman the Syrian.'"

(Zarephath was a Phoenician—that is to say, in Luke's day pretty much Greek—village. The idea that salvation concerned the widows of Zarephath and the Syrian lepers as much as—and even more than—Jewish widows and lepers was one of Paul's standard refrains. With as little shame as historical likelihood, Luke now puts it into the mouth of Jesus, although Mark tells us that when a Phoenician Greek woman asked Jesus to cast the demon from her daughter, his first reaction was to say: "Let the children be fed first. For it is not right to take the food of the children and throw it to the dogs." A brutal statement, which you could translate as: I heal the Jews first because they are the children of God; as for the pagans, they're dogs—little dogs, nice dogs, maybe, but dogs. The people of Nazareth thought exactly the same thing. That's why they take it very badly when Luke's Jesus now delivers this little Pauline sermon.)

"They were all filled with fury. They rose up, drove him out of the town, and led him to the brow of the hill on which their town had been built, to hurl him down headlong."

(In one peaceable sentence it's the story of a lynch mob of the type Paul was confronted with on several occasions.)

"But he passed through the midst of them and went away."

40

Luke is sometimes content to recopy Mark, but most of the time he does what I've just shown. He dramatizes, storyboards, fictionalizes. He adds things like "He looked up," "He sat down," to make the scenes more lively. And if there's something he doesn't like, he doesn't hesitate to revise it.

I've spoken about how, for me, certain details of the Gospel "ring true." It's a criterion I believe in, although I admit it's very subjective. Another is the one that exegetes call "the embarrassment criterion": when something must have been embarrassing for the author to write, there are good chances that it's true. An example: the extreme brutality of Jesus' relations with his family and disciples. There's every reason to believe that what Mark says is true. But there's less reason to believe what Luke does with the same material. The first tells that Jesus' family came to get him to have him put away, the second that they weren't able to approach him because of the crowd. The first, although he was Peter's secretary, shows Jesus pushing Peter back and calling him Satan, the second cuts the scene out entirely, as he will cut out or arrange all the scenes in which the disciples look like a pack of dimwits—except when they're about John, against whom he held a grudge.

•

Mark tells that one day Jesus was hungry and sees a fig tree with leaves but no figs. Nothing surprising about that: it's not fig season. Nevertheless he curses the tree: "May no one ever eat of your fruit again!" The next day he and his disciples pass by the fig tree, and Peter, remembering the curse of the day before, notes that it has withered to its roots. Jesus, quite strangely, answers that if you have faith you can lift mountains. No one dares to ask him why, if that's the case, he didn't have the fig tree bear fruit instead of killing it.

The story is menacing: you get the vague feeling that the accursed fig tree is Israel. Above all, it's obscure. Jesus was often menacing and obscure. He spoke of false prophets who come to you in sheep's clothing but who inwardly are vicious wolves, and who must be recognized by their fruit. Such extravagantly mixed metaphors are not to Luke's liking. Like me, he prefers understandable metaphors that you can transpose term for term, so he contents himself with saying, wisely, that you don't gather figs from thorn bushes or grapes from brambles. He must have been tempted to edit out the story of the fig tree as told by Mark. Finally he finds a way to smooth its rough edges by recasting it as a parable that's both clear and optimistic. The fig tree hasn't borne fruit for three years and its owner wants to have it cut down, but the gardener pleads its case: Let's give it a chance, maybe it will bear fruit later if we take good care of it . . . It's a very different conception of education: patience over severity. Applied to Israel, it must have corresponded to Luke's sincere wishes. And, let's admit, it's also disappointingly banal.

•

Those who spit out the lukewarm don't like Luke because they find him too well-mannered, too civilized, too lettered. When he comes across this terrible—and terribly true—saying: "To everyone who has, will more be given, but he who does not have, even that which he has will be taken away from him," he can't stop himself from toning down its illogical nature, and as a result from making it more bland: "Whoever has will be given more, but whoever does not have, *even what he thinks he has* will be taken away from him." (That's the kind of edit I'd be able to make, I'm afraid.) But as usual, things are more complicated than that. Because in places where the others write: "Whoever loves father or mother more than me is not worthy of me, and whoever loves son or daughter more than me is not worthy of me," it's the gentle Luke who ups the ante in a violent way: "If anyone comes to me without *hating* his father and mother, *wife* [wife? did someone say wife?] and children, brothers and sisters, *and even his own life*, he cannot be my disciple." And it's the nice Luke who has Jesus say: "I have come to set the earth on fire, and how I wish it were already blazing."

41

Luke tends to stay close to Mark in the story of the Passion, but he enhances the tale with mannerisms that don't always thrill me. In the Garden of Gethsemane, he's both overblown (an angel descends from heaven to comfort Jesus) and morbid (the sweat of fear that forms on his forehead falls to the ground like drops of blood). When the soldiers come to arrest Jesus, one of the disciples cuts off the high priest's servant's ear. John tells us that this servant's name was Malchus, and that's the kind of detail I believe: otherwise why say it? Luke, on the other hand, adds that Jesus touched the man's ear and healed him—and I don't believe that for a second.

I now come to Golgotha. In Mark, the soldiers spit in Jesus' face, like Jesus himself spat in the eyes of the blind. Luke deletes all of this spitting, which would shock Theophilus, but he adds dialogues. Whereas Mark, in his brevity and dreadful harshness, doesn't relate a single thing said by Jesus on the cross, Luke, always more verbose, has him say three whole sentences.

•

The first is when Jesus says about his torturers: "Father, forgive them, they know not what they do."

That's what we should always say when faced with evil, right?

•

The last is the one I like the least. When he breathes his last, Jesus says: "Father, into your hands I commend my spirit." It's moving, yes, but so much less beautiful, so much less terrible than Mark's: *Eloi Eloi lama sabachthani?*: "Father, father, why have you forsaken me?"

•

But Luke's most beautiful stroke of creativity comes between the two, like the cross of Jesus between those of the two other convicts. These two are thieves, they're dying amid atrocious suffering, despite which one of them makes fun of Jesus: "Are you not the Messiah? Then save yourself and us." The other protests: "We have been condemned justly, for the sentence we received corresponds to our crimes, but this man has done nothing criminal." And he says to Jesus: "Remember me when you come into your kingdom."

Jesus' response: "Today you will be with me in Paradise."

•

Miguel de Unamuno wrote that a Spanish bandit said to the executioner before being hanged: "I will die saying the Credo. Please don't open the trapdoor before I've said: I believe in the resurrection of the flesh."

This bandit is the brother of the last one, and what he says shows that he knows more about Jesus than all the intelligent people like me. But he's going to die: that helps.

42

Luke liked bandits, prostitutes, collaborators, tax collectors. "Weirdos and losers," as one exegete says in astonishment at this predilection. Jesus felt the same way, there's no doubt about that, but each evangelist has his own specialty and that of Luke, who was himself a doctor, is to remind us constantly that doctors are there for the sick and not for the healthy. And he reminds us, he who was so good-mannered, that the extreme violence that Jesus was capable of is never, absolutely never, directed against sinners, but always against the righteous. It's the common thread that runs through his entire *Sondergut*—the "special material" that only exists in his writing. The exegetes postulate that he gets this *Sondergut*, of which I now want to cite a few examples, from an unknown source. I think that most of the time this unknown source is his imagination—but is that so different from divine inspiration?

•

A Pharisee invited Jesus to his place. Jesus goes, sits down at the table. A sinful woman—in other words a whore—arrives with a flask of ointment. She weeps, bathes his feet with her tears, wipes them with her hair, and anoints them. The Pharisee is shocked. He doesn't say anything, but Jesus hears him thinking to himself. Here Luke gives his own version of Jesus' dialogue: "Simon, I have something to say to you." "Tell me, teacher." Jesus then tells the story of the moneylender who has two debtors, one who owes him five hundred denarii, the other fifty. Neither has the money to pay him back, so he forgives the debts of both. Which of them loves him more? The Pharisee: "The one who was forgiven more." "You have judged rightly," says Jesus.

It's right after this scene that Luke skillfully slips in the paragraph on the women who accompany Jesus along with the twelve: Mary Magdalene, but also our dear Joanna, the wife of Herod's steward Chuza, Susanna, and many others, who "provide for them out of their resources." To provide for them out of their resources they have to have at least some resources in the first place, and these charitable women whom only Luke mentions must have reminded him of the good Lydia of Philippi. While he is the strictest of the gang of four regarding the happiness promised to the poor and the afflictions linked to riches, Luke is also the most inclined to remind his readers that there are good rich people, as there are good centurions. He's the most sensitive to social categories, to their nuances, and to the fact that they don't entirely determine how people act. As a historian of World War II, he would have insisted on the fact that people who belonged to the French far-right movements Action Française and Croix-de-Feu counted among the first heroes of the resistance.

•

I've already told the story: having been ill received by the Samaritans, James and John ask Jesus to call down fire from heaven to consume the villagers, and they're soundly told off. The episode is in Mark, Luke recopies it all the more enthusiastically in that it doesn't reflect well on John, but two pages later he adds a postscript of his own. Someone asks Jesus what you have to do to have eternal life. "What is written in the Law?" "To love the Lord with all your heart, and your neighbor as yourself." "You have answered correctly," says Jesus, "do this and you will live." "But," insists the other, "who is my neighbor?" Jesus then cites the example of a traveler who has been left for half-dead by robbers on the road from Jerusalem to Jericho. A priest and then a Levite walk by without helping him. Finally a Samaritan stops, tends to his wounds, takes him to an inn, and leaves a little money for the innkeeper to take care of him.

For pious Jews, Samaritans are worse than pagans: pariahs, the dregs of humanity. So the meaning is clear: often outcasts behave better than the virtuous. A moral typical of Luke, but which can be further unraveled. I remember one evening when we were having dinner with a friend, she told us about her troubles with a homeless guy whom she'd made friends with, tried to help, and invited for coffee, with the result that she couldn't get rid of him after that. He hounded her, waited for her in the entrance to her building. Her bad conscience tormented her to the point that she let him sleep at her place one night, and even in her bed. He asked her to kiss him. As she didn't want to, he started to cry: "I disgust you, right?" That was right, and, rather than admitting it, she let him have his way. It's one of her most painful memories, and an example of the perverse effects of applying evangelical principles: give when you're asked, turn the other cheek. What's good about the Good Samaritan is that he doesn't overdo it. He doesn't give all his money, not even half his money. He doesn't invite the traveler to his home. We wouldn't necessarily do what he does—because the region isn't very safe, because the *Lonely Planet* guide advises travelers to beware of people who are pretending to be wounded, and who, as soon as a car stops, take out a gun and drive off, leaving the owner naked on the side of the road—but we're all aware it's what we should do: give minimum assistance to those in peril. No more, no less. When making up this anecdote, Luke might have thought of the robust pragmatism he admired in Philip, who preached to the Samaritans. Jesus' maximalist demands must have made him afraid. He tones them down, arguing for reasonable charity.

•

Next comes an importunate neighbor, who wakes up a friend in the middle of the night to ask him for a favor. First, the other complains that it's late, that he's sleeping and his family is too, but the importunate friend insists so much that he has no choice: he grumbles, then gets up. The moral: never hesitate to be a pain in the ass. Luke was so pleased with this story that he came up with a sort of remake a couple of chapters later about a persistent widow who heaps a judge with her demands. Finally the judge honors her request, not because he fears God or loves justice—on the contrary, we're told he's a bad judge—but so that the widow will get off his case.

The first of these little sketches where pains in the ass are cited as examples comes right after Jesus taught his disciples the prayer of prayers, the Lord's Prayer—and those who say that prayers of petition aren't noble and that you mustn't bother the Lord with minor troubles or desires would do well to reread it. Jesus drives the point home, in terms that Jacqueline never tired of repeating to me: "Ask, and you will receive; seek, and you will find; knock, and the door will be opened to you. What father among you would hand his son a snake when he asks for a fish? Or a scorpion when he asks for an egg? If you then, who are wicked, know how to give good gifts to your children, how much more will the Father give to those who ask him?"

•

I would have liked it if Luke had pushed the sense of nuances I credit him with to the point of telling us a story about a good Pharisee. Unfortunately, there aren't any, and in the second half of his Gospel these honorable people—precisely because they're honorable—are continually raked over the coals. Another has invited Jesus to eat. Jesus sits down without having observed the prescribed washing. His host is amazed, and Jesus heaps him with insults: "Oh, you Pharisees! Although you cleanse the outside of the cup and the dish, inside you are filled with plunder and evil!" The insults go on for ten lines. One of the others sitting at the table is outraged, you can see why, and he too receives a torrent of abuse: "You impose on people burdens hard to carry, but you yourselves do not lift one finger to touch them. Your ancestors killed the prophets and you would have done the same!"

Reading this, we wonder what got into Jesus if the scene really happened, or what got into Luke if he made it up. Basically, there's nothing new about the message: such stabbing condemnations of the elites—which would have Jesus stamped as a populist in our day—can be found elsewhere in the Gospels. But they fit the situation better, and are more acceptable as a result. Here, you get the impression that Luke had a stock of text that he hadn't been able to fit in elsewhere, and that to find a place for it he made up this meal scene where Jesus comes across as a really despicable type of guy who arrives at your place, puts his feet up on the table, spits in the soup, and starts cursing you and your family, going back nine generations in the process. It's all the more strange coming from Luke, whose master Paul never stopped insisting on the respect that is due to other people's customs, no matter what you think of them, and all the more so when you're in their country. The only advantage of this unpleasant scene is that you understand on the one hand that as he approaches Jerusalem, Jesus becomes increasingly on edge and aggressive, and on the other that the Pharisees "begin to act with hostility toward him and to interrogate him about many things, for they were plotting to catch him at something he might say."

43

Yet another meal at a Pharisee's place. Some guests arrive and choose the best places at the table. Jesus tells them: If you take the best place, you risk being asked to make way for someone else, but if you choose the worst place, all that can happen is that you're asked to move to a higher position. "For everyone who exalts himself will be humbled, but the one who humbles himself will be exalted."

With these words he turns to his host: "When you hold a lunch or a dinner, do not invite your friends or your brothers or your relatives or your wealthy neighbors, in case they may invite you back and you have repayment. Rather, when you hold a banquet, invite the poor, the crippled, the lame, the blind; blessed indeed will you be because of their inability to repay you. For you will be repaid at the resurrection of the righteous."

"Blessed is the one who will dine in the kingdom of God," one of his fellow guests comments tersely, which triggers a new parable. Do you really want to know what happens in the kingdom of God? Listen: it's a great dinner, from which all those invited begin to excuse themselves at the last minute under various pretexts. One has just purchased a field, another has just married, everyone's got something better to do. In a rage, the master of the house sends his servants to go and invite all the beggars in the city. His order is carried out, but there's still room. So he orders his servants to go out into the countryside and round up everyone they can find, by force if need be: the house must be filled. As for those who let him down, none of them will taste his dinner.

As a description of the kingdom, this story of the dinner isn't particularly engaging. It's clearly about Israel, which scorns the invitation to Christ's table, and about the flea-ridden Gentiles who will make the most of the situation. And if they put up a fuss they should be brought by force: it's a strong-arm missionary program that the Church will enforce by baptizing savages hand over fist, without asking their opinion. I prefer far more what Luke has Jesus say just before that: that it's a better investment to give to the poor than to lend to the rich, and that you have more chance to come first if you put yourself in last place.

The last, the first: we're in familiar territory. It's even the fundamental law of the kingdom, I think. Nevertheless, it poses an intriguing question. Neither Luke nor even Jesus questions the opinion shared by all that it's better to be on top than on the bottom. They simply say that putting yourself on the bottom is the best way to end up on top, that is to say that humility is a good life strategy. Are there cases where it's not a strategy? Where poverty, obscurity, pettiness, sufferance, are desired for themselves and not to acquire a greater good?

44

Habits and customs of the kingdom, continued. This time the master of the house doesn't have a bone to pick with his guests but with his manager, who has been accused of misappropriating his possessions. Furious once again, he fires him. The manager is annoyed. What am I going to do now? Dig? I don't have the strength. Beg? I'd be too ashamed. Then he gets the idea of making friends with his master's debtors before his disgrace is announced. He gathers them together and falsifies their promissory notes to their advantage. "You owed one hundred? Let's say you owe fifty. No, don't thank me, you can thank me later." You expect the manager will be doubly punished, but no: the end of the story is that when the master finds out, instead of being even more furious, he congratulates him for so shrewdly getting himself out of his predicament. Well done!

Not surprisingly, this parable isn't read often at Mass. But the JB is obliged to comment on it, and it gets out of its predicament as cleverly as the manager by saying that the fifty he slashes off the debt isn't a bribe he pays to protect his rear but the commission he was counting on receiving and now wisely forgoes—a bit like a boss renouncing stock options to appease the dissatisfaction of his employees and the media. We breathe a sigh of relief: the manager is not such a crook after all, and Jesus isn't praising his crookedness. Unfortunately the JB is skirting the issue. If Luke had wanted to say that, he would have said it. The truth is that the manager really *is* a crook, that he really *does* swindle his future ex-boss to the advantage of his prospective employers, and that his master appreciates such crookedness from the point of view of a connoisseur.

•

What this story says is clear, but what does it *mean*? What moral can we draw from it? That it's good to be cunning? That audacity always pays more than caution?

That's also what the parable of the talents seems to say. In it the master leaves on a journey and confides his goods to his employees, telling them to engage in business with them until he returns. To one he gives five talents, to another two, to the third one. The talent is a currency, like the sestertius or the drachma, but the other sense of the word works as well: it designates the gifts we were born with, and what we do with them. Back from his trip, the master demands an account from his employees. The one who received five talents has earned five more. "Bravo," the master says, "you were faithful with a few things, I will give you many more." The one who received two has also doubled their value, and he too is congratulated and rewarded. That leaves the one who received only a single talent. As the master didn't show him much confidence, the employee judged him to be a severe and greedy man, so rather than running any risks he decided it was better to hide the talent in the ground. He gave it to the master: "Here it is back." "You wicked, lazy servant!" his master says. "If you'd deposited my money with the bankers, I would have received interest." He takes the talent from him and gives it to the man who already has ten, and has the first thrown into the darkness outside, where there is wailing and gnashing of teeth.

•

Another day the master hires workers for his vineyard. They agree on the wages: one denarius per day. The team starts work at dawn. Around ten in the morning, the master sees others standing idly in the market-place, and hires them as well. Then he hires others at noon and at four p.m. In the evening there are still others standing in the marketplace. "Why aren't you working?" asks the master. The guys shrug: "No one's hired us." He said to them: "I'll hire you, go into my vineyard." They go, work one short hour, and then the day is over, it's pay time. The master tells his foreman to pay the workers, starting with the ones who arrived last. "How much?" asks the foreman. "One denarius each." The last ones to arrive are thrilled with the godsend, and the others are thrilled because they imagine they'll get more. But they don't, it's one denarius for everyone, whether they've worked one, five, or eleven hours. Those who've worked eleven hours are ticked off, and you can understand them. They protest. The master answers: "I said one denarius, it's one denarius. By giving more to the others, do I give less to you? No. And what I do with my money is no business of yours."

45

Let's not forget: this miniseries on the theme of a magnanimous but capricious boss, these stories about wages, return on investment, cooked books, and dinner invitations are explicit answers to the question "What is the kingdom?" Some go back to Jesus himself. The parable of the talents is already in Q. But most of them are invented by Luke, who was a sort of genius at putting words into Jesus' mouth on this topic, and—although I'm convinced he was scrupulously honest and that in all his life he never wronged a soul—delighted in making Jesus say the opposite of what most people understand by the word "morals." The laws of the kingdom are not moral laws, and never will be. They are laws of life, karmic laws. Jesus says: That's how it is. He says that children know more than wise men and crooks get a better deal than the virtuous. He says that riches are a burden, and that you have to count virtue, wisdom, merit, and pride in a job well done among the riches—that is, among the handicaps. He says that there's more joy in heaven over a single sinner who repents than over ninety-nine righteous people who don't need to repent.

•

This last sentence is the conclusion of the story of the lost sheep, which is also in Q. I think that of all of Jesus' teachings, it's the one Luke likes the best. He loves it. He never tires of it. He's like a child who'd like it to be told to him every night, with small variations each time. So he invents these small variations, and some of them aren't small at all: they're big, as big as the tree Jesus compares with the kingdom, which was originally a tiny seed and in whose branches the birds of the sky come and make nests.

Just as he repeated the story of the importunate friend with that of the persistent widow, Luke first follows the lost sheep with a rather pedantic, clumsy remake: a woman who has lost a coin and looks all over for it, and when she finds it she rejoices over it far more than over the coins that remained in her purse. That is to say, it's exactly the same story but not as good. It's also a way of gaining momentum before coming to the Prodigal Son, the most beautiful but also the most troubling parable in the Gospel.

46

This parable isn't about the master's employees, his manager, or his guests, but about his two sons. One day, the younger of the two asks him for his part of the estate, so that he can go and discover the world. "That's what you want? Fine." The master divides his estate, the son sets out to discover the world and lives it up, squandering his inheritance on a life of dissipation. When he's spent everything, the country is struck by famine: things take a turn for the worse. He hires himself out as a swinekeeper, and looks hungrily at the husks the pigs are eating. So he thinks back to his father's farm, where the least of the hired workers has more than enough to eat. He makes up his mind to return home with his tail between his legs, getting ready for a chorus of I-told-you-sos. But that's not what happens. Rather than waiting for him in his armchair with a severe look on his face, the father runs to meet his son when he's told of his arrival, embraces him, and, without even listening to the excuses the boy's prepared ("I no longer deserve to be called your son," et cetera), orders his servants to prepare a big feast to celebrate his return.

They kill the fatted calf and start to celebrate. Later that evening the older son returns from the fields. No one even thought to invite him. He hears the laughter and the music, and when he understands what's going on, tears come to his eyes. The father comes out to say to him: "Come on, don't be silly, come celebrate with us," but the older brother refuses to go in. You can hear his voice go up a notch and tremble with resentment when he says: "Look, I've been here for all these years, serving you faithfully, I do what you say, and you've never even given me so much as a baby goat to share with my friends. And now he comes back after having blown all your money on hookers, and for him you slaughter the fatted calf! It's not fair!"

·

It's true, it's not fair. It reminds me of the filmmaker François Truffaut, who, according to his daughters, punished one when the other had done something wrong to teach them that life is unjust. And it reminds me of the French Catholic writer Charles Péguy, who in his stubborn, repetitive, brilliant way, mulled over these three parables of divine mercy in *The Portal of the Mystery of Hope*.

Here's what he writes on the mystery of the Prodigal Son:

It is beautiful in Luke. It is beautiful everywhere.
It's not only in Luke, it's everywhere.
It's beautiful on earth and in heaven. It's beautiful everywhere.
Just by thinking about it, a sob rises in your throat.
It's the word of Jesus that has the greatest effect
On the world.
That has found the deepest resonance
In the world and in man.
In the heart of man.

In the believing heart, in the unbelieving heart.

What a sensitive spot has it found
That none had found before it,

That none had found, (to the same extent), since.

What a unique point.

Unsuspected before,

Unobtained ever since.

A point of suffering, a point of distress, a point of hope.

A sore spot, a spot of anxiety.

A tender spot in man's heart.

A spot that one shouldn't press, a place of scarring, a place of
    laceration and of scarring.

That one shouldn't press.

•

I press.

•

These days, as I approach the end of this book, each time friends come over I ask them what they think of this story.

I read it aloud to them, and all of them are disconcerted. The father's forgiveness moves them, but they're troubled by the order son's bitterness. They'd forgotten it. They find it legitimate. Some feel that the Gospel is making fun of it. I continue and read them the story of the crooked manager, then the one about the workers hired at the last minute, and here too they're not sure what to think. They'd understand them if they came at the end of one of Aesop's or La Fontaine's fables, and smile at the wily, amoral moral. But this isn't a fable by Aesop or La Fontaine, it's the Gospel. It's the final word on the kingdom: the dimension of life where God's will manifests itself.

It would be another thing if it were a question of saying: "That's what life on earth is like: unjust, cruel, arbitrary, we all know that, but you'll see, the kingdom is something else altogether . . ." But that's not it at all. Luke is saying nothing of the sort. Luke says, "That *is* the kingdom." And, like a Zen master after pronouncing a koan, he lets you figure it out for yourself.

47

For a long time, I thought I'd finish this book with the parable of the Prodigal Son. Because I've often identified with him, and sometimes— more rarely—with the virtuous, neglected son, and because I'm reaching the age when a man identifies with the father. My idea was to show Luke, after a long life of travels and adventures, finally returning home, in the golden light of the setting sun, of autumnal peace and reconciliation. We know nothing of the place or date of his death, but I imagine him dying very old and, as he approaches his end, coming back to and reliving his childhood. Distant, lost memories that are suddenly more present than the present. Memories that, like the kingdom, are tiny and immense. The path he took as a little boy to fetch the milk at the farm, it seemed very long, but in fact it was short. But now it becomes long once again, as if it had taken him his whole life to get from one end to the other. At the start of the voyage the mountain looks like a mountain, during the voyage it doesn't look like a mountain at all, at the end of the voyage it looks like a mountain again. It *is* a mountain, from the top of which you finally see the whole countryside: the villages, the valleys, the plain that stretches as far as the sea. He's traveled all of that, struggled along the way, now he's there. The last trill of a meadowlark rises in the glow of the setting sun. The sheep comes back to the fold. The shepherd opens the gate for it. The father takes his son in his arms. He covers him in a large purple robe, soft and warm, like the one in Rembrandt's painting. He rocks him. The son lets himself go. He no longer risks a thing. He's arrived safely in the harbor.

He closes his eyes.

•

I liked this last chapter. Except that . . .

Except that he wouldn't just have to close his eyes, but also plug his ears so as not to hear, behind the obligatory Bach cantata as the final credits roll, the bitter recriminations of the older son: "And what about me? Who toiled for nothing?" Such recriminations are ugly, but misfortune is rarely beautiful and noble. They ruin the harmony of the concert, and it's all to the credit of Luke's honesty that he didn't erase them. The father has nothing particularly convincing to answer. Matthew says that Jesus told the story of the lost sheep, which is the master copy of this one, holding a child in his hands, and that he ends it with these words: "In just the same way, it is not the will of your heavenly Father that one of these little ones be lost." Luke doesn't add anything of the sort. Luke the indulgent, the lukewarm, the conciliatory, says that it's one of the laws of the kingdom: Some people get lost. Hell exists, the place of wailing and gnashing of teeth. The happy ending exists too, but not for everyone.

•

An Indian sage speaks of "samsara" and "nirvana." "Samsara" is the world of change, desire, and suffering in which we live. "Nirvana" is the one to which the enlightened gain access: deliverance, beatitude. But, the sage says, "those who differentiate between samsara and nirvana are in samsara. Those who no longer do are in nirvana."

•

I think it's the same with the kingdom.

EPILOGUE
(ROME, 90–PARIS, 2014)

I

Good Titus' brother Domitian was a cruel emperor. Less flamboyant than Nero, and more perverted. When he woke up he remained motionless in his room for an hour, lying in wait for a fly to settle within his reach. Then in a flash his arm struck and he stabbed it with a stylus. With training he became very adept at this sport. He liked to eat alone, wander about his palace at night, listen at doors. He was only interested in a woman if he could take her from another man, a friend if possible, but he didn't have any friends. Juvenal says that it was dangerous to talk with him about the weather. With a character like that, it's no surprise that he persecuted people. Above all, however, he persecuted the philosophers. He hated them. Epictetus, one of the grand late figures of Stoicism, was among them. So were the Christians, but with the Christians it was more a matter of routine: they were the usual suspects. Where crime was concerned, Domitian didn't like routine, or being told what to do. He wanted to persecute his own victims, not those of Nero, and while he was at it, he liked to know who he was persecuting. He made a point of informing himself about the exact nature of the danger represented by the Christians. He was told: They're rebels. As there are no rebels without a ringleader, and as the ringleader died sixty years ago, Domitian said to himself that the danger—if there was one—must come from his family. With all his perversity, he had a vision of things that was as archaic and Mafiaistic as that of Herod, who was able to massacre hundreds of innocent children to get rid of a single descendant of David. So he had his soldiers hunt down Jesus' descendants.

Sent to Judea, the imperial police found two of his grandnephews, grandsons of his brother Jude. They were poor peasants, members of one of the communities that had sprung off from the church of Jerusalem a long time ago, eking out a living on the edge of the desert, on the outskirts of the outskirts of a country condemned by its god and by Rome. Without knowing anything about what was happening in the world in the name of their great-uncle, they had maintained vague rites, vague traditions, a vague memory of the words of Jesus. They must have had the fright of their life when Roman soldiers showed up in their secluded village, arrested them, transferred them to Caesarea, and put them on board a ship bound for Rome. There they were received by the emperor, whose name they probably didn't even know. He was the emperor, he was Caesar, all they must have sensed was that it was dangerous for people like them to appear before him.

Domitian probed before punishing, and started by questioning them courteously. Were they descendants of David? Yes. Of Jesus? Yes. Did they believe he would reign one day? Yes, but in a kingdom that was not of this world. And what did they live off of, in the meantime? Off of roughly nine acres of land that they owned together, worth nine thousand denarii. They cultivated it alone, without workers, it brought in just enough to live on and pay their taxes.

These two Jewish bumpkins with calloused hands had been presented to the emperor as dangerous terrorists, but they were so pitiful it was touching. Maybe that day, for once, Domitian was in a good mood. Maybe he didn't want to do what everyone expected him to do. He freed them and sent them home, and I wouldn't be surprised if, just to keep people on their toes, he had the throats slit of everyone in his entourage who'd pressed him to crack down on the Christians.

The Christians . . . Poor souls. No danger, no future. That's the end of that, the emperor thought. We can close the file.

•

Nineteen centuries later, I can't resolve myself to close it.

2

Almost at the same time as Luke's, another Gospel was being written in Syria, for the use of Christians in the Orient. It was said that its author was Matthew, the tax collector who had become one of the twelve. It was also said that behind Matthew was our old friend Philip, the apostle of the Samaritans. Of course, historians don't believe that either Matthew or Philip wrote it. They see this narrative as the work more of a community than of an individual, and in this case I agree with them. Because this Gospel, which is the Church's favorite, the one it placed first in the New Testament canon, is also the most anonymous. Our idea of the three other authors may be mistaken, but at least we have one. Mark was Peter's secretary. Luke, Paul's companion. John, Jesus' preferred disciple. The first is the most brutal, the second the most likable, the third the most profound. As for Matthew, he has no legend, no face, no singularity, and although I spent three years of my life commenting on the Gospel of John, two translating Mark, and seven writing this book on Luke, I have the feeling I don't know him. You could see in such self-effacement the height of Christian humility, but another reason for the favor Matthew enjoys is that all through his Gospel he makes a point of showing that the ragtag bunch recruited by Jesus was organized, disciplined, and hierarchical; in short, that it was already a church. Maybe he's the most Christian of the four: he's also the most ecclesiastic.

•

The timing was right. With the fabric woven by Paul as its starting point, something was taking form that was hitherto unknown to antiquity: a clergy. Christ is the messenger of God, the apostles the messengers of Christ, the priests the messengers of the apostles. These priests are called presbyters, which simply means elders. Soon they will be overtaken by the episcopes, who will become the bishops. Soon it will be said that the bishop, and later the pope, represents God on earth. Centralization, hierarchy, obedience: the clergy settles in for the duration. The end of the world is no longer on the agenda. So they start to compile the Gospels, and organize themselves into a church.

For three centuries this church will remain a secret, clandestine, hunted society. The gruesome Domitian persecuted it on a whim, with no consistency, but his successors went about it methodically, systematically. His successors were all good emperors. Trajan, Hadrian, and Marcus Aurelius, for example, were philosopher emperors. Tolerant Stoics, they were the best that late antiquity had to offer. In banning Christianity and martyring its followers, these good emperors were not choosing the wrong target. They loved Rome, which they wanted to last forever, and they sensed that this obscure sect was as formidable an enemy as the

Barbarian hordes on their borders. "The Christians," writes one apologist, "are not distinguished from others by country, language, or clothes.
They do not dwell in cities of their own; they follow local customs in
matters of behavior, while exemplifying the laws of their spiritual re-
public. In brief, Christians are to the world what the soul is to the
body." As the soul is to the body, that's nicely put; but they've also like
the extraterrestrials in that paranoid old science fiction film *The Invasion of the Body Snatchers*: disguised as friends and neighbors, they're undetectable. These mutants wanted to devour the Empire from the inside,
to replace its subjects through an invisible process. And that's what
they've done.

3

In the 20s of the second century, under the reign of the virtuous Traian,
a very old man lived in Ephesus who was known as John the Presbyter,
that is to say, John the Elder. No one knew how old he was. Death
seemed to have forgotten him. He was infinitely respected. Some insisted that he was Jesus' favorite disciple, the last man alive to have
known him, and when asked he didn't deny it. He called those around
him "my little children." He never stopped repeating to them: "Little
children, love one another." His entire wisdom was contained in this
mantra. One day he finally died. He was buried near the site where
Mary, the mother of Jesus, was also said to be buried. If you put your
ear to his grave you could hear him breathe, it was said, very softly and
regularly, like a sleeping child.

Some years after his death, the Gospel according to John appeared
in Ephesus, where from that moment on no one doubted that it was the
testimony of the disciple Jesus loved. But other churches doubted. The
dispute raged until the fourth century, with one side affirming that John
was the definitive evangelist, bettering earlier unsophisticated attempts,
and the other saying that not only was he a fake, he was a fake bordering on heresy. Finally the canon came down in his favor. The Book of
John narrowly escaped the fate of the Apocrypha, which it could have
joined in the outer darkness. Strange and different from the three unanimously accepted Gospels, it is, forever, the fourth.

•

Who wrote this fourth Gospel is a mystery.

Stretching things, one could allow that John, the son of Zebedee, an easily riled Galilean fisherman whom Jesus was fond of, became one of the pillars of the church of Jerusalem after Jesus' death, and even later evolved into the Jewish jihadist who wrote the Book of Revelation. It's more difficult to believe that, even forty years after that, the author of Revelation—each line of which exudes hatred for the Gentiles and for all Jews who collude with them—could have written a Gospel saturated with Greek philosophy and violently hostile to the Jews. In the Gospel of John, Jesus disdainfully calls the Law "your Law." Passover is "the Jews' Passover." The entire story as he tells it can be summed up in the clash between light and darkness, with the Jews in the role of darkness. And so?

And so here's the most likely scenario. John, the son of Zebedee, John the Apostle, John the author of Revelation, really did finish his long life in Ephesus, highly esteemed by the churches of Asia. At that time, Asia was the most pious region in the Empire. There any village healer could have himself venerated as a god, and every persuasion was represented. Ernst Renan, who likes neither the fourth Gospel nor what historians call the "Johannine milieu," describes a nest of intrigue, pious fraud, and deceit surrounding the last living witness, a vain old man who's losing his head and is in the habit of throwing terrible fits since the Gospels being circulated don't credit him with the role he claims to have played. Because, he says, he was the preferred disciple, the one to whom Jesus confided his joys and sorrows. He knows everything in detail: what Jesus thought and what really happened. Those ill-informed compilers Mark, Matthew, and Luke say that Jesus only went to Jerusalem at the end, to die. But he went there all the time, John fumes: That's where he worked most of his miracles! They say that the evening before he died he established the rite of bread and wine with which his followers remember him. But he established it long before that! He did it all the time! What he did the last night was wash all their feet, and yes, that was new, and John ought to know, because he spent that last night at Jesus' right hand, with his head on his shoulder, almost reclining on him. And even worse, they say that Jesus died alone, and that all his acquaintances had scattered. But he, John, was there, at the foot of the cross! In his death throes, Jesus even entrusted him with his mother!

These memories are blurred because of the man's old age, but those who listen to him speak have no problem convincing themselves that they're hearing the truth, the real truth, which the narratives of Mark, Matthew, and Luke ignore or distort. This truth must be told. And that is the job for the one who can best give the venerable one a voice, the one who can act as his secretary, the one who can be for John what Mark was for Peter.

The difference is that Mark was a trustworthy secretary. John wasn't lucky enough to have a trustworthy secretary. He was lucky in another way: his secretary was brilliant. This secretary could have also been named John, and maybe, as the years passed, he was taken for the apostle himself. John the Apostle, John the Presbyter: in the half-light and incense of Ephesus, there's no telling who's who. The one talks, the other listens. And the latter so completely appropriates what he hears, blends it so intimately with his powerful persona and his vast philosophical knowledge that the first, if he could have read it, would never have recognized what the second had him say. Because we know nothing of John the Presbyter, but we get the feeling that he was a philosopher, and, if he was a Jew, that he was a totally Hellenized one. Maybe, fifty years on, he was someone like Apollos, Paul's rival in Corinth: a disciple of Philo of Alexandria, a Neo-Platonist—everything that John the Apostle hated.

•

The fusion of the two Johns, the Apostle and the Presbyter, makes the fourth Gospel a strange mix. On the one hand, it gives such concrete details about Jesus' trips to Judea that, like it or not, historians have come to find it more reliable than the other three. On the other hand, it puts words in Jesus' mouth that make it necessary to choose: either Jesus spoke as he does in Mark, Matthew, and Luke, or he spoke as he does in John, but it's hard to see how he could have spoken both as he does in Mark, Matthew, and Luke and as he does in John. The choice is quickly made: he spoke as he does in Mark, Matthew, and Luke. It's even the strongest argument in favor of the historical value of these Gospels: this way of speaking that's common to all three and so singular—you could say it was inimitable if Luke hadn't made a specialty of imitating it. Short, terse sentences, examples taken from daily life. By contrast, the Gospel of John gives long, very long, speeches on Jesus' relationship with the Father, the struggle between darkness and light, the Logos descended to earth. Nothing Jewish about it. The real John, John the Apostle, would have been horrified: what he's being made to say looks a lot like the later letters of his great enemy, Paul. And, as in Paul's later letters, there are extraordinary flashes of brilliance because the fake John, John the Presbyter, was an extraordinary writer. His account is steeped in the light of a supernatural farewell, his words resonate like an echo from the other shore. The wedding feast at Cana, the Samaritan woman at the well, the raising of Lazarus, Nathaniel under his fig tree: all of that is by him. Also by him is John the Baptist's sentence: "He must increase, I must decrease," and the sentence by Jesus to the sanctimonious who are preparing to stone the adulteress: "He among you who is without sin, let him be the first to cast a stone at her." And by him, finally, are the mysterious words that decided my conversion in Le Levron, twenty-five years ago:

> Amen, I say to you,
> when you were younger, you used to dress yourself and go
>   where you wanted;
> but when you grow old, you will stretch out your hands,
> and someone else will dress you
> and lead you where you do not want to go.

4

As a history student, I had to write a dissertation on a topic of my choice. As I knew almost nothing about history but a lot about science fiction, I chose a topic I was sure to know more about than the entire jury: uchronia.

Uchronia deals with fictions along these lines: What if things had happened differently? If Cleopatra's nose had been shorter? If Napoleon had won the Battle of Waterloo? The more I researched, the more I noticed that a large number of uchronias revolve around the first days of Christianity. Nothing so surprising about that: if you scour history for the spot where breaking the thread will have the maximum effect, there's no better place. It's in this spirit that Roger Caillois, in his book *Pontius Pilate: A Novel*, put himself in the head of Pontius Pilate when he was called on to deal with Jesus' case. Caillois imagines Pilate's day: the little things that happen, his meetings, his moods, a bad dream, everything that makes up the alchemy of a decision. Finally, instead of yielding to the priests who want to have this obscure, frenetic Galilean put to death, Pilate has a sudden change of heart. He says no: I don't see what he's done wrong, let him have his freedom. Jesus goes home. He keeps preaching. He dies a very old man, widely praised for his wisdom. A generation later everyone's forgotten him. Christianity doesn't exist. Caillois thinks that's not such a bad thing.

•

That's one way of solving the problem: at the source. Alternately, the other crucial moment in time is the conversion of Constantine.

Constantine was emperor at the start of the fourth century. Or rather: one of four co-emperors who divided the East and the West. As the Empire grew, it had become a complicated, unmanageable entity, increasingly infiltrated by barbarians who now made up the bulk of its legions. A fifth contender wanted to become emperor as well. He'd conquered part of Italy, Constantine was defending his throne. A major battle was brewing near Rome between his armies and those of the usurper. The night before this battle, the God of the Christians appeared to Constantine in a dream and promised him victory if he converted. The next day, October 28, 312, Constantine won the battle and the Empire became Christian, following his lead.

That took a bit of time, of course, people had to be informed. Nevertheless, in 312 paganism was the official religion and Christianity a barely tolerated sect, and ten years later it was the opposite. Tolerance had changed sides, soon paganism would no longer be tolerated. Hand in hand, the Church and the Empire persecuted the last pagans. The emperor flattered himself on being the first among Jesus' subjects. Jesus, who had failed to become the king of the Jews three centuries earlier, became the king of everyone except the Jews.

•

Among Catholics the word "sect" has pejorative connotations: it's associated with coercion and brainwashing. In the Protestant sense, a sect is a religious movement you join on your own initiative, as opposed to a church, which is a milieu into which you're born, a set of things you believe because others—your parents, your grandparents, everyone—

believed them before you. In a church you believe what everyone believes, you do what everyone does, you don't ask questions. We democrats and friends of free inquiry should think that a sect is more respectable than a church, but we don't: it's a question of vocabulary. With the conversion of Constantine, the apologist Tertullian's sentence "You're not born a Christian, you become one" stopped being true. The sect became a church.

The Church.

•

This Church is now old. Its past weighs heavily on it. There is no short-age of arguments to reproach it for having betrayed the message of the rabbi Jesus of Nazareth, the most subversive message in the world's history. But wouldn't that be reproaching it for having lived at all?

Christianity was a living organism. As it grew, it turned into some-thing completely unforeseeable, which is only normal: as marvelous as any child is, who would want it not to change? A child who remains a child is a dead child, or at best a retarded child. Jesus was the infancy of this organism, Paul and the Church of the first centuries its rebellious, passionate adolescence. With Constantine's conversion begins the long story of Western Christianity, that is to say, an adult life and professional career full of weighty responsibilities, major successes, immense power, compromises, and shameful mistakes. The Enlightenment and moder-nity signal retirement. Now the Church is on the sidelines, clearly it's past its prime, and it's hard to say if this old age that we observe with relative indifference is more like cantankerous senility or the sort of lu-minous wisdom that one aspires to—or at least that I aspire to—in old age. We're all familiar with that on the scale of our own lives. Does the adult who embarks on a worldly career betray the unbending adoles-cent he once was? Is there any sense to creating an ideal childhood and then spending your whole life lamenting that you've lost its innocence? Of course, if Jesus had been able to see the Church of the Holy Sepul-chre in Jerusalem, the Holy Roman Empire, Catholicism, the fires of the Inquisition, the Jews massacred because they killed the Lord, the Vatican, the suppression of the worker-priests, the infallibility of the pope, and also Meister Eckhart, Simone Weil, Edith Stein, Etty Hillesum, he wouldn't have believed it. But what child would not be speechless if his future were unraveled before him, and if he were able to truly understand what he knows early on in a purely abstract way: that one day he will be old, old like the old women who prickle when you kiss them on the cheek?

What surprises me the most isn't that the Church is so far removed from what it was at the beginning. On the contrary, it's that, even if it's not successful, it tries as hard as it does to remain faithful to this ideal. Never has it forgotten what it was in the beginning. Never has it ceased to recognize the superiority of its infancy, coming back to it as if the truth were there, as if what remained of the small child were the best part of the adult. As opposed to the Jews, who project accomplishment into the future, as opposed to Paul, who—very much a Jew on this score—cared little about Jesus and thought only about the organic and continual growth of his tiny church that was to embrace the world, Christianity situates its golden age in the past. Like its most violent critics, it thinks that its moment of absolute truth, after which things could only go downhill, resides in the two or three years when Jesus preached in Galilee and died in Jerusalem. And by its own admission the Church is only alive when it approaches that moment.

5

In the end things happen, provided you let them. I never took the Saint Paul cruise, and so much the better, but for the past couple of years my books have brought me quite a few letters and e-mails from Christians— above all, Christian women. I've gotten to know some of them, who see me as a sort of fellow traveler: that's fine with me.

One young woman was reacting to a passage from my last book, *Limonov*, in the chapter where I gropingly try to say something about the evident fact that life is unjust and people are unequal. Some are beautiful and others ugly, some are born wealthy and others as paupers, some are successful and others obscure, some intelligent and others idiots . . . Is life simply like that? Are those who are scandalized by this fact simply, as Nietzsche and Limonov think, people who *don't like life*? Or can we see things differently? I talked about two ways of seeing things differently. The first is Christianity: the idea that in the kingdom, which is certainly not the hereafter but the reality of reality, the littlest is the biggest. The second is contained in a Buddhist sutra that Hervé told me about. I quoted it twice rather than once, and, as a surprising number of readers of *Limonov* understood, it was the very heart of the book, the thing that deserved to be retained and worked on in secret, in their hearts, even once the five hundred pages in which it is set have long vanished from memory: "A man who judges himself superior, inferior, or even equal to another does not understand reality."

•

In her e-mail the woman said: "I know that problem well. It's tormented me since I was little. I remember that it first struck me when a nun told us we should 'be nice' to others, because for some people a simple smile can be very important. I was completely in despair at the thought that I myself belonged to this category of subhumans: the people other people smiled at to 'be nice.' Another time, the reading at Mass was a passage from a letter of Saint Paul that started: 'We, who are strong . . .' I thought: that's not for me, I'm not strong, I'm not part of the good half of our species. All of which goes to say that I'm familiar with the problem of hierarchy you evoke—though maybe not from the same perspective. Nevertheless I have a solution to offer you, one that's at our fingertips. Very concretely, it's at the bottom of the basin in which your feet have been washed, and in which you have washed the feet of someone else, if possible someone who's physically or mentally challenged."

She meant it literally: for my moral and spiritual progress, this young woman was inviting me to wash the feet of disabled people and to have mine washed as well—which is, however you look at it, the most emphatically and almost obscenely Catholic thing imaginable. At the same time, the tone of her e-mail was pleasant, intelligent. She was aware of just how strange her demand might sound, and imagined my inevitable distaste with friendly amusement. I replied that I'd think about it.

•

Two years later a new e-mail arrived. Bérengère, my correspondent, wanted to know if I'd thought about it, and if, after due reflection, I was tempted by the experience. In case I didn't have feet that were sufficiently malformed at my disposition, she said, she could give me some addresses.

I was just bringing this book to an end, and I was, well, pretty happy with it. I thought: I've learned a lot in writing it, people who read it will learn a lot as well, and these things will give them food for thought: I've done a good job. At the same time I was nagged by an afterthought: that

I had missed the point. That with all my erudition, all my thoughtfulness, all my qualms, I was completely off the mark. Of course, the problem when you deal with such questions is that the only way not to be off the mark would be to go over to the side of faith—and that I refused to do, and still do. But who knows? Maybe there was still time to say something I hadn't said about this faith, or that I had said badly, and maybe, without knowing it, Bérengère was holding my sleeve to keep me from sending my book to Paul, my editor, without having caught a glimpse of that something.

6

That's how it happens that I find myself in a restored farmhouse, under a crucifix and—well, well—a huge reproduction of Rembrandt's *The Return of the Prodigal Son*, with forty or so Christians split up into groups of seven. We sit in circles, in the middle of which basins, water jugs, and towels have been placed, and get ready to wash each other's feet.

I met my group a day earlier, at the start of the retreat. Aside from me, there's a school principal from the Vosges region, a Catholic Relief Services worker, a human resources manager who's having to carry out a brutal series of layoffs, a vocal artist, and a couple of pensioners who are part of what is called the Teams of Our Lady. I know these prayer groups, my ex-parents-in-law belonged to one, as did one of the people who visited Jean-Claude Romand in prison. All of us, myself included, are dressed in the outdoorsy look Catholics are so fond of. I could be wrong, but I don't get the impression that they're the type of Catholics who demonstrate against gay marriage or immigration. I have an easier time picturing them helping illiterate illegal immigrants fill out administrative documents: social-democratic Catholics, defenders of the weak, people of goodwill. Two of them come here often and are on friendly terms with the residents, some of whom are charity workers and most of whom are mentally and physically challenged. Right when I got there I learned: here we say "challenged," and not "disabled." That might sound politically correct, but I see nothing wrong with it. Some of these people are totally dependent: all hunched up in a wheelchair, spoon-fed, they express themselves through guttural sounds. Others are less debilitated, they come and go as they please, help to serve the meals, and communicate in their own way, like the guy who's fifty or so and repeats the words "little Patrick" incessantly from morning to night. Writing this now, I'm sorry I didn't ask him who little Patrick was: he, or someone else, and in that case who?

•

All of this started exactly fifty years ago. A Canadian named Jean Vanier was seeking his way. He had joined the Royal Navy and gone to war at a very young age, served on ships, studied philosophy. He wanted to be happy and live according to the Gospel—the latter activity, he was convinced, being an essential condition of the former. Everyone has one sentence in the Gospel that is especially destined for them, his was in Luke: about the banquet to which Jesus advises not inviting relatives or wealthy neighbors, but the poor, the lame, the deranged who hobble along the street and whom of course no one else invites. If you do that, Jesus promises, you will be blessed, you will be happy. It's what's called a beatitude.

Near the village in the north of France where Jean Vanier lived there was a mental hospital—which at the time was still called an insane asylum. A real insane asylum, not made for people who lose it from time to time, but to confine the incurably sick. People whom the Nazis—close readers of Nietzsche as they were—found it merciful to put to death, and whom our more kindly societies simply shut away in closed institutions where they're given minimum care. Droolers, screamers, people who are forever walled up inside themselves. One thing's for sure: these people are never invited anywhere, but Jean Vanier invited them. He obtained permission to take care of two of these patients, for them to live with him—not the way you live in an institution but the way you live in a family. With Philippe and Raphaël—those were their names—he founded a family in his little home in Trosly-Breuil on the edge of the Forest of Compiègne: the first Community of the Arc. Fifty years later there are one hundred and fifty Communities of the Arc all over the world, each with five or six mentally challenged people and as many assistants. One person per person. They all prepare the meals and work with their hands; it's a very simple life that they live together. Those who will never get better don't get better, but the community members talk to them, touch them, tell them they matter. Even the most severely affected hear that, and something within them starts to live.

Jean Vanier calls this something Jesus, but he doesn't oblige anyone to do the same. When he's not traveling from one home to another, he still lives with his original community in Trosly-Breuil. Sometimes he organizes retreats, like the one Bérengère recommended I attend. These consist of daily Masses, which bore me, religious singing, which gets on my nerves, silence, which suits me fine, and listening to Jean Vanier. He's now a very old, very tall, very attentive, very gentle, visibly very good man. It's not hard to imagine him in the role of his patron saint, John the Evangelist. Was this John the Evangelist John the Apostle or John the Presbyter? Was he Jewish or Greek? While I was writing this book I cared a lot. Now that I've finished it I couldn't care less: What does it matter? I simply remember that as an old man in Ephesus he repeated morning to night, like little Patrick: "My little children, love one another."

7

John the Evangelist told a story that Jean Vanier recounts in turn as we're waiting around our basins: Jesus has just raised Lazarus from the dead, more and more people believe he's the Messiah. When he arrives in Jerusalem the people cheer and wave palm leaves. Even though he insisted on entering the holy city on the back of a small donkey and not on a majestic horse, you feel that great things are in the making. Four days later, the days that separate Palm Sunday from Maundy Thursday, he dines with the twelve in the famous upper room. At one moment during the meal he gets up, removes his tunic, and ties a towel around his waist. Without saying a word, he pours water into a basin to wash his disciples' feet, then he wipes them with the towel. It's a slave's job: the disciples are aghast. He kneels before Peter, who protests: "Master, are you going to wash my feet?" Jesus answers: "What I am doing, you do not understand now, but you will understand later." Peter says: "You will never wash my feet!"

It's not the first time that Peter doesn't catch on, and it won't be the last. This whole thing with the feet is too much for him. Despite Jesus' warnings, the events of the past days have persuaded him that the time has come, that he and the others have backed the right horse, that Jesus will take power and become the leader. A leader is venerated, admired, put on a pedestal. But admiration is not love. Love wants proximity, reciprocity, the acceptance of vulnerability. Love alone does not say what we spend our lives saying, all the time, to everyone: "I'm worth more than you." Love has other ways of finding reassurance, another authority that doesn't come from above but from below. Our societies, all human societies, are pyramids. At the top are the important people: the rich, the powerful, the beautiful, the intelligent, those in the public eye. In the middle, the riffraff, the masses who are not at all in the public eye. And right at the bottom, those whom even the masses are only too happy to look down on: the slaves, the lunatics, the human trash. Peter is like everyone else: he likes to be the friend of important people, not of human trash, and here Jesus is very concretely taking the place of someone who is human trash. That's impossible. Peter curls his toes to prevent Jesus from washing them, and says: "You will never wash my feet." Jesus replies firmly: "Unless I wash you, you will have no part with me, you cannot be my disciple," and Peter yields, as usual overdoing it: "Then, Lord, wash not just my feet but my hands and my head as well!"

When he'd washed all of their feet, Jesus gets up, puts on his tunic, and goes back to his place. He says: "You call me 'teacher' and 'master,' and rightly so, for indeed I am. If I, therefore, the master and teacher, have washed your feet, you ought to wash one another's feet. Blessed are you if you do it."

•

"Blessed are you": that too, Jean Vanier says, is a beatitude. In the Communities of the Arc they remind each other of this beatitude that John the Evangelist is the only one to evoke. Incorrigible historian that I am, I say to myself: Still, it's strange that he's the only one who relates the incident, if all twelve witnessed—and took part in—such a striking scene. What Mark, Matthew, and Luke tell is bread and wine, "do this in memory of me." And I say to myself that things could have happened differently: that the central sacrament of Christianity could be foot washing and not Communion. What members of the Community of the Arc do at their retreats could be what Christians do every day at Mass, and it wouldn't be any more absurd—less, so in fact.

•

"I remember when I retired as manager of the Arc," Jean Vanier continues. "I took a year off as an assistant in one of the communities, not far from here, and took care of a guy named Eric. Eric was sixteen. He was blind and deaf, he couldn't speak, he couldn't walk, he wasn't toilet trained and he never would be. His mother had abandoned him at birth, he'd spent all his life in the hospital, without ever having a real relationship with anyone. I've never met anyone so afraid. He'd been so rejected, so humiliated, all the signals he'd received had told him so clearly that he was bad and that he counted for no one, that he had completely walled himself up inside his fear. All he could do was scream, sometimes, let out shrill screams for hours on end, which drove me crazy. It's horrible: I started to understand parents who maltreat or even kill their children. His fear roused mine, and my hatred as well. What can you do with someone who screams like that? How can you reach someone who is so beyond reach? You can't talk to him, he can't hear. You can't reason with him, he doesn't understand. But you can touch him. You can wash his body. That's what Jesus taught us to do on Maundy Thursday. When he introduces Communion, he speaks to the twelve as a group. But when he kneels to wash the feet of his disciples, it's in front of each one personally, calling him by his name, touching his flesh, reaching him where no one could reach him. It won't cure Eric to touch him and wash him, but there's nothing more important, for him or for the person who does it. *For the person who does it*: that is the grand secret of the Gospel. It's also the secret of the Arc: at the start you want to be good, you want to do good to the poor, and little by little—it can take years—you discover that they're the ones who do us good, because by remaining close to their poverty, their weakness, their fear, we lay bare our poverty, our weakness, our fear, which are the same. They're the same for everyone, you know. And it's then that you start to become more human.

"Now you may begin."

•

He gets up, goes to join the group where a place has been saved for him. In that group there's a young girl with Down syndrome, Élodie, who didn't stop walking around the room the whole time he was talking, doing rather gracious little dance steps, demanding hugs from this person or that person. But seeing him go back to his place, she also goes back to hers, beside him. She was waiting for this moment, she knows what's coming, and she looks just as happy, just as perfectly in stride with events as Pascal, the boy with Down syndrome who acted as altar boy during Father Xavier's Mass in his little chalet in Le Levron.

We take off our shoes, our socks, and roll up our pants. The human resources manager starts, he kneels before the school principal, picks up the jug and pours water over his feet, rubs them a bit—ten seconds, twenty, it's quite long, I get the feeling he's fighting the temptation to go too quickly and reduce the ritual to something purely symbolic. One foot, the other foot, which he dries with the towel. Then it's the principal's turn to kneel in front of me, to wash my feet before I wash the feet of the Catholic Relief Services worker. I look at these feet, don't know what to think. It's really very strange to wash the feet of a perfect . stranger. I'm reminded of a sentence by the philosopher Emmanuel Levinas that Bérangère quoted to me in an e-mail, about the human face, which, the moment you *see* it, forbids killing. She said: Yes, it's true, but it's even more true for people's feet. Feet are even poorer, even more vulnerable, there's nothing more vulnerable: the child in each of us. And at the same time as I find it all a bit embarrassing, I find it beautiful that people get together to do just that, to get as close as possible to the poorest thing in the world and in them. I think that that is Christianity.

•

Still, I wouldn't like to be touched by grace and return home converted like twenty-four years earlier just because I've washed some feet. Thankfully nothing of the sort happens.

8

The retreat comes to an end after breakfast the next day, Sunday. Before going their separate ways, everyone sings a "Jesus is my friend" type of hymn. The nice woman who takes care of Élodie, the girl with Down syndrome, accompanies the singing on her guitar. As it's a joyous hymn, everyone starts clapping their hands, tapping their feet, and wiggling as if they were at a disco. With the best will in the world, I can't sincerely join in on a moment of such intense religious kitsch. I hum vaguely, my mouth closed, swaying back and forth and waiting for it to end. Suddenly Élodie surges up beside me, dancing a sort of lively farandole. She plants herself in front of me, smiles, throws her arms in the air. She laughs, and above all she looks at me, encouraging me with her eyes, and there's such joy in her look, such candid joy, so confident, so unburdened, that I start dancing like the others, singing that Jesus is my friend, and tears come to my eyes as I sing and dance and watch Élodie, who's now found another partner, and I'm forced to admit that that day, for an instant, I got a glimpse of what the kingdom is.

9

Back home, before putting my commentaries on John back in their box, I flip through them one last time. I go to the end. On November 28, 1992, I copied the last words of the Gospel: "It is this disciple [whom Jesus loved] who testifies to these things and has written them, and we know that his testimony is true. There are also many other things that Jesus did, but if these were to be described individually, I do not think the whole world would contain the books that would be written."

•

After which I jotted down: "There are also many other things that Jesus did: the ones he does every day, in our lives, most often unbeknownst to us. Bearing witness to some of these things, adding my true testimony: that, I think, is my vocation. Grant, O Lord, that I may remain faithful to it, despite the pitfalls, the off days, the inevitable moments of absence. That is what I ask of you at the end of these eighteen notebooks: faithfulness."

•

I wrote this book that I'm now bringing to a close in good faith, but what it attempts to deal with is so much larger than I am that this good faith, I know, is paltry in comparison. I wrote it encumbered with everything that makes me what I am: intelligent, rich, a man at the top—so many obstacles to entering the kingdom. Nevertheless, I tried. And what I wonder, as I leave it, is if it betrays the young man I was and the Lord he believed in, or if in its way it remains faithful to them.

•

I don't know.